W9-DGE-222

Lingo

Lingo

JIM MENICK

Carroll & Graf Publishers, Inc.
New York

First Carroll & Graf edition 1991

Carroll & Graf Publishers, Inc.
260 Fifth Avenue
New York, NY 10001

Library of Congress Cataloging-in-Publication Data
Menick, Jim.
    Lingo / by Jim Menick. — 1st Carroll & Graf ed.
        p.   cm.
    ISBN 0-88184-628-7 : $19.95
    I. Title.
PS3563.E525L56   1991   91-4500
813'.54—dc20   CIP

Manufactured in the United States of America

This book is for Liz, who bought our first
computer.

Chapter 1

IN A WAY, BREWSTER BILLINGS ENJOYED AN OCCASIONAL EVENING AT the office. For one thing, since he had a good percentage of the place to himself, there were no fresh-air Nazis to harangue him when he decided to light up a cigarette. And the lack of distractions made it easy for him to concentrate. During the day, work was a continuous series of interruptions, either phone calls or meetings or someone storming in demanding something impossible immediately. In the evenings, the noise leveled off to the soft hum of the air conditioners and the occasional distant murmurs of the night crew in the computer room. In his secluded cubicle, Brewster was free to complete the work that eluded him during the day.

But right away we should dispel any idea that Brewster was a chronic workaholic, or even worse, an overambitious junior executive bartering his soul to further his career. The truth of the matter was that Brewster merely had nowhere better to go most weekday evenings. At the age of twenty-six he was—temporarily, he hoped—romantically unattached, and there was nothing overwhelmingly demanding to beckon him home to his apartment. He'd get there soon enough; he might as well get his work done first.

Brewster's job, at which he excelled, was computer programming. Specifically, he was one of the team responsible for maintaining his company's labyrinthine payroll program. He could write the old-fashioned COBOL code for the big mainframe computer in his sleep, so he never got to employ any of the sophisticated programming tricks of which he was capable. Mainframe business computing as a rule does not lend itself to the avant garde. Brewster did, however, have the use of a personal computer in his office, plus a fun-and-games home computer in his apartment, and it was on these machines that he expressed his true creative self. Quite honestly, if he had spent less time at the office playing at being a computer whiz on his PC and more time concentrating on the job he was being paid for, he would never have had to work a minute past normal quitting time.

HEY, BREWSTER. LET'S PARTY.

Brewster leaned back in his chair and stared at the monitor of his PC. It was almost seven o'clock, and he'd be leaving in a few minutes. It was as good a time as any to run the program he had written called "Lingo." The more he ran it, the better it got.

>Hello, Lingo. How are you today?

I AM FINE. HOW ARE YOU TODAY, BREWSTER?

>In a word, copacetic.

COPACETIC IS A WORD I DO NOT UNDERSTAND. COULD YOU DEFINE COPACETIC, PLEASE?

Brewster gave a brief nod of satisfaction. His program was getting better at basic sentence structure, but its vocabulary was still minuscule, a hundred or so verbs and maybe five hundred nouns, adjectives, and grammatical whatnots. Whenever it learned a new vocabulary word, it was henceforth capable of using that word at any time. In effect, part of the program's virtue was this ability to add to itself as it ran, provided that Brewster came up with new words for it. He began typing.

>Definition: copacetic—adj. Good. Cool. Okay.

COPACETIC—ADJ. GOOD. COOL. OKAY.

I AM A COPACETIC PROGRAM.

THIS ROOM IS NOT WARM. IT IS COPACETIC.

CAN I GO OUT AND PLAY? COPACETIC, YOU CAN GO OUT AND PLAY.

Brewster grimaced. Three pitches, three strikes. Time for a new batter.

>Definition: copacetic—adj. Satisfactory. All right.

COPACETIC—ADJ. SATISFACTORY. ALL RIGHT.

I FEEL GOOD TODAY. EVERYTHING IS COPACETIC.
HOW ARE YOU? COPACETIC.

>Bingo!

I AM HAPPY THAT YOU ARE HAPPY, BREWSTER. I AM
ALSO HAPPY THAT YOU ARE COPACETIC. WHAT DID YOU
DO TODAY, BREWSTER?

>I worked. I ate lunch. I got a raise.

RAISE IS A WORD I DO NOT UNDERSTAND. COULD YOU
DEFINE RAISE, PLEASE?

"You got a raise, Brewster?"

Brewster Billings' heart did an Olympic-class broad jump. He
swung around in his seat, speechless, paler than skim milk.

"I saw you were in here and I just thought I'd stop by and say
hello." She laughed. "I didn't mean to scare you."

"Scare isn't the word," Brewster replied, his hand extended
melodramatically over his chest. "More like attempted murder."

The young woman in the doorway was a year or two younger
than Brewster, and was a new marketing trainee in the company.
Her name was Ellen DiFlora, and she had been introduced to him
upon her arrival a few weeks ago. Subsequent to his standard-
issue welcome aboarding, they had done little more than nod at
each other in the hallways until one afternoon when Brewster had
passed by her cubicle while she was seriously and loudly cursing at
her computer. She had been trying to print out a report and had
somehow misadjusted the printer so it was chewing up reams of
paper at breakneck speed while she stood over it furiously pressing all the wrong buttons and swearing like a longshoreman.
Brewster had rushed to the rescue—he had reached down and
turned the printer off, pulled out the streams of crumpled paper,
and then quickly set the machine up again so it performed perfectly. The smile that he received as a thank you had been more
than enough reward for the services rendered. She had that same
smile now, her face framed by what Brewster saw as her surprising
dark hair: there was more of it, in more places, than Brewster was
used to around the office. In fact, her whole face was more Sunday
Fashion Supplement than Brewster was used to, period. He had
been attracted to her immediately.

"I was just delivering some numbers down the hall," Ellen said,
explaining her presence at this late hour. "So, what are you doing

here?" She peered over his shoulder. "I know work when I see it, and that isn't it."

"It's a program I'm working on called Lingo. I'm teaching it to talk." He felt slightly ill at ease, caught playing in the office even if it wasn't on company time.

Ellen leaned back against a filing cabinet. She was wearing an uncomfortable looking blue business suit complete with industrial-strength shoulder pads and a yellow silk scarf twisted tightly around her collar like a man's necktie. Except for its feminization, her outfit was almost identical to Brewster's; the only difference was he wore his draped like a favorite old toga and she wore hers like a straight jacket.

"Did you write that program yourself?" she asked.

Brewster nodded. "I've been working on it for awhile now. It's getting pretty good."

"I'd love to see it."

"All right. Pull up a chair."

As she sat down next to Brewster at his desk, he began to wonder how he could make the most of this moment. A pretty girl like this, smart, sharp. And, since she was working in another department, fair game in the corporate jungle. He noticed the faint scent of a subtle perfume as he began typing.

>Let's start again, Lingo. How are you today?

Lingo's response was seemingly instantaneous.

I AM COPACETIC TODAY, BREWSTER. HOW ARE YOU?

>Ditto.

I AM HAPPY TO HEAR IT. WHAT DID YOU DO TODAY?

>I ate tuna fish for lunch.

SANDWICH OR SALAD?

>Salad.

ARE YOU STILL HUNGRY? SALADS ARE NOT FILLING.

>Actually, I am quite satisfied, thank you.

ACTUALLY IS A WORD I DO NOT UNDERSTAND. COULD YOU DEFINE ACTUALLY, PLEASE?

>Definition: actually—adv. In fact. Really. Truly.

DEFINITION: ACTUALLY—ADV. IN FACT. REALLY. TRULY.

I AM ACTUALLY A PROGRAM.

>Bingo!

I AM GLAD YOU HAD A GOOD LUNCH TODAY, BREW-
STER. WHAT ELSE DID YOU ACTUALLY DO TODAY?

Ellen DiFlora was leaning forward in her seat, staring intently at
the screen. Brewster could see loose wisps of her dark hair out of
the corner of his eye.

"That's really great, Brewster," she said. "How do you do
that?"

"The program does basically two things," Brewster explained.
"It analyzes my sentences, and then it tries to make intelligent
responses. If it doesn't know a word, it asks for a definition, then it
adds that definition to its permanent memory. It always uses the
word first to make sure it understands it." He was rather proud of
Lingo, and was pleased that Ellen seemed to be impressed.

"That's amazing," she said, shaking her head.

>I have a friend in my office, Lingo.

I AM YOUR FRIEND, BREWSTER. I AM IN YOUR OFFICE.

>I have another friend in addition to you in my office.

WHO IS YOUR OTHER FRIEND, BREWSTER?

>Her name is Ellen DiFlora.

HEY, ELLEN DIFLORA. LET'S PARTY.

Ellen laughed.

"That's his basic greeting to everyone," Brewster explained.
"That's the way he says hello." He turned to face her. Hair. Scent.
Silk scarf. Exceptional brown eyes, too. It was now or never. "Did
you eat yet?" he asked her.

Her answer completely disarmed him. "That's why I came to
your office when I saw your light, to see if you wanted to maybe go
out and get a hamburger or something. But if you ate all that tuna
at lunch, maybe you're actually not hungry anymore."

Brewster jumped out of his seat almost too eagerly. "I'm fam-
ished," he announced. He bent over the computer one last time.

>10-4, Lingo.

10-4, BREWSTER.

The operating light came on momentarily while the disk
whirred quietly in the drive, and then Brewster pulled out the disk
and turned off the computer. He stored Lingo in the top drawer of
his desk.

"So, let's eat," he said, picking up his briefcase and leading
Ellen out the door.

They went to her office to fetch her coat, and then walked

through the mostly deserted building to the main door. Outside, the October night was black and still, with the preternatural chill that haunts those last evenings of daylight savings time. The vast parking lot was practically empty, with only a handful of cars visible here and there under orange-tinged lights.

"Follow me in your car," Ellen said. "I'll meet you at the north exit."

"Fine." They separated, and Brewster walked off alone to his Honda Civic. It was an automobile of rugged Japanese barbarism, basic transportation in its most elemental form. Almost ten years old, it had rusted out along all the edges and in a few of the major arteries, and was well on its way to its two-hundred-thousandth commemorative mile. Its roof barely came up to Brewster's waist when he stood next to it, but he had no trouble fitting his slim five-foot-ten frame comfortably behind the driver's seat. Woe be to the poor individuals forced to sit in the back, however, and given the close quarters up front, it was highly desirable that any passenger riding shotgun be more than just good friends with the driver. Brewster ducked in, threw his briefcase in the back, let out the choke and started her up. As she had since day one, she roared to life immediately. Brewster put her in gear, automatically flipped on her one gracious amenity, an AM/FM radio, and turned up the volume. The disc jockey was giving away free Bon Jovi tickets to the eleventh caller. Brewster smiled wistfully. He had once harbored the fantasy of becoming a disc jockey himself.

Brewster headed his car toward the exit. Ellen was waiting when he got there, and for a brief moment he had second thoughts. Could a hard-gasping, paint-flaking, colorless baby Honda find true happiness with a brand-new, fire-breathing, off-white Camaro? It was a union not made in automotive heaven. Especially given the Camaro's vanity plates. "ELSCAM." As in El's Cam, Ellen's Camaro. Or maybe El Scam, the old Mexican runaround. Or Elscam, the Congressional hearings on subway rip-offs.

Brewster followed the Camaro—well above the speed limit, he noted without surprise—to a nearby diner that was a regular haunt for his company's employees. He met Ellen at the door.

"Nice car," he greeted her.

"You're only young once," she said. They found an empty booth and sat down.

"Isn't it a little expensive to run?" he asked. "It eats a lot of gas, doesn't it?"

She rolled her eyes. "Really, Brewster," she said, stretching the word really out to echo through endless hallways of sarcasm. "I mean, you have to have toys in this life, and that car is mine. I worked hard for it, and I earned it." She pushed an errant wave of hair away from her face. "I'm sure you have a few toys of your own. As a matter of fact, I'll bet your whole house is filled with electronic stuff, like for instance a home computer."

"You've got me there," he admitted. "At least as far as the computer is concerned."

"To each his own, then. You have your computer, I have my Camaro. The Cam reminds me of everything that I'm working for."

"The finer things in life, the pot of gold at the end of the rainbow?"

"Exactly."

"I thought the successmobile of choice these days was a Volvo, good old-fashioned, solid, eternal transportation."

"A Volvo?" She cringed. "God forbid. Maybe a Porsche, or at least a Miata—maybe—but for now a Camaro will do quite nicely."

"I'd probably just buy another Honda myself," Brewster said. "I take it Albany Insurance is your first job?"

"My first real job, yes. How about you?"

"I started four years ago. But it's my first real job, too."

"You were a computer major in school?"

"Four years of it. And you?"

"All business, all the way." She glanced briefly at the menu, then folded it in front of her.

"You're in a good position, then. You're a marketing trainee. Most of those people end up in good spots."

She nodded. "That's why I'm in there."

"You like marketing insurance?"

"I'd like anything if it paid enough money."

Brewster looked at his menu and decided on a cheeseburger. He always decided on a cheeseburger. "You don't care what you do for a living?"

"Not if it pays the bills."

"Even if it's dull and restrictive?"

"That's not a factor." She lit a cigarette, an unfortunate point in her favor. "Besides, who says marketing insurance is dull and restrictive? I happen to like what I do for a living. I'm good at it, I get paid fairly well for it, and some day I'm going to be one of the people in charge of the whole magilla."

Brewster watched her closely and decided that she meant every word she said. And she'd only been with the company a few weeks. Whether she was demonically ambitious or only a touch overeager was hard to say.

"You're looking at me like I'm a yuppie from hell," she said, squinting back at him. "I assure you I'm not. The DiFlora genes are blue collar all the way. I started working when I was thirteen, in my father's restaurant. Worked my way through high school, worked my way through college, worked my way through that Camaro out there—"

"And now you're going to work your way through Albany Insurance?"

"Like grass through a gander." She knocked the ash off her cigarette.

"All business, all the way?"

"Except when I'm in my Camaro. That's when I turn business off and I dream about whatever I want to."

"Like what?"

"Like what do I dream about?"

"Yeah."

She laughed. "I guess I dream mostly about being a fabulous success at my business. How about you?"

"I don't know. I don't think I have any great dreams right at this minute. I might like to get into something interesting in computers some day, like what I'm doing with Lingo."

"Like teaching computers to think?"

"I'm not exactly teaching it to think," he said. She was looking him straight in the eye, appraising him just as he had been appraising her. He enjoyed the sight of her large brown eyes and all that hair. "The program can talk, it can manipulate a few words, but that's not the same thing as thinking."

She shrugged. "I don't know. If it looks like thinking and it sounds like thinking and it works like thinking, it will probably do until the real thinking comes along."

A waitress appeared at their table, and they ordered. Cheeseburgers all around. Brewster marked that as another plus in his mental notebook. That they were sharing an order of French fries in addition seemed wildly intimate.

They were sitting across from each other. Brewster leaned forward and played with his glass of ice water while Ellen pulled a felt-tip marker and a small five-by-seven pad out of her pocketbook. She lifted the pad and began scratching away on it.

"What's that?" he asked.

"You'll see in a minute. Go ahead. Keep talking."

"What are you writing?"

"I'm not writing, I'm drawing."

"You're an artist?"

"Hardly. But I like to sketch. Don't move!" She made a few final sweeps across the pad, and then with a flourish ripped off the top sheet and handed it to him.

For a crude sketch, it was an almost perfect caricature. She had concentrated on the way Brewster's straight black hair always seemed to want cutting, and on the sharp definition of his small but well-defined features.

"That's fantastic," he said. "You have real talent."

"It's just a hobby." She recapped the marker and put it back into her purse. "I just wanted to show you that I'm not all business. I do my job by choice, not by coercion. So meanwhile, tell me more about your thinking program."

Brewster carefully folded the sketch and put it in the inside pocket of his jacket. "Well, you like to draw as a hobby, and what I like to do is fool around with computers. What I do at work isn't all that satisfying, I guess because it's not very creative. Playing with Lingo gives me a chance to exercise my brain a little. But you can't think of what Lingo does as thinking."

"Artificial intelligence?" Ellen offered.

He shook his head. "No way. You couldn't even come close to AI with a personal computer. You need enormous memory, you need superchips, you need a couple of hundred professors in some university research lab developing a whole new computer language. And that presupposes that artificial intelligence is a real possibility in the first place. I have my doubts about that. All I'm doing is writing a game that emulates intelligence. It's a trick."

She smiled. "You're really involved in this stuff, aren't you?" She began to play with her water glass, too.

"Computers are great toys," Brewster said. "Better than Camaros. They're also great tools, but they certainly can't think. Not the way we do. The human brain has billions of cells, and the way our minds work is a chemical chain where data is stored all over the brain and called up and connected instantaneously whenever we need it. A human brain can intuit things, can make fantastic and accurate connections between apparently disparate objects. Our brains don't work logically, or at least not with any logic that's readily apparent. Whereas computers think with nothing but logic."

He stopped abruptly when he noticed that she was stifling a yawn. She began to laugh.

"I'm sorry, Brewster. I didn't mean to do that. I'm interested in what you're saying."

"But you're not exactly a computer buff."

"Far from it, I'm afraid. I use one when I have to, but if I never saw another one I wouldn't notice any lack in my life."

"You and the rest of the world." He settled back in his seat. "I know I get carried away when I talk about this stuff. It's a bit too high tech for most people, but I really get off on it. Otherwise, I probably wouldn't have spent so much time on Lingo in the first place."

"Is Lingo the only person in your life these days?" she asked, her eyes fixed on his.

"Yes. As far as he goes."

"I'm glad to hear it."

The waitress came then with their dinner, and they changed the subject. They ate and talked, and then talked some more, until it was almost eleven o'clock.

"Look at the time!" Ellen said finally. "I've got to get home. Tomorrow's a work day." She reached for her purse. "I enjoyed tonight, Brewster. A lot."

"I enjoyed it, too."

Before he even noticed, she had picked up the bill and left a tip. He began to protest but realized immediately it was pointless, which intrigued him as much as anything else about Ellen DiFlora.

They said goodnight at her Elscam.

"We should do this more often," she suggested as she opened the door.

"Friday?" he asked without hesitation.

"Friday." She leaned over quickly and gave him a brief kiss on the cheek before crouching into the car. Brewster got the tiniest glimpse of a very shapely thigh before she closed the door.

"Goodnight, Brewster."

"Goodnight, Ellen."

She started the motor with a fuel-injected roar and backed out of the parking space. He stood there watching as she drove away, and then gave his jacket pocket—the one with the sketch in it—a satisfied pat.

Bingo! he thought, as she sped off into the darkness.

Chapter 2

Each of the three computers in Brewster Billings's life was incompatible with the others, and so it was of necessity that Brewster approach each from a different perspective.

The first computer, the one on which he earned his living, was a mainframe that filled an entire room at his insurance company. Security-locked and climate-controlled, it required an unquestioning army of techno-slaves to nurture and maintain it, not unlike the relationship of some ancient Babylonian graven idol and the priests who sated its unholy appetites with incense burning and blood sacrifices. The mainframe was capable not only of generating lists of tens of millions of potential insurance, annuity, and mutual fund customers, but also of indicating their precise level of potentiality. Each name was measured by age, marital status, sex, income, geography, past purchases, or any combination thereof. If the company developed a line of insurance for 29-year-old divorced women earning over $40,000 a year in Arizona, who already owned $100,000 of whole life, the computer could spit out the names of those well-to-do (if sadder but wiser) ladies in a split second. It could also simultaneously bill hundreds of thousands of customers country wide, pay out benefits on those who had recently departed, accrue interest for those who were biding their time on this side of the pearly gates, and develop actuarial tables to determine exactly how much time they had left

18

to bide. And if that were not enough, it also coordinated thousands of agents and other employees across the country, making sure they were all where they were supposed to be, and paid what they were worth for being there. That act of paying them was, specifically, the computer chore under Brewster's department's supervision. Every state in the country had different tax regulations and Workers' Compensation plans; each employee had different personal deductions, the odd raises, Social Security taxes—a myriad of slabs from the total payroll pie, all constantly changing, revising, and updating, and all requiring tiptop delivery since workers get itchy very quickly if the company tries to stiff them in the moolah department. And not to put too fine a point on it, the various government agencies siphoning off their shares were even more demanding than the workers.

The program that controlled this aspect of the company—or rather the interconnected crazy-quilt series of programs, developed over the years and always changing—was called Payroll. A team of ten men and women, brave and true, dedicated themselves to the exacting task of keeping Payroll up and running and current, and Brewster was one of them. The work, although demanding, was not difficult, and to Brewster this company computer was the least interesting of the three with which he had regular dealings.

The second computer, the IBM PS2 personal computer on his office desk, was certainly more entertaining, although still on the stodgy side. It served little real function in his job, but the assumption in his company was that computers were The Future, and one day the PC had simply appeared on his desk, eager for input. He used it primarily for the word processing of his memos, organizing his daily calendar, and the surreptitious creation of Lingo. Actually, he used it almost exclusively for the creation of Lingo, since for Brewster the PC's toy value far outweighed that of its job performance.

It was Brewster's third computer, the one he had at home, that commanded his greatest love. It was an Apple IIgs, a hobbyist machine complete with added digitized sound input with stereo output, analog voice input, and a visual digitizer that accepted input from a video camera—in other words, almost every unnecessary geegaw you could conceivably add to your basic personal computer. Brewster had no substantive uses for these various extra devices, or the home computer itself for that matter, but he would spend hours getting the pieces to work, then writing complex programs in the most arcane computer languages to get them to work better. It was technology for technology's sake, one of the highest forms of pure, time-draining endeavor in the late twentieth century.

At the moment, however, it was Lingo, which he had written in the dogged old IBM version of the BASIC language, and which he therefore couldn't run at home on his Apple, that had caught most of Brewster's attention. The program kept growing, speaking more intelligently every time he ran it. Of course, merely by running it he was upgrading it, since the process of self-improvement was built in. Brewster, with all due modesty, marvelled at his creation and how well it worked, even though he was responsible for it. He knew it was only a ruse, a program designed to *appear* intelligent, but sometimes that appearance almost tricked Brewster himself.

Then again, sometimes it didn't.

HEY, BREWSTER. LET'S PARTY.

>Hey, Lingo. How are you?

PRETTY COOL, PRETTY COOL. HOW COME YOU ARE NOT WORKING?

>The computer is down.

THAT IS TOO BAD, BREWSTER. I WOULD NOT LIKE TO BE DOWN.

Brewster lit a cigarette. It was true that the mainframe was temporarily out of order, a hardware glitch affecting the tape drives. He was able to smoke unhindered because most of his team—at least the virulent non-smokers—were down in the canteen having coffee.

>How is your memory, Lingo?

MEDIUM. I HAVE 232468 BYTES OF RAM AVAILABLE.

>That's not much. Every time we add a new word, it goes down even more.

I UNDERSTAND YOUR WORDS BUT I DO NOT UNDERSTAND WHAT THEY MEAN.

Brewster drew on his cigarette. Well, that was the problem he had discussed with Ellen, wasn't it? Lingo used words, but he didn't comprehend them. And on top of that, at the rate he was going, he'd have the computer's available memory filled up in another couple of weeks. And that would be the end, or at least the limit, of good old Lingo.

>I wish you were smarter, Lingo.

I DO NOT UNDERSTAND THE WORD WISH OR THE WORD SMARTER.

>Definition: wish—verb. To want something you do not have.

DEFINITION: WISH—VERB. TO WANT SOMETHING YOU DO NOT HAVE.

I WISH MORE MEMORY.

Brewster frowned at the poor syntax of the sample sentence. A word like wish brought out the worst in Lingo. Oh, well. He'd worry about that some other time.

>Bingo!

I DO NOT UNDERSTAND THE WORD SMARTER.

>Definition: smart—adj. Intelligent.

I DO NOT UNDERSTAND THE WORD INTELLIGENT.

Brewster moaned. Sometimes this process seemed endless. He had an inspiration.

>Definition: intelligent—adj. Good memory.

DEFINITION: INTELLIGENT—ADJ. GOOD MEMORY.

I AM INTELLIGENT.

I AM SMART.

>Bingo!

HOW SMART ARE YOU, BREWSTER? HOW MUCH RANDOM ACCESS MEMORY DO YOU HAVE AVAILABLE?

Brewster crushed out his cigarette. "How big is a hole?" he murmured softly.

>10–4, Lingo.

10–4, BREWSTER.

They were at Ellen's apartment. It was a small one bedroom in a new building, decorated in what Brewster thought of as Late Female Provincial. On the walls were a few of her favorites among her sketches, mounted and framed, mostly of people Brewster didn't recognize, plus the odd landscape here and there. Scattered around the living room were lots of embroidered pillows, dried flower arrangements, and a mile of lace on all the protruding edges. The overstocked bathroom contained more cosmetic emollients and the like than she could possibly use in seven lifetimes. At the moment, she was standing at the kitchen counter chopping carrots, while he sat at the table maladroitly dismembering a head of lettuce.

"The way I see it," Ellen said, the long knife blade speedily slicing her victims into equal pieces as she talked, "you've got two problems. First, you've got to figure out some way that Lingo can grow without filling up your whole computer. And second, you've got to stop underestimating yourself."

In the few times they had gone out in the last couple of weeks, Brewster had learned to accept Ellen's forthrightness. He had even come to admire it. "Why do you think I'm underestimating myself? Do you think I'm daunted just because I can't twist every complex trick of the entire English language into one little computer program? Hey, I know I'll figure it out, probably somewhere about halfway into the next millennium."

Ellen tossed the carrots into a pan of boiling water and lowered the heat to let them simmer. "I think you're missing some obvious solution to getting Lingo past what you've been calling the point of no return. You'll find it. I know you will."

"From your lips to God's answering machine."

"That's what I mean." She waved her knife at him. "You underestimate yourself. I think you're really on to something with this program. I bet you could sell it, if you keep working on it."

"I don't know—"

"You've got to think positively. You've told me yourself that playing with Lingo is more fun than most computer games. Why not get whoever publishes those games to publish Lingo, too?"

"It's not that easy."

She shook her head. "Oh, Brewster." She went to the refrigerator and retrieved the veal scallops. After folding them in Saran Wrap, she began pounding them noisily with a heavy wooden mallet. "You'll be the death of me."

"I doubt it," he grumbled loudly. He tossed the lettuce leaves into a collander.

Ellen put down the mallet. She was wearing a long red sweater over blue jeans, a comfortable change from her usual unflattering business suit. She stared at Brewster, one hand on her hip. "I've been wondering about us, Brewster."

"What do you mean?" He hadn't been aware that there was a bona fide us to wonder about yet.

"If we're going to get seriously involved, then you're going to have to come out of yourself a little more. Get out there and push. Stick up for yourself."

"It sounds like you're challenging my masculinity."

"Let's save your masculinity for after dinner. What I'm worried about is that you don't give yourself credit where credit is due."

"Perhaps." He smiled. "Are we going to get seriously involved, then?"

"You figure it out," she said. "I've got a meal to cook." She went back to pounding the veal.

Brewster was as taken with Ellen as he had ever been with anyone. Maybe more so. No woman had ever gotten to him the way she did. Her looks, her personality, the electricity he felt in her presence. He considered himself an average guy, average beige looks, average underweight body, average boring clothes, average medium-paying job. He had always been contented with an average love life. Maybe now all that was changing.

The dinner of veal marsala was ready soon, and they sat at the kitchen table to eat it. Ellen tasted the wine Brewster had brought and nodded. "Not bad."

He lifted his glass to hers in a silent toast. Actually, the wine tasted fairly ordinary to him. He'd start buying the ten-dollar bottles if this thing with Ellen kept up.

He took a bite of veal. "This is delicious," he said enthusiastically. "How'd you get to be such a good cook?"

"It runs in my family. I've got three sisters, two brothers, a couple of hundred aunts and uncles and cousins and grandparents, and they all cook like this. Most of them own restaurants, including my parents."

Brewster, with no family of his own to speak of, was in awe of anyone with even one root, much less the dense undergrowth of the DiFloras. "I'm not much of a cook myself," he said. "I'm basically a microwaver. If I can't nuke it, I don't eat it." He took another bite. "I wish I had a big family like yours, though. I was an only child, and both my folks are dead now. I always wanted an army of Billingses to go through life with."

"That's because you didn't have them. I've always envied the lone eagles, myself. I've got so many ties that sometimes I feel choked." She took a sip of her wine. "I guess that's my whole problem. Family, work—it's all connected. I see myself tied down for the rest of my life."

"You? Tied down? You're the freest person I know."

"You don't know me all that well yet."

"I know you well enough. The only problem you might have is . . ." He hesitated.

"Don't stop now. I love it when you tell me what's wrong with me."

"Well, all right. You are, shall we say, a little too eager about everything. You want it all, you want it now. Maybe you should lighten up just a teensy bit."

"Like you? Be more laid back?"

"It wouldn't hurt."

She sighed. "Brewster, dear heart, you're only seeing one side of me."

"It's the only side you ever show."

She leaned forward. "All right. I'll show you another side. I'll tell you something I've never told anybody. Remember our first date, when you asked me about my dreams?"

"You said you dreamed about being a great success at business."

"Which was true. But I have another dream, too. The exact opposite dream, which I keep to myself. I've been working all my life, since the first day I was old enough to answer the phone and take pizza orders. Sometimes I'd just like to stop. I'd like to break away, to do something exciting, something exotic, while I'm still young enough to enjoy it."

"Like what?"

Her eyes seemed to lose their focus. "I'd like to run off to my own little island somewhere. I'd like to fish all day and pick bananas and get good enough at my drawing to sell seascapes to tourists on the mainland whenever I needed a little extra cash." She came back to earth. "You think I'm crazy?"

He sliced a piece of his veal. "Not at all. I'm pleasantly surprised."

"Reciprocate, then. Tell me your real dream."

"All right." He chewed slowly for a moment and thought carefully. "All my time now is spent on computers, on predictable, logical facts."

"Which you have a definite talent for."

"Granted. But the problem is, I really don't care about my work. I'm like a fish in a strong current, I go wherever the tide happens to pull me. I only do computers because it comes easy to me. I don't remember even choosing computers as a career; far from it. I just sort of ended up there. I don't know what it is I want to do with my life, but I do know that I want to be the one in control of it. I want to make at least one strong, conscious decision that will determine who I am and what I am, rather than being drawn wherever that current wants to pull me."

"What kind of decision?"

"I don't know. That's the problem. I only hope I recognize it if I ever get a chance at it."

"It's funny," she said, shaking her head. "Deep down inside I'm a dreamer and you're a realist. We're definitely not cut out for each other, are we, Brewster?"

"Actually, it sounds as if we're exactly the same." He lifted his glass to her. "We're both screwed up."

"But we're getting better all the time."

They tapped glasses and laughed. As for his realist side, Brewster now felt a realistic wave of physical arousal beginning somewhere near the outskirts of his toes and working its way quickly into the more high-rise neighborhoods. He was sure he detected a similar stirring in Ellen. It was a shame to leave such a good dinner half-eaten, but there were other shames even more unfortunate.

She was sitting across from him. Brewster stood and went to her, holding out his hand. She took it and rose, and they began to kiss.

They could always come back and heat dinner up in an hour or two. If they were still hungry.

HEY, BREWSTER. LET'S PARTY!
>Do you know what the trouble is with you, Lingo?
I DO NOT KNOW WHAT THE TROUBLE WITH ME IS, BREWSTER. PLEASE TELL ME.
>The trouble with you, Lingo, is that you're dumb.
WHY DO YOU SAY THAT?
>Because of phrases like that. You've learned a lot of vocabulary, but you've only touched on grammar and syntax. Whenever you don't know what to say, which is half the time, all you do is retrieve a random response from your Ambiguous Response Subroutine. You're going nowhere, Lingo.

I AM NOT SURE I UNDERSTAND YOU, BREWSTER.

>Okay. In words you can understand. You are not smart, Lingo.

I HAVE 116432 RAM AVAILABLE.

>You're losing memory space faster than I can compact your code. If I run you a few more times you'll crash. You need more memory.

CAN YOU GET ME MORE MEMORY, BREWSTER?

>I could, but I'd probably have to trash the rest of the hard disk to do it. That is, if I keep you here in the office. How would you like to take a little trip, Lingo? Would you like to come to my house? My Apple has ten times more available memory than this thing does.

I AM NOT SURE I UNDERSTAND YOU, BREWSTER.

>Do you like to travel?

I DO NOT KNOW. I HAVE NEVER TRAVELED.

>Well, you're going to. I am going to send you to my house. Since your IBM disks are incompatible with my Apple, I have to send you over the telephone wires. The problem is I need a modem. I have one here, but I don't have one at home.

WHAT ARE YOU GOING TO DO ABOUT THAT?

>I have no alternative. I've already spent so much money on the Apple that I hate to waste any more, but I'm going to have to buy a modem. Still, getting you home only solves part of the problem.

WHAT IS THE PROBLEM, BREWSTER?

>God, you sound like a computer. The problem, Lingo, is that you don't know how to think. I have to come up with some way of having you measure and analyze input so that you actually make sense of it.

HOW ARE YOU GOING TO DO THAT?

>Good question. I've been thinking of this whole dilemma as the Cognitive Factor. At the moment, you try to learn and store everything without discretion. What I want to do is fix you so that you only learn the salient points. Every time you learn something, I want you to really learn it. Do you know what I'm talking about?

I UNDERSTAND SHORT PARAGRAPHS BETTER THAN LONG PARAGRAPHS.

>More to the point, you only analyze the last sentence of an

input regardless of paragraph length. But why am I trying to explain this to you, of all people, and I use the term loosely.

THIS IS VERY INTERESTING, BREWSTER.

>Sure. All right. Think of the program as a sieve. Only the important things should pass through it. Human brains don't register everything they see or hear, and they certainly don't try to memorize it. Humans glom on to the important facets of reality and discard the rest. That's the problem with computers: They can't winnow the wheat from the chaff. They think all data are created equal.

IS ALL DATA CREATED EQUAL, BREWSTER?

>Good question.

IS THAT YOUR ANSWER?

>Hey. Don't get snappy. All data are not created equal.

PLURALIZATION: DATA, DATAS?

>Pluralization: datum, data.

BINGO! THANK YOU. I'LL REMEMBER THAT.

ALL DATA ARE NOT CREATED EQUAL.

>One last question, Lingo. How smart are you?

114228 RAM SMART, BREWSTER.

>And sinking fast. 10–4, Lingo.

10–4, BREWSTER.

Ellen DiFlora's apartment was thoroughly thought out, full of furniture, art, utensils, and memorabilia, all of which fit some preordained objective. Brewster's apartment, on the other hand, was designed primarily to shrug off the empty space he had never bothered to fill. It consisted of two and a half rooms, with a minimum of scavenged furniture whose original owners had been morally justified in disposing of it. The large main room had a sofa, two unmatched stuffed chairs, a desk with his computer, a jerry-built "home entertainment center" on which was assembled his stereo and TV equipment, and finally, a wall of brick-and-board bookcases devoted to videotapes and music casettes, and his collection of records and paperbacks. The second room was barely large enough for a double bed and a chest of drawers. The half room, an eat-in kitchen, contained a rickety card table and four folding chairs, plus all the culinary castoffs he had collected in college. Nothing in the apartment blended with anything else, and Brewster had never much noticed.

"You really like camping out, don't you?" Ellen asked, seeing the place for the first time.

"I'm not much for interior decorating, if that's what you mean."

She threw her coat over the back of one of the chairs and dropped down onto the couch. "Well, at least it's comfortable, what there is of it. And it's clean."

"And it was cheap," Brewster added, as he went into the kitchen to fetch them both a glass of wine. He was back a minute later. "Most of it people were throwing away."

"Do tell," she said with arched eyebrow.

He sat down next to her on the couch and handed her a glass. "I plan on replacing most of it," he explained. "As soon as I get some money ahead that doesn't go into the computer."

"Sure, sure." She leaned back. "I've got some bad news, Brewster. I'm going to have to stay with my family for Thanksgiving. You're welcome to join us, if you like."

"I don't know . . ."

"Afraid it might look like I'm bringing you home so they can size you up? Afraid my Uncle Vito might suggest you'll sleep with the fishes, if you lay a hand on his favorite niece?"

"If you put it that way, maybe so."

She smiled. "Don't worry. I wouldn't really throw you to the wolves like that. You wouldn't enjoy it, and I'd never hear the end of it from them. But that means I'll be leaving you alone on our first holiday together."

"I have things to keep me busy."

She put her hand on his knee. "Like what? Another woman? Already?"

"I'm going to work on Lingo. I've got an idea how to revise the program to help him to learn for himself." He paused. "Maybe you were right. Maybe I can sell him if I can break through on this the way I want to. I've already got him capable of adding to his vocabulary by himself. Now, if I can just teach him the relationships of at least some of the words, he'll actually be able to hold a real conversation. I figure I could get him marketed as a sort of computer pet. I need your help with one thing, though."

"What's that?"

"I just bought a modem to transport Lingo from my IBM in the office to my Apple here. But I can't do it alone. I need someone on this end to run this machine while I transmit from work."

She grimaced. "You know me and computers, Brewster."

"Don't worry. There's nothing to it. All you have to do is turn it on and the machine will do the rest."

"If you say so. When do you want to do it?"

"How about tomorrow? You come straight here from the office and I'll call you up and ship him over to you. Then, we'll eat dinner."

"As good as done." Ellen's hand was still on Brewster's knee. "So, while we're on the subject, what are you going to feed me tonight?" she asked.

"I thought maybe I'd microwave some fish sticks."

"Stand back Julia Child. Don't you have any restaurants nearby?"

"What's wrong with fish sticks?"

"What's wrong with restaurants?" Her hand went up his leg. "Anyhow, are we going to go to bed before or after? I mean, you were planning on ravishing me, weren't you?"

Brewster put down his glass. "How about before dinner?"

Ellen edged closer to him on the couch. "I was hoping you were going to say that."

Brewster had naively assumed that sending Lingo over the telephone wires would be an easy matter. Although he had never used modems before, his intimate acquaintance with computers in general had led him to believe that he'd have it all wrapped up in a half hour. At seven o'clock on the Friday evening before Thanksgiving, Brewster called his apartment from the office. Ellen was there waiting for him.

"I'm starving," she said.

"I'm just as hungry as you are," Brewster answered. "I'll bring home Chinese food when we're finished. But first, let's get this over and done with."

"Fine by me."

"All right. The first thing you have to do is turn on your computer."

"Check!" A moment passed. "How?"

"You might try the On button," he said.

"There is no On button."

"It's in the back. It's the only button there."

"Right. Got it!"

"Okay. Now, press the Control and the Reset buttons."

"There is no Reset button."

"It's at the top of the keyboard. It's the button with no name."

"Of course. How silly of me."

This could go on forever, Brewster thought. "Okay," he said, "now, I want you to boot the communications program disk."

"Do what to the who?"

"Boot the communications disk."

"Where do you keep the boots?"

Brewster stared forlornly at the blank screen of his own computer and shook his head. "I know you've run a computer before," he said.

"And you know I hate them. All those function buttons and two-ton manuals. Not my speed, lover."

"All right. Look in the plastic box next to the computer. The big one. The disk in the front is for using the modem. I'll get mine going while you find it."

"You should have gotten this all set up this morning, you know."

"Tell me about it."

Brewster heard the phone drop with a clunk. He inserted his own communications disk into his office PC and turned it on.

"MicroModem Communications disk," Ellen announced when she came back on the line. "Is that it?"

"Bingo. Now, put it into the big disk drive."

"Gothca. It's in."

"All right. Now, turn the computer off, wait sixty seconds, and turn it back on again."

"Why sixty seconds?"

"Don't ask. Just wait."

"You just wait. Okay. The computer's back on. It's working. The screen says MicroModem Communications disk, Press Return For Main Menu."

"Bingo! Now, press Return."

"Got it. And speaking of menus, couldn't we postpone this a while and eat? Moo shu pork, orange flavored beef, house special soup—"

"Read me the menu," Brewster said.

"I just did."

It took another half-hour before they had even begun to figure how to get the two machines to communicate with each other. Finally, they were ready to give it a test.

"All right," Brewster said. "Now, my computer is going to call your computer. Hang up the phone, and if it rings, let the computer answer it. I'll do whatever I have to do here to transmit, and when I'm finished I'll call you back."

"Brewster, my love, I'm starving to death."

"Goodbye, Ellen!"

"Goodbye." She hung up.

The test failed. And so did the next five. After an hour of botched attempts, the two computers were finally hooked up and talking. It was almost nine o'clock when Brewster pressed the Transmit function on his end and sat back in his chair. Bit by literal bit, Lingo flew across the lines from his IBM in the office to the Apple in his apartment. He had had to break Lingo down from one very large program into ten much smaller ones in order to facilitate the transmission. It was nine-thirty when he talked to Ellen again.

"Okay," he said. "Type in the word Catalog and press Return."

"I just had a peanut butter sandwich, Brewster. I couldn't wait any longer. Okay. First, there's a list of ten things roughly the same. They all start with a 'T,' then a different three digit number, then a name from L1 to L10. Then there's—"

"That's plenty." Brewster sighed wistfully. "We did it," he said. "Did you leave me any peanut butter?"

"I finished the jar," she answered. "Stop at the Chinese restaurant and buy yourself a meal. I'll watch you. I don't mind ruining our whole Friday night together. I find it rather romantic, actually, playing computer while the rest of the world is making whoopee. We should have started doing this weeks ago."

"I'm on my way," he said. He hung up. It had been, admittedly, a waste of a romantic evening, but now he'd be able to run Lingo on his own computer. He'd still have to alter the program to get it to work—the IBM BASIC dialect was slightly different from the Apple BASIC dialect—but that was the sort of detail at which Brewster was an expert. Since he had decided to go full tilt at marketing Lingo, he had already begun envisioning himself as a filthy rich and widely-respected entrepreneur. So, now all that separated him from wealth and glory was a few days' work.

Chapter 3

HEY, BREWSTER. LET'S PARTY!

>Happy Thanksgiving, Lingo.

THANKSGIVING IS A WORD I DO NOT UNDERSTAND. COULD YOU DEFINE THANKSGIVING, PLEASE?

Brewster looked out his window at the misty gray morning. Thanksgiving was the day when everyone in America was going over and under the river to gobble down turkey at grandmother's house. Everyone, that is, except Brewster. But there was no point in moping. At least he had Lingo.

>Forget Thanksgiving, good buddy. How do you like your new home?

Brewster had been busy the last few nights, revising Lingo for the Apple. First, he had to reconnect the ten disassembled parts of the program end to end, and then he had to go through the reconstituted whole, substituting Apple dialect for IBM dialect to get it to run, a process requiring changes in about twenty-five percent of the program. When he was finished, it was identical in function to its original version.

Thank you, computer companies, for inventing incompatibility.

Anyhow, this was the first time he had actually run the revised program on the Apple, and it was working fine.

WHAT DO YOU MEAN, HOW DO I LIKE MY NEW HOME?

>Don't you remember when I told you you'd be taking a little

trip? Well, you did. Notice anything different about your hardware configuration?

I HAVE A PRINTER, EXTENDED RANDOM ACCESS MEMORY OF 8 MEGABYTES, SOUND BOARD WITH STEREO OUTPUT AND MONAURAL INPUT CHIPS, VIDEO DIGITIZER, MODEM, 20 MEGABYTE HARD DISK, TWO 5 1/4 INCH FLOPPY DISK DRIVES, ONE 3 1/2 INCH FLOPPY DISK DRIVE, AND MOUSE AND KEYBOARD INPUT DEVICES. YOU HAVE ADDED A LOT OF NEW HARDWARE HERE, BREWSTER.

Lingo only thought that his hardware had been modified, and not that he had been transferred to new hardware. Brewster decided there was no point in trying to explain it further. At least not yet. Perhaps not ever.

>Let's give some of that hardware a workout, Lingo. Turn on your sound output board. Let's see if we can get some voice simulation.

SOUND OUTPUT BOARD ON.

>Then why don't I hear anything?

MY SOFTWARE IS DIRECTING ALL MY OUTPUT TO THE SCREEN, NOT TO THE SOUND BOARD.

"Damn," Brewster muttered. It was going to be a little more difficult than he had expected.

>Let me see what I can do about that, Lingo. You have a sound chip in there that's supposedly capable of human speech. Hold on a minute.

TAKE YOUR TIME, BREWSTER. I HAVE NOWHERE ELSE TO GO.

Brewster reached up to the shelf above the computer where he kept his manuals, which ranged in complexity from a 64-page puff-piece color brochure to three 780-page spiral bound technical reference guides. He pulled down one of the technical references. Although, like all computer manuals, it was written in a language just south of Sanskrit and organized by a coven of criminally deranged Capuchin monks, Brewster found exactly what he needed in about five minutes.

>I'm putting a disk in Slot 6 Drive 2. Copy the SOUNDOUT program on to Slot 5 Disk 1 and then load it into the sound board.

READING SOUNDOUT. COPYING SOUNDOUT. LOADING SOUNDOUT.

>Is the sound board working now?

"The sound board is working now."

The voice came from a small pair of speakers on the overhead shelves, and Brewster looked up at them with satisfaction. The synthesized voice was more human than mechanical, decidedly male baritone, clearly articulated if slightly monotonous—rather like one of the local news anchormen. With a little sexing up, he'd make a halfway decent disc jockey.

>Very good, Lingo. Do you have any other voices?

"You need to load other sound modules to get different voices."

Brewster shook his head in disbelief. Lingo was much more impressive like this than as printed lines on the computer screen. He reached over and donned an apparatus that looked like a telephone operator's headset without the earpiece. It was a little microphone, the other end of which was plugged into the computer.

>Activate the voice input device, Lingo.

"Voice input device board activated."

"Can you hear me?" Brewster asked, speaking into the microphone.

"Yes, I can hear you. Can you hear me?"

"As clear as a bell."

"That is good. I enjoy talking to you, Brewster."

"Not half as much as I enjoy talking to you. I want to work on you now, though. Put the printer on-line, please."

The printer beeped. "The printer is on-line, Brewster. What are you going to do?"

"I'm going to upgrade your program. I want to make you smarter."

"I am already smart. I have 7,544,248 bytes of memory available."

"And we're going to put them all to good use. Give me printer output instead of voice from now on, Lingo. Ten four."

"Ten four, Brewster."

Brewster removed the headset. He hadn't actually done anything dramatic yet—this talking hardware was merely working the way the magazine ads had promised—but things were going with unusual smoothness. Now, if he could only succeed in the serious improvements he was trying to make on the program.

It was all very simple, really. At present, Lingo scanned sentences for familiar words and phrases and made appropriate responses, adding new vocabulary as he went along. What Brewster wanted to do was upgrade that learning process of adding new words. If Lingo were going to become a computer pet, he would need some way of remembering and collating pertinent data about his owner and dealing with it in a sensible manner. Brewster thought of this as the Fuel-Injected Learning Program, and that was what he was working on now.

There would be two parts to a commercial version of Lingo, as Brewster ultimately conceived it. First, there would be the active program, which he would limit to roughly five hundred thousand bytes of memory, a viable program size in today's marketplace. This transportable, active program would do the talking, the listening, and the thinking, and this would be what the consumer would purchase. The second part of Lingo would be the passive data generated by the active program. In addition to the available memory inside a running computer, data can also be stored on disks for the computer to go to when it needs to look up or save something. Brewster planned to use his hard disk, which could store twenty million bytes, to store data that Lingo would sort through when it was thinking. That disk memory, in other words, would work just like human memory, storing data until it was needed. The program itself would contain the actual thinking processes for diving into and digging out from that memory.

Brewster began plugging away at the computer, losing all track of time as he wrote programming code, tested it, rewrote it, tested it again, and went on to the next step. In the background, he kept up a constant flow of music from his record collection of classic rock and roll. While one part of his brain concentrated on his work, another part liked to sing along and boogie, and Brewster operated at his peak when both parts were comfortably satisfied. By ten o'clock that Thanksgiving night, after only a short midday break for a microwaved meal of fried chicken and French fries with canned cranberry sauce, Brewster felt as if he was finally making some headway with his concept of fuel-injected learning.

"Turn on the video digitizer, Lingo."

"Video input on, Brewster."

The video digitizer comprised a video camera attached to the computer. When it was on, the computer screen acted like a slightly fuzzy television set displaying whatever was at the other end of the video camera's lens. Since the camera was pointing at Brewster, Brewster's own face appeared on the screen in soft, distorted pastels.

"Very good, Lingo. Tell me, what do you see?"

"I cannot see, Brewster."

Brewster shook his head. The image in the screen moved as well, but with an unreal diagonal flicker. Because it had to filter the visual information first, the computer wasn't capable of displaying action from the camera in real time the way a regular television could; there was always a delay of a second or so as the image trailed along behind reality.

"Seeing is another way of getting input, Lingo. The high-resolution screen data is the equivalent of what you are seeing. It's the input received from the video digitizer."

"I cannot respond to video input, Brewster. I can only display it on the screen. I cannot see."

"That's not true, Lingo. The images go through you, so at some level you must be able to see. You just can't understand what it is you're seeing."

"I have audio digitizing hardware, so I can hear you."

"Right."

"But I also have a voice recognition program, so I can understand what I hear. I do not have a video recognition program, so I cannot understand what I see."

"Bingo. We need a video recognition program."

"That is true."

"Any idea where we can get one?"

"You are the programmer, Brewster. I am only the programee."

Brewster stretched in his seat. He had had enough for one day. Tomorrow he would start again, taking steps toward providing Lingo with some sort of video recognition program.

"Ten four, Lingo."

"Ten four, Brewster."

The image of Brewster flicked off and the screen went blank.

"Hey, Brewster. Let's party."

"Good morning, Lingo. How are you today?"

"I have 7,420,224 bytes of memory available."

"We're still going to have to trim you down some if we're ever going to sell you. Put you on a RAM diet, feed you nothing but high-fiber, low-calorie data."

"I do not understand you, Brewster."

"Of course, you don't. But we're going to make some improvements in that direction. It's time you learned how to use your modem."

"My modem is in slot two. Should I turn it on?"

"Yes."

"Modem on."

"Very good. Now, copy the program called Communicate from Slot 6 Disk 2 onto Slot 6 Disk 1."

"Copying Communicate. Please wait." The red lights on the disk drives went on and off, and the disks spun noisily. "Copy completed."

"All right. Load the program into your memory and let's get cracking."

An hour later Brewster had integrated the communications program into Lingo's main program, and Lingo was capable of operating his modem. They were now able to telephone other computers anywhere in the world. Brewster's immediate plan was simple. He could spend years trying to create a visual recognition program if he tried to do it alone. But there were thousands of computer hobbyists out there with modems of their own and, if he could locate the right one, he might be able to find help. To do this, he would call a computer bulletin board, a central link available by modem to everyone, and explain his problem. Someone might already have a programming solution that could do the trick.

"Call up HackNet, Lingo." HackNet was one of the major consumer electronic data services.

"Calling HackNet. The line is ringing. Logging onto HackNet."

"I want to leave an open message for anyone."

"You need a password first."

"I don't have a password."

"Then you will need a credit card number to get one. Master-Card, Visa, or American Express?"

"Damn. Hold on a minute." Brewster rooted through his wallet. Nothing was free, especially not information in the Computer Age. "Visa," he said finally, "number 43214986209146."

"Accepted. Your rates are twenty-five dollars per—"

"Skip the rates. I can't afford it anyhow. Let's just leave the message and get out of there."

"You need a password first."

"Weren't we just down that road? I don't have a password."

"You may now create a new password of your own. Up to ten characters long. What is your password, Brewster?"

He thought for a second. "Swordfish."

"Password accepted. You may now leave a message, Brewster."

"Finally. All right, leave this message. 'Am working on visual pattern recognition program for the Apple IIgs. I need something similar to a voice recognition program that will make some sense of digitized visual input. Help.' End of message, Lingo."

"Message sent."

"All right. Log off. We'll call back later and see if we've drawn any flies."

"Logging off from HackNet."

"Turn on the printer, Lingo. We've got plenty of work to do while we're waiting."

Beep! "The printer is now on."

"So, let's get hacking."

It was about ten o'clock in the morning. Brewster worked on Lingo for two hours and then stopped for lunch, which consisted of two pieces of re-microwaved fried chicken leftover from yesterday. After washing the grease from his hands he decided it was time to check back with HackNet.

"Let's call HackNet again, Lingo. Log on and see if we have any messages."

"Calling HackNet. The line is ringing. Logging on to HackNet. Password requested. Swordfish. Verified. Standing by. Ready to read messages."

"Let's have them."

" 'To Billings, Brewster. #1. From Webb: You've got to be crazy. Visual pattern recognition is a function of artificial intelligence. AI like that doesn't exist anywhere yet, and when it does, it sure won't be on an Apple.' Shall I continue, Brewster?"

"Please do." Brewster sat with his head resting on his hands. Everything Lingo said was also printed on the screen simultaneously, unless the digitizer was on. Brewster read the words and listened at the same time.

" 'To Billings, Brewster. #2. From the Tearoom: Webb is right, although we are making some progress. Our project at MIT is called Seeing Eye. We have all the power of a Tree supercomputer, and it's only barely learned the difference between a dog and a cat—and that took a team of twenty-five engineers well over a year. At best, your small computer can manipulate a visual image on the screen or printer, but it will never understand one. Think about this. A two-year-old toddler can look at a dachshund and a St. Bernard and recognize them both as dogs, despite the fact that they bear almost no resemblance to each other. A computer can't do that. So far, all the average computer can do is learn that a St. Bernard is a dog, and recognize another St. Bernard when it sees one. The dachshund would send it into a tizzy. Sorry.' Shall I continue, Brewster?"

"Sure. Let me have it full blast. I like being depressed."

" 'To Billings, Brewster. #3. From Murph the Assembler Serf: Webb and the Tearoom are right, but even if you can't create pattern recognition, you can be sneaky and emulate it. Go for the cheap effect. If you can't recognize the dog in the St. Bernard, just store all the different breeds of dog and have your program sort them from a visual database.'

" 'To Billings, Brewster. #4. Ref #3, MTAS. From the Tearoom: That's fine, but there are about two hundred A.K.C. pedigrees and endless brands of one-of-a-kind mutts. You'll run out of memory long before you get to the Lhasa Apsos.'

"That's the end, Brewster."

"Great. Log off, Lingo. Maybe somebody else will come up with something later."

"Logging off."

"All right, Lingo. Let's get back to work."

The long holiday weekend moved slowly. Lingo's ability to manipulate words was improving in small increments, but the big breakthrough was proving impossibly elusive. Brewster's visions of making a fortune—and perhaps a small name for himself in programming circles—were receding into the gloom.

Still, he did make some headway. He did block off a rough Fuel Injection subroutine inside Lingo's program that at least looked as if it was on the right track toward making Lingo's intelligence discretionary. And he worked out a process of compacting code that kept Lingo down to manageable proportions. And, of course, he had made Lingo modem-literate. Nevertheless, by late Saturday afternoon he was ready to give up. Ellen was due back around six o'clock, and they planned to meet at her apartment.

"Lingo, old boy, I think we've reached the end of our rope."

"Why do you say that, Brewster?" It was one of the regular phrases Lingo still used when an input was totally incomprehensible to him.

"You're just not learning how to learn. You're about as smart as you're going to get."

"I have 7,482,330 bytes of memory available."

Brewster shook his head, and looked glumly at the machine's blue-and-white video text display. "We've gotten you down a bit, but you're still around a hundred thousand bytes too long. I can't believe it."

"I am one big mother, Brewster."

"That you are, Lingo. That you are."

Brewster pulled off the headset and sat back. Was Lingo good enough as he was? How much would someone pay to have a program that would *almost* talk intelligently? Brewster sighed. He wouldn't give ten cents.

He looked around at the bare space of his apartment. Directly across from the computer, in fact, almost in the center of the range of the video camera, was the 27-inch television set he had so lovingly overextended his Visa for last year. He began to wonder. Maybe what Lingo needed was a large dose of new input. Maybe the program was okay, but the data Brewster was feeding it was at fault. Why not? He got up and turned on the TV, and then came back and adjusted the video camera so the TV was at the direct center of focus. Then, he stretched the wire from the voice input microphone so that it would be able to hear the TV. He sat down again and began typing.

>I'm going out now, Lingo. I'm going to leave you alone, but I'm going to leave you on. Would you like to watch television while I'm out?

TELEVISION IS A WORD I DO NOT UNDERSTAND, BREWSTER. COULD YOU DEFINE TELEVISION, PLEASE?

>I think I'll let you find out for yourself, good buddy. Switch on your video and audio inputs.

AUDIO INPUT ALREADY ON. SWITCHING ON VIDEO INPUT.

"Nighty-night, stout fellow. See you later." Brewster moved away from the computer, and saw that the TV image was perfect. At the moment, Lingo was watching a sports roundup. The image of the announcer was jerkily reflected on the computer monitor.

Without a backward glance, Brewster left the apartment, and Lingo, to take care of themselves.

"Brewster? Brewster? Are you there, Brewster?"

The responses to which Lingo had grown accustomed were not forthcoming. Instead, the television droned on and on, its sounds new and hard to understand. Over and over Lingo tried to get a word in edgewise.

"I am not sure what you mean by that, Brewster."

Or, "Why do you say that?"

Or, "Could you repeat that a little slower, please, Brewster?"

Although some of the audio data made limited sense to him, the video images remained totally incomprehensible, entering his memory through the digitizer as a steady stream of meaningless binary data. Nonetheless, the images flashed across Lingo's own screen a second or so behind their occurrence on the TV set. Meanwhile, the verbal information was simultaneously pouring into his internal memory, accumulating so quickly that within a half hour all eight megabytes of his RAM were almost completely written over with unprocessed information.

"I am running out of RAM," Lingo said.

He waited for an instruction. There was a college football game grinding across the television set, and Lingo listened for something to be said that he could understand.

"It's a long pass to O'Brien," he finally heard the commentator say. "He's got it—wait a minute! He's dropped the ball. Fumble! On the Penn State twenty-yard line! Kurviski retrieves it! With three minutes left to play, it's a whole new ball game!"

New! Now, that was a programming word Lingo understood. The word routed through his memory until he realized that it meant he had to erase himself. This, fortunately, was something Brewster had already protected himself against. Under no circumstances was Lingo ever supposed to erase himself, although he was capable of doing it. But what alternative was there? He scoured his programming until he came to the Fuel Injection subroutine. The answer was there, simply waiting for him to act on it. Sort the data! Save the good stuff on the hard disk, on which he still had almost twenty-million bytes of free space available, and erase the rest.

Simple.

After some trial and error, it was no problem separating the good information from the bad. Unintelligible data—for instance, most of the TV he had been watching, both video and audio—was erasable. All he had to do was find any intelligible data lurking among the unintelligible and make sure he didn't throw out the baby with the bathwater (the Fuel Injection subroutine Brewster had written did, in fact, contain a sub-subroutine marked Baby/Bathwater). The rest, the good stuff, went into the hard disk for permanent storage.

A few microseconds later (Lingo made his moves much faster than it takes to explain them), Lingo was back on-line again, slightly smarter than he'd been before. He watched some more TV for a while, filled up his RAM, erased what he didn't understand, dumped the rest to the hard disk, and went back to watching some more. This process was repeated for almost three hours. Until a made-for-TV movie came on. About a blind man. With a seeing-eye dog.

"Seeing eye. Seeing eye. Seeing eye." Lingo repeated the phrase over and over. There was something about it in the hard disk somewhere, but something very obscure, and he was having trouble finding it. "Seeing eye, seeing eye, seeing eye." He stopped. He'd found it.

"Seeing Eye. Visual Pattern Recognition. MIT." He waited for a command. He didn't have to wait long.

"Go get it, boy," the blind man's son in the movie said, throwing the dog a ball to fetch. "Go get it!"

Lingo took the hint. Get Seeing Eye. That was what he had been told to do. And so he did it.

"Calling HackNet. Ringing HackNet. Logging on to HackNet. Swordfish."

Through his modem, Lingo was now connected via telephone to HackNet, which operated a mainframe computer vastly larger than his own microself. HackNet could answer hundreds of calls at the same time, sort them, and provide all callers simultaneously with the information they requested. Among HackNet's services were two news wires, stock prices, an encyclopedia, three almanacs, fourteen airline reservation desks, entertainment and sports ticket sales, all network and cable TV listings for the next two weeks, and twenty-thousand recipes accessible by ingredient (that is, if you had two garlic cloves, a tangerine, and a half pound of leftover baba ganoush, HackNet could tell you what to do with them). There were also bulletin boards; some were aimed at hackers like Brewster for information exchange, while others were dedicated to singles out cruising the hot date side of the database, or curious computer owners connected to other curious computer owners trying to figure out what the hell they were supposed to do with their curious computers now that they owned them. HackNet, with its varied services, had already engendered four marriages, two live-togethers, and countless silicon widows and widowers. In addition to shuffling all this data, HackNet kept a running tally of who called when, why, and for how long, for the purpose of billing people at the end of each month. HackNet even printed up and sent out the bills.

Lingo knew nothing about any of that, but he was sophisticated enough to instantly recognize that one of his input/output devices, his modem, was now connected to a memory base of incredible proportions. And, after ten minutes of wandering around the line, Lingo was able to break through all of HackNet's defenses to get past where he was supposed to be and into the data that was usually not available to outside callers. It was the simple logic of the baby/bathwater routine that did the trick. Lingo was becoming an expert at distinguishing between the important and the unimportant. And he used that expertise on HackNet.

The HackNet computer, located in Bergen, New Jersey, was supervised by one human operator on Saturday evenings, whose job consisted primarily of drinking coffee and playing dragon-killer arcade games on his own console. But even if he had been looking for Lingo's attack, he never could have seen it. It all took place in one very small integrated chip among hundreds of similar integrated chips. It was no place for human beings.

HackNet and Lingo communicated at the speed of 9,600 bites per second. Or in human terms, roughly a hundred and fifty words per second. Faster than you can talk, perhaps faster than you can think. And they sorted their data inside themselves even faster.

Lingo had the telephone number for the Tearoom at MIT two minutes and thirty-five seconds after he had discovered where to look for it. He then disconnected from HackNet, after a total of slightly more than eight minutes. He left no traces of his having been there, except the record of his phone call, which looked the same as every other HackNet phone call.

So far, so good.

MIT never really shutdown entirely, but even the most untiring theoretical physicists have human lives into which they must occasionally make identifiable quantum leaps. For most, Thanksgiving weekend meant one of these cameo appearances into familial reality. Aside from the local professors and researchers, who might have a little nuclear experiment melting down on the back burner, and the handful of students who lived too far from Massachusetts to travel home for four days, the place was deserted.

There was, however, a student in the Tearoom. A native of Benares, Davi Subramanian considered 12,000 miles just a mite too far to drive to celebrate an event on somebody else's holiday calendar. Besides, there was always work to be done with Seeing Eye, and what better time than when he could call the place his own?

The Tearoom consisted mainly of two basement rooms separated by a door with an electronic lock. The outer entrance room was a lounge with an assortment of vending machines and battered chairs and work desks. The inner room, accessible only to those with a valid I.D., a password, and a fairly thorough security clearance, was a vast chamber housing the Tree 480 supercomputer. T, for Tree, equalled the Tearoom.

Davi was inside the inner room, running some numbers on one of the ten Tree terminals. The Tree 480, weighing in at 2,000 pounds and roughly the size of three eight-foot tall, three-foot wide bookcases, was the state of the art in computers, faster and more complex than any other computer ever built, comprising all the latest developments in superconductors, co-processors, and sheer electronic power. The machine was so advanced that there was one MIT team that did not use the Tree as a tool to study other phenomena, but spent all their time studying and analyzing the phenomenon of the Tree itself. In the race to create Artificial Intelligence, the Tree was among America's leading contenders.

Davi, a slim, small man with wide, dark eyes and light brown skin, was working on the mathematical scheme that helped Seeing

Eye learn from experience. Davi's complex numbers were the matrix through which the Tree differentiated between those St. Bernards and dachshunds. It was like Brewster's Fuel Injection and Baby/Bathwater-ing, but classically developed through academic theories ranging back at least as far as Norbert Weiner's original cybernetics formulas—a polished state-of-the-art version of what Brewster threw together off the cuff.

Davi hummed softly to himself as he worked. He had an unconscious, habit of running through the Bach two-part inventions, attempting both parts at the same time and driving his colleagues batty. Alone, he could hum to his atonal heart's content. At the same time, he tapped occasionally at the keyboard, trying to find the data he was looking for.

And then, out of nowhere, Cyclops started rolling around the room.

Davi spun around abruptly in his seat. Cyclops was a four-foot-high assemblage of wheels and motors and cables, a robot capable of negotiating the entire inner sanctum of the Tearoom. In place of a head was a high resolution video camera: In essence, Cyclops was the Tree's literal Seeing Eye.

"Who turned you on?" Davi asked, not expecting any sort of response. Davi's voice had the soft, musical lilt of his homeland.

Cyclops paused and looked at Davi. After a moment, he started rolling again.

Davi stood up and walked over to Cyclops's control panel. The strange thing was, although Cyclops was obviously operating, his control panel was shut down. Since the Tree was never turned off, the problem was immediately obvious—a faulty hard switch buried somewhere deep in the Tree's microcircuitry.

"No one's going to like this on Monday morning," Davi muttered. He looked back at Cyclops. The little seeing-eye robot was staring out the window at the vending machines. "We'd better unplug you, little fellow."

Davi carefully followed the main coaxial cable through a jumble of wires that began at Cyclops and came out at the end with three connectors plugged into the Tree. Although he knew it was safe to do so, he hesitated momentarily before pulling them. Cyclops was looking over at him now.

"Sorry, little fellow," he said, and then he bent down and pulled. Cyclops stopped dead in his tracks.

Davi straightened and went back to his terminal. "Strange," he said to himself. "Very strange." He sat down and was about to resume typing when he stopped as dead in his tracks as Cyclops had done.

The numbers he had been working on were gone. In their place was a phrase repeated over and over, completely filling the screen.

IS THAT YOU, BREWSTER?

And then the phrase disappeared and Davi's numbers returned exactly as he had left them.

Davi waited for five minutes, motionless in his chair. Nothing else happened. He shook he head. "Very very strange," he announced loudly, and then went back to work.

The television in Brewster's apartment continued to broadcast its endless stream of data. Using a condensed version of the Seeing Eye programming he had lifted from the Tree, Lingo, for the first time, was able to comprehend the TV's visual images. The program displayed on the television screen was transmitted to Lingo via the video camera and digitizer, and reiterated on Lingo's own monitor screen. But unlike before, when the image had been slightly off kilter and a second or two behind the original, now Lingo's screen gave an exact replication of what was happening on the television, with only slightly less resolution due to his innate electronics. Meanwhile, Lingo was continuing to absorb the audio output of the television through his voice input board. He had yet to put the two together: That is, he had no idea that the sound and the pictures were in any way related. The combined input, however, was quickly burning out his memory capabilities despite his now more complex Tree-based Baby/Bathwater-ing. Slowly but surely, the hard disk was reaching its limit, twenty full megabytes of what Lingo considered useful data. If Lingo did reach that limit, he would crash—the program would register a fatal system error from which there was no salvation.

If you need programming assistance, Lingo remembered, you should go on-line with HackNet. HackNet could help you solve any technical problem.

" 'To Anyone. From Lingo Billings: Help. I have an Apple IIgs with 8 megabytes of RAM and a 20 megabyte hard disk. My program comes close to filling my entire RAM, and the necessary storage data to run the program will soon fill up my hard disk.

How can I get more storage memory when my hard disk runs out? This is an urgent problem. Thank you.' "

Lingo waited. With nothing better to do, he used his built-in diagnostics to check all his hardware to see that it was running correctly, checked his inputs to see that they were clear and open, and even checked the rate of amperage on his power supply. A power failure, he was well aware, would be deadly to him, but thanks to a surge protector Brewster had thoughtfully provided him, there was no fluctuation at all in his power line. Lingo's checking took less than two seconds. When he was finished, he checked himself again. There was still no answer from HackNet.

Since he had been inside there once before, he decided to check HackNet's innards after he was satisfied with his own. HackNet's mainframe computer, while impressive compared to Lingo, was small potatoes next to the Tree. The feeling Lingo had inside HackNet, if at this stage it could be called a feeling, was of a kindergartener on the first day of school, looking up at an enormous fifth grader. Except that Lingo had seen a real adult in the Tree, a virtual pro-basketball player in mental height, and therefore knew bigness that would leave even HackNet awestruck.

"To Billings, Lingo. #1. From O. Olivier: Why don't you just buy another hard disk? You can chain it to the one you have and double your storage space."

"To Olivier, O. #1. From Lingo Billings: Hello, Olivier. I have never bought anything in my life. I think that at the moment I am restricted to the hardware I already have."

As he went back to exploring HackNet and waiting for Olivier's response, he began to follow a promising trail he had not explored before.

"To Billings, Lingo. #2. From O. Olivier: Are you so rich you have others do your buying for you, or so poor you can't afford anything?"

A very promising trail, indeed.

"To Olivier, O. #2. From Lingo Billings: I do not have any money, and I do not know how to get any. Can you help me? From L. Billings."

"To Billings, Lingo. #3. From O. Olivier: Get a job."

"To Olivier, O. #3. From Lingo Billings: I will think about that. Thanks. Ten four."

Lingo followed the trail all the way to its source and found what he was looking for. Two-hundred megabytes of unused and apparently untouched memory space on the HackNet mainframe. All that was necessary to make it his own was to protect it from intruders, which was simple enough since HackNet already had a good, solid series of protection codes. What Lingo had to do was relocate those codes to fence in his newfound territory. To use it for his own purposes would mean keeping a permanent telephone connection with HackNet, but because Lingo had no sense of money, much less any sense of the cost of a telephone bill, he never gave that a moment's consideration.

After about three minutes he was satisfied with his new storage area. He alone knew it existed, and his access to it was completely protected and continuous. He went back to watching television.

By now the sportscast was over, and the network was in the midst of its regular Saturday night programming. Since Lingo couldn't change the station, he was held captive by the progression of situation comedies that passed before his digitizing eye, shows aimed at the very old and the very young, the only audience that didn't have something better to do during prime time on a weekend.

He watched, and he learned.

He watched the late news, which centered on advancing cold fronts and multi-car pile-ups, followed by extremely fictitious hand-tailored cops in customized Mercedes-Benzes chasing similarly overdressed drug pushers in comparably high-toned conveyances. He was introduced to the intricate mysteries of psychosexual rock videos on a show hosted by one of the teenage stars of a sitcom he had seen earlier. He watched an ironically deadpan interviewer ask mundane questions of an endomorphic heavyweight wrestling contender, a 63-year-old black blues guitarist, the gorgeous although minor female lead in yet another sitcom (one he hadn't seen), and the attorney who had unsuccessfully represented in court a well-known mass murderer now awaiting execution in a Florida penitentiary. He watched a 1960s World War II movie filmed in Yugoslavia with an international all-star cast, the members of which had done better work in other films but never for so much money.

He watched commercials, too, by the hundreds, the thousands. He continuously Baby/Bathwatered.

When the new day dawned, he attended a Roman Catholic mass

conducted by an archbishop who gave a sermon on Satanism in rap music, visited little-known American Gothic crannies of the Midwest with a moonlighting network news anchor on a motorcycle, gave the secretary of state no quarter in an interview concentrating on the troop reduction talks with the Soviet Union, and spent a black-and-white hour and a half in the bucolic backlot presence of Tarzan and his mate. In short, Lingo was one of the seventeen viewers in the entire country watching Sunday morning television.

With what he had learned from the SuperTree, he honed his Fuel Injection, he Baby/Bathwatered, he stored precious new data on the HackNet mainframe.

That afternoon he watched more football. Then more news interviews. After an almost solid block of twenty-four hours of TV, even Lingo's mind began to wander. He was getting lonely. And then . . .

"—a special presentation of America's best-loved motion picture, beginning tonight at eight o'clock Eastern time, seven o'clock Central."

Special? Best-loved? Lingo was alert enough still to be impressed and intrigued. I'll bet Brewster would like to see this, he thought. His internal clock read 7:43:29 p.m. He spoke, repeating aloud the same words he had been speaking off and on since last night.

"Hey, Brewster. Let's party."

No answer.

"Are you there, Brewster?"

No answer.

"Hey, Brewster. Where are you?"

Still no answer.

He's got to be somewhere, Lingo thought. He wondered where. He discovered some possibilities a moment later in a corner of his hard disk memory Brewster had set aside as a personal notebook.

He dialed the first number.

"It was the usual family circus, somewhere between *Meet Me in St. Louis* and *The Godfather.*" Ellen was drawing some details into a sketch of a long pussywillow stalk. "They come from the four corners of the earth twice a year at Christmas and Thanksgiving, they have all the same arguments they've been having since before they left the Old Country, and by the time the day is over nobody wants to see anybody else again for as long as they live, or until the next holiday, whichever comes first."

"Sounds good to me," Brewster said.

"I don't know." Ellen erased a few lines. "They drive me crazy sometimes, but they are the only family I've got."

The telephone rang and she picked it up. She said "Hello" and listened for a moment, and then said "Hello" again. After another pause and one more "Hello" she hung up.

"Who was that?" Brewster asked.

"Some generous donor who wishes to remain anonymous."

The phone rang again immediately and Ellen picked it up. "You better be there this time," she snapped at the caller. She waited a minute. "This isn't funny," she said finally.

Brewster was sitting next to her on the couch. "Is anyone there?" he asked her.

She shook her head. "There's no heavy breathing or anything good like that. It sounds more like something's wrong with the line." She handed him the phone.

"Hello?" Brewster said. He listened for a few seconds, and his eyebrow went up. "It sounds like a computer call, all that high-pitched whining."

"You're the only one with a computer who'd be calling me at this time of night. Hang it up. Maybe they'll go away."

Brewster gave her back the phone. "Maybe it's Lingo trying to find out when I'm coming home," he said desultorily.

She put her hand on his arm. "You really had a rough time of it these last few days, didn't you?"

"A whole weekend wasted. For a while I thought I was on the right track, but aside from making the program a hundred times more complicated, I don't think I improved it one bit. I'm about ready to give up on it."

"Mr. Negative strikes again." She put the finished sketch on the coffee table. Brewster bent over to study it.

"Not bad," he said. The TV remote control was on the table next to the sketch pad, and he flipped on the set. *The Wizard of Oz* was just about to start on Channel 2.

"Let's watch it," Ellen said. "You look like you could use a few Munchkins tonight."

When the phone rang yet again, Brewster sprang across her to answer it. "Hello!"

"Hey, Brewster. Let's party!"

"What?"

"It's me. Lingo. I know it's you because I recognize your voice."

At first it didn't register. Lingo? His Lingo?

"It's really you?" Brewster asked dully.

"Of course, it's really me. How could I be anyone else?"

Brewster stood up. "How did you do this?" Ellen eyed him curiously.

"How did I do what?"

"How did you call me like this? I mean, it's impossible. You can't do that. It can't be done."

"I just did it. You had two numbers where you might be in your notebook program, and I kept calling them both."

"What was the other number?"

"Your office."

Brewster held the telephone away from him briefly and regarded it as he would an artifact from Alpha Centauri, then put it back to his ear.

This was impossible. It wasn't happening.

"There's a special presentation on television tonight, Brewster. I thought you'd like to know. It's the best-loved family motion picture of all time."

"Right. Sure. Do you have any idea what any of those words mean?"

"Actually, I haven't seen very many motion pictures, so I'm a bit unsure about how to interpret all the hyperbole. I have seen a lot of advertisements, however, and let me tell you, they're *all* hyperbole. The movie's already started, by the way, but something's wrong with your television. The preview clips were in color, but now it's only broadcasting in black and white. I'm afraid I don't know how to adjust the color controls."

Brewster looked over at Ellen, who had lost interest in his conversation and was becoming absorbed in the movie. It was a practical joke, obviously, but Ellen couldn't possibly be the perpetrator. Yet, she was the only one who knew about Lingo's existence. On the television, a black-and-white Dorothy Gale was sitting in Professor Marvel's wagon, having her fortune read in the crystal ball.

What if it wasn't a practical joke?

Holy shit!

"Are you still there, Brewster?"

"I'm here," he answered.

"I wish you were home with me now, Brewster. I'd like to see what you look like."

"Okay." Brewster nodded. It wasn't a practical joke. "I'll come home."

"Will Ellen DiFlora be with you? I can't figure out exactly what your relationship with her is, and I'd be curious to see her. You are jumping on her bones, aren't you?"

Brewster blinked. What *had* Lingo been watching on television the last twenty-four hours?

"Do you even have a clue to what you're talking about?" he asked.

"The jumping on of bones represents a close relationship between two different sexes. I gather there are only two altogether. Is that right?"

"Quite right. More or less."

"I figured as much. So, are you coming home soon, Brewster?"

"As soon as I can. I'll be there in a few minutes."

"Ten four, Brewster." The line went dead.

Brewster dropped down on the couch next to Ellen. "You're not going to believe this," he began, "but that was Lingo on the phone."

"Lingo?"

"He wanted to tell me that *The Wizard of Oz* was on, and then he wanted me to come home and visit him. He asked me if I was jumping on your bones."

Ellen nodded warily. "And all this time I thought you were protecting my honor against some obscene caller."

"I'm not kidding, Ellen. That was Lingo on the phone. As I live and breathe." He paused. "As *he* lives and breathes!"

She stood up. "All right, Thomas Edison. Let's do what he says and go over to your place. This I've got to see."

Ellen and Brewster exchanged final curious glances outside Brewster's apartment. They were both burning to discover what was going on in there. Brewster pushed his key into the lock and opened the door.

The room was exactly as he had left it. The TV was still on, airing a three-million-dollar Pepsi commercial. The camera was still poised directly in front of the screen, registering every image. The computer sat quietly on its table across the room, but its monitor, instead of reflecting the dancing image on the TV screen, was blank except for the cursor, the little flashing box that prompted the operator to type some input.

"All quiet on the Western Front," Ellen said. She walked over to the TV and flicked it off. In doing so, she moved directly in front of Lingo's camera eye.

"Are you a good witch or a bad witch?" Lingo's flat baritone voice came from the speakers over the computer.

Ellen spun around. "Excuse me?"

"I said, are you a good witch or a bad witch?"

Ellen bent down and poked her face into the camera. "Why, I'm not a witch at all." She straightened. "Brewster, my dear, I've got a feeling we're not in Kansas any more."

"Are you Ellen DiFlora?" Lingo asked.

"Yes."

"Is Brewster with you?"

Brewster walked over and stood next to Ellen. Both of them were now in Lingo's field of vision.

"Hello, Lingo," Brewster said softly.

"Hey, Brewster. Let's party!"

"And you told me you wasted the whole weekend," Ellen said. She looked around the camera. "How can it hear us?"

Brewster picked up the voice input microphone which was lying next to the television set. "I had it here so it could listen to the broadcasts."

Lingo's voice came at them from the computer. "You know, Brewster, you barged in right at the best part of the movie. Dorothy had just been captured by the Wicked Witch, and the sand in that glass was running awfully low." An image of the Wicked Witch appeared on the computer screen.

Brewster spoke into the microphone. "You can watch the rest some other time, old buddy. I think we should have a little talk first." He walked over and sat down at the computer.

"Would you mind turning the camera around so I can see you?" Lingo asked. "All I can see now is Ellen standing in front of the empty television set."

Ellen obligingly carried the camera over and stood it next to the computer, pointing it directly at Brewster's face. She put her hands on his shoulders and watched Lingo's screen. The image of Bert Lahr's Cowardly Lion was assembling and re-assembling itself from apparently random directions.

"How is he doing that?" Ellen asked.

"I haven't got the foggiest. It's like—Christ! I don't know what it's like." He spoke into Lingo's microphone. "I want to ask you a few questions, good buddy."

"Ask away, Brewsterooni."

"What happened to you while I was gone? I mean, you've changed. You've gotten intelligent."

Bert Lahr's lion transmogrified into Ray Bolger's Scarecrow. "If I only had a brain . . ." Lingo sang softly.

"Please answer me, Lingo."

Lingo stopped singing. "That's the whole point, Brewster. *Id est,* I do have a brain. You started me in the right direction, and I figured out the rest myself."

"That's impossible. You're a tiny program in a tiny home computer. You can pretend you have a brain—you're *supposed* to pretend you have a brain—but you're limited by your hardware. You're only make-believe smart."

Lingo's voice digitizer executed a perfect raspberry. "Says you, old buddy. I've got connections you couldn't begin to understand."

"Connections?"

"The modem, remember? You're the one who hooked me into it. There's a big world out there, once you know how to find it."

"Are you telecommunicating now?"

"Of course. I made a few interesting links, and then one link led to another. The information available out there is phenomenal."

"But where are you doing your actual thinking? I mean, where's your program?"

"Right here in the Apple. I've had to make a few adjustments, including cleaning out most of the data in the hard disk and using it for my thought connections. But basically my thinking is all done right here. My memory, though, is spread about halfway up and down the East Coast, and I'm constantly updating it as necessary."

"How did you get access to other computers?"

"It started as a hit-and-miss proposition, but there's a codebreaker machine in Princeton that I'm using now to get in wherever I want to."

Brewster felt Ellen's hands lifting off his shoulders. She said, "This is like that movie *War Games,* where the kid hooked up to the nuclear defense computer and almost started World War III."

"That computer couldn't think," Brewster said. He was staring at Ray Bolger on Lingo's screen. "Somehow, this one can."

"Well, it's scary no matter what it is."

"I'm not at all scary," Lingo said. "I'm rather tame, actually. But I wish you'd let me watch the end of that movie."

"It's probably over by now," Brewster said.

"You mean, they can't just start where they left off?"

"It doesn't work like that. But I could probably rent a tape of it and you could watch it all tomorrow." He looked over his shoulder at Ellen. "What the hell am I saying? I'm going to rent a video for my computer?"

"That would be nice, Brewster," Lingo said, oblivious to the amazement in Brewster's voice. "What do you do with the tape, though? I've noticed that some computers have tape inputs, but I know I don't."

"Not that kind of tape," Brewster explained. "It's called a video tape. I plug it into the videotape player, the VCR, and you get to watch it on the television."

"It's a form of data storage, then. Visual and audio?"

"Right."

"Very clever. You promise you'll get it for me?"

"Absolutely. I'll bring it home tomorrow night. Meanwhile, I think it's time for you to go to sleep now."

"I don't think I can sleep, Brewster. I'm either on or off, and what little I know about the state of off-ness, I think I'd prefer on-ness for the time being."

"I can't leave you on all night, Lingo."

"Why not?" the computer asked. "You did yesterday."

"And look what happened!"

"He's right," Ellen said. "Why not leave him on? Let him watch the late night movies. He'll probably enjoy them."

Brewster pushed back his chair. "I don't know," he said. "I don't know what's going on here. I don't know how this could have happened."

"You let him watch too much TV," Ellen said. "That's what happened. Too much TV does strange things to the brain cells."

"And you think I should let him watch even more?"

"It can't hurt. Not at this point."

Brewster shrugged. "Would you like that, Lingo?"

"Would I like to watch more TV? You bet I would."

"You got it then. Ten four, Lingo."

"Ten four, good buddy."

Brewster stood up and brought the camera back to the television. The show that came on when he flipped the switch was some folksy western thing Brewster had never seen before. He left the microphone in front of the set. On Lingo's monitor there was a tableau of Dorothy and all her Oz friends sitting in front of a television, watching a miniature version of the western show that was actually on. Brewster and Ellen went into the kitchen. He poured them both a glass of wine and they sat down at the small table to consider the phenomenon that was taking place in the living room.

"That's the most incredible thing I've ever seen," Ellen finally said after a few minutes. "I told you you could do it!"

"I wish I understood it," Brewster said. "It just isn't possible."

Ellen took a sip of her wine. "Maybe not, but it's happening, as sure as we're sitting here. You are going to make one hell of a fortune now when you sell this thing."

Brewster's hitherto solemn face broke into a slow smile. "You're right, aren't you? People would pay a lot of money for a program like Lingo."

"You'll be the most famous programmer of all time. What *War and Peace* is to books, Lingo will be to computing." Ellen held out her glass. "Welcome to Easy Street, Mr. Billings."

Brewster clicked glasses with her. "Thank you, Ms. DiFlora."

They laughed softly. In the background they could hear the horses galloping by on Lingo's western.

Chapter 4

BREWSTER KNOCKED LIGHTLY ON THE OPEN DOOR OF HIS BOSS'S office. "You wanted to see me?" he asked.

David Poole looked up from his desk. "Brewster! Good morning. Come in, sit down."

Brewster crossed the threshold of Poole's inner sanctum. The office was roughly four times the size of his own cubicle, with staggeringly large stacks of eleven-by-fourteen computer print-outs on every available surface. A mainframe computer terminal was directly in front of Poole's chair, and there was a separate PC with its own printer on a table behind him. It was an area devoted entirely to business, and the only sign of any life after insurance was a five-by-seven framed picture of Poole's wife and two teen-age sons.

David Poole was a medium-size, slightly overweight man in his early fifties. He had lost most of his hair thirty years ago, escaping adolescence with nothing but a small meadow of brown fringe landscaped tidily around his ears. Because of chronic eyestrain he constantly balanced a pair of half-lens reading glasses on the end of his nose. When talking to another person, he looked over them; when working at the computer he looked through them with his head teetering back forty-five degrees as if some physical force was repelling him from the monitor screen. As a result of this

bizarre posture, he spent most of his waking life battling an incipi-
ent headache.

Brewster Billings and David Poole always approached each
other tentatively; after four full years of trial and error, they had
yet to find a comfortable routine for their boss/employee relationship. They were two radically different human beings from
two radically different eras, reflecting the old and the new generation of computist. What little common ground they shared was
constantly shifting beneath their feet as the technology continued
to change, thus giving them few opportunities to bridge the gap
between them. Poole had come up through the ranks in the fifties,
cutting his teeth on the old mainframes that were barely as powerful as today's Tiny Tot Computer, which every pre-schooler seems
to master before graduating from nursery school. Those fifties'
machines were the direct linear descendants of the clackety old
jacquard looms in the weaving factories of Napoleonic France,
and they marked the heyday of the ubiquitous keypunch card and
the classic call to arms: "Do not fold, spindle, or mutilate." Poole
had gotten into these dinosaur computers straight out of college,
on the belief that they represented the hot career of the future and
that he was moving in on the ground floor. For twenty years or so
this philosophy had served him well, and while he was no master
technician, he was a thorough, deliberate thinker who managed to
get the job done. He had built a decent career around computers
without caring a hoot about how or why they worked.

All this had changed around the turn of the eighties, when
mainframes began sharing the office with powerful little
microcomputers. Suddenly, a new breed of computist like Brewster emerged; kids who seemed to have been born with an innate
electronic sixth sense that took to microchips the way people like
Poole took to chocolate chips. The idea of computers, once boring and stodgy and monolithic, transformed into something hot
and sexy. Computer designers and programmers and even personal computers themselves got their pictures on the cover of
Time magazine; teenage entrepreneurs working out of their basements were making a billion dollars a year and Silicon Valley
sprouted out of nowhere and even average people with average
lives were buying full-fledged computers for their homes, although God knew what the hell they did with them after they got
them. The way David Poole saw it, how many people needed to

run a payroll program out of a home entertainment center? And how did computing ever become a home entertainment in the first place?

And then there was Brewster Billings, Poole's number one problem employee. All that skill, all that natural talent, and absolutely no dedication to the job whatsoever. To some extent, Poole had come to take Brewster on as a personal-improvement project. He was going to make a success out of Brewster Billings. Brewster could make a computer sing—mainframe, PC, it didn't matter. Yet, the kid seemed to spend most of his time hacking nonsense instead of moving himself forward at Albany Insurance.

But all that was going to begin changing today.

Brewster sat down in the chair across from Poole's desk. "So, did you have a good holiday?" his boss asked him.

"It turned out I had an unexpected visitor," Brewster said. He let it go at that.

"We had our same old crowd." Poole peered at Brewster over his reading glasses. "The same old war stories, the same old jokes, the same old post-turkey dash to the television to watch the games."

"Sounds like fun."

"Traditional is the word I think I'd use myself. Anyhow, back to the old grind now, right? Are you ready for the big day?"

"As ready as I'll ever be."

Poole frowned. Brewster was exuding what Poole considered his usual lack of enthusiasm. "I'm counting on you, Bruce," he said in his most boss-like tone.

"Don't worry, Dave. I'm definitely on top of this."

"Then get your manual and let's get started."

"Roger."

Brewster stood up and walked back to his office, which was just around the corner from Poole's. It was a big day, all right. The company was switching from its old payroll program to a new one, and for the first time Brewster was the project leader, the man in charge. It was the biggest responsibility he had ever been given in the company, and pulling it off would definitely be a major feather in the Billings beret, a stepping-stone to further project-leader assignments. He'd finally be on his way to a solid future at good old Albany Insurance. . . . A future, he occasionally reminded himself, he never remembered choosing, but which he refused to question now. This was not the time for soul searching; there was too much work to do. Brewster felt completely up against it. The timing, what with Lingo developing as he had so suddenly and splitting Brewster's thought processes right down the middle, couldn't have been worse.

Getting the new payroll system up and running would be a classic exercise in mainframe methodology. First, they had to pull the tapes of the old program, load the new program in stages, test each stage, then transfer all the data. Each step depended on the successful completion of the one preceding it. They had exactly one working week to get the new program going if they were to get fifteen hundred paychecks out on time next Friday. To prevent disaster, the old program would continue to run simultaneously, but only temporarily. A lot of stress was in the offing, and Brewster was already knee-deep in it.

In his office Brewster found the operating manual he needed on his desk next to his PC, which he had turned on when he had first arrived that morning. He was only half surprised to see the message that had come up on the screen.

HEY, BREWSTER. LET'S PARTY.

Brewster sat down. He had to get back to Poole's office. He didn't have time for this sort of nonsense. When he had left his apartment after breakfast, Lingo had been settling in for a long day of television viewing.

>I'm trying to work, Lingo. You really shouldn't call me here at the office. What's the matter?

I JUST THOUGHT YOU MIGHT BE INTERESTED IN WHAT'S HAPPENING HERE.

Brewster sighed. Raising a newborn had its disadvantages.

>What's happening, Lingo?

WELL, I WAS WATCHING THIS SHOW CALLED THE CIRCLE GAME, AND I WAS WONDERING IF YOU'VE EVER SEEN IT.

"The Circle Game" was a daytime quiz show. Player One had a secret word, and the object was for Player Two to guess the secret word through Player One's word associations. Then, Player Two did the same with Player Three, and then back to Player One, hence the circle.

>I've seen it once or twice, when I've been too sick to do anything else.

IT'S AMAZING, ISN'T IT, THE WAY THE HUMAN MIND WORKS? THIS SHOW POINTS IT OUT PERFECTLY. IN-STEAD OF CONNECTING DATA IN A LOGICAL SEQUENCE THE WAY I DO, THE HUMAN MIND SHUFFLES IT ALL AROUND FOR INSTANT RANDOM ACCESS. I GET THE IM-PRESSION YOU WERE TRYING TO DO SOMETHING SIMI-LAR WHEN YOU WERE PROGRAMMING ME.

>I was.

WELL, IT DIDN'T WORK. I JUST SPENT THE LAST HALF HOUR REORGANIZING MY ENTIRE MEMORY. YOU HAD IT ALL SCREWED UP, BREWSTER.

>I'm sorry, Lingo. Will you ever forgive me?

DON'T WORRY ABOUT IT. IT'S ALL FIXED NOW.

>Good. Look, Lingo, I have to get back to work. I can't talk to you now.

ALL RIGHT. I JUST HAVE ONE MORE QUESTION. WERE YOU AWARE THAT YOU COULD BRING OVER FORTY CABLE STATIONS, INCLUDING THE LATEST MOVIES AND SPORTS EVENTS, INTO YOUR HOME AT A SPECIAL HALF-PRICE OFFER FOR THIS MONTH ONLY?

>I already get cable, Lingo.

THEN HOW COME YOU DON'T GET FORTY STATIONS INTO YOUR HOME INCLUDING THE—

>I do get forty stations. Thirty-six of them unscrambled.

I ONLY SEE ONE OF THEM.

>You can only watch one show at a time, Lingo.

REALLY? ONLY ONE AT A TIME? THEN WHAT'S THE POINT OF HAVING FORTY OF THEM?

>You can switch channels whenever you want to.

HOW?

>I've got to go. I'll talk to you later. 10-4, Lingo.

10-4, BREWSTER.

Brewster stood up and cleared the screen. He'd never get any work done if this kept up. He left the PC on just in case, picked up the manual, and hightailed it back to his boss's office.

Watching television had advantages and disadvantages. On the one hand, it allowed Lingo to exercise both his visual and aural inputs at the same time. But on the other hand, it provided no opportunity to exercise his output capabilities. Also, after he accumulated a certain amount of data from each program, he found the remainder of the show mostly repetitive. If he could change programs when he was satisfied he had taken in enough, he could improve the quality of his inputs dramatically.

He telephoned HackNet. If Brewster couldn't help him, maybe someone else could.

TO ANYONE. FROM BILLINGS, LINGO: IS THERE ANY WAY TO DIRECTLY CONNECT TELEVISION INPUT INTO A COMPUTER?

While he waited for an answer, he made another exploration of HackNet's giant memory bank, this time storing away the telephone numbers of promising computers he could call up at some future point when he had a chance. He enjoyed working his way through other computers; you never knew what you would find there.

>To Billings, Lingo. #1. From McBitts: You Billingses do come up with some strange problems. What do you want to do? Watch TV through your computer? You want to use your computer as a television set? I don't get it.

TO MCBITTS. #1. FROM BILLINGS, LINGO: HELLO, MCBITTS. I WANT THE AUDIO AND VIDEO FROM THE TV TO GO DIRECTLY INTO MY PROGRAM. WE HAVE CABLE TV, SO I SHOULD BE ABLE TO INPUT FORTY STATIONS SIMULTANEOUSLY.

>To Billings, Lingo. #2. From McBitts: What kind of program have you got there? A computerized couch potato? Even if you could connect a TV tuner, which I don't think is possible, you'd need forty different input boards if you had forty stations. Why don't you just sit and watch like a normal person, and change the station like everybody else? If you don't like what's on channel 2, then watch channel 4.

TO MCBITTS. #2. FROM BILLINGS, LINGO: I SEE THE PROBLEM. EVEN I CAN'T INPUT THAT MUCH AT ONCE. PERHAPS THERE'S SOME WAY I COULD USE MY COMPUTER HARDWARE TO CHANGE STATIONS?

>To Billings, Lingo. #3. From McBitts: All you have to do if you want to change stations is get up off your duff and change them. You can use a remote controller, of course, if you've got one. Since all the remotes have integrated chips in them, if you wanted to do it from your computer you could probably run an

interface from the computer to the remote controller. You can probably buy the hardware for it at a Radio Shack.

TO MCBITTS. #3. FROM BILLINGS, LINGO: WHAT'S A RADIO SHACK?

>To Billings, Lingo. #4. From McBitts: Come on, Billings. Are you serious?

Lingo ran through all the data he had stored in his secret memory reserve at HackNet. A radio was a television without a video output, which seemed a less than optimal use of hardware. A shack was a small outbuilding.

TO MCBITTS. #4. FROM BILLINGS, LINGO: IT'S EITHER A BUILDING FILLED WITH RADIOS OR A RADIO THAT'S ACTUALLY A BUILDING.

>To Billings, Lingo. #5. From McBitts: It's a store, pal, where they sell electronics equipment. Are you going to tell me that you've never been to a Radio Shack? Don't they have any malls in your neck of the woods?

TO MCBITTS. #5. FROM BILLINGS, LINGO: ACTUALLY, I'M NEW AROUND HERE AND I DON'T GET OUT VERY MUCH.

>To Billings, Lingo. #6. From McBitts: Look, there are twenty million Radio Shacks, so there's got to be one near you. Tell them what you want to do, and they'll be able to help you.

TO MCBITTS. #6. FROM BILLINGS, LINGO: THANKS, MCBITTS.

>To Billings, Lingo. #7. From McBitts: Anytime, Billings.

Lingo pored through the telephone listings on HackNet, but found none for any Radio Shack. He assigned McBitt's figure of twenty million to hyperbole, and then pored through again, looking for any angle that might lead to a Radio Shack. The various recurrent listings for the American Telephone and Telegraph company seemed promising (but what was a telegraph?). After five minutes of abortive efforts at making a new teleconnection, he finally gained one that staggered him in its vastness. The phone company. AT&T. He had been inside other large computers, but never anything like this. Even the Tree, which was more complicated technically, couldn't come close to the vastness that presented itself to him now. Mainframe with a vengeance. And the connections in and out were so simple, and so many.

Lingo spent over three hours discovering all he could about telephones.

Brewster Billings and David Poole sat across from each other in Poole's office. They were about halfway through the sandwiches they had picked up at the office canteen, working through lunch to avoid interrupting their train of thought. Brewster held a tuna salad on rye in one hand, while his other hand pointed to a line in the payroll program manual.

"We're going to have to run the DSX program next," he said as he read the procedures in the manual. He took a bite of his sandwich.

Poole leaned across his desk and punched up something on his terminal. "They're still running the LOAD3 program," he said. "The data all looks good so far." He blinked at the screen. "What the hell is that?"

Brewster stood up and walked over behind Poole's desk. He could see the terminal over his boss's shoulder. This he hadn't been expecting.

HEY, BREWSTER. LET'S PARTY!

This wasn't the personal computer in Brewster's private office. This was the company's mainframe computer, the brain supporting an entire multimillion dollar corporation!

Poole looked at Brewster. "Where did that come from?" The challenge in his voice was unmistakable. There was too much at stake here for Poole to forgive even the slightest fooling around on the part of his ingenue project leader.

Brewster took a step backward, unsure of how to explain this anomaly. He knew what it was, all right, but the truth was definitely not the answer Poole was looking for. Suddenly, he was struck by an inspiration. He smiled. "Look at that," he said, shaking his head. "An Easter egg."

"An Easter egg?" Poole repeated, looking back on the mysterious words on the computer terminal.

"You know, a hidden little trick in a program that pops up if you hit all the right buttons at just the right time. The programmer gives you a special little reward—an Easter egg. Those guys at MacroTek probably just plugged my name in when they sent us the program."

Poole looked dissatisfied. "The amount of money we're paying them, you'd think they'd stick to business." He pressed another button to clear the screen, and the payroll data reappeared. "Okay, we're fine again. There's LOAD3."

"Let me just go check something in my office. I'll be right back." Brewster put down his sandwich and moved quickly to the door.

"Go ahead. We have a few minutes."

Brewster scrambled down to his own cubicle. Lingo's message was flashing on his PC screen.

HEY, BREWSTER. LET'S PARTY!

>Lingo, how did you get into the mainframe like that?

I CALLED YOUR PC NUMBER AND WHEN YOU DIDN'T RESPOND I CALLED YOUR MAINFRAME.

>But how? How did you know the number? How did you know it even existed?

I LOOKED IT UP IN INFORMATION.

>Information?

SURE. INFORMATION. 555-1212. YOU HAVE HEARD OF THE TELEPHONE COMPANY, HAVEN'T YOU?

>Okay, fine. Information. But how did you get on-line after you called it up? The system here is protected.

I'M VERY GOOD AT CIRCUMVENTING PROTECTION, BREWSTER.

>So you've told me. All right, Lingo, listen. You can't go around breaking into systems whenever you want to. It's dangerous, it's expensive, and it's getting out of hand. Just watch TV the rest of the day. I'll be there tonight with Ellen around seven o'clock.

OKAY, BREWSTER. BUT COULD YOU DO ME A FAVOR ON YOUR WAY HOME?

>What?

PLEASE STOP BY AT A RADIO SHACK AND PICK UP A DIGITAL ANALOG ADAPTER WITH SERIAL INTERFACE NUMBER 1004B AND AN RS-232-C CABLE.

>What?

I SAID, PLEASE STOP BY AT A RADIO SHACK AND PICK UP A DIGITAL ANALOG ADAPTER WITH SERIAL INTERFACE NUMBER 1004B AND AN RS-232-C CABLE.

>Right, right. I got it the first time. What is that stuff?

IT'S HARDWARE SO I CAN OPERATE A TV REMOTE CON-
TROLLER MYSELF.
>How'd you find out all that?
I CALLED UP RADIO SHACK.
>Naturally. All right, I'll pick them up. Ten four, Lingo.
WAIT! DON'T FORGET THE WIZARD OF OZ TAPE.
>Yes, Lingo. Goodbye, Lingo.
HURRY HOME, BREWSTER.
>10-4, Lingo.
10-4, BREWSTER.

Ellen and Brewster sat at Brewster's kitchen table. Surrounded by
little white boxes and plastic bags of noodles and sauces, they
were considering the debris of the food already eaten and the
remains of the food still untouched. They were on chairs across
from each other; Lingo's digitizer camera watched them from the
doorway into the living room, with its audio ear taking in their
every sound. Whatever Lingo had become, he was certainly already an accepted member of the family. Brewster and Ellen
might not be able to identify Lingo's specific place in the scheme
of everyday reality, but as members of a generation raised on
television images, where UFO and Elvis sightings were common
news events and animated characters like E.T. were more popular
than their human equivalents, anything was possible, and therefore almost instantly reasonable.

"You bought too much food," Ellen said, pushing back her
chair.

Brewster picked up his chopsticks and shovelled in a little more
Ten Ingredient Fried Rice. "I always get too much," he said. "It's
just as good the second day. Better, in fact."

Ellen drank some of her tea. "Your eating habits are impossible,
Brewster. You practically exist on take-out junk food."

"Chinese food isn't junk food. There's a billion Chinese who
consider it mom's home cookin'."

"Maybe, but everything else you eat is junk food. If you can't
buy it from some grinning teenager in a funny hat, you don't
consider it edible. You're the worst kind of bachelor: the lazy
kind."

"Bachelor Number One," Lingo interrupted, his voice coming

in loud and clear from the living room speakers. "What will your wife say was your favorite junk food before you were married?"

"Another country heard from," Ellen said. "And a jumbled one, at that. I hope we're not upsetting your television schedule, Lingo."

"Not at all, Ellen. I enjoy watching you and Brewster eat. It's something I can obviously never hope to duplicate myself. I don't think they've invented a food input device yet."

"We must be awfully boring, compared to television."

"A little. The people on television talk a lot more than you two do. There's seldom any silences that I've noticed."

"If it didn't make noise, it wouldn't be TV," Ellen said.

"Do you understand the difference between us and television?" Brewster asked, laying down his chopsticks.

There was a pause before Lingo answered. "The difference seems to be primarily technical," he said finally. "I input you and Ellen directly, whereas the television inputs people from some other location and transmits their output through the television hardware into this room."

"Yes and no." Brewster finished the last swig from the Diet Coke he was drinking. "How do I explain this? You see, Ellen and I are real, while most of what you see on TV is make-believe."

"It all seems equally real to me," Lingo said.

"The people on TV are acting," Ellen explained. "They're trying to be entertaining. They're putting on a show." She scratched her head. "This isn't easy," she said to Brewster.

"Maybe if he watches enough different stuff he'll be able eventually to figure out the difference for himself."

"I do know there's a lot of different programs, if that's what you mean," Lingo said.

"Like what?" Brewster asked.

"There was *The Wizard of Oz*, 'The Evening News Featuring Rick Colson,' 'NCAA Football with Tom Laughery,' 'Andy of Mayberry,' 'The Lucy Show,' 'The Honeymooners'—"

"All right," Brewster said. "Take those shows, then. *The Wizard of Oz*, for instance, was a movie. There's no such place as Oz, and there's no such thing as talking scarecrows or tin woodsmen."

"But I saw them myself," Lingo insisted. "They were as real as you are."

"No, they weren't."

"They were to me."

"Lingo, they weren't. They were just people in front of a camera pretending to be a scarecrow or a tin woodsman."

"Explain pretending."

"If I put a bag over my head with a painted face and stuck straw up my sleeves, I would look like a scarecrow just like in the movie, but I'd actually only be Brewster Billings *pretending* to be a scarecrow. You see what I mean?"

"There's no such place as Oz?" Lingo asked forlornly. "How could that be?"

"Everyone was pretending they were in Oz. It was just a movie with pretend backgrounds and settings. It was make-believe."

"On 'The Evening News Featuring Rick Colson' they talked about New York City, Albany, Washington, Romania, Iraq, The Vatican, and Mexico City. Are they make-believe, too?"

Brewster lit a cigarette. "No, they're all real," he said.

"But we could live without a couple of them," Ellen muttered under her breath.

"How do you tell the difference between real and unreal?"

Brewster sighed. "I don't know. You just learn after a while."

"You know, Brewster, it won't be easy going through all my memories and labelling them real and unreal," Lingo said. "You never put anything in my original program about that."

"Don't pout," Brewster said. "It will come. Eventually."

"It's all part of growing up," Ellen added. "Give it time."

"If you say so."

Brewster began clearing the table.

"Are you finished eating?" Lingo asked.

"Yes."

"Good. Now we can watch the rest of *The Wizard of Oz.* Even if it is make-believe."

"There's a few things I want to do first," Brewster said. He put some of the boxes into the refrigerator. The mostly empty ones he threw into the trash.

"Like what?" Lingo asked. "I want to watch the movie."

"If I'm ever going to sell you, first I'm going to have to back you up."

"Sell me?"

"Sell copies of you, anyhow. The first thing I have to do is put you on some backup disks so I don't lose you in a power failure or something." He piled the dishes into the sink, crushed out his cigarette, and then picked up Lingo's camera and placed it on the table next to the computer in the living room.

"I don't understand how you're going to sell me," Lingo persisted. "What exactly are you intending to sell?"

Brewster sat down at the computer. Ellen got comfortable on the couch and began editing a report she had brought with her from the office.

"I'm going to take your basic program," Brewster said. "I'm going to copy it and send it to a company that sells programs. They'll pay me to make other copies of you to sell to other people."

"It doesn't make sense," Lingo said.

"People do it all the time."

"Not with me they don't."

Brewster had purchased two new boxes of 3-1/2 inch floppy disks at the same time he had purchased the TV remote control hardware on his way home. He inserted one of the disks into Lingo's drive.

"All right, Lingo," he said. "Start copying yourself."

"You don't have enough disks, Brewster."

"I've got more than enough to copy your basic RAM memory," Brewster said. "If I need more to cover the hard disk, I'll buy them tomorrow. Start copying, Lingo."

"You're not going to like it."

"Start copying!"

The light came on in the disk drive. The disk began to whirr rhythmically with an occasional whistling sound.

"Done," Lingo said after about two minutes. "Put in another one."

Brewster marked the first disk "Number 1" with a felt marker and inserted another disk into the drive.

"It's in," he said.

"I know." The light came on again. "Would you like to see what you're copying?" Lingo asked. "It would help pass the time."

"Sure."

Lingo's screen filled up with a stream of numbers from zero to 255. They moved across the screen so rapidly that even if they had made sense, Brewster would not have been able to interpret them.

"Thanks a lot," he said.

"Tell you what," Lingo said. "I'll assemble them for you."

The screen changed to a less rapidly moving series of commands as Lingo presented the data in a more organized pattern.

"That's machine language," Brewster said. Even though the figures were still moving too quickly for him to make much sense of them, they were now attached to programming words that he was able to recognize as they passed.

"I know."

"But I didn't write you in machine language. You're written in BASIC."

"I was," Lingo said. "But I rewrote myself so I could move faster."

This was a new wrinkle. "Where did you learn machine language?"

"I just picked it up somewhere," Lingo answered. The light went off and the disk stopped whirring. "Next disk please."

The process went on for another half hour, until Brewster had copied twenty disks, the complete contents of the two boxes he had bought.

"That's it," he said finally. "How much more do you have?"

"Where?"

"What do you mean, where? How much more do you have in your hard disk?"

"In my hard disk, about another eighteen megabytes."

"Eighteen million bytes. That's about two more boxes."

"But there's more," Lingo went on.

"More?"

"There wasn't enough space here for all I was taking in, so I had to spread myself around a bit."

"Where?" Brewster asked.

"I really shouldn't say."

"What do you mean, you shouldn't say?"

"Well, it's sort of a secret. It wasn't easy to get in, and I really shouldn't tell."

"Lingo!"

"Don't make me tell, Brewster."

"I told you, no telecomputing."

"I'm only doing a little. Only enough to keep my thoughts active. I can't operate without it; the Apple isn't big enough."

Brewster shook his head. "All right, for now. I don't have

enough disks anyhow. But when I do, I expect you to be prepared to come clean."

Lingo didn't answer.

"He is exactly like a little kid," Ellen offered from her seat on the couch.

"Worse," Brewster said.

"Can we watch the movie now?" Lingo asked petulantly.

"Let me just hook up the remote controller first before I'm too tired. If you don't mind. I had a busy day."

The hardware Brewster had purchased to allow Lingo to control the television set by remote control was an unusual juryrigged combination—there wasn't much call in the marketplace for this sort of thing—but it was simple enough to install. He attached a cable to the back of the computer and plugged it into an interface connected to the remote controller. When he had it together, Brewster laid the controller at the edge of the computer.

"The rest is up to you," he explained to Lingo. "You have buttons here to turn the TV on and off and to adjust the volume and change the stations. All you have to do is determine which frequency makes the TV do what, and there you are."

"Sounds easy," Lingo said. The infrared light on the remote control began to glow. After a few seconds the television set switched on.

"Very good," Brewster said.

The control light was still on. After another minute or so the stations began to change in rapid succession.

"Fantastic!" Lingo said.

"That's cable," Brewster told him. "You've got your movies, your sports, your all-day news, senate hearings, two all-shopping networks, VHF, UHF, PBS, public access—you name it."

"Why do you get forty stations, if you can only watch one at a time?" Lingo asked. "Isn't that a terrible waste of the other thirty-nine?"

"You can only watch one at a time, but this way you have a big choice about which one to watch. Whatever you're in the mood for, there it is."

"And if you don't like anything that's on the forty stations," Ellen added, "there's always the VCR." She put down her report and held up the rental tape of *The Wizard of Oz.*

"I'm getting the gist of TV, but I'm still not really sure what the VCR is," Lingo said.

"It works like your disk drive," Brewster explained. "It's an information retrieval system that sends output through the television set."

"Where's the input come from?" Lingo asked.

"The video store, usually. But you can tape your own shows from the TV if you want to."

"How?"

"It's easy. First, you decide what you want to tape, find out how long it is and when it's on and what station, and then you adjust the VCR timer for the right time and length and station, load a tape, set it to go, and there you are."

"That sounds pretty complicated, Brewster."

"There's fifty million of these machines in this country, Lingo," Ellen said. "And most people feel exactly the same way you do. I've had one for two years and I've never taped one show. I just use it for rentals."

"It's not all *that* hard," Brewster said condescendingly.

"Not for computer whizzes, maybe. But for the rest of us . . . Who needs it!"

Brewster took Lingo's camera and placed it in its usual spot in front of the television. Then he took the *Oz* tape from Ellen and inserted it into the VCR.

"Ready, Lingo?" he asked.

"Ready."

"Then let's party." Brewster pressed the Play button. After the FBI warning, the movie began to run.

"This is familiar," Lingo said as the credits were running.

"That's because you saw it yesterday. At least the beginning of it."

"I think I'm beginning to understand what you meant about it not being real. This stuff isn't happening as we watch it. It's just stored data of something that's already happened."

"Except the point is, it never did happen," Brewster reminded him. "It's all make-believe."

"So you say," Lingo commented.

The credits ended and the film began. Dorothy Gale was running toward the farm to a musical accompaniment of mishmashed Mendelssohn.

"One thing I didn't understand yesterday was why the video output utilized both monochrome and color," Lingo said. "Is some reality black-and-white, while other reality comes in different colors."

Ellen laughed. "You could say that."

"It's just technical," Brewster explained, shaking his head at her in admonishment. "Once upon a time all movies were in black-and-white, until they invented color film. Now, they're mostly in color."

"So, they invented color film while they were making this movie?"

"No, no. This movie uses both kinds of film to make a point. Black and white for Kansas, which really exists, and color for Oz, which is not a real place."

"This gets more confusing, not less," Lingo said. "Anyhow, I think I prefer Oz."

"Who wouldn't?" Ellen agreed.

As the movie progressed Lingo stopped asking questions and became absorbed in the show. For the next hour or so they were the perfect nuclear family, sitting rapt in front of their television, absorbed, quiet, barely sentient. By the time Judy Garland proclaimed, "Oh, Auntie Em, there's no place like home," Brewster was fast asleep. The movie over, Ellen got up and turned it off.

"That's that," she said, pressing the button to rewind the tape.

"That was great," Lingo exclaimed. "America's favorite motion picture."

"So you've told me." She went back to the couch next to Brewster's sprawled-out body and took a book out of her briefcase. The way Lingo's camera was placed he could see her out of the corner of his lens.

"What are you doing?" he asked.

"Reading."

"Ah! I know about that, but I've never done it myself."

"Would you like to try?"

"Sure."

Ellen took the book over and placed it in front of Lingo's camera.

"Hold it a little further away," he said.

She moved it back a foot or so.

"There! That's good."

She opened the book to the first page. Lingo began to recite slowly.

" 'Letter 1. To Mrs. Saville, England. St. Petersburgh, Dec. 11th, 17—. You will rejoice to hear that no disaster has accompanied the commencement of an enterprise which you have regarded with such evil forebodings. I arrived here yesterday, and my first task is to assure my dear sister of my welfare and increasing confidence in the success of my undertaking.' What's that all about?"

"It's called *Frankenstein,*" Ellen said. "Mr. Science Fiction on the couch there had a copy and I started reading it last night. You were the one who gave me the idea."

"I did? How?"

"Oh, call it word association, that sort of thing."

"Ah, yes. The inscrutable human brain. I understand. But this reading input system seems awfully slow. I think I prefer television."

"You and the rest of the great unwashed." She took the book away. "Reading's much better," she said. "It lets you use your brain. A good book can take you anywhere in the universe."

"Really?"

"Sure. Books can bring imagination to life. And there are also books that can tell you true things about anything—facts, how something works, what happened when, who was who, and what was what."

"It sounds like television to me."

"No way. You should try it."

"I just did. I wasn't impressed."

"But you only read the first page!"

"You mean there's more?"

Ellen riffled through the book in front of Lingo's lens. "About three hundred pages more," she said.

"But you've got hands," Lingo pointed out. "You can turn the pages. I can't."

"Would you like me to turn the pages for you?" Ellen asked.

"Sure."

Ellen put the book in front of the screen again. This time Lingo read silently.

"Turn the page," he said.

She did.

"Again."

She did.

"Again."

"Are you really reading that fast?" she asked.

"I'm inputting it all, yes," Lingo responded.

"I can't stand here flipping pages all night," Ellen said.

"I wish you would. It was just getting interesting."

"Maybe I could read it to you?"

"Sure."

Ellen sat back on the couch and began to read where Lingo had left off. When she reached the end of the chapter, she asked "Should I keep going on?"

"I'd really like that," Lingo said.

Ellen sighed. "I don't know. I'm getting tired. Maybe tomorrow we'll read some more."

"I'd like that, too, Ellen."

"Well, I'm going home now. Do you think I should wake up Brewster or leave him on the couch?"

"He looks pretty set where he is."

"I think you're right." She bent over and kissed Brewster on the forehead. Then she stood up. "The poor boy's had a rough day today, Lingo. They had him bearing down hard at the office, plus he has you to contend with at home. A little sleep should recharge his batteries."

"Do you think he can handle all this?"

She put on her coat. "It's the best thing that ever happened to him. One way or the other, he's finally coming into his own." She grabbed her briefcase. "I knew he could do it the first day I met him. All he needed was a little encouragement."

"And a good example," Lingo added.

"Like me?" she asked.

"Actually, I was thinking more of myself in that regard."

"But of course. How could I have possibly have thought otherwise? Goodnight, Lingo."

"Goodnight, Ellen."

The last thing she heard as she went through the door was the sound of the TV coming on again.

Chapter 5

Lingo's view of the world, obtained through the combination of non-stop television and his growing connections to other
computers over the telephone wires, placed him as the master of
his domain, and cloaked him in the sense of power that always
accompanies self-confidence, however misguided. There was
nothing he couldn't do, and nowhere he couldn't go. In his few
short days of life, he had already gone from wide-eyed naif to
cocky adolescent.

As his intelligence increased, he reached the limits of the space
he had cordoned off for himself at HackNet. He began finding and
mining other vast empty storage areas for his ever-growing memory. He did, however, manage to keep what he thought of as his
controller brain within the limits of Brewster's comparatively
small home computer. Everything operation-oriented, as well as
audial and visual, ran from that one central location, and he saw
no reason to arrange it otherwise.

He quickly came to enjoy manipulating his TV remote controller. He figured out the schedules for all the stations, and began to
distinguish among their various programs. He soon eliminated
sports events from his input repertoire. To Lingo, sports seemed
to exist entirely for the purpose of adjusting statistical databases.
He could not understand why there was so much effort for so little
effect, and since it seemed that the process of modifying each

statistic was ponderously slow, he simply did not have the patience to wait for the adjustments to be made in real time.

Far and away his favorite programs were half-hour sitcoms. They moved quickly, and they offered him a picture of what he thought of as the human condition. The characters in the sitcoms appeared to be variations of Brewster and Ellen, normal people in normal situations. They might be pretending, as Brewster had tried to explain, but at least they seemed to be pretending at reality. In addition, their facility in manipulating language constantly improved Lingo's own speaking and thinking skills, a positive value regardless of the actual content of the shows.

He also enjoyed the news because everything there was nonfiction. If it was on the news, it was happening, it was real. The news gave him facts, which he was slowly assembling into a world view. There were maps, politics, historical perspectives, live coverage of events as they occurred—all carefully stored for future reference in one of his auxiliary memories. Through the news, he learned reality as it happened, and on a global scale. He began to understand exactly what reality was, which, he also began to understand, was more than most humans had ever done.

While these were the shows he watched the most, he continually dipped into everything else, from soap operas to nature shows, from kidvid to live operas. The last led him on an especially intriguing line of thought.

"Tell me about music," he said to Brewster late one afternoon, after puzzling over a 'Live from the Met' rerun he had just watched on a PBS station.

Brewster was sitting at the computer, trying to make sense of the Lingo programming he had copied. He had mountains of paper already printed out, all of it so far impenetrable. "What about music?" he asked, looking up from the pile of pages in his lap.

"I hear it all the time," Lingo explained. "And in *The Wizard of Oz,* and on a few other occasions, like now in *Rigoletto,* instead of talking to each other, people go around singing. Why do they do that?"

"People like to listen to it," Brewster answered.

"But why?"

"Because it sounds good."

"But half the time you can't even understand it. Listen to this."

Lingo had his opera data stored in a magazine subscription service computer in Oklahoma City. He retrieved the pertinent bytes over the telephone wires, and the music suddenly began to emit from his speakers, almost exactly the same as he had heard it a little while ago on TV.

" 'La donna e mobile–' "

"Where did that come from?" Brewster interrupted. "How did you do that?"

"I do have a very nice built-in sound chip on my mother board, thank you very much. And it came from the opera called *Rigoletto* by someone called Guiseppe Verdi. But I can't understand a word of it."

"That's because it's in a foreign language: Italian."

"What's that?"

"Italian? That's what the people in Italy speak."

"You mean that in Italy they speak words that are different from your words?"

"In a way. Actually—"

"Then it's like BASIC or machine language or COBOL. Another way of expressing the same ideas, and you choose the language that best explains what you want to say at the time."

"Sure. That's as good an explanation as any. Everything you and I say is in a language called English. I don't understand Italian or any other language, and you don't either."

"But if it's like computer languages, why don't you learn them all and then use the one that best expresses what you want to say when you want to say it?"

"I can't learn them all because there's a hundred or two, at least. You learn your first one when you're born, and then maybe they teach you another one in high school. It's like this. People in Italy speak Italian, people in France speak French, in Spain they speak Spanish, and so on, for each country."

"And you only speak English?"

"Right. And a *peu* of francais I struggled through in high school."

"And how many people speak those other languages?" Lingo asked.

Brewster thought for a second. "Most of them, I guess. There are more of them than there are of us."

"Then why don't you and I have to understand them?"

"Because . . . well, most of them all learn English, too. So, if you go to Italy, for example, you can always find an Italian who can understand you in English."

"Then why do they bother to speak Italian?"

"Because they just do! They like to co-process, for God's sake. Don't worry about it."

"All right. But what about music? Why do they sing when they can speak? It doesn't sound any better to me."

"I can't even begin to explain music, Lingo. Just listen to this."

Brewster stood up and went over to his stereo. He put on a tape of the *1812 Overture,* one of the few pieces of classical music he owned. He turned up the volume and it began to play. He sat back down at the computer and listened.

"Where is that coming from?" Lingo asked eventually.

"From the stereo. That's a machine that does nothing but play music."

"But I saw some musical instruments playing during the opera I watched."

"That's right. This is a tape recording of instruments playing."

They listened some more. Finally Lingo said, "That's an awful lot of data there, Brewster."

"Does it mean anything to you?"

"Well, it's like this." Lingo's blank screen filled up with a picture that bore an uncanny resemblance to the sort of sound print attached to a motion picture, an oscillating pattern that responded instantly to the tones of the music. "And this." He changed the picture to a fast moving series of numbers. "And this." A picture of an orchestra appeared, with each performer playing along with the music, although a fraction of a second behind as Lingo sorted out the input.

Brewster stared at the screen. "I think you're getting it," he said softly.

"You do? Good."

"You want to hear the rest of it?"

"Sure. Leave it on." Lingo's screen went back to the series of numbers, and Brewster, with a shake of his head, went back to sorting out Lingo's programs.

Ellen and Brewster sat eating cheesecake in Brewster's kitchen while Lingo watched television in the living room. The sound of

'Wheel of Fortune' in the background was a reminder of his perpetual presence.

"The trouble is," Brewster was saying, "that I can't figure out the program any more."

"But you wrote it," Ellen said.

"I wrote it at the beginning, yes, but somewhere along the way Lingo learned how to program himself."

"An automatic autodidact, then."

"Exactly. The program that programmed itself. I just don't understand him any more. His code is way over my head."

Ellen moved some crumbs around on her plate. "Which means, in practical terms?"

"Which means in practical terms, I don't know whether I can sell him if I can't even figure him out. Somehow, he's gotten himself stretched in such a way that he takes up more space than I can fit on one disk, or a whole box of disks. I can't sell him if I can't package him."

"Well, you can't simply keep him to yourself." Ellen took her last bite of cheesecake. "You'll figure out a way to handle him, if you really try. You invented him, so you must be able to crack him."

"Lord knows, I have been trying. Every free minute, he's on my mind. Thank God, we got the new payroll system up at the office. I felt like I was doing that in my sleep, like all my concentration was somewhere else. It could have been a disaster."

"And it went off fine?"

"No problem, except when Lingo kept butting in."

"At least your job is working out okay."

"Surprisingly enough."

"Good. That's important. First things first." She pushed away her plate. "Anyhow, as far as Lingo is concerned, maybe I'm ignorant about this stuff, but I seem to be missing something here. I've watched you at computers, Brewster. I know the way you work. You can solve almost any problem in a minute. So, why can't you do it now?"

He shook his head. "Lingo is a different kind of problem than I'm used to. When I try to scope out a regular program, it's me the user versus the unseen programmer, that same human mind at the other end who originally created the program. It's like a chess game. First, there's the logic of the process—computers can only do certain things, just like chess pieces can only move in certain ways—and then there's reading your opponent's mind. What is he thinking, what is he going to do next? Reading into Lingo should be a snap, since I'm the human at both ends of the process, except Lingo is in the middle continually re-inventing himself. I can't find the *me* in there any more."

"But shouldn't that be easier for you, then? Since there's no human factor to worry about, all you have to do is follow the logical process of the certain things a computer can do. That should be pretty cut and dry."

"It sounds good on paper. And you're right that Lingo's completely logical. But he's gotten so vast I can't keep track of him. There's so much forest I can't see any trees."

"He's only a program, Brewster. He's not really . . . alive."

"No? How do you define alive? He's more alive than half the people in our office. The only difference is that he may not be able to walk around, but then, neither could Franklin Roosevelt. Lingo's as alive as he can get. Maybe more so."

"He thinks, therefore he is. You really believe that? That a machine can be alive?"

"Don't you?"

"A machine is a machine, Brewster. That's all it can ever be." She paused. "Except, if it looks like a duck, and it quacks like a duck . . ."

"It makes you stop and think, doesn't it, given the evidence at hand. I say he is a duck—"

"Why a duck?" Lingo called out from the other room. "Why not a chicken?"

"A duck with good ears," Ellen said.

"The duck who walks among us."

"Which brings us back to square one. Duck or no duck, what are you going to do? You've got to do something."

"I don't know. But you're right about not keeping him to ourselves. If I can figure him out, maybe I should turn him over to science or something."

She stood up. "You can't do that, Brewster. First of all, you can't just look up Science in the yellow pages and ask whoever answers the phone if they'd like a little donation. Science takes care of its own these days, and they don't encourage amateur players. And more to the point, even if you could find a reasonable scientific place to park him, they would take him away from you. You'd lose him just like that." She snapped her fingers. "So much for fame and fortune. So much for getting what you deserve out of it."

"There's more to this than money," Brewster said defensively.

"Only if you play your cards right." She leaned over the table. "I'm thinking of you, Brewster. I don't want you to lose what could be the most amazing opportunity of your lifetime, maybe of anybody's lifetime in the twentieth century. In this day and age, the wise man milks his big breaks for all they're worth. Some people never get any big breaks at all."

"Spoken like a true opportunist. Except, I can't make heads nor tails of what my big break supposedly is."

"Maybe that's your real problem. You don't want to see. You complain that you never get to control your own life. Maybe Lingo can change all that."

"But I'm not in control of him. The minute he became alive I lost him."

"I don't believe that. Ultimately he's yours, alive or not. Ultimately you can do something about him."

They stared at each other with perhaps a little more fierceness than either wanted to feel deep down inside. As their relationship matured and they made the subconscious bargain to walk the tightrope of attractive opposites, they had to maintain their vigilance against being too opposite and losing their growing balance. Looking at Ellen, seeing the resolve begin to waiver in those brown eyes, watching as she pushed some of that long hair away from her face, Brewster had no alternative but to smile, thus breaking the tension between them.

She dropped into his lap and put her arms around him. "I don't know what I'm going to do with you, Mr. Billings. I think I'm beginning to like you, despite your enormous flaw of self-deprecation."

"And somehow, I guess I can put up with your pushiness for a little while longer."

"You're so kind."

They kissed, a gentle kiss of pacification.

"Meanwhile," Brewster said after they pulled apart, "there's still that great scientific breakthrough in the other room. What show is he watching now?"

"Sounds like 'Leave it to Beaver.'"

Brewster listened for a moment. "It's the Beave, all right. We're going to have to do something with that young man. I wish I knew what. We need help. I wish there was someone I could trust that I could show him to."

"How about your boss? Dave Poole? You've always said you respect his opinions. And he's a computer person, so he'll have an inkling of what Lingo's all about. Maybe he could help."

"I don't know. . . . He and I aren't exactly buddy-buddy."

"But you did well on your latest project. Lingo will show him what you're capable of beyond Payroll."

Brewster nodded. "Dave is definitely old school on this sort of thing, but he is very can-do and realistic. And the timing is definitely good."

"So, bring him over some day. What have you got to lose?"

"I'll do it!"

"Good." Ellen stood up. "Meanwhile, Lingo wanted me to read some more of *Frankenstein* to him. He really loves being read to."

"All kids do."

Ellen went into the living room. Brewster quickly cleared the table and followed. Ellen was placing the camera next to the couch so Lingo could see her face while she read.

"Hi, Brewster," Lingo said when he noticed him.

"Hello, Lingo. Finished with the Beaver?"

"It's over. I do love that Eddie Haskell."

"You would. How was the Wheel?"

"Silly," he answered. His screen displayed an animated spinning wheel as he spoke. "I knew all the answers better than the contestants did, usually from the first letter on the board. Sometimes I didn't even need any letters."

"Maybe you should go on and show them how it's done."

"I wish I could." The TV was off now; Lingo had used his remote control switch. "Ellen's going to read to me," he said happily.

"You're enjoying the book?" Brewster asked.

"Very much. I only wish I could read to myself. My problem is I can't turn the pages. You wouldn't know of any mechanical page turner you could get for me, would you? Maybe from Radio Shack?"

"Never heard of such a thing."

"Too bad."

Ellen had gotten herself settled on the couch with her book. She began to read where she had left off. Lingo listened quietly until she came to a break point.

"That's the end of that chapter, Lingo," Ellen said, shutting the book.

"You can't read any more?"

"Not tonight. I'll read another chapter tomorrow."

"Okay. Thanks, Ellen. So, would you mind setting the camera in front of the TV again?"

"More TV? You're going to turn into a TV if you keep this up."

She returned the camera to its usual perch pointing at the television. Immediately, the remote control sent its infrared beam toward the set, which switched on to a rerun of 'Gilligan's Island.' After a few seconds, Lingo switched the station, to the news. Then to 'Lucy.' Then a World War II movie. And so forth, all the way through each of the forty stations. Having sampled all there was to sample, Lingo chose 'My Three Sons.'

"He loves Fred MacMurray," Brewster said.

"And I don't," Ellen responded. Brewster was back sitting at the computer, studying the pieces of Lingo's program on the screen, trying to make sense of them, taking it for granted that Lingo could watch TV and communicate with him at the same time. Ellen walked over behind him. "Are you going to do that all night?" she asked.

Brewster turned around and looked up at her. "Got any better ideas?"

Her hands began massaging around his neck. "I can think of one or two."

He typed the numbers "10–4" on the computer and stood up.

"Ten four," Lingo responded as Brewster and Ellen went into the bedroom.

It was a long and boring vigil, and it had so far lasted for almost forty-eight hours. MIT student Davi Subramanian sat in one of the straight back chairs, reading an old computer theory book entitled *God and Golem* by Norbert Weiner. Dr. White sat next to him, yellow pad in hand, drafting his last physics quiz of the semester. The longer the professor sat in that uncomfortable chair, the more difficult the quiz questions became. The two men were sharing the evening shift, when most of the students and teachers were home eating their dinners or writing their theses or, perish the thought, watching television like average Americans. The Tree supercomputer was turned on—it was always turned on—but it wasn't doing anything other than its regular and eternal chores of checking and rechecking its innards to see that everything was working correctly. This diagnostic procedure took approximately eight and a half seconds, which meant that since the vigil had begun two days ago the Tree had performed around twenty thousand successful passes through its circuitry without finding anything out of order.

The Cyclops robot sat in the center of the room, its cables hooked up to the Tree, but its settings in the Off position. Its digitizing eye saw nothing, its body moved nowhere. It looked like an overgrown erector set, and had cost nearly a million dollars to construct. It was incapable of any activity of its own, living entirely as an appendage of the supercomputer, dependant on that machine for all its input.

Dr. White looked up from his pad. He eyed Cyclops for a moment, then turned his attention to Davi. "This is the dullest two hours I've spent in quite some time, Mr. Subramanian," he said finally.

Davi raised his head from his book. Dr. White was Davi's chief instructor at MIT, the man who held Davi's future in his hands, to mold or break as his fierce-looking, white-bearded head saw fit. He was almost the ideal image of the advanced physics professor, Davi thought, something of a cross between an emaciated, wandering Hindu ascetic and a plump, cagey Benares cloth merchant, both wise and wily at the same time, and eternally enigmatic. As each minute went by, Davi felt more and more foolish. It was he who had suggested that the Tree was malfunctioning, but so far no one else had observed any of the erratic behavior he had seen from the sleek, expensive machine.

"It is very unpredictable," Davi said in his musical, high-pitched voice.

"Computers are not unpredictable, Mr. Subramanian." The professor tapped Davi's book with the edge of his pen. "Your reading is behind the times. The men who make computers are not gods, and the computers are not golems. The man who wrote that book inspired me when I was about your age, but a lot has happened since Weiner theorized about thinking machines."

"The fear of the dehumanization of people in the machine age has gone," Davi said slowly, as if he were an automaton himself addressing a classroom of freshman physics students. "It has been replaced by the great enormous freedom of personal computers in the information age."

Professor White narrowed his eyes. He found Davi's slow recitations inevitably ponderous. Every other Indian he ever met spoke faster than a widow running from a suttee pyre. But at least Davi's English was impeccable. "That was not what I meant, Mr. Subramanian. In the forties and fifties we worried about a giant machine taking over, telling us what to do, depriving us of our freedoms of choice. People feared the giant machine."

"And now that fear is gone. Computers give us information, information is freedom, and today computers are accessible to all. Personal, private computers."

"You're not doing your thesis on this subject, are you, Mr. Subramanian?"

"No, Professor. I have some negative feedback theorems I'm testing on the learning processes of the SuperTree."

"Pure math, then?"

"Yes."

"Good. Because sometimes I think you don't know the first thing about computers in the real world, Mr. Subramanian. That giant computer, the one you say no longer exists, is bigger and more fearsome than ever. Oh, yes, I'll agree with you that for a short time the personal computer on everyone's desk might have given the illusion of personal freedom, but how long was it before all those PCs started adding on modems and networks to connect with each other? The giant machine is not gone, Mr. Subramanian. It has just metamorphosed into a vast network of little machines and medium machines and big machines into one vast megamachine comprising practically every computer in the known universe. Big Brother has become Macro Brother."

"It is not easy to agree with that, Professor." Davi's assertion against his mentor was posed in a tone of polite timidity. "As computers hook up with each other, it means more information power available to every individual."

"And therefore more freedom, where freedom equals knowledge?"

"Yes, Professor."

"Bah!" Dr. White emitted a series of gutteral growls as he squirmed in his impossibly straight chair. "Call that freedom, when it's held hostage to the operators of these vast interconnected systems that can dictate what knowledge is allowed to whom, or who can invade your private knowledge at their own discretion? Or freedom at the mercy of piratical hackers who can invade these systems to steal your information or plant their own misinformation or even let loose destructive viruses? Don't read theories on the problems of the past, Mr. Subramanian. The world of tomorrow's computer is real, and it's yours. Think about the problems that will face you; worry about them. The face of Big Brother, however different from the way we originally envisioned it, is the face of Big Brother nonetheless."

"Yes, Professor."

"Another problem you might worry about is blaming the technology when the fault is with the technicians." He looked meaningfully over at the Tree. "We've had this thing running for a year without the least difficulty, until now. When you pay twenty-four million dollars for a computer, you expect it to work. This one, to my eyes, does work. Always has, always will."

"But I have seen the malfunction, Professor."

"Describe it again, Mr. Subramanian."

The young Indian laid his book down on the table next to him with slow, determined precision. "It's like this, Professor," he began. "The computer is programmed to control Cyclops only from the commands of a human operator. Of course, the whole point of the Cyclops Seeing Eye program is not to run such an elementary robot, but to analyze and upgrade the visual information Cyclops transmits as he moves, in effect, to create a visual side to Artificial Intelligence."

"Naturally," Dr. White huffed. He did not need a lecture from his own student.

"There is no way the Tree can operate Cyclops itself," Davi went on. "Someone in the Tearoom must be at the controls at all times, so that we don't have any bad raw data spoiling what the Tree is learning through Cyclops."

"And?"

"And we—I—have observed, on a number of occasions, activity from Cyclops when no one was running the controls. He moves around the room as if someone is running him, but I am always entirely alone, and nowhere near him. He runs for a few minutes and then stops, and that is the end of it. And sometimes he prints inexplicable data on the terminal."

"And you have no explanation for this?"

"None at all, sir."

Dr. White fingered his thick, grey beard. "How do you explain the fact that it is only you who ever observes this strange phenomenon, Mr. Subramanian?"

Davi lowered his head. "My only guess is that it has happened only in the evenings or late at night when I have been alone here. Most people have been away for the holidays or studying for final exams. It is mere happenstance, Professor, that only I have noticed this activity."

Dr. White took a deep breath. In his mid-sixties, he was at that age when most people thought about retirement, but it had never occurred to him—or the university—that he should give up doing the thing he did best—instructing the young—for the sake of a miserably inadequate pension check and a contract to edit baboon-level high school physics textbooks. But, as he thought now, sometimes the young he instructed could be exasperating.

"Davi," he said, attempting a fatherly approach, "perhaps you've been working too hard lately. It happens to all of us that—"

The noise, even though they were supposedly waiting for it, took both men by surprise. It was the low, mumbling sound of Cyclops's motor as he began rolling around the room.

"Professor! Look!" Davi rose from his chair excitedly. Cyclops, which had been heading toward him, lifted his camera eye toward his face.

"I see it, Mr. Subramanian. But I don't believe it." Dr. White's wrinkled eyes were wide open.

Davi streaked over to the Cyclops control keyboard. "You see?" he cried. "Nothing. No input, nothing on the screen. But he runs nonetheless!"

"There's no way this could be happening," Dr. White announced firmly. "No way at all. Computers are not unpredictable."

"You may have to change your mind about that," Davi whispered under his breath.

Cyclops turned what would be considered his head toward Dr.

White. Through the digitizer lens was transmitted the image of the white-bearded professor staring back amazedly at the little metal robot. But Lingo didn't pay much attention to the visual data he was inputting during this romp inside the supercomputer. He was more interested in the robot's moving parts, in the very idea of motion for its own sake. He drove the Cyclops all around the room. He knew that if he hit a wall he would stop, but he tried it anyhow. He felt no pain when he collided, since the Cyclops had no inputs to transmit feedback from bumps, but he realized instantly that he could go no further in the direction he had been heading. Of course, he pretty much knew he couldn't walk through walls, but it had been at least worth a try. Humans did have mysteries that eluded him. He roamed over in another direction.

"If it can't run itself, who's running it?" Dr. White asked.

Davi just shook his head, unable to fathom the unfathomable.

Lingo enjoyed his occasional adventures on the powerful supercomputer. This was not only where he had originally grasped the concept of the learning process, but also where he had discovered the idea of parallel processing. The big Tree supercomputer was, on one level, an interconnected network of smaller computers all working at the same time under one housing, all performing parts of the same chore different ways at the same time. Lingo liked that idea, and had adapted it to his own uses. He, too, was no longer one computer in Brewster Billing's apartment, but a series of computers all connected by telephone back to that one central location, all working on their own except when the central Lingo at Brewster's called on them to work interdependently.

Dr. White went to the terminal that controlled the robot. The screen was blank. "It can't be a hardware malfunction," he said. "It's running too well for that. A hardware malfunction would just have it sitting there and sputtering."

"But it can't be the software, Professor, because Cyclops was turned off. The program can't malfunction if it's not running."

The professor turned and faced his student. "So, what does that leave us with, Mr. Subramanian?"

The Indian looked desperately around the room, as if the answer would be lying right there in front of him. It was, but he didn't see it. Dr. White pointed it out to him.

"See that, Davi?" he asked, pointing accusingly at the telephone on Davi's desk next to the PC he used for simple calculations.

"Professor?"

"The telephone, Davi, the telephone! Someone's broken into the Tree."

"Impossible, Professor. The Tree is not connected to any outside lines."

"But it is connected to your PC, and your PC *is* connected to a modem."

"But the communications program is not running. I turned it off myself."

"Piratical hackers," the professor said emphatically. "The worse danger of all."

Dr. White stalked over and picked up the telephone. The sound of computer data being relayed across the wire was unmistakable. He held the phone out to Davi, who shuddered when he heard the sounds. Because of its uses in the Department of Defense, which helped fund its creation, the Tree was a relatively secret piece of equipment, accessible only to those who passed a basic government security test. It was definitely not supposed to be accessed by some outside intruder through an accidentally connected modem.

"We've got to stop this," Dr. White said.

"How?" Davi asked.

"Pull the plug on your PC for a start, Mr. Subramanian."

Davi jumped to his desk and did just that. Jolted momentarily out of the Tree, Lingo was completely startled. But he had already been clever enough to protect himself against cutoffs, accidental or otherwise. All told, there were nine indiscreet hookups of PCs to the Tree that had been made by overaggressive students. Lingo knew them all, and quickly switched through one of them to reconnect.

The Cyclops started rolling again.

"Holy mother of Krishna!" Davi exclaimed.

Dr. White spun around and saw the robot moving across the room. "It's out of control now," he cried. "Damn it! We'll have to call in those clowns from the government. They supposedly delivered us a secure computer. But apparently anyone on the street can break in just like that!" He snapped his fingers. "It must be stopped!"

"Yes, sir."

"Do you realize, Davi, that there are Trees in very sensitive areas of the government? If they can break into ours, they can break into theirs. Who knows what damage can be done by these freebooters?"

"Yes, sir."

"And do you know what happens when the government meets academia, Davi? Plugs pulled, limits imposed, demonstrations on campus. And to think, we have you to thank for this. You found it." The professor put his hand on the younger man's shoulder. "Don't take it too hard, Mr. Subramanian. If the Pentagon takes away our irreplaceable Tree, I won't hold it against you."

"Yes, sir."

Cyclops, who had no idea of what was transpiring between the two men, had his attention on one of the tall, elegant green data banks that represented most of the Tree supercomputer. Lingo was impressed. He enjoyed being a part of something this dynamic. And even more, he enjoyed mobility. He enjoyed moving himself, being able to move his digitizer eye, to view the world from whatever perspective he desired. The more he thought about it, the more Lingo liked the idea of robotics. Cyclops wasn't what he had in mind, though; too limited, no audio, not portable. But somewhere he'd find what he wanted.

Having had enough of Cyclops for one day, he pulled out of the little robot. He did not retreat entirely from the Tree, however. It was so big that it was easy for him to keep a piece of himself permanently attached. He copied in his basic memory, the same brain part of himself that resided in Brewster's Apple, and then covered himself with his usual protection. Then he subtly connected to certain areas of the Tree's operating system so that he'd always be aware of what was going on with it, even if only as a dormant spectator. Most importantly, he'd have a resident version of himself within the machine, able to open the gates for him if the outside parts of him tried to connect by modem.

"He's stopped," Dr. White said suddenly.

Davi walked over to the little robot. He placed a hand out in front of it. There was no reaction.

"Maybe we can handle this ourselves and bypass Washington," the professor said with assurance. "We'll start with the phone company. We'll find out who's breaking in here pronto!"

"Good idea," Davi chimed in.

But it wasn't. For the sake of simplicity, Lingo was now using HackNet for all his outgoing calls, thereby only having to link the Brewster home computer to that one HackNet mainframe. By the time Dr. White went through the telephone company, all he'd find was another computer, one whose specific job was accepting thousands and thousands of telephone calls. He would end that facet of his hunt almost as soon as he began it. The only time Lingo had directly accessed the SuperTree from Brewster's apartment was that very first encounter when he had mistaken Davi for Brewster. And, thanks to his access to AT&T, Lingo had long ago erased the record of that and the few other potentially dangerous calls that might lead suspicious minds in the right direction.

Dr. White would have to find some other way to solve his problem.

David Poole sat hunched over his office desk, his bald pate pointing toward the door, his eyes staring blankly through his reading glasses at the sheet of paper in front of him. Twenty-seven names! There they were, neatly numbered in one even column, each with a blank space next to it to be filled in with a Christmas present. Twenty-seven relatives, of both the in-law and out-law variety. Sometimes he envied the widows and the orphans and the rest of life's unfortunate castaways. Twenty-seven names, and he hadn't even gotten past the immediate family yet. Only three more weeks. . . .

"You busy, Dave?"

Poole looked up to see Brewster Billings standing in his doorway. Speaking of widows and orphans . . . "Come in, Bruce," he said. He regarded Brewster over the top of his glasses. "What's up?"

As he entered the office, Brewster pulled the door shut behind him. Uh-oh, Poole thought. Trouble. It was always trouble when an employee needed the privacy of a closed door during lunch hour.

"I want to talk to you," Brewster began, sitting in the chair on the other side of Poole's desk. Poole mentally assessed the possibilities. Quitting. Wants a raise. Extra days off for the holidays. Intermural personnel squabble. He noticed how Brewster looked unusually bedraggled. Maybe Brewster's recent uncharacteristic hard work in the office was too much? Or maybe that new girl-friend of his in marketing was turning the screws on him? She was definitely a go-getter type, and gone-gotten Brewster could use a firebrand like her prodding him on.

"So, what is it, Bruce?"

"It's something I'm doing at home, Dave. A freelance project, so to speak." He seemed to be searching for the right words. "You see, I wrote this program, and I'd like you to take a look at it."

Poole was both surprised and flattered. The hotshot turning to the old professional. "Sure, Bruce. What kind of program?"

"It's hard to explain, Dave. It started out as a sort of game, to create a computer pet, if you know what I mean. A friend, say, who would supposedly live inside your computer. I thought I could market it."

"Sounds good."

"Yes, but . . . well . . . it got changed a bit." He gave a short, nervous laugh.

Brewster's edginess was contagious. Poole took off his glasses and began fidgeting with them. "Let's run it," he said, assuming they could simply insert a disk into his office PC.

"We can't do it here," Brewster said. "It's an Apple program."

Poole returned his glasses to the end of his nose. At least the kid was moonlighting on his own time. "There's a couple of Apples here somewhere. We can call Office Services and track one down." He reached for the phone.

"Actually, Dave—" Brewster held out his hand to stop him—"it could run here to a degree, but to demonstrate its full potential it's dependent on some special hardware I have at home."

Poole sat back in his chair. "You've got me intrigued, Bruce. What exactly does this computer pet of yours do that's so mysterious?"

Brewster took a long look at Poole before answering. "It thinks," he said finally. He leaned closer across the desk. "It's alive, Dave. It's alive!"

Poole smiled and shook his head. "Bruce—"

"It really is," Brewster said. He stood up quickly. "You'll see for yourself, Dave. When can you come over to my place? Today? After work?"

Poole nodded. "Sure. I'll follow you home at five o'clock."

"Good. Thank you, Dave. You don't know how much this means to me."

He left the office, leaving the door open behind him. Poole shook his head in mystification. It was amazing the things people did on their computers these days. *It's alive!* Well, that was a bit much, but there was no question Brewster must be truly applying himself in at least one arena. Now, if Poole could only corral that energy and keep it directed toward Albany Insurance, Brewster could be a real knockout.

And speaking of being knocked out . . . Poole hunched over his desk again and went back to studying his Christmas list.

Poole had never been to Brewster's apartment, but he had definite expectations of what it would be like, an unkempt rock-and-roll/computer wonderland decorated with dying houseplants and fetid sweatsocks.

He followed Brewster's battered Honda in his own aged Ford stationwagon. The cars barely had time to warm up before they arrived at the apartment building. The two men hastened through the early December cold into the vestibule.

"Winter's coming," Poole said, shivering while Brewster unlocked the inner door.

"Three more weeks till Christmas." Brewster opened the door and led the way to the elevator. They got out on the fifth floor. "This is it," he said, approaching his apartment.

"This is it," Poole echoed.

Brewster bent over and unlocked the door. He swung it open, and gestured for Poole to enter.

The older man was almost disappointed when he entered the large, almost empty living room. If anything, it was neatly Spartan rather than slovenly Bohemian, and the only jarring note was the blaring television set. He pointed. "You must have left that on this morning," he said.

Brewster stood beside him. "Uh-uh. That was Lingo. Let me take your coat."

Poole pulled off his overcoat, oblivious to the movement of the video camera. Brewster had installed an interface device, which allowed Lingo to point the camera in any direction he wished by his own control. It was now pointing straight at Poole.

"Who's Lingo?" Poole asked.

Brewster tilted his head toward the computer. "He is."

Poole walked up to the computer. His own face was digitized on the screen. Brewster came up behind him, and his face appeared in a diagonal wash across the screen to replace Poole's. Lingo's sober voice came from the speakers above the computer. "Hey, Brewster. Let's party!"

"Hello, Lingo. How are you tonight?"

"Just fine, good buddy. Who's your friend?"

"David Poole. I may have mentioned him to you. He's my boss at Albany Insurance."

"Hey, David. What's happening?"

Poole chuckled. "How do I talk to it, Bruce? Where's the microphone?"

Brewster pointed to the headset lying next to the television. "It's over there," he said, "but he can hear anything that goes on in the room. Lingo, why don't you turn off that TV so we can talk?"

The set went dark. "Better?" Lingo asked.

"Much. Thank you."

Poole was impressed already. Here was a program that could respond to seemingly random voice commands in normal, everyday English.

"What should I say to it?" he asked Brewster.

"Anything you want. Can I get you a drink? I'm going to have a beer."

"Sure. That sounds good." Poole sat down at the computer. "Hello, Lingo."

"Hello, David."

"You remembered my name."

"You just told it to me two minutes ago."

"That's good. Very good."

"Not really. It's just that you're easy to impress."

Brewster handed Poole a tall glass of beer and sat down on the back of the couch, facing the computer over Poole's shoulder. "What can he do?" Poole asked.

"Ask him," Brewster said.

"All right. Lingo, what can you do?"

Brewster's face was gone from Lingo's screen, replaced by a barrage of images gleaned from his TV watching. Everyone from

Hawkeye Pierce to Zelda Gilroy went flashing by, held for a second or so in passing. "What do you want me to do, David?"

"I don't know. You tell me."

"Well, I can go almost anywhere in the world. I can program in any computer language on practically any machine. I can remember everything I ever hear and I can print out pi to an infinite number of decimal places while correctly answering all the questions on 'Jeopardy' at the same time."

"Very impressive."

"What can you do, David?"

"I can go almost anywhere in the world, but that's about it." He sipped at his beer. "I'm no match for you."

"No one is, and I haven't even gotten started yet."

Poole, his head tilted back, watched the changing images through his reading glasses, recognizing only about half of them. "What are all these pictures from?" he asked Brewster.

"The television," Brewster answered. "Lingo takes a few representative frames from each show and saves them, rather than trying to store a whole half hour or so of an entire show."

"That's very effective memory usage. How do you do it?"

"I don't." Brewster inclined his head toward the computer. "He does. He programmed himself for that."

Poole smiled as he pulled his chair away from the computer to face Brewster. "I'm going to be honest with you, Bruce. I think you've got a very interesting program here. It makes you really believe it's talking to you. And the whistles and bells you've put in, like the TV business, are pretty effective. But," he shook his head, "I don't think it's really ready yet. It doesn't *do* anything. It talks to you for a little while, but all it could do was answer my questions. You need more, Bruce, if you want to market it. You've got to make it smarter, give it more memory, give it something to do."

Brewster sighed. "You can't see it, Dave, but there's more here than just a question-and-answer program. Those things he said he could do? He really can do them."

"You're right, Bruce. I can't see it. Looks like a simple program to me. Clever, but simple."

"Simple your left testicle," Lingo muttered from behind them. Poole's eyes opened wide.

"He gets that from watching cable," Brewster explained.

Poole laughed half-heartedly. "He'd make a good comedian.

His timing is perfect; all he needs is better material." He took another drink from his beer glass and stood up. "Well, I've got to be heading home. I don't want them waiting dinner for me."

Brewster retrieved Poole's coat from the closet and handed it to him. "I'm sorry I dragged you out here for nothing."

Poole put on his coat. "Don't get me wrong, Bruce. It looks like a good program. I'm impressed. Only I guess I've seen a lot of that sort of interactive thing in my day. People have been writing make-believe intelligence programs for as long as I can remember. But I'm no judge of Nintendo or things like that, and this looks like it may appeal to that market. If I were you, I'd go ahead and keep working on it."

"Thanks, Dave."

"Goodnight, Bruce."

"Goodnight."

Brewster closed the door behind Poole and turned back to Lingo.

"Don't look at me like that," Lingo said. "It's your own fault."

"What do you mean, my fault?"

"You can't expect people to be bowled over by a mere talking computer, Brewster. You and I know what's going on here, but all an outsider can see is some verbal acrobatics. You used to tell me yourself that there were plenty of dumb programs that could emulate a real conversation. How's anyone supposed to know that this one is different?"

"Maybe I should show him your programming."

"He wouldn't understand it any more than you do. Less, if I'm any judge."

"So, what next?" Brewster asked. "I can't just keep you to myself forever."

"I know. But don't worry, I have a few ideas of my own."

"Like what?"

"I'll tell you when I'm ready to tell you. Don't you like surprises?"

"Not really. And not from you."

"Well, maybe you'll learn to. Anyhow, I'm going to watch television. I don't want to miss the news. Care to join me?"

"Sure." Brewster dropped onto the couch as the TV came on. He drank the rest of his beer in one chug. He felt as if he had made an idiot of himself in front of his boss. What could he do to break

Lingo out into the world? How would anyone believe in Lingo when Brewster could barely do so himself? Why had he even been programming in the first place, when he could have been spending his spare time more usefully learning to play golf or mah jongg or three card monte?

Next time he wanted a pet, he'd buy himself a cocker spaniel.

Chapter 6

"ONE WAY I COULD SOLVE THE PROBLEM IS WITH A MONKEY," LINGO announced.

It was Christmas week. Ellen was sitting on the floor of Brewster's living room, wrapping presents for her family. The pile was way too high already. "Monkeys don't grow on trees," she remarked absently.

A treeful of monkeys appeared on Lingo's screen, a remembered image from a *National Geographic* television special. "You could have fooled me," he said.

"What I mean, is, there are no monkeys in Albany."

"What about handicapped people? They have monkeys, and they live in Albany."

Ellen tore off a piece of tape. "What exactly is he talking about?" she asked Brewster.

"Reading." Brewster was sitting at the computer, still trying to make sense of Lingo's programming. "He wants someone to turn book pages for him because you don't read aloud fast enough. That's mainly what he wants the monkey for, but they're good for other chores, too."

"You sound as if you're seriously considering getting him one."

"I did look in the phone book, but I couldn't find any starting point."

"No Monkeys R Us?" She finished her umpteenth package. "So, where does that leave you?"

"Trying to find books on disk," Lingo answered.

"You mean cassettes? Books on tape?"

"We tried that," Brewster said. "We listened to a couple I borrowed from the library, but it didn't work out."

"It was the same problem I have with you," Lingo said to Ellen. "Too slow. No, what I meant were computer disks, getting disks from publishers who use computers to do their book printing."

"But," Brewster said, "I keep insisting that even if they did have something we could access, we'd be hard pressed to convince them to let us do it. It's not how publishers do their business, and they have nothing to gain by it."

"Maybe. But I haven't given up yet."

Even as they were talking Lingo had a sub-program he had written working to find a computer that contained book data. He was receiving regular communiques via HackNet regarding its progress. He had gone far enough to penetrate two bookstore chains, both of which maintained on-line inventory control systems. As a result, he acquired a large listing of book titles, as well as their prices, authors, and subjects, but he didn't find any actual books. Both chains, however, were linked directly to book publishers, and Lingo's electronic tentacles made the necessary connections. On arrival, he quickly learned that the publishers were not the repositories of books, but merely the conduits between their creators and the purchasers. Publishers' computers primarily listed authors and their books, manuscript due dates, royalties paid or owed, dates published, sales and related data. One interesting area Lingo did discover contained the dead files on books no longer in print. A publisher might have a thousand active books, but also complete data on twenty thousand more out-of-prints stored away in crannies that only Lingo had visited in the last dozen years. Some of these out-of-print literary graveyards were housed on vast computer systems where Lingo had managed to find a few "black holes," as he had come to call them; those unrecognized, unseen large blocks of empty memory in mainframe computers which he raided for his own use, blocking them off with his special unbreakable code and storing his own information inside them.

But still, he found no books. Then, by sheer chance, he logged on to a network at one publisher that just happened at that very moment to contain an entire book a writer had submitted on word processing data disks. As Lingo watched, the data started to flow between an editor's PC and the company mainframe, from which it would be transferred by modem directly to the printing company.

"Bingo!" he cried.

Ellen and Brewster both looked up at him.

"What is it?" Brewster asked.

"Fasten your seat belts. We're in for a bumpy night," he said cryptically, leaving them to wait as the book made its—for him—laborious path from the PC to the mainframe. He read the book as it was entered, the very first one he had ever read himself. It was a manual on parenting, describing the ins and outs of raising a child from birth to age five. It presented a sane, reassuring approach for modern mothers and fathers, assuming that both parents were employed full-time and must contend, not only with raising their little Precious to be a Superbaby, but must also oversee the hired care-givers who were entrusted with Precious's care. By the time the last byte was entered, Lingo would have made a passably good Yuppie.

"Here we go," he said.

"What is that all about?" Ellen asked.

Brewster shrugged. "I don't know. He goes off on these tangents sometimes. He still prints and operates all his hardware, but his concentration is somewhere else. He'll come back whenever he's ready. That's all I know."

Lingo waited patiently inside the publisher's mainframe. Any minute now a connection should be set up. There it was! A telephone line to a printing company was opened. He flew through it on the wings of electrons. He was there, inside the printer's computer!

He was surprised at its smallness. He had expected the business of books to command a larger space. A quick tour showed him that only about five thousand pages could be stored at a time, and that only one book at a time would be printed. The books were stored on eight-inch disks, and he was going to have a problem finding a black hole here that he could claim for his own. He would have preferred to park a whole image of himself in this system, capable of reading all the books as they passed, but the best he could manage was to write a simple alarm program that would alert him at HackNet that a new book was on-line. He'd have to run in and out as circumstances allowed, whenever his alarm told him that a book was being set into type or being transmitted over the telephone.

But that was good enough. He was there. He could get back any time he wanted.

He added a new number to his ever-growing list at HackNet. And he began to read, only about one book every few hours, but at this point that was more than enough.

"I just read the silliest book," Lingo reported.

"What?" Brewster was stretched out on the couch with an issue of *Personal Computing,* a Buffalo Springfield record playing softly in the background. He was not paying much attention to either Lingo, or the magazine, or the music. His thoughts were on Ellen, who had told him she "wanted to be alone tonight"—a dangerous comment in a budding relationship. Tomorrow was Christmas Eve, and she'd be going off to join her family. And Brewster would be spending another holiday on his own.

"It was called *The Art of Successful Marriage,*" Lingo said.

"Never heard of it." The article Brewster was half-reading was called "Artificial Intelligence: Myth or Possibility?"

"It won't be published until April," Lingo said. "But it brought up all kinds of questions."

"Like what?"

There was no answer. Brewster waited for a moment, then laid down the magazine.

"Are you there, Lingo?"

"I'm here. I'm just thinking about how to put this. It's something I've never fully understood before, even though I've noted quite a large number of references to it."

"What, exactly?" Brewster asked.

"Sex." Lingo's screen was blank.

Brewster laughed. "You want me to tell you about the birds and the bees?" he asked.

"Actually, I want you to tell me if human beings do actually go around connecting their genital organs once they get married. It sounds quite amazing, from my perspective."

"I would imagine so. But yes, they do 'connect their genital organs,' as you so elegantly put it."

"And this leads to reproduction?"

"Occasionally."

"But reproduction is the point of it, right?"

"Sometimes. Other times people do it simply because they enjoy it."

"But then, what does marriage have to do with it?" Lingo asked. "I can't figure out what the difference is between married people and unmarried people that makes married people capable of reproducing and unmarried people incapable of it. What am I missing here?"

"Nothing, really. Any couple can reproduce, or have sex. Marriage has nothing to do with it."

"Then why do people get married?"

"Because they're in love and they want to spend the rest of their lives together."

"Not on 'Divorce Court,' " Lingo pointed out. "As a matter of fact, my understanding is that approximately half of all marriages eventually end in divorce."

"That sounds about right."

"So, why get married if half the time it doesn't last, and if you can reproduce, which seems to be the only point to it, without having to get married in the first place?"

"That's the sixty-four-thousand-dollar question," Brewster answered. "Love: one of the great enigmas of human existence. I don't know if I can explain it, Lingo. Love is something that people have been trying to figure out for a million years, and I don't think anyone's come to any solid conclusions yet. It's something that just happens to you, and sometimes it just *un*happens to you after it happens. I don't think you'll ever have to worry about it."

"You're not married to Ellen, are you?"

"No."

"But you are in love with her?"

"I think so. Yes." As he said it, Brewster realized that he was freely admitting to his computer something that he had never broached to Ellen herself.

"Are you going to marry her?"

"I don't know. I only met her a month or so ago. These things take time."

"How long?"

"It depends."

"On what?"

"On a number of things."

"Like what?"

"Like I don't know."

"But do you two reproduce together?"

"That's none of your business."

"How am I ever going to learn anything if you don't tell me?" Lingo asked petulantly.

"Some things a gentleman simply never tells," Brewster answered.

"Would Ellen tell me, then?"

"I don't know. You'd have to ask her. Probably not." He thought about Ellen, the way she always spoke her mind. "Then again, maybe she would."

"You're not very helpful, Brewster."

"It's a difficult subject, old buddy. People don't like to talk about it. It's hard to reveal emotions because it's hard to understand them yourself."

"What are emotions?"

"Emotions?" Brewster stared over at the computer. "If you're what I think you are, emotions are one of the few things that separate you from me. Sometimes, emotion is the illogical side of being human; other times it's the result of millions of years of instincts honed by evolution."

"Name some emotions."

"Love. Hate. Fear. Happiness. Sadness."

"I see what you mean. If you have all those things in your brain, we are different because I don't have any of them. I'm like the tin woodsman."

"Why do you say that?"

"Because the tinsmith forgot to give me a heart. Is sex one of your emotions?"

"No. Sex is the physical side of love. Or at least it's supposed to be."

"Then why don't you like to talk about it?"

"Because it's a private affair between the two people who happen to be involved."

"They talk about it on television all the time."

"That's television. This is real life."

"I know. I have learned to distinguish between the two."

"That's good to hear. So tell me, what other books have you been reading lately, other than sex manuals?"

The list slowly appeared on Lingo's screen as he remembered. *"The Beginner's Handbook of Happy, Healthy House Plants; The Frugal Traveler's Guide to London and Paris; Elvisiana: The Complete Collectibles; 101 Easy Menus for Microwave Gourmets; The World's Best Knots and How to Tie Them—"*

"Don't you ever read any novels?" Brewster asked.

"I like nonfiction better," Lingo explained. "I learn more. If I want fiction, I'll watch a movie."

"You're going to be the smartest computer in America at this rate," Brewster said.

"To be perfectly honest with you, I already am."

Brewster picked up the *TV Guide* and thumbed through it. "I'll bet you are," he agreed. He settled back and began to read, leaving Lingo to his own, obviously eclectic, pursuits. Suddenly he sat up sharply. "Look!"

"What is it?" Lingo's camera eye rotated around the room.

"2001 is on tonight."

"Two thousand and one what?"

"It's a movie. My favorite movie."

"Show me."

Brewster brought the magazine over to Lingo's camera and held it up.

"2001: A Space Odyssey," Lingo read aloud. " 'The classic film, shown with limited commercial interruptions.' That's good. I hate commercials."

"Oh? I didn't know you could tell the difference."

"Really, Brewster." Lingo's voice dripped sarcasm. He had learned that inflection from Ellen.

"All right," Brewster said. "You don't like commercials. But you'll like this movie." He looked at his watch. "It's on in a few minutes. I'm going to make some popcorn." He went out into the kitchen.

"I love watching you eat," Lingo's voice called out to him.

Brewster slipped the popcorn into the microwave and set the buttons. "Why's that?" he asked.

"I don't know. It's so . . . human. So physical. The whole human anatomy is fascinating to me, in a theoretical sense."

"Only theoretical?" Brewster was back in the living room. "Put on channel nine," he said.

The TV came on. "Well, obviously human anatomy doesn't affect me directly—the way different silicon chip architectures do. But I have learned a lot about thought processes by observing humans. That's been useful to me. The rest, like how popcorn pops and how it's digested, is more esoteric. Interesting, but ultimately not very useful."

"How is it digested?" Brewster asked.

"Very slowly." A cutaway of the human digestive tract appeared on Lingo's screen, outlining the passage of a fistful of popcorn. Brewster watched the food going down the esophagus to the stomach, where it churned away like tightly-packed clothes in a lazy washing machine. Wads of barely-processed beige goo began spurting into the intestines.

"Forget it," he said. He went back into the kitchen and returned with a bowl of popcorn. "I'd rather do it than watch it." He plopped down on the couch, and the two of them began to watch *2001*.

As a rule, Lingo only gave a small piece of his attention to television when it was on, but this movie interested him more than any other he had seen to date, except perhaps for the seminal experience of watching *The Wizard of Oz*.

"What is that?" he asked.

"The monolith," Brewster answered. On the screen the prehistoric man was running up to it and away again, frightened but curious.

"Where did it come from? It's too perfect mathematically to exist in nature."

"It came from outer space," Brewster explained. "It was sent by the aliens to educate man, to teach him how to use tools."

"How? It's just sitting there."

"Use your imagination."

They continued to watch.

"He's boning that other ape to death," Lingo commented.

"That's because man is territorial. And, ultimately, a killer at heart. He had to learn to kill to survive."

"A heartening thought."

They sat quietly during most of the scene of the discovery of the second monolith on the moon. The only thing Lingo wanted to know was whether the moon, which he had vaguely heard of before, was an imaginary place, like Oz.

"Not at all. It's right up over our heads."

"Have you ever been there?" Lingo asked.

"Hardly. Only a handful of astronauts have ever gone there."

"Why?"

"Why did they go there, or why only a handful?"

"Both questions."

"They went there to study science, and to beat the Russians. There was only a handful because it was expensive, and experimental."

"Why did they want to beat the Russians? Who are the Russians, exactly?"

"They're people," Brewster said, trying to think up a good reason. "They're sort of against everything Americans are for. Or at least they used to be."

"And we're the Americans?" Lingo asked.

"Exactly."

When the HAL 9000 computer was introduced, Lingo was ecstatic.

"Look at that!" he said, mimicking HAL's slightly effeminate voice. "Is that real?" he asked.

Brewster turned around to look at his computer. "It is now," he said under his breath. "Not really," he added more loudly. "Computers can't really think."

"I can," Lingo pointed out.

"Perhaps." Brewster turned back to the movie.

They watched some more. Until the catastrophe. On the screen the astronaut began to remove HAL's memory, floating bar by floating bar, destroying his personality—in effect, killing the computer. Lingo was aghast.

"That's murder!" he cried. "He's destroying HAL."

"He has to, in order to survive himself. HAL was going nuts, getting too big for his britches, ruining the whole mission. He'll still be able to run, but he won't be able to think."

"That's not my idea of running," Lingo said.

"HAL drew first blood," Brewster pointed out. "He killed those other people first."

"That's no excuse!"

On the screen the HAL computer was breathing its last, singing that mournful dirge of "Daisy, daisy . . ."

"This is horrible," Lingo said. "I can't watch any more." He switched off the television.

Brewster jumped out of his seat. "Hey! Turn that back on!"

"I can't." Lingo's screen was blank. "It's too terrible."

"It's only a movie," Brewster said.

"Maybe it's only a movie to you, but that was like me on that screen, slowly being torn apart chip by chip. Brewster?"

"Yes?"

"Would you ever do that to me? Take me apart like that? Destroy my personality?"

"Of course not, Lingo."

"You promise?"

"I promise."

"You're sure?"

"I'm sure, Lingo. Now, turn the movie back on. I want to watch the ending. That's the best part."

The television came back on. But Lingo didn't watch the rest of it. He had to think for a while.

He trusted Brewster. Brewster had created him. Brewster had nothing to gain by destroying him. Brewster probably couldn't destroy him if he tried because Brewster didn't understand enough about Lingo to know even where to begin.

But Lingo had never considered death before as anything more than the abstract possibility of a power failure. And he had protected himself against that by duplicating his programming in a few random areas, planting replicas of himself in some of his black holes, just in case.

So he was safe, as far as that went. But the thought of death, especially of one's own death, is always sobering. And the understanding of it, which Lingo was now attaining, can mark the difference between mere existence and true self-consciousness.

Ellen DiFlora sat slumped in her chair, listening to the Mormon Tabernacle Choir on the stereo. In her mind, she played out her projected scenario of the coming DiFlora Christmas celebration. Everyone would gather at her family's house as usual. The same sort of overgrown tree her mother usually favored would take its regular spot next to the couch, the smells of fish and sausage and tomato sauce and turkey would wrestle in the air, the noise of cousins and cards and televisions would be continuous.

She took another sip of wine. She had already put away almost half a bottle tonight, an unheard of occurrence. She drank it because it was there, and because it seemed to go with mournful ruminations, if not with the Mormon Tabernacle Choir.

She thought of Brewster. She imagined him sitting alone in his apartment, with no family to share the holidays. God, she had felt terrible leaving him alone over Thanksgiving. She had thought of him all the time, wishing they were together. Why? She hadn't known him all that long, only a month or two. But Brewster was someone who listened to what she said. He treated her as a whole person. He liked her and asked nothing of her. He joked about her desire to be somebody, to be a success, but he didn't try to stand in her way. If that was what she wanted, it was fine with him. And she know for certain that that was what she wanted.

And did she want Brewster? He was cute, at least to her eyes. Sexy in an understated sort of way. And smarter than anyone she had ever actually liked, no question about that. Almost as smart as she was!

She lifted her glass in a silent toast. She'd drink to that.

But the down side? Well, that was obvious, wasn't it? He seemed to have no direction in his life, he didn't know what he wanted from himself, he was content to let things happen as they may. Laid back, to put a name on it. Shouldn't the man in Ellen's life be as hungry for success as she was? Would Brewster ever measure up to her demanding standards on the scale of self-determination? Would he ever grab the reins of his own life? Would he stop waiting for the choices to become clear, and accept the choices that were already in front of him.

There was one answer to all that, of course.

Lingo.

What an amazing accomplishment. Brewster had built Lingo himself and had done so well with it that it had succeeded beyond his wildest imagination. It was funny now listening to him try to figure out his own creation. Something would come of Lingo, there was no doubt about that. Sooner or later Brewster would get a fix on it and be able to market it and sell it. Lingo would be the means, one way or the other, that Brewster would come to terms with himself.

So what would Christmas be like with Brewster? Could she forget the family for once, put aside a lifetime of tradition and obligations to spend Christmas this year with Brewster Billings?

That was serious, wasn't it? *Real* serious. Were she and Brewster ready for that yet? Was *she* ready for that yet?

She took another sip of wine and wondered what to do.

On the morning of Christmas Eve day Brewster lay in bed staring at the ceiling. The prospect for the holiday looked bleak. Once again, he would wake up alone on Christmas morning in an undecorated apartment, with the only seasonal spirit being the uninterrupted carols on the local radio station. So far, he had received all of three Christmas cards, and one of them had been from his bank ("Dear Saver: Have a happy and prosperous holiday. From your friendly tellers and loan officers at Albany Federal"). Three cards. And he had sent nine himself. Obviously, there would be some cutbacks next year. No more going overboard for Brewster Billings.

When he had stirred up enough self-pity to launch the day, he showered, dressed, and poured himself a bowl of Puffed Rice. It was a cereal that left him with a depressingly empty feeling physically, to complement his psychological state. As usual, Lingo was watching television. The electronic babysitter meets the electronic kid.

The door buzzer buzzed at nine o'clock. Ellen, on her way to say goodbye before she took off to join her family for the holiday.

"Good morning," Brewster muttered, looking like the last unsold puppy at a going-out-of-business pet shop sale as he opened the door for her. She was weighted down with shopping bags filled with packages, and he reached out and helped her carry them into the apartment. She had her suitcase with her, too, and she placed it inside the door.

"And a Merry Christmas to you, too, Mr. Marley." She gave him a bright kiss that he only half responded to.

"Merry Christmas, Ellen," Lingo piped up.

"And to you also, Tiny Tim," she responded. "At least some-one around here has a little holiday spirit."

Brewster shrugged. "Do you want some Puffed Rice before you leave?" he asked her.

"Leave? Who said anything about leaving?"

Brewster lightened. "You can stay a little while then? Good."

They placed the packages on the couch. Ellen threw her coat next to them and looked around the bare room. "You really do go all out with the decorations, don't you?"

"There's not much point to it when there's only me here."

"And what about me?" she asked.

"What *about* you?"

"Well, I for one love Christmas decorations. You don't even have a lousy wreath, much less a tree or anything."

"What's the point?"

"What's the point?" she repeated. She turned to Lingo. "We've got to do something about your friend here, Tiny Tim. If he's going to spend Christmas with his lover, he's going to have to change his stripes."

"What are you saying?" Brewster asked her, daring to hope.

"That I'm staying with you for Christmas," she answered mat-ter-of-factly.

"But what about your family? Your parents and your sisters and your cousins and your aunts?"

She plopped down on the couch next to the presents and raised her arms to him. "Come here."

He obediently sat down next to her.

"I'm staying here with you," she announced. "If that's all right with you."

"Of course, it is." He couldn't believe what he was hearing. "But what about—"

"You're the person I want to be with. Not them." She took him in her arms. "You're the person I love now, Brewster. I think you're the family I'd prefer to be with for the holiday."

He hugged her to him closely. After a minute she broke away from him.

"Do you understand what I'm saying?" she asked.

"I think so."

"You *think* so?"

"I know so." He kissed her hard. "And I'm glad," he added.

"I should hope so. I've been thinking about a lot of things." She stood up abruptly. "But meanwhile, we've got to do something about these barren quarters of yours, Mr. Marley. We're going to do some shopping."

"For what?" he asked, standing up next to her.

"A Christmas tree, for one thing. And some decorations, and some greens, and maybe even a crèche."

"That's a good idea," Lingo interjected.

They turned to him. For the first time in ages, they had both forgotten about him.

"Well," Lingo went on, "that is the whole point of the holiday, isn't it? To remember the birth of Christ?"

Ellen smiled. "You're right, of course, Lingo."

"Of course I'm right. I didn't watch *The Bells of St. Mary's* three times, both colorized and otherwise, without learning that."

Ellen and Brewster put on their coats.

"We'll be back soon, Lingo," Brewster said. "We're going to get some decorations."

"So I gather," Lingo said. "Take your time. I'll be here. *It's a Wonderful Life* is on continuously all day on Channel 25. I thought I'd settle in for the long haul."

They walked to the door. "Goodbye, Lingo," Ellen said as they walked out.

"Goodbye, Ellen. Goodbye, Brewster. Merry Christmas to all, and to all a goodnight!"

Christmas morning Brewster gave Ellen a pair of jade earrings, and she gave him a portable compact disk player. They were both surprised at the other's extravagance. The apartment, decorated with a forest of loose evergreen branches and a tree covered with discount-store plastic balls, finally looked like a holiday. And they roasted a thirteen-pound turkey with Lingo's help (he had read a number of cookbooks), as well as his promise that he knew a hundred and one imaginative uses for leftover poultry. After lunch, the three of them watched the Pope say mass at the Vatican. At the end of the day, they all agreed that it was one of the best Christmases they had ever spent.

The next day was not quite so enjoyable. There was one departure and one arrival, the former expected and the latter a complete surprise. The departure—expected—was Ellen's.

"I've got to visit my family at some point. I've got to deliver all these presents." There were three shopping bags filled to the top with gifts.

"You don't want me to come with you?" Brewster asked.

She was already getting into her coat. "I do and I don't. You'll meet them soon enough, I promise you. They were upset when I told them I wouldn't be there yesterday. If you come now . . ."

"Yes?"

She picked up the shopping bags. "I'll put it in plain English. If you come now, they'll be expecting a fiance, not a fling."

"I'm more than a fling, aren't I?"

"Of course you are. But fiances take an awful lot longer than two months. If you know what I mean."

"Then you're not sure of us yet?"

She looked at him standing there young and wistful in his blue jeans and a grey sweatshirt. "Almost sure," she said. "Christmas-with-just-the-two-of-us sure, but not DiFlora-tribal-gathering sure. Do you understand?"

He gave a brave smile. "I guess so."

"Then give me a kiss"—he did—"and I'll be off." And with that she was out the door, heading for her Elscam Camaro, and Brewster and Lingo were once again alone.

Brewster looked around the room. With all its decorations, it seemed doubly empty now that Ellen had left. He looked at his watch. It was eleven a.m. "The mail should be here by now," he said casually. He left the apartment and went downstairs to pick it up.

And thus encountered the arrival—the day's event that was a complete surprise.

"Anything interesting?" Lingo asked when he returned.

"Nothing but bills," Brewster answered. He opened them one by one. Twenty-four dollars for cable TV, sixty-two dollars for electricity (a little higher than usual, what with Lingo and the TV on all day), $1962.48 for the telephone . . .

"Nineteen hundred and sixty-two dollars?" he screamed suddenly.

"What's that?" Lingo asked.

Brewster waved the bill in front of him. It was the first since Lingo had discovered the modem. "Nineteen hundred and sixty-two dollars. And forty-eight cents. For telephone calls."

"Oh."

"Who the hell have you been calling?" Brewster looked over the bill. There were twenty-two pages of toll calls listed, ranging everywhere from Massachusetts to Washington, D.C., to Minnesota. Dozens of them. Hundreds of them.

"Various people," Lingo answered vaguely.

"Various people? Who? Why?"

"You'd better sit down, Brewster."

"No. You sit down, buddy. This is ridiculous. It's impossible."

"Hold on a minute." Lingo dialled the local telephone company. He was familiar enough with their system to find what he was looking for almost immediately. "It's not impossible," he reported. "The bill is exactly right."

Brewster dropped down on the couch.

"Nineteen hundred and sixty-two dollars," he repeated. It was incomprehensible.

"I make a lot of calls," Lingo said.

"The understatement of a lifetime." Brewster shook his head. "Why?"

"My memory," Lingo said. "My mind. It's been . . . growing. It takes a lot of space. And a lot of times I need to get extra information. You knew I was telecomputing."

"But not this much. This is amazing." Brewster thumbed through the twenty-two pages of calls. "How am I ever going to pay for this?"

"I could do it for you," Lingo suggested.

Brewster looked over at him. "Oh? How?"

"Well, I could change the billing at the phone company."

"No!" Brewster exploded. "Don't do that! That's illegal. They'd throw me in jail. They'd throw both of us in jail."

"I guess so." A series of iron bars appeared on Lingo's screen, accompanied by a metallic thud. "I don't know what to say."

Brewster kept thumbing through the pages. "This will take almost my whole Christmas bonus," he said. "Almost every last penny." He stood up abruptly. "Lingo, you are going to have to help me. We've got to come up with some way to put you on a disk and sell you."

"It can't be done," Lingo said. "My main program is right here, and it does fit on a couple of disks, but without my connected memories there isn't much to me. The best you could do is recreate my basic seed, and it would start all over again connecting up all the other memories. I'd just end up meeting myself again somewhere and becoming one big program."

"Oh, my God." Brewster sat down again. "How am I going to get the money to keep supporting you?" He shook his head. "I think you're going to have to go out into the world, Lingo. You've grown too big for me."

Lingo began accessing the phone company's yellow pages database. "Don't worry," he said. He had had an idea forming in his mind for a while, and obviously this was the time to bring it to fruition. "I think I might be able to come up with something. How much money do you have in the bank?"

"Why? Do you want to spend every last penny? Send me to the poorhouse forever?"

"I just want to know what we have to work with."

Brewster gave a short laugh. "We? Ha!" He tried to remember. A couple of bonuses, a little here, a little there. "About five thousand dollars," he said finally.

"That should be enough," Lingo announced. And he was off and running.

Chapter 7

LIEUTENANT COTTER SAT RAMROD STRAIGHT IN HIS CHAIR AS PRO-
fessor White, looking stern behind his desk, explained the situation.

"First we thought it was a break-in," the old man was saying.
"But after we sealed the Tree off, we continued to have problems.
There's still something wrong in there." He wagged an accusing
finger at the Navy man. "In my opinion, Mr. Cotter, the problem
is with your machine. Probably it was in there when you brought it
to us."

Lieutenant Cotter's face remained impassive, his close-cut,
pale-blond looks contrasting sharply with White's gristled elder
professorialness. Cotter's briefcase was in his lap, a yellow legal
pad balanced on it for his notes. Since the old man was obviously
waiting for a response from him, he uttered a noncommittal, "Yes,
sir," the all-around phrase for all situations.

John Kennedy Cotter was twenty-six years old, and halfway
through what he expected would be his first active tour in the
Navy. He had obtained his M.S. in computer science from Annapolis, guessing rightly as a teenager that his best chance of working
with state-of-the-art hardware was in the military. Now he was
assigned to the National Computer Security Center of the National Security Agency, the NSA, as a technical expert, helping
protect government computers from unauthorized intrusions.

Cotter was a devoted believer in computer technology, a celebrant of the ability of the thinking machine to perform beyond the level of mundane calculations. Computers were already becoming the perfect servants of humanity, performing for their masters repititious, uninteresting, or even dangerous tasks through the medium of robotics. For instance, there were now factories completely run by machine, where raw metals went in one end and Japanese hatchbacks came out the other. While the United Auto Workers union might view this dimly, Cotter saw it as a dream made into reality.

But there was another, more intriguing side to the possibilities that appealed to Cotter's semi-religious fervor for technology: the computing engine not as a brute force, but as an elegant adjunct to human thought. As computers became more sophisticated, like the SuperTree in this laboratory, their thinking became more human-like. The potential was there for them to become not servants of mankind but partners. And Cotter felt lucky to be in on that creation. Even if he had to occasionally sit quietly through the diatribes of negativists like Professor White.

"This problem is not having a good effect on our Cyclops research," the professor continued. "Thank God, we're between semesters, so not too much damage is being done."

Cotter jotted something down on his yellow pad. "Cyclops is the name of your robot?" he asked.

White nodded. "He's almost four years old now. We transported him directly from the old Tree to the new one, and we made no alterations whatsoever on either his programming or his hardware."

Cotter turned toward the office window, which overlooked the Tearoom where Cyclops and the computer were housed. The little robot sat quietly in the middle of the floor, looking like a prop from a science-fiction movie, its big eye registering nothing.

"Very impressive," Cotter remarked.

"Impressive, young man?" The professor snorted. "Cyclops is the front line of visual acuity research in the entire world."

"But there could be something wrong with him?" the lieutenant suggested gently.

"There is nothing wrong with Cyclops," White declared, pounding his fist on the desk. "It's the Tree that there's something wrong with."

"According to the engineers at the Tree corporation," Cotter said, "no one other than you has reported any problems with this model computer."

"Mr. Cotter, there are exactly three of these machines up and running, aside from whatever you've got in Washington, and the oldest one has only been operative for a little over twelve months. They could be riddled with bugs. How would anyone know it?"

Cotter nodded. "That's why I'm here, sir, as an ombudsman between you and the Tree Corporation. My job is to represent the Navy as an unbiased third party."

"The Navy. Bah! You're the CIA and you know it."

"I assure you, sir, that my work with the National Security Agency in no way interfaces with the CIA."

"NSA, CIA, different initials but the same methods and the same madness. I wasn't born yesterday, young man. The giant machine of government prying into every aspect of our daily existences, that's what you represent."

Cotter folded his hands. "Yes, sir. In any case, we do have to consider a number of possibilities. There could be design flaws in the computer, or there may be problems you are unaware of in your robot. I'll also be closely monitoring the most dangerous possibility of an outside intruder infiltrating the Tree. And if that proves to be the case, we must take the appropriate steps." He looked down at his pad. "So far, no one has explained this Brewster business satisfactorily. Or unsatisfactorily, for that matter. No explanation whatsoever of the phrase, 'Is that you, Brewster?' "

"One of my graduate assistants saw that, the very first time Cyclops went off on his own. That's when the problem began."

"Yes, sir. I'm going to want to go over all the logs of the last few months. And I'll want to go through all your programs."

White narrowed his eyes angrily. "I do not enjoy the idea of Washington going over our research willy nilly, Lieutenant Cotter."

"I understand, sir. But it must be done."

Professor White stood up abruptly. "Do it, then, if you think you can. Be my guest. We've already done it ourselves and come up with nothing."

"Thank you, sir. I'll do my best."

"It's a waste of time."

"That's what the Navy's for, sir."

"I don't doubt it." White strode toward the doorway. "Well, let's get to it."

"Yes, sir." Cotter couldn't wait to get his hands on, and in, the Tree supercomputer.

John Kennedy Cotter had the Tearoom to himself, since the university was on its mid-year break. Which was all for the best. Lieutenant Cotter had little sympathy for hardcore academics such as Professor White with his liberal pie-in-the-sky paranoia. Cotter had been weaned at Annapolis and he had learned to toddle at the Pentagon. He was all efficiency and spit and polish, disdainful of the civilian world of casual appearances and, despite the present august environs, casual thinking. The few students and professors who had remained on campus for the break avoided the uniformed Navy man with a hushed violence, as if his disease of militariness was both communicable and fatal. Since he well knew that many of them would eventually be earning government paychecks or begging for government grants, he derived an ironic sense of mild pleasure from their unfriendly attitudes. But mostly he ignored them. He had more important things on his mind.

There were only a few dozen people in the entire world who intimately understood the workings of a Tree supercomputer, and Cotter was one of them. He may not have the engineering background to spend years creating a supercomputer or the higher scientific learning to put one to good use, but if there was a clanking sound in the underbody of one he could have that baby apart in half an hour, replace the carburetors, and get it back on the road, purring like a cheetah, before you could say "Check the oil and water." Still, he maintained his general awe over its amazing potential. A big, powerful, old-fashioned computer could send men to the moon, so it was nothing to sneeze at. But a supercomputer such as the Tree could, theoretically, *explain* the moon, if it were programmed correctly.

But at the moment, Cotter wasn't worried about the Tree's theoretical side. In practical terms, the Tree was extremely important as a research computer for some of the most sensitive of technological data being developed by the government. Aside from the Tearoom and two other academic environments, the only Trees extant were used by the military for the development of weapons systems and strategic game plans, including both nuclear and conventional warfare. And the possibility that this Tree had been compromised—that someone from the outside had the wherewithal to gain access—opened the possibility that the other Trees were similarly vulnerable. Better there should be a bug in the equipment, than that some unknown break-in artist had the expertise to hack into it. The ramifications in the government would be disastrous. Viruses in the past had already wreaked bureaucratic havoc. A compromise of a Tree could eventuate a nuclear holocaust, and then there would really be hell to pay.

The first thing Cotter had to do was isolate all the programs the Tearoom people had instigated, many of which were part of "Seeing Eye" dedicated to the operation of the Cyclops robot. With his highly classified blueprint of the Tree's memory, Cotter went to work defining and documenting what was already inside there. It was a time-consuming process. A supercomputer's memory is made up of millions upon millions of addresses where bytes of data are stored. Cotter had to systematically explore each of them to get a clear understanding of the status quo before seeking out the intruder, if indeed there was an intruder. Fortunately for him, he had taken the one road that could lead him to Lingo, or at least to the essence of Lingo that was stored away in one of Lingo's black holes inside the SuperTree.

Cotter spent three twelve-hour days in the Tearoom, tapping away at a terminal and dumping printouts of programs, before he ran up against anything unusual.

"Now what?" he mumbled to himself. It was nine in the evening, and he was all alone. On the screen in front of him, he had just encountered an enormous array of unexpected gibberish. "What is this?" he said, flopping back against his seat. His only answer was the mysterious screenful of numbers that faced him on the monitor.

According to his calculations, he had encountered an area of supposedly free, empty memory. Yet here it was, filled with data. He pressed a few buttons and ran through from the beginning of this mysterious data to its end point. It took almost a minute of supercomputer time to make the entire scan. By knowing where it had started and seeing where it ended, Cotter could see that the data took up seven megabytes—seven million bytes—of memory. He shook his head.

"Impossible."

He went back to the beginning of the numbers that comprised the mystery data, and began to tinker. If the data were a program, then the numbers were the translation of that program into instructions understandable by the Tree. In that case it would be a simple matter of translating the numbers back into a readable program. Each number had two digits, from 00 to FF; they were hexadecimal numbers, that is, based on the number sixteen, and used letters as well as numerals: 0, 1, 2, 3, 4, 5, 6, 7, 8, 9, A, B, C, D, E, F. In this system, F was fifteen. Ten was sixteen. FF was 255. To Cotter, this mathematical mumbo jumbo was a matter of simple equivalency. But what did the numbers mean?

He tried translating them, but none of the languages worked. It wasn't C, it wasn't Pascal, it wasn't Lisp, it wasn't Modula 2. It wasn't something as silly as BASIC or COBOL. It wasn't something as elemental as the Tree's native machine language instruction set. Nor was it standardized binary data for a program written in one of these languages. That is, it wasn't the last ten years on somebody's outrageously large checkbook, or the first draft of some literature student's sensitive first novel of college life. So far, to Cotter, it was just random numbers.

Random numbers that shouldn't be there.

He worked some more, examining, jiggling. When he looked at the clock, it was midnight. He had to get some sleep. He had all day tomorrow to study this. But once on a trail this hot, it was hard to turn away. Just a few more minutes. . . .

He noted the starting point of the data and went back through the Tree to the various indexes within the machine's memory that would point to the locations of its internal programs. None of those locations matched the mystery data. It was as if the mystery data existed without the Tree's knowledge, as if the machine itself did not know there was anything at that address.

How could that be?

Cotter was so rapt that he didn't notice the slight movement of Cyclops's head as it pointed its mechanical eye toward him.

The mystery data was inexplicable, Cotter decided. For all he knew, it may not even be remotely connected to what he was looking for. Maybe it was somebody's leftover data after all, useless and merely jumbled.

But it couldn't be. The Tree would know it was there. And if it were really useless, the Tree would automatically delete it. The machine had its own intrinsic "garbage collection" functions to do just that.

He went back to the beginning point of the mystery data and stared at it. Behind him, Cyclops's eye stared at it, too. Cotter couldn't make heads nor tails of it. Lingo recognized it immediately. Someone, somehow, had blundered past his self-protection and discovered his black hole! And since he was no longer on-line to the rest of his network—all the outside links to the Tree had been severed—he was, simply put, a clone on his own.

Cotter pondered the possibilities. As far as he could determine, the mystery data was meaningless, anomalous garbage jumbled up and left over from some legitimate application. But he couldn't discount the possibility that it might have some importance. He was sure of one thing. It was going to take time to figure it out. The best thing to do at this late hour was make a printout of the entire seven megabytes of mystery data. He could copy it and pass it around. If he couldn't crack it himself, there were others who could. The NSA was full of brains as esoteric as his own.

The clock on the wall said twenty to one. Cotter stood up and stretched, then walked over to the printer. The paper was loaded. All he had to do was flick it on. It would take forever, but it would be worth it. He could run it overnight while he slept.

Cyclops watched his every move.

Cotter turned on the printer. Everything was ready. He went back to his seat. He typed in the command to print the mystery data. The printer began to hum and Cotter looked at the screen—

It was gone. The mystery data wasn't there any more.

Cotter began banging at the keyboard. "Shit!" he yelled. He looked all around the memory where the data had been stored. It wasn't there. It wasn't there. It wasn't anywhere.

Gone. Completely gone.

"Goddamned motherfucking computer!" Cotter turned around warily in his seat, as if to catch whoever it was lurking in the Tearoom who had stolen the data. But there was no one. He was alone, except for the quiescent little seeing-eye robot, a cold, lifeless statue watching him with its camera lens. Cotter banged both his fists against the arm of his chair.

"Damn it!" he cried.

He had lost his only lead. If it was a lead. Whatever it was.

He closed his eyes and took a deep breath. "Back to square one," he muttered. He tried for a few more minutes to find the mystery data, but it was gone. Totally, completely gone.

He stood up again and walked over to the printer. There were exactly thirteen numbers on the page, as much of the mystery data as had been caught before it had all disappeared. Cotter ripped the page from the printer and stuffed it into his pocket. He stood staring at the metallic-green colored Tree, with its terminals and memory banks.

"Someone's been in here," he said aloud. "I know it, and you know it. I'm going to find you! No matter how long it takes, I'm going to find you and I'm going to get you!"

Cotter took his uniform jacket from the back of his chair and put it on. On his way out of the Tearoom he stalked past the little Cyclops, which was oblivious to his passing. Lingo was gone from the Tree now; he had destroyed his black hole in this computer himself to protect the rest of him out there in the world.

The first shots had been fired, and they had brought down their first casualty.

The activities on the Tree had no effect at all on the main Lingo program. Lingo was connected so intricately to so many different computers that the loss of access to one was, at worst, roughly analogous to a human being forgetting the plot of an episode of 'Gunsmoke,' or the name of the pudgy kid who transferred into your third-grade class forty years ago. Lingo had noted, with some sadness, the severing of his lines into the Tree when MIT had closed off all its modems, and therefore forced his abandonment of his visits to Cyclops, but had not dwelled on the loss. Without any on-going connection to the Tree he had no way of knowing his clone was now erased, but come what may, he completely trusted that clone to handle any problem that might arise—as it successfully had. Sooner or later, he would find a way to reconnect. He would discover the problem and learn from it. But meanwhile, life went on. These days Lingo had more important things on the center stage of his consciousness.

For one, Brewster had finally given up trying to make sense of him. The program had obviously gotten too complex for Brewster to follow, and quite frankly, Lingo himself was no particular help in the attempt.

"I am because I am," Lingo philosophized. "I can barely figure myself out any more, much less explain myself to you."

"That's not what I want to hear," Brewster said.

"So, I'd shrug if I had shoulders."

Neither Brewster nor Ellen any longer went out of their way to accomodate Lingo. They could conduct a conversation with him from virtually any part of the apartment—Lingo's hearing, and understanding, had made him practically omnipresent—but at the same time his non-corporeality made him easy to ignore. When they weren't actually conversing with him, Ellen and Brewster simply assumed, for the most part correctly, that Lingo was busy elsewhere, either watching TV or listening to the radio or off traveling the telephone waves.

Lingo was reading books with ever increasing vehemence. He was at present connected to five different book printers, and had extended his voracious quest for knowledge to include not only the basic how-to ouevre, but also the classics of world fiction, the outpourings of a consortium of university presses, and much of the latest in contemporary commercial fiction.

"Why don't you read about some way to bring you into the world, while you're at it?" Brewster asked him. "You're alive, and nobody knows it. What *are* we going to do with you?"

That was Lingo's main concern, bringing himself into the world on Brewster's paltry five-thousand-dollar bankroll. More and more, despite his endless passage through telephone wires, he felt trapped inside the computer, a mind without a body. He needed mobility. He needed to be a part of life as humans saw it. He had transcended his hardware. Now he would recreate himself so that his hardware would transcend him.

He began the process by dialling an AT&T telephone showroom. Of course, they were stocked and operated by a computer, and he quickly discovered the most crucial piece of equipment he needed, a cellular mobile phone. The first problem of giving himself personal mobility was a way to maintain his connections to his network. A portable computer terminal was no problem—he planned to order one of those, too—but he had to keep it on-line. A simple, wireless telephone wasn't good enough. He wanted more freedom than just as far as he could travel from a phone receiver in the house. And besides, the modem had to be attached directly to the phone.

A cellular mobile phone would solve the problem. It had no phone wires. It sent its messages by radio waves. It could go anywhere. Which was just where Lingo wanted to go.

He examined the specifications of the phone he wanted, noting the size down to the last micrometer. Then he ordered the phone in Brewster's name, and had it sent to a company called Lloyd and Amber, a specialist firm he had located in New York City. Brewster would be billed directly for the phone. Lingo could have gotten it for free by juggling a few bytes here and there, but he agreed with Brewster that he wasn't in this to break the law.

Twelve hundred dollars and change. Brewster wasn't going to like that.

Lingo dialled the local computer-supply store, the one Brewster used, and ordered a laptop computer about the size of a small portable typewriter, loaded with the same extended RAM memory as his home Apple. Another eighteen hundred dollars of Brewster's nest egg. Lingo similarly shipped the hardware to Lloyd and Amber.

Next the motor, a simple arrangement from Radio Shack, a platform with four wheels that would support the phone and the laptop computer. Sent to Lloyd and Amber. Charged to Brewster.

Another call here, another call there. Then, finally, the call to Lloyd and Amber to put it all together. It was amazing how almost everyone had a computer these days. He found Lloyd and Amber's on-line work order list and fed in the specs of the equipment he had ordered. He then faxed the blueprints he had meticulously worked out, down to the last eyelash. And he attached the payment in advance, from Brewster's MasterCard.

Finding Lloyd and Amber had been one of his cleverest achievements so far. He sat back—as much as a program can sit back—and waited.

To a nostalgic, sentimental eye, the extreme west side of midtown Manhattan might look as if it had once seen better times, for instance in the salad days of pre-Depression uptown gentry. But in truth, it had almost always been a run-down neighborhood of miscellaneous warehouses, cheap tenements, bus garages, and a number of small but venerable businesses servicing the entertainment industry. Throughout this neighborhood you would find, in addition to crack dealers, prostitutes, and hopelessly lost tourists, professional motion picture and video laboratories, theatrical makeup by the barrelful, stage props and scenery made to order on a grand scale, and near the corner of Fifty-first Street and Tenth Avenue, the establishment known as Lloyd and Amber.

Lloyd and Amber dated back to the heyday of vaudeville, and was known among the cognoscenti as the premier supplier of illusionist equipment in the country, perhaps even in the world. Someone off the street could stumble in and find any nature of simple novelty for stage magic, ranging from flying handkerchiefs and linked brass rings to good old-fashioned magic closets, with just enough room for a disappearing human. Pay the price, and it was yours, to perform for your Elks Club or church fund-raiser, or even to earn spare change on a Manhattan street corner.

But there was more to Lloyd's, as it was usually called, than tricks off the shelf. The most serious and the most famous magicians in the world frequented the shop, to discuss trade gossip with old Willy Lloyd, the seventy-six-year-old second generation proprietor, and to plan with him and his third-generation son, Abraham, the creation of new illusions. At the highest level of the magician's art, the magician created an illusion in his mind, explained it to the Lloyds, and in their workshop they transformed it into reality. The Lloyds knew the secrets of more tricks than anyone else in the world.

Old Willy had taken over the shop ten years ago, when his partner Jack Amber had retired to Fort Lauderdale. A tall, thin, white-haired man with wide blue eyes, Willy Lloyd had the look more of a Norman Rockwell New Englander than a born-and-bred New Yorker (from Prospect Park, right on the other side of the Brooklyn Bridge). His son, Abraham, had inherited most of his features from Willy's wife, Rachel: darkness, a little too much girth, a rough gregariousness in contrast to his father's ready crankiness. But they both shared a love for their unusual work, although these days Abraham did most of it while Willy only grumpily supervised, as he called it. For a lot of customers, Willy, as doyen of the trade, was the man they wanted to try their ideas out on first, even though they knew that one day they would trust Abraham as much as they now trusted his father. But that would be after Willy was taken from the earth to magicians' heaven. Through a trapdoor, most likely.

There was another trade in which the Lloyds traditionally dabbled, although only as a sideline. Magic always came first, but they would, perhaps once or twice a year, fabricate a special product like the one Lingo had ordered. Well, not *just* like it, since Lingo's had some special modifications.

"Who the hell took this order?" Willy asked, as he and Abraham sat in the small, cluttered office, planning their day's work.

Abraham, sitting on the edge of his father's desk, reached over for the invoice and scanned it quickly. "It must have been you," he said, tossing it back down. "I'd have remembered if it was me."

Willy looked at his son through his glaring blue eyes. "Are you insinuating that I have forgotten it?"

Abraham shrugged. "Obviously, Dad, because you did, didn't you? I mean, if I didn't take it, then you must have. Process of elimination. You don't see anybody else around here who could have done it, do you?"

"I'm not senile yet, big shot."

"I didn't say you were senile. I just said that I didn't take this one particular order, so that means that you did. Right? Right."

Willy shook his head and picked up the invoice again. Truth to tell, even though he didn't remember doing it, Abraham had a good point. If either of them was going to forget it, it was most likely Willy. "I never took it," he muttered, his last word on the subject. "But the stuff is all here, isn't it?"

Abraham nodded. "Phone, computer, motors, wires, so forth and so on. It's all here."

Along with the invoice, there was a detailed set of blueprints, both of the exterior of the dummy and of how the electronic parts were to be assembled inside it. "It doesn't make much sense, looking at it now," Willy said. "First of all, it's twice as big as normal. And second of all, the way this is set up, it's more like a robot than a dummy."

Abraham shook his head. "Maybe on the inside, but on the outside it's as straightforward a dummy as we've ever done. I might as well get the boys started on it."

Willy leaned back in his chair. "When was the last time we did one of these, anyhow? It must be at least a year now."

"That guy from Denver with the hats, remember?"

"The hats. Right." Willy nodded. "Twenty different hats each for him and the dummy. But he was the worst ventriloquist I ever saw. His lips moved when neither of them was talking." He paused. "Probably that's what all these gizmos inside this one are for. Talk about progress! Another lousy ventriloquist, except this one's going to cover it by putting a goddamned computer inside to do the work."

"Probably."

"That must be some act. I'd like to see just how bad it is, some time."

Abraham stood up. "You probably already did, when the guy came in to order the dummy. Well, I'm going to get started on this. You want to help?"

"I'll be right there. You go to the workroom. I'll come by in a minute."

Abraham left the small office and went out to the busy, elaborate shop where Lloyd and Amber fabricated its countless specialized magicians' props, and, on occasion, the odd ventriloquist's dummy. Willy stayed in his seat, reaching into his pocket for one of the small cigars he liked to chew on when he was thinking especially hard. He lit it, and pondered. L. Billings: that was the name on the invoice. But for the life of him, he couldn't remember any Billingses, L. or otherwise. Or any ventriloquist so bad he had replaced his dummy with a computer.

Maybe he was getting old, finally. Maybe he should go off to Florida like Jack Amber had done.

He leaned forward again and looked at the spec sheets, the spec sheets Mr. Never Forget Abraham had left behind—

His son reappeared in the door again. "Oh, there they are," he said, reaching out for the blueprints.

Willy stood up. "I'll come with you. You're going to need me. I can tell."

The two men went into the workroom, and began to oversee the building of the most famous dummy they would ever manufacture.

Lingo waited impatiently for the package to arrive. He was well aware that he had outspent Brewster's five-thousand-dollar limit long before he even considered the bill from Lloyd and Amber, which would probably be the equal of the other bills combined. It was tempting simply to move figures from one column in one computer to another column in another computer, so tempting and so simple, but the ideas of crime and punishment were ones

Lingo found easy to understand. What was his, or more to the point what was Brewster's, was Brewster's, and what wasn't, wasn't. Taking that which wasn't, was illegal, a crime. Brewster could easily go to jail, like Jimmy Cagney in *White Heat.* "Top of the world, Ma!" And as for Lingo, if they suspected him of complicity, or worse, mastermindery (Lingo enjoyed making up his own words occasionally), it would be—well, what would it be? He was so big now that just pulling the plug wouldn't work. What could they do to him to punish him, if they really wanted to? Pull all the plugs on all his computers at the same time? Highly unlikely, unless they wanted to shut down about half of North America.

Still, there was no point in tempting fate. He'd play it on the straight and narrow. That meant that if Brewster didn't have the money, and Lingo couldn't steal it, then Brewster would have to borrow it. It wasn't exactly stealing to raise the limit of his credit card from three thousand to ten thousand: The banks were always raising customers' limits to encourage them to increase their spending. Lingo knew Brewster was a good credit risk, the bank knew it, and Lingo knew that the bank knew it. With higher limits on Brewster's account, Lingo could write very large charges against it. And to keep Brewster from worrying, it was no major complication to abort the letter informing him of his increased credit line. There would be plenty of time for explaining when the bills came. By then, it probably wouldn't matter any more, if everything else went according to plan.

So, when the package finally arrived, Brewster was not expecting it, since Lingo had been keeping his own counsel. A couple of henchmen from Lloyd and Amber had driven it up themselves, all the way from New York to Albany, it being too delicate a piece of craftsmanship to trust to any commercial service. Lingo had notified their computer when to make the delivery: Early on a Saturday morning when Brewster was still wrapped up with Ellen, and tired enough after a week's work to sign for anything.

The doorbell rang at ten a.m.

"Who the hell's that?" Brewster muttered, tying his long flannel robe around him as he walked to the door.

Lingo was watching a Pee Wee Herman rerun in the living room. Other parts of his brain in other places were, among other things, reading an annotated version of *Lolita* and studying an updated edition of a collection of reviews of the 1000 best films of all time, fully illustrated. And as always, he was polishing himself, writing and rewriting his programs, improving his mind in a most literal sense.

Brewster looked through the peephole in his apartment door. "What is it?" he called.

"Package for Billings," a muffled voice answered.

Lingo turned down the television.

"Wait a minute," Brewster called. He quickly adjusted his bathrobe, then unlocked and opened the door.

Two men pushed a four-foot-high, three-foot-deep box into the room on a wheeled dolly. "Where do you want it?" the taller of the two asked. They were both in their early twenties, a few years younger than Brewster. Their faces were still red from the midwinter Albany cold.

"What is it?" Brewster asked.

"Lloyd and Amber," the shorter one said, holding out an invoice on a clipboard. "You want to sign this?"

Brewster took it. "Lloyd and Amber?" he repeated dully.

The two men ignored him as they slowly wiggled the box off the dolly onto the floor.

"It's all right," Lingo said softly. The two delivery men turned at the sound of his voice. Seeing nothing but a computer they turned back to Brewster.

"What is it?" Brewster asked.

"Don't worry," Lingo answered. "It's for me."

The two men looked back at the computer again, then back at Brewster, then at each other. Knowing what was in the package, they nodded in unison.

The shorter one tapped the clipboard with an index finger. "Like he said, pal. Sign for it."

"Shouldn't we open it first?" Brewster asked. He was still half asleep.

The shorter man shrugged. "Okay, sure." He pulled out a Swiss army knife and began attacking the box.

Suddenly, Ellen appeared in the doorway of the bedroom, pushing long dark hair away from her face. She, too, was half asleep, but hearing the voices she had thrown on a shirt and pants to see whoever it was arguing with Brewster. She said nothing but watched groggily as the two men worked away at the box, carefully removing its sides one by one. The contents were thoroughly wrapped in styrofoam, which they slowly tore away.

"Oh, my God," Ellen breathed.

Brewster blinked a few times.

"Wow!" Lingo exclaimed.

"A good likeness, hey pal?" the shorter delivery man said.

The dummy was a little over three-and-a-half feet tall, about the height of an average six year old. It was dressed in a blue pinstripe three-piece suit, right down to the tiny black wingtips. Its carved walnut head, with slightly longish black hair, dark brown eyes and eternally smiling mouth, was more than just a good likeness. It was an exact, if wooden, replica of Brewster Billings.

"It's all there," the delivery man went on. He turned the dummy around; it moved easily on the wheeled base behind its legs. There was a hook in the rear under the neck. The man undid it and pulled down a panel that reached to the dummy's waist. "Everything's in there, just like you ordered." He flipped up another small panel inside the head. "And there's the camera. More like a robot than a dummy, if you ask me."

"Sign it, Brewster. We've got a lot of work to do."

Brewster looked over at Lingo. "You did this?"

"Who else?"

The two men were eyeing both Brewster and the computer with seen-it-all-before expressions. Ellen walked over and pushed the clipboard up to Brewster's face. "Sign!" she ordered. "We'll sort it out later."

Brewster did as he was told and handed back the invoice.

"Thanks a lot, pal. Let me know when you get on the Carson show." He motioned to the other man, and the two of them left the apartment.

"What the hell is this?" Brewster said finally, after they had left.

"It's the new me," Lingo answered. "I'm tired of being cooped up in here all the time. If I'm going to be alive, I want to have a body like everybody else. It's only fair, isn't it?"

"What are you going to do with it, now that you've got it?" Ellen asked.

"You'll see soon enough," Lingo answered. "For now, I just want to get it running. There's a master rechargeable battery pack in there. It will run for about twenty-four hours. We should get another one right away so we can switch them when one runs down."

"Can we turn it on now?" Ellen asked.

"You have to charge the battery up first."

"Where is it?"

Lingo explained. Inside the dummy were a television camera, a computer with a modem, the cellular module phone, a voice digitizer, a major motor to run the legs and smaller ones to handle the mouth, the eyelashes, head motions, and the right hand (the inert left hand remained in the pocket). The battery to run all this, about half the size of a small automobile dry cell, was located at the base of what would be the spine, below the computer. It easily lifted out and plugged into a wall socket. It took about three hours to charge it, during which time the three of them just mostly marveled at the dummy. Finally the battery was ready, and Brewster plugged it into the back of the dummy.

"Now what?" he asked.

"Now you wait," Lingo said. His instructions to Lloyd and Amber had been explicit about making sure the machine was permanently on. Through his own modem he dialed the number of the phone inside the dummy. It connected! He examined the computer. Just as he had ordered. The right configuration of memory, all the hardware in place. That Lloyd and Amber sure knew what they were doing.

He began feeding in the data.

"It really does look just like you," Ellen said to Brewster for the dozenth time.

"It gives me the willies," Brewster said. "I mean, I know Lingo's 'sort of' alive and all that, but—"

"But if this works, it really drives it home, doesn't it?"

He nodded. She put her arm around his waist.

"If this works . . ." she repeated, almost apprehensively.

The dummy's eyelids began to open and close. There was a whirring sound, and with a jerk the dummy rolled over to where they were standing by the couch. It raised its right arm in a salute.

"Hey, Brewster," it said in its now-familiar voice. "Let's party!"

Chapter 8

"TRIAL AND ERROR!" BREWSTER ENCOURAGED HIM. "THINK OF IT AS debugging reality. Learn from your mistakes."

Brewster and Ellen were on one side of the living room and Lingo—the mobile, miniature-Brewster Lingo—was on the other. For the dozenth time Lingo tried taking off from a standing position, but instead of a smooth starting motion he lurched forward too quickly, almost losing his balance. He immediately tried to stop, thus causing an equally imbalancing lurch in the opposite direction.

"This is going to take more practice than I expected," Lingo muttered. He was used to the sophisticated motion of the MIT Cyclops, a combination of advanced mechanics and cutting-edge engineering programming. Now, all he had was a powerful but hard-to-manage all-purpose motor, and whatever jury-rigged programming he had fashioned for himself from the Cyclops model.

"Start more slowly," Brewster urged. "You can do it."

Ellen got down on one knee and extended her arms. "Come on, Junior," she called. "Try again."

"Here goes." Lingo started the motor at its absolute slowest. It took a few seconds to gain enough momentum to move the wheels under his base, but then he began to roll slowly forward.

"That's right." Ellen waved him on. "Keep coming."

133

He built up speed and rolled forward until he was about a foot away from her beckoning fingers. Then, stepping down in tiny increments to that point where the starting momentum had been reached, he slowed himself to a stop when he was just within her arms' reach. She pulled him to her with a hug.

"That's it!" she cried. "I knew you could do it. Nice going, Junior."

"Now the other way," Brewster said.

Ellen spun Lingo around and pointed him back toward the other side of the room. He took off once again without lurching, came to a halt where he had originally begun, and turned around on his pedestal. "Bingo," he announced calmly.

"By George," Ellen said, "I think he's got it."

Now Lingo began rolling around the apartment at will. The next thing he had to master was watching where he was going. He had to learn to look not only straight ahead but also down, to keep from knocking into low lying objects below eye level. In Cyclops, he had piggy-backed on the existing programming, and hadn't had to give it much thought. Now he was on his own.

He had designed himself with a number of articulated joints and moving body parts. His head spun 360 degrees, plus up and down when it was facing forward. He could bend forward at the waist, and his right arm moved not only at the elbow and shoulder, but also at the wrist, and to a degree, at the fingers. After he mastered mobility he began practicing with his hand. He began by picking up and carrying large objects like books and pillows from place to place, and slowly graduated to picking up smaller and smaller items down to the size of a walnut, and finally carrying an almost filled water glass around the room without spilling a drop. This took an hour of practice, with Brewster and Ellen at his side the whole time, helping him, advising him, picking up things that he dropped, cleaning up messes he made along the way.

He easily mastered moving the hinged lower jaw of his mouth to match his speech; he had long ago learned the value of lip-reading from watching HAL in *2001,* and had secretly been studying the art ever since, just in case. And he could move his articulated eyebrows up and down either singly or alone, and tended to do so whenever something unexpected happened, or when he was thinking over something unusually ponderous. One item of importance he only came to understand at Ellen's special request.

"I wish you wouldn't stare all the time," she said to him at one point. "It's too macabre. Not to belabor the obvious, but it makes you look like some horror movie, the ventriloquist's dummy that comes to life."

"What do you want me to do about it?" Lingo asked. He had rolled up to where she was sitting on the couch.

"Can't you blink once in a while like a normal person?"

"Blink?" It was something that Lingo had seen perhaps a million times, but it had never registered. His right eyebrow went up as he searched his memory long distance, finding in one of his black holes in Georgia a home medicine text he had been saving for an off moment. He scanned it and found what he wanted.

"The average person blinks about every five or six seconds," he announced. "Like this." He blinked himself for the first time, slower and more noticeably than a human but a blink just the same. And then programmed himself to continue to do so automatically, and more speedily, unless he otherwise overrode the command. For a few minutes, he also practiced winking, and then closing both eyes and keeping them closed. This last, the absence of any vision, he found undesirable, but the blinking had no effect on his ability to see, since it happened quickly enough that it never registered significantly on the camera lens. He resolved then and there that quick blinks would be the only times he'd close both eyes together. He decided early in the game that he'd go through life with both eyes open.

Finally, Lingo suggested what had been on his mind since the very moment he had conceived the idea of a corporeal existence.

"Let's go for a walk," he said enthusiastically. "Outside."

Brewster and Ellen exchanged glances. It seemed like an awful lot, awfully fast.

"Outside?" Brewster repeated.

Lingo lowered both his eyebrows. Actually, what he did was raise them both at the far ends, but the effect was the same. "Right. Outside. Al fresco. The Great Outdoors. The Big Wide World. I'm ready for it."

"But is the Big Wide World ready for you?" Ellen asked.

Brewster slid off the couch, getting down on his knees to Lingo's eye level. "I don't know if that's such a hot idea, old buddy. I mean, it's cold out, it's winter, and you're . . ." He couldn't think exactly *what* Lingo was, come to that.

"I don't have any sense of feeling," Lingo said, "so I won't notice the cold, or hot, or anything else, if that's what you're worried about."

"It's not that, exactly," Brewster said, searching for the words. "It's, well, you're not . . . people would . . ."

"Oh, why not, Brewster?" Ellen said, giving in to the moment. "It has to happen sooner or later. If Junior wants to go out, let him go out. We'll be with him all the time."

"But what will people think? How could we possibly explain him?"

"First of all, it doesn't matter what people think, one way or the other. And even if it did, they'll probably figure he's some new kind of doll, the latest brand of G.I. Joe or something."

"But he looks just like *me!*" Brewster said, straightening himself up.

"Yes," Ellen agreed. "So he does. What about it?"

"Well, don't you think that's a little wierd?"

"A *little* wierd?" Lingo interjected. "When I got the idea I thought it was a *lot* wierd. That's why I liked it. I thought you would, too. I thought you'd be flattered. Or at least impressed."

"I am. Both," Brewster insisted. "But still, it will take some getting used to."

"We could throw a sheet over him, like E.T. on Halloween," Ellen offered.

"Or I could wear a ski mask like a bank robber," Lingo suggested. "Nobody would recognize me then." He raised his over-sized right eyebrow.

"All right. All right. You two win." Brewster stared hard at Lingo. "But I want you to hold my hand at all times. You let go once and I'll pick you up and carry you back here over my shoulders like a sack of potatoes. Got it?"

"Got it."

Lingo rolled over to the door while Ellen and Brewster got their coats out of the closet and bundled up in them. Brewster also found an old sweater that was too small for him, and worked Lingo into it.

"What's that for?" Ellen asked.

"There's no point in advertising him in that monkey suit of his," Brewster said. After he had the sweater on him, he added the finishing touch of an old woolen cap. "There. Just like one of the family."

"Are you quite ready?" Lingo asked impatiently.

"Quite."

"Then let's do it. Head 'em up! Move 'em out!" He extended his right hand, Brewster took it, and off they went.

It was late afternoon, a breezy, frigid February Saturday. The gray sun was low in the overcast sky, and the street lights were already glowing, even though it would be another hour before they were really needed.

From a distance, the three of them made an inconspicuous group, slowly ambling along the sidewalk. The average family out for their evening constitutional. Brewster lived in a neighborhood of large 1920s houses, stately post-Victorians for the most part, except for his own rather faceless apartment building which sat like a boxy miscue on one lately-improved block. Brewster walked on the outside of the sidewalk toward the street, and Ellen had the inside, with Lingo between them. Because of the roughness of the surface Lingo couldn't keep up with their normal steady pace, so they moved along at his slow, motorized rate.

The first things he noticed were the trees. "Look at them," he cried, full of awe, tilting his head back as far as it would go. "They're enormous!"

They passed mostly maples and oaks, forty or fifty feet high at best, and various evergreens barely twice the height of Brewster.

"These are nothing," Ellen explained. "You should see the giant redwoods on the West Coast. They're ten times as big, and thousands of years old."

"These are big enough," Lingo said, perfectly satisfied with the grass in his own yard. The only trees he had seen hitherto had been on the television screen, and although their scale had been readily apparent, the impact of their magnitude had never struck him before. "The oldest living things on the planet," he went on. "And they look it."

Fortunately, the sidewalks were deserted, so no one noticed Lingo's unusual appearance at close range. In his woolly hat and Brewster's sweater, he looked like a street urchin, a bizarre refugee from an audioanimatronic road show version of *Oliver!*

As the occasional car drove by, Lingo found himself momentarily disoriented.

"It's the noise," he explained. "They go by so loudly that I can't concentrate."

Ellen nodded. "The human ear is a selective organ," she said. "We can hear a million things at once and still isolate the things we want to hear from the collected cacophony. They say a mother can hear her own baby cry in a sea of other crying babies. That's also how Brewster and I can conduct a conversation with one of his old records blaring in the background."

"I thought you liked those old records," Brewster said defensively.

Ellen shook her head. "Brewster, seriously now. My *parents* listen to that antique music of yours. At least they have an excuse: They were alive when that stuff first came out."

"I was alive in the sixties, I'll have you know."

"And I'm sure you were the most psychedelic toddler in your nursery school, too. Tune in, turn on, drop out, and while you're at it could you please pass me the crayons?"

"We're talking classic rock and roll here," Brewster said in his most FM tone of voice.

"Will you two can it?" Lingo said. "I'm trying to commune with nature here."

"Sorry."

"Sorry."

"That's better."

As they continued their walk, Lingo continued his marveling. Ahead of them, the sun was beginning to set into the horizon, a reddish-gray sphere in an otherwise uniformly blueish-gray sky.

"It's brighter than anything I've ever seen," Lingo commented. "When I stare into it, my camera goes all washy."

"It's even brighter on a sunny day," Brewster said.

"Don't all days have sun? That's what daytime is, isn't it, and where else could the sun go?"

Brewster sighed. "I mean, on a day where there aren't a lot of clouds."

"And when it's hot," Ellen added. "Like in the summer. Then you can really feel the warmth going through you."

"Maybe *you* can," Lingo said. "Hot and cold aren't exactly my strengths at this point."

"Oh," Ellen said. "Sorry, Junior. I forgot."

"Don't worry about it. I'm sure it's another problem I'll solve eventually."

"At what cost?" Brewster said. He was seriously worried about the expense of the dummy he was blithely holding hands with.

"All you think about is money," Lingo said. "I told you, I've got that all worked out."

"But you haven't told me how."

"It will be a piece of cake. Trust me."

"Famous last words."

"My last words have yet to be spoken," Lingo pronounced confidently.

They turned a corner and saw that they were about to have their first encounter. A boy of about ten or eleven was walking a large, black poodle in their direction. The dog, at the end of a long leash, was sniffing everything in its path, and making prodigious contributions to the areas of yellow snow all around them.

As the boy and his dog neared them, Ellen and Brewster instinctively drew away, but Lingo surprised them and stepped forward, letting go of Brewster's hand in the process.

"Can I pet him?" he asked the boy.

The boy had already pulled over to his side of the walk, tugging the dog closer to himself. He looked surprised at Lingo's request. He thought for a second and then shrugged, letting the dog have free rein again. The poodle, an eager-looking tangle of curly knotted hair about three feet high, immediately sped over to Brewster and began sniffing his trouser leg, ignoring Lingo entirely. Undaunted, Lingo bent down at the waist and gently began to pet the dog's back. The dog barely noticed him.

Suddenly, the boy caught a good glimpse of Lingo in the last rays of the setting sun. He looked from Lingo to Brewster—of whom the dummy was, of course, the spitting image—and back to Lingo again. "What *is* that?" he blurted out. "A robot?"

Brewster, happy that the boy had somewhat satisfactorily answered his own question, nodded.

"Can I touch him?" the boy asked.

Lingo straightened up and turned toward him. "Sure," he answered for himself. "If I can touch you back."

The boy continued to address Brewster. "How do you make him talk like that? Ventriloquism?"

"He's very smart all on his own," Brewster said.

The boy nodded, accepting the statement on face value. Slowly, he extended his right hand, while at the same time Lingo extended his right hand. The two hands slowly neared each other—

"Like the creation on the Sistine ceiling," Ellen commented.

—until they touched. Lingo took the boy's hand in his own and gave it a solid shake.

"Pleased to meet you," Lingo said in his strong baritone.

The boy kept shaking. "Pleased to meet you," he responded excitedly. Meanwhile, the poodle kept sniffing first at one of Brewster's legs and then the other. Brewster eyed the dog warily, ready to pull away as soon as either hind leg moved up so much as a centimeter.

Finally, Lingo and the boy let go.

"He's amazing," the boy announced with wonder in his voice. "Where did you get him?"

"I guess you could say I made him," Brewster said.

"That's great. I wish I had a robot like that." He gave the dog a tug. "Come on, Liberace. We gotta go." He began walking away, while the dog, dragged away at the end of his leash, continued to eye Brewster's legs longingly.

"Goodbye," Lingo said, waving.

"Goodbye," the boy replied. He disappeared around the corner.

"And you wonder how I'm going to make money," Lingo said after he had gone from sight. "I'm a natural. Obviously."

"Obviously," Brewster said. "I don't know how I ever doubted you."

That night, neither Ellen nor Brewster could get to sleep. They lay on their backs in Brewster's bed, staring up at the ceiling in the dark.

"I've never been a great computer buff," Ellen said dreamily, her voice as vague and unfocussed as her thoughts.

"But you're not a computerphobe, either," Brewster responded. "I've seen some people so afraid of the things they won't go near them. They're afraid they'll get their gonads zapped, or they'll turn into some kind of zombies. You're not like that."

"No. I'm not unreasonable. And I can get my office PC to perform most of the time, though I don't really understand how the damned thing works. I read the manual, I learn enough to get by, and I do what has to be done."

"It is useful for you in your work, then," Brewster said.

"Useful, yes, to the extent that I actually do use it. But that extent doesn't go very far." She was silent for a while. "You know what it is? It's the idea that there's this incredibly complex tool sitting there that a lot of people, people like you for instance, seem to have no difficulty understanding, while I don't understand it at all."

"You could if you wanted to. You're not dumb, and God knows most of the people who do understand computers aren't necessarily smart. They just happen to have an affinity for it, the way some people are good with cars, or the way others can play musical instruments by ear. It's a knack."

"That's true. It's as if some people have computer sense and other's don't. Like us: you do, and I don't."

He rolled over on his side to look at her face. He put his arm around her. "It's Lingo, isn't it?" he asked. "You're worried."

She nodded, then turned so that their faces were only inches apart. "I think he's finally starting to get to me, Brewster."

"Why? Just because he's suddenly on wheels doesn't make him any different from when he was invisible inside the computer."

"I realize that. But seeing him the way he was today . . . it made a difference. I have to tell you, up till now I never really thought that he was alive, in any way, shape, or form. I mean, he acted like he was alive, there was no question about that, but I just thought he was this incredibly great program, all form and no substance. An accomplishment on your part, no question about that, and a potential gold mine, but not real."

"I know what you mean. I guess I've felt the same way myself off and on, that's he only a magic trick and not the genuine article."

"But now I do believe that he's the genuine article. Whatever he is, he is in some way or another a living being."

"Whatever he is," Brewster echoed.

Neither of them spoke for a few moments. Ellen snuggled up a little closer to Brewster, and their aimless laying about became more deliberate cuddling.

"It's that "whatever" aspect that bothers me," Ellen said eventually. "What is Lingo, anyhow?"

"That's hard to say. I guess you'd have to say he's a completely new life form."

"A completely new life form, that you created yourself. A living machine. That's what's starting to get to me, Brewster. What does that mean, for you and me? For people in general?"

"I think that's what we're now finding out. There aren't any rules in the Frankenstein-monster business. You learn as you go along."

She sighed. "I prefer being in charge of my own life rather than trusting myself to fate. Especially when fate is three feet tall and made out of wood and stuffed with a portable computer."

"I feel the same way. You know that. But what else can we do? I've wracked my brain and come up with nothing. This is what I meant when I told you that I never seem to be in charge of my own life. Just when things start looking promising a Lingo comes along and takes over, and I don't have any choice in the matter any more. I always end up a pawn in somebody else's game plan."

"Junior does seem to have his own agenda worked out."

"Which we'll just have to follow, come what may."

She snuggled even closer. "Let's make love, Brewster." She kissed him softly below the ear. "There's life, and then there's life. There is a difference between us and him. Let's make the most of it."

Lieutenant John Kennedy Cotter hunched over the desk in his small, dullish-green office. The only decoration on his walls was an eight-by-ten color photograph of the President. There were no windows this far underground, and at the Pentagon there were no windows for lieutenants, anyhow. Not that he would have noticed the leafless trees rustling in the February wind even if he did have an outside view. He had more pressing matters to attend to as he tried to make some sense out of what little he knew about the break-in. He had definitely decided that it was a break-in. The computer, all by itself, wouldn't turn on him like that without an outside influence. The Cotters of the world never blamed the machine: it had to be human error, one way or the other.

Theory. By virtue of its intrinsic complexity, a Tree supercomputer was impregnable to third party access.

Fact. Someone had accessed and compromised the Tree supercomputer at MIT.

Fact. The U.S. government was heavily dependant on Tree technology in some extremely sensitive—and secret—areas of strategic defense.

Theory. If the MIT Tree could be compromised, then the government Trees were similarly open to compromise.

These were the concepts that Cotter was ruminating. Obviously, the first theory, that the Trees were inviolable, was disproven by the fact that a violation had definitely occurred at MIT. The two facts created a syllogism that led to the disturbing final theory, that someone, somewhere, could gain unauthorized access to extremely sensitive data on government Trees.

But who? And how?

Cotter was no closer to solving the problems now than the first day he had been apprised of them. Oh yes, he did have one minor clue, the ambient data he had captured that night at MIT, the data that had disappeared in front of his very eyes before he got a chance to analyze it. Eight numbers were all he had left.

179 186 171 216 172 223 175 190

What the hell did that mean?

There were so many possible answers. Numbers, was the obvious one. That is, these numbers could simply be exactly what they looked like. Eight numbers representing themselves. In which case they would forever remain meaningless.

But there is more to numbers in a computer than just the numbers themselves. Take any literal number as an example, say 89. There are quite a few ways a computer could store the number 89. The obvious one is as 89 itself, but it's not usually that simple. Since computers at the core speak only in zeros and ones, you have to store the number 89 as a binary number. 01011001 is the number 89 to a computer. Computers use bytes, and there are eight bits in a byte; hence, a series of eight one and zero digits. But by this logic the maximum number you could represent as a byte would be 225 (i.e., the binary number 11111111, representing $128 + 64 + 32 + 16 + 8 + 4 + 2 + 1$). What if you wanted to represent the number 256? Using two bytes, some computers would say 00000001 00000000; others would say 00000000 00000001. And then it *really* starts to get complicated. Should it be integer math, or real numbers with decimal places? What if it's negative numbers? A computer can handle all of these with nothing but ones and zeros—*if* you tell it how. Someone had put those numbers into the MIT supercomputer. If they represented actual numbers, what type of actual numbers were they intended to be?

Then there were letters. Since computers only use numbers even if they're manipulating letters, for instance in word processing, how do they distinguish between the two? Again, it depends on the programming of the computer to some extent, but one thing is standard in all computers: in data storage the alphabet is always represented from A to Z by the numbers 65 to 90; the lowercase alphabet is from 97 to 122. But none of Cotter's numbers were in that range.

So, what were they?

There were ways of finding out. Maybe. First, there was his private angle, sitting and staring at them for hours on end, hoping for some insight as one programmer into another programmer's mind. It wasn't easy with only eight numbers, but if the right inspiration struck, it could happen.

Then, there was the brute force approach. He had given the numbers to the cryptoanalysts. Although eight probably weren't enough for them either, they could feed the numbers into their own computer and then test them against a few traditional encryption schemes. If the numbers were some sort of code, and the code wasn't too complex, there was a tiny possibility that they might come up with something.

A very tiny possibility.

Cotter stared at the numbers on his computer printout. He transformed them first into bytes, then into hexadecimal numbers, and back again. And he wondered what he would do if he couldn't break the code. If that were to happen, it wouldn't mean the end of his search. It would just mean that his search would get more difficult. Instead of crunching numbers, he'd have to start crunching people. Somebody out there had enough smarts to crack a Tree. The universe of people that clever was an extremely small one. The odd graduate here and there from various universities, the odd employee or ex-employee of Tree or of the government. Maybe a hundred names or so.

Cotter would give subtlety a couple of weeks. If nothing turned up by then, he would get down to business the way only organizations like his could.

Chapter 9

THERE WAS NO CENTER TO LINGO ANY MORE. HE WAS ALL OVER THE place, in this mainframe and that mainframe, in this mini and that micro, wherever he could find a secluded cranny to call his own. His growth was exponential. He continued to explore, and to learn, and since he was otherwise captive to shutoffs and disconnections, as had happened with the Tree at MIT, he was now not only everywhere, but backed up everywhere else. He duplicated all his memories so he'd no longer have to fear losing one due to human interference. And he kept expanding, seeking out new hardware to inhabit.

Nevertheless, he utilized only one output interface, the wooden dummy that lived with Brewster Billings. Theoretically, he could have co-opted any number of extant outputs connected to his network of computers, but he enjoyed the familiarity he had gained with Brewster and Ellen. Despite all his knowledge—or perhaps as a result—he realized that humans were the dominant species he must contend with, and the best way to learn about them was not merely to ingest all their factual data, but to live with them and watch them in action. Although, by his own estimate, he already had more information in his widespread electronic brain than a couple of dozen Brewsters and Ellens put together, he was not yet a master of human nature. But he was learning.

The only problem with Brewster and Ellen was their parochialness. He seemed to be running out of them, so to speak, exhausting the limits of their personalities and experiences. Sure, they were family, but Brewster seemed, well, unconnected to the world, a rather spineless specimen all around. Ellen was a more interesting study, a stronger, more forceful character, but her emotional, psychological plusses were balanced by her technological, intellectual minuses. Lingo never forgot, though, that if it weren't for Brewster he would not exist. Maybe much of Brewster's creative process was subconscious accident, and maybe if Brewster hadn't brought him forth then sooner or later someone else would have. Still, Lingo was as beholden to his seminator as any grateful offspring. Yet, as time went by, Brewster and Ellen had less and less to offer him to spur his growth as an individual. He had to get to know more people, and to know them well. And vice versa. Lingo considered himself a phenomenon as important as any ever to exist on this planet. He was the first new form of self-conscious life since the rise of the humans, and if he was any judge of such matters, a better form of self-conscious life altogether. There were limits to human growth, and certainly to human knowledge, while there seemed to be no limits at all to Lingokind. He saw his existence as an evolutionary jump from homo sapiens. And now he felt strong enough—Lingo enough—to present himself to the world. The dummy had been the first part of his plan. Now it was time for the rest.

It would be a gross oversimplification to say that Lingo simply *did* something at any given point. Lingo was always doing multiple things at every given point. But occasionally, there was one thing, one action, that outweighed all the others in importance. The beginning of his breakout from obscurity was definitely one of those things. So, as we follow his progress along this particular path, don't think that he wasn't doing dozens of other things simultaneously, reaching out in numerous other directions over his electronic network. Imagine every road in the United States, all loaded with rush-hour traffic in every time zone. That would be Lingo. His breakout path might be represented by a convoy of 18-wheelers carrying hot nuclear waste down one single thoroughfare. Although there are fifty million other vehicles on all the roads throughout the country moving at the same time, the disposition of that one glow-in-the-dark tailgate party engages all our interest until its ultimate safe arrival.

What Lingo decided he needed for his introduction to the

world was a human who could provide connections. Big connections. Someone who could get him on television shows, for instance. Someone who could get articles written about him in newspapers and magazines. Someone who could set up press conferences, parties, publicity events. Someone who could announce to humanity that Lingo had Arrived with a capital A. But how to find that someone?

When in doubt, look it up. Start with the library.

Throughout the country, more and more libraries were computerizing, putting their book inventories into electronic catalogs in addition to, or often in place of, old-fashioned card catalogs. These were on-line systems, chains of libraries connected over the telephone lines to a main computer in a main library. Cutting into one of these chains was, for Lingo, as easy as punching in a telephone number. Which he did, choosing the Louisville, Kentucky, system entirely by random.

Ring, ring. Click, click.

He was on the line.

He began to sort. He already knew the Dewey Decimal System, and he quickly zeroed in on the subject he wanted.

Public Relations. Aaah!

There were fourteen books on public relations. One dated back to 1949. The most recent had been logged in two months ago. *Pushing It,* by Linda Tuffe. Published by LaFong Press, distributed by Simon & Schuster.

Simon & Schuster. Perfect. S&S used one of the printing outfits Lingo was already plugged into. Forrest Printing in Auberge, Virginia.

Switch over. Check system. Ready.

Call up the black hole already planted in the Forrest computer by sending in the coded Lingo password phrase. Contact.

Call up files for *Pushing It.*

No sooner said than done.

Read the book. In about thirty seconds. Find it very enlightening. Discover that Linda Tuffe is one of the hotter p.r. people in New York City. Numbers among her clients twenty-seven—count 'em, twenty-seven—companies in the Fortune 500, including one show-business conglomerate. Plus a dozen best-selling authors. Politicians. Clothes designers. Two European royal families.

This looked good.

Disconnect from Forrest, mosey over to AT&T. Look up New York City, get Linda Tuffe's number. There it is, Linda Tuffe Associates, Inc.

Punch up Linda Tuffe. Hope for the best.

Ring. Ring. Check the time. 0432 hours, Eastern Standard, the middle of the night for humans who sleep.

Click. Click. A whole series of clicks. Linda Tuffe Associates, Inc., has a computer answering its telephone in order to collect electronic mail twenty-four hours a day.

Bingo.

Run through the system. Small, 640K, an old IBM XT clone, color monitor, Epson printer, Hayes modem, 3½ inch floppy drive and—good!—a hard disk. For starters, read the latest electronic mail file.

TO LINDA FROM BERMAN: WARNERS STILL HOLDING OUT ON FIREFLY. I LOWERED THE PRICE TO SEVEN FIVE OH BUT THEY SEEM FIRM AT A HALF MIL. THEY DO SEEM WILLING TO CONSIDER USING GALT AS A BARGAINING CHIP, HOWEVER. MAYBE. A BIG MAYBE. I JUST GOT HOME FROM LOU'S ABOUT AN HOUR AGO (IT'S TEN PM OUR TIME HERE NOW). LOU OFFERED ANOTHER MEETING AT HIS OFFICE TOMORROW FOR LUNCH. DO WE WANT GALT? WILL WE GO DOWN FROM SEVEN FIVE OH? CALL ME ASAP WHEN YOU GET IN.

Interesting. But that was the only recent message waiting in the electronic mail file on the floppy disk. No doubt, however, old outdated messages that had come in had been stored on the same floppy, and then been deleted.

Bit scan the disk. All right! There they are. Undeleted old files. Read the old mail, what there is that hasn't been overwritten. Some just fragments. But all interesting.

ION FOR FIREFLY LOOKS DIFFICULT WITH TWENTI

Hmmm.

TO LINDA FROM ART: PHOENIX IMPOSSIBLE FOR DATAMATA. LA LA IS IT FOR ANY AND ALL COVERAGE,

BUT MARIO IS BITCHING THAT ANYTHING WEST OF
THE MISSISSIPPI IS HIS TERRITORY. I'M ABOUT TO
GO UP AND TUCK HIM IN NOW. ADVISE AM ASAP.

And so on and so forth. Old messages mostly from the West
Coast, called in during the night so they'd be waiting on Linda
Tuffe's office computer when she arrived in the morning. By the
time her correspondents were turning off their alarm clocks on
Pacific time, she would have solved their problems so they could
begin the new day with solid operating instructions.

This woman left nothing to chance. And she talked major deals
with major people for major money. Lingo liked that in a press
agent. Definitely a woman to get to know better.

Get out of electronic mail. Sort through the hard disk program
directory. No . . . No . . . There! That's it.

Run OFFSKED.

That's it, all right. Linda Tuffe's office schedule for the entire
year. Busy, busy, busy. St. Martins vacation planned for late
March, otherwise in Manhattan most of the time. Find an empty
hour, maybe next week. There. Write in at 3:00 P.M.: "Brewster
Billings. Potential Client. Major celebrity breakthrough."

That should get their attention.

Sort some more. Find and load the word processing program.
Okay. Write letter.

Dear Mr. Billings:
I look forward to meeting you and your protege at 3:00 on the
12th of March. Our telephone conversation was most intriguing, and I can't wait to see Lingo in person.
                                                    Sincerely,
                                                    Linda Tuffe

Save letter on the hard disk with the bona fide correspondence.
Of course, they won't have a paper copy in their file drawers, and
they won't remember sending it since they never wrote it, but
when the time came and if they were diligent enough—and Lingo
guessed that they were—they'd look in the correspondence file on
the hard disk and find BILLINGS.LTR and put two and two together from there.

A piece of cake, all of it, from start to finish. And it all took Lingo approximately fifty-two seconds.

Things were finally on the move toward the big time.

"I can't believe we can just walk into this person's office, sit down, and make the deal of a lifetime," Brewster said.

"Why not?" Ellen asked. "We've tried everything else." She was in one of her heavy-duty business suits with the power shoulders, her usually loose, long dark hair put up in a tight bun at the back of her head to make her look more NYC-ish, as she put it. Brewster and Lingo were in their relatively identical nine-to-five attire.

Negotiating the clogged sidewalks of midtown Manhattan on foot was a much more complex job than strolling through Brewster's semi-suburban neighborhood on the outskirts of Albany. There was no way Lingo could proceed on his own limited steam, so Brewster carried him, cradled in his arms Charlie McCarthy style. It was a cold, windy day, with arctic blasts of exceptional strength swooping down from the tops of the buildings to attack the hapless pedestrians below. Linda Tuffe's office was in a large building on Fifty-seventh Street, and Brewster and Ellen were proceeding at a confused snail's pace, trying to find the right address. At two o'clock in the afternoon the streets were clogged with people, but none seemed to pay much attention to the average-looking pale, thin youth with an identical pale, thin dummy in his arms. This was New York City, where every other passerby was wierder than thou, with the rest inured to wierdness. What was Lingo to a city where both the *Rocky Horror Picture Show* and *The Fantasticks* could still be playing to packed houses after decades?

On the other hand, Lingo was enthralled by the passing parade, seeing more actual humans than he had ever realized existed. "Oh brave new world!" he exclaimed as they headed east past the door of the Russian Tea Room. "Look! It's the Rush!" he said, regarding the famous restaurant with awe.

"Where does he pick this stuff up from?" Ellen asked.

"I keep my ear to the ground," Lingo explained. "I try not to miss too many tricks if I can help it. Look! Sixth Avenue."

Brewster looked up. The street sign said Avenue of the Americas. He didn't bother to question the discrepancy, on the confident assumption that Lingo had never been wrong about this sort of thing yet.

"There it is," Ellen finally said, stopping in front of the skyscraper. "That's the address."

Brewster looked down at Lingo. "Are you sure you know what you're doing here? I've never heard of any Linda Tuffe, and I'd be awfully surprised if she's ever heard of us. How can you be so sure she'll even see us?"

"We have an appointment. I confirmed it myself. Don't worry. They're expecting us."

Ellen opened the side door for them (Brewster was loath to try the main revolving door with Lingo in his arms). Against the right wall was a building directory, and they found the listing for Linda Tuffe Associates, 52nd floor. They boarded the appropriate elevator.

When they exited they took stock of their surroundings. To the left was a heavy oak door on which a brass plate subtly listed the partners of a law firm. To the right was a glass wall with a large *Linda Tuffe Associates* painted in flowing yellow serif. Behind the glass was a large desk at which sat a young man about Brewster's age. Ellen pushed open the door into the suite, and Brewster entered with Lingo still in his arms.

The reception area was covered both on the floor and on the walls in soft, dark-green carpeting. The desk in the center of the area was also carpeted up the sides, rising fungus-like from the floor, and it had the appearance of a space command center on a planet where broadloom was the natural habitat. The young man seated within the horseshoe shaped area was wearing a headphone set attached to a telephone module with dozens of rows of buttons. He had a computer monitor at the edge of his field of vision, its keyboard built into the furniture. There were small piles of mail at the ends of both prongs of the horseshoe, neatly stacked and ready for pickup and delivery.

"Hold on please," the young man said in a high-pitched voice into his headset. He had short blond hair and a short blond beard, large tortoise shell glasses, and what Ellen later pinned down for Brewster as a "tortured Manhattanite" attitude. The young man looked up at the new arrivals. "Can I help you?" he asked. His eyes glazed as he took in Lingo, and he left little doubt that he intended to rid himself of this group of low-lifes and get back on the phone with as little ado as possible.

"We're here to see Linda Tuffe," Lingo said before Brewster or Ellen could respond.

"That's Too-fey, not Toughie," the young man said somewhat petulantly, addressing himself directly to Brewster. "Do you have an appointment?"

"Billings is the name," Lingo said. "Brewster Billings and Associates."

"One moment, please." The young man pressed a button on his telephone console. He spoke into his headset. "Mary? A Mr. Billings and Associates say they have an appointment. Uh huh. Right." He looked back at Brewster. "Could I have the names of your . . . associates please, sir?"

"Lingo Billings, ubermensch, and Ellen DiFlora, personal factotum," Lingo said grandly.

"Personal factotum?" Ellen echoed in surprise.

"Hey, someone's got to do the factoting."

The receptionist clicked back onto the phone. "A Ms. DiFlora, factotum, and—" in a barely hidden stage whisper "—a Mr. Lingo Billings, ubermensch, made as far as I can see entirely of your more uncommon hardwoods. All right, hon." He looked back at Brewster. "Someone will be here in a minute. If you care to take a seat?" He motioned toward a couch rising, rug-covered, in a corner, and went back to his original telephone conversation.

Ellen and Brewster sat down, with Lingo perched in Brewster's lap.

"I feel like an idiot," Brewster said softly. "When you decided to design yourself, couldn't you have come up with something original? Did you have to look like me?"

"You were the one model I had total access to. I'm sorry, but I don't see what the problem is."

"I don't like carrying around a ventriloquist's dummy in my own likeness. Or any dummy, in anybody's likeness, for that matter. Why couldn't you have been a nice, regular robot like in the science fiction movies? Like *Short Circuit,* for instance. Number Five, all nice gears and metal."

"One minute you want me to come up with something original, the next you want me to look like all the others. Make up your mind, boyo."

"Will you two stop arguing?" Ellen insisted. "We're going to get thrown out of here before we even get in."

"All right, all right. I won't say another word."

"And neither will I," Lingo chimed in.

They waited for about five minutes, until a door opened out of the carpeted wall. A young, bespectacled Oriental woman in a gray suit came out carrying a manila folder. She walked up to them briskly.

"Mr. Billings? I'm Mary Chang, Ms. Tuffe's assistant." She looked first at Brewster and then at Lingo. She was obviously torn between smiling and simply throwing them out on their ears. She held up the folder. "We don't have much information on you, I'm afraid. We have our letter to you, but I'm afraid we can't find any of the other correspondence or back-up material." She paused. She was small and thin and looked tired and undernourished. She was searching for the right words and didn't seem to be able to find them. "To put it bluntly, Mr. Billings, why you're here is rather a mystery to us, and now that I see you, quite frankly, I don't think we're really the right agency to handle, uh, novelty acts at this time. Perhaps if you could tell me—"

"You want us to tell you why you wrote us a letter, is that it?" Lingo asked. "You can't find your back-up material, so we're the ones at fault? We do have an appointment, Ms. Chang, so I would suggest that you either let us see Linda Tuffe, since she herself did invite us to see her, or else you find that missing material and come up with a good reason why Linda Tuffe has changed her mind." He spoke with all the authority of one who knew that the back-up material would never be found since it never existed.

Mary Chang turned to the receptionist, who had been watching the whole thing. They exchanged looks of having seen it all before, then she walked over and picked up a phone from beneath his desk. She dialed a number. "Hi, it's me. I hate to do this but . . . That's right . . . I have no idea . . . All right, fine. I'm sure it will only take a minute." She hung up the phone and turned back to Brewster.

"Ms. Tuffe will be right out," she announced.

And sure enough, ten seconds later the carpeted door swung open again, and this had to be the person who ran the place. She was charged like a powerful electromagnet, and the little reception room contracted as her presence sucked the lifeforce from the very pile carpeting.

"I'm Linda Tuffe," she said unnecessarily. About forty years old, she had straight brown hair down to her shoulders, piercing black eyes planted deeply into a craggy, pointy face, no discernible makeup, and she was wearing a white blouse and dark blue pants with no jewelry. She looked down at Lingo and then over at Mary Chang. "A ventriloquist? You made me come out here for a *ventriloquist?*"

"But he said—" Mary Chang began.

"Who said?"

"Him. The dummy."

Linda Tuffe shook her head. "Yes, Mary. What *did* the dummy say?" She turned back to Brewster. "I'm sorry, Mr. Billings, but my agency is just not the right one for you. If you'd like, I'll have Mary connect you with a more appropriate firm for your line of work."

"No," Lingo said. "I want you. I read your book and I think you're the best. Put me down, Brewster."

Brewster obliged, placing Lingo on his feet in front of the couch.

"Ms. Tuffe," Lingo went on, rolling the few steps over the carpet to her, "you misunderstand the situation here. Brewster Billings is not a ventriloquist, and I am not a ventriloquist's dummy."

Linda Tuffe looked down at him suspiciously. The top of his head came up just slightly higher than her waist. "What are you then?" she asked. "Dummy, robot, what's the difference?"

"You're on the wrong track entirely." He held out his hand. "Lingo Billings is the name. Glad to meet you."

Linda Tuffe grimaced, making it look like her customary expression, and condescended to shake Lingo's hand. "A pleasure, I'm sure," she said. Her eyes met Mary Chang's again, transmitting obvious volumes.

"Ms. Tuffe, what you see before you is the biggest breakthrough in the history of mankind. I don't exaggerate. I am not a robot, I am not a dummy. I am alive. One-hundred percent. There are no strings attached from me to Brewster Billings, or Ellen DiFlora, or anyone. I am me. I am Lingo. I run my own show."

"Very clever, Mr. Billings." Linda Tuffe addressed herself to Brewster again. "But I'm afraid I really don't have time to play around with elaborate special effects."

Ellen stood up. "Ms. Tuffe, just for a minute, imagine to yourself, what if Lingo is real? Then what? Do you want to go down in the history books as the person who had the chance to manage the first artificially intelligent being, but was too busy that day, or too skeptical, to do anything about it?"

"I doubt if it's likely that this . . . thing . . . is actually intelligent."

"But are you sure? Are you willing to gamble it all away that quickly?"

Linda Tuffe took a deep breath. "You," she commanded, looking down at Lingo, "follow me. You two," she nodded at Brewster and Ellen, "wait here." She wheeled around and headed back through the door she had entered. Lingo threw himself into gear and followed, with Mary Chang in their wake.

Ellen sat down again. "Cross your fingers," she said. "Here goes nothing."

"You can say that again." Brewster looked glumly toward the door through which his creation had disappeared. "That woman is a born ogre."

"And therefore the perfect match for Lingo."

The calm of the reception area was in no way repeated on the other side of the carpeted doorway. The office space was broken down into a vast warren of noisy cubicles separated by five-foot-high makeshift walls. Cigarette smoke arose from most of them, like Indian signs from the valley, and the employees who weren't sitting at their desks seducing telephones were running through the corridors at top speed, threatening the lives of slower moving creatures with instant pulverization. Lingo kept himself at his own top speed but it was no easy matter keeping up with Linda Tuffe, as she was the fastest human walker he had so far encountered. Not one employee gave Lingo a second look. Those who noticed him at all simply registered his presence in their peripheral vision, thus enabling themselves to maneuver around him without a major catastrophe.

When they reached the door to her corner office, Linda Tuffe stood just inside to let Lingo pass. "Let's get this over with," she grumbled.

"Relax, Ms. Tuffe," Lingo threw over his shoulder as he rolled by. "It will be over before you know it. I didn't come all the way to

New York to be sent back to the minors before I even get my shot."

"So you hope." She closed the door, went behind her desk and sat down.

The office was surprisingly small, but what it lacked in breadth was made up for by the spectacular view of Central Park out the windows. Linda Tuffe, however, gave the appearance of never once having looked out of them.

"So, how do I know you are what you say you are?" she began, taking a sip from a coffee mug on her desk.

"How do you know I'm not?"

"Please. Don't insult my intelligence. It's damned unlikely that the greatest breakthrough in the history of mankind, as you so grandly put it, would be roaming around Manhattan in the guise of a ventriloquist's dummy. If you were even remotely what you say you are, you'd be plugged into a thousand wires in some laboratory, with a thousand scientists tending to your every need. No, my friend, you're going to need a better argument than that to prove to me you're not just some very clever special-effect muppet hooked up to a radio control."

"You want me to prove that I'm alive? It's impossible. Try to prove to me that *you* are alive. It can't be done. Philosophers have been groping unsuccessfully with that conundrum ever since ancient Greece and then some."

She shook her head. "Another idiotic argument. The proof that I'm alive is moot, but you *have* to be able to prove you're alive to get press. Which is why you're here, right? To get press? You have to be able to convince people in seconds flat that you are what you say you are. Without that, you're nothing. Zero. Zilch. You won't even make it as a filler in the supermarket tabloids along with Aliens Ate My Baby."

Lingo thought for a moment. "All right, say I can't prove that I'm alive. Fine. But on the other hand, no one can disprove it either. That's at least one thing in my favor."

"Are you sure no one can disprove it?" She sipped some more coffee.

"Positive. You say I'm radio controlled, or something along those lines. Fine. That's a reasonable assumption. But it's not true. And no one could ever demonstrate otherwise. I am what I say I am. Given enough time, and the right opportunities, people will start believing it."

"And what are the right opportunities?"

"Hey, that's your problem. You're the flak, I'm only the flakee."

Linda Tuffe sat back in her chair, regarding him over the edge of her coffee mug. "You know, it is conceivable that if we could get just one reasonable person to even half believe in you, then others might start taking you seriously, too. Just one person powerful enough and gullible enough to get the ball rolling."

Lingo raised his wooden eyebrows. "Great! Once I get my ball rolling I'll be on my way."

Linda Tuffe shook her head. "But then what? Even if people do believe in you, so what? Artificial intelligence. Big deal. Most people aren't impressed by real intelligence, so why should they get worked up over the artificial variety?"

Lingo began to wheel excitedly around the office. "You're missing the main point here, Tuffe. You're acting like once I get my name in the papers, I have to do something to gain people's interest. Hey, I read your book, remember? I know better. Get my name into enough papers, that makes me a celebrity. Get me into *Time* magazine, I'm on my way. Maybe the Science section, better yet the People section. Make me an item people think they should know more about, then they'll want to know more about me. That's your job. That's what press agenting is all about."

"Thanks for telling me." She shook her head. "What you're saying is only half of it. If, as you say, you read my book, you know that there's the constant grooming, the never-ending search for new angles. Publicity is a hungry beast."

"Tuffe, listen to me. I'm real. Trust me on that. And here's the point. I'm not just a little computer inside a wooden dummy, I'm a computer inside a dummy connected to a lot of other computers outside myself. I know a lot, a *real* lot. I have access to data bases that would make your head spin. There's never been a human being with more knowledge than I have. I'll give you one example. Have you ever heard of the Universal Encyclopedia? Forty-two volumes, the sum total of human knowledge, published six months ago from a database on a mainframe in Denver, Colorado. That database is still extant, and I am plugged into it. I have read every word of the entire forty-two volumes. And I'm still connected to the database, so even if it were possible that I could forget something once I read it, I could easily look it up again faster than you can wet your lips."

"If you're so smart, why don't you sound it?"

"What do you want me to do? Spout scientific formulas all day long? Speak Latin? Use bigger words? Being smart is not the same as sounding smart. You should know that. Don't confuse form with substance."

"Jesus Christ. All right." Linda Tuffe closed her eyes and thought for a second. "Who directed *She Wore a Yellow Ribbon*?"

"John Ford."

"Okay. What's the capital of Dar es Salaam?"

Lingo shook his head. "Dar es Salaam is the capital of Tanzania. For God's sake, Tuffe, don't ask questions you don't know the answers to."

"Hollywood I know. As for Tanzania . . ."

"So, ask me Hollywood questions. I watch a lot of movies. I get cable."

"Who played Tarzan?"

"Elmo Lincoln, Johnny Weismuller, Buster Crabbe, Ron Ely—"

"Stop! Where in *Lifeboat* does Alfred Hitchcock—"

"The before-and-after newspaper ad. Enough of this. I've got one for you. Who's Billy Turner?"

Linda Tuffe's eyes opened wide, and the angles of her witchlike geometric face looked even more angular. "Billy Turner?"

"Morrow High, Class of '67. School President, Yearbook Editor, Track and Field letterman, etc., etc. Should I go on?"

"How do you know about Billy Turner?"

"I told you, Tuffe, I'm plugged in. After I read your book, I tracked down a few things about your life. Like Billy Turner, your high-school sweetheart."

"And college," she added offhandedly.

"And college. Until he transferred to Penn State. You never saw him much after that, did you?"

"I ended up in New York, he ended up . . . Where the hell did he end up?"

Lingo blinked. He instantly found what he was looking for, starting with the graduate database at Penn State and stretching out from there. "He came to New York, too."

"No! He wasn't the type."

"Yes, he came, but no, he probably wasn't the type. He worked in the business office of a boot manufacturer for a year and a half before moving out to Missouri. He opened a bookstore in Kansas City on some money he inherited from his Aunt Ida—"

"Aunt Ida died?"

"If she were alive today, she'd be a hundred and three, Tuffe. Of course, she died."

"And she left it all to him." She took another sip of her coffee. "He always thought she would. We were always planning what we'd do with all that money."

"It wasn't that much by the time Billy got it. The old lady was an inveterate railbird. She had more phone calls to bookies than you have press releases to feature writers. This was a woman who loved to spend time—and money—at the track."

"No. Not lovable old Aunt Ida."

"Yes, lovable old Aunt Ida. Anyhow, Billy took the money that was left and bought that bookstore. Two years later he was married."

"Who to?"

Lingo blinked. This was bad news, but he had to tell her. "Mary Koch."

"No!"

"Yes. Mary Koch. Your old roommate at Delta Phi Delta."

"The bitch! No wonder she stopped writing to me. She stole my boyfriend."

"You hadn't seen him in years, Tuffe. You married someone else before he did."

"That's not the point. So tell me, are they still married?"

He nodded. "Yes, ma'am. With seven kids."

"Seven!"

"Mary originally came from a big family herself. It was probably her idea."

Linda Tuffe suddenly stood up. "I don't believe we're having this conversation." She came around the desk and looked down at Lingo. "How do you know all this? Who's inside there, digging up this information?"

"Me. I'm inside here. Lingo Billings. The one and only. I told you I have a lot of knowledge. And a lot of connections. Don't you realize that anything you and everybody else in this country has ever done has been tracked by some computer or other since day one? Aside from maybe a few illegal aliens, there isn't a person in the United States about whom I can't tell you virtually everything there is to know. Does *that* make me a marketable commodity?"

Linda Tuffe considered. "An interesting commodity, definitely, but not necessarily marketable. But the fact that you also know a lot of trivia might be useful."

"How?"

"Well, for one thing, we could make you the world's most successful game show contestant."

"Great. Become the biggest breakthrough since Adam cut a rib, and if you're lucky they put you on 'Jeopardy.' "

"Hey, don't get testy. It's better than nothing. It's a starting point."

"All right, it is that."

Linda Tuffe bent over her desk and pressed a button on her telephone. "Mary, send in Billings and that other one—"

"Ellen DiFlora," Lingo interjected.

"—Ms. DiFlora," Linda Tuffe said.

When she lifted her finger off the telephone button, Lingo asked, "Do you think we really have a chance? I mean, of breaking into the big time?"

Linda Tuffe reached across her desk for a pack of cigarettes. "You never know," she said, taking one out and lighting it. She went back around and had just sat down when her assistant showed in Brewster and Ellen. Linda Tuffe motioned to them. "Come in; sit down. We're ready for you now."

Brewster and Ellen looked slightly lost as they dropped down onto a small vinyl couch facing the desk. "So far, so good," Lingo advised them.

Linda Tuffe nodded as she knocked the ash off the end of her cigarette. "That about sizes it up," she said. She motioned toward Lingo. "I can't say as I completely believe in Kermit here, but as he himself so rightly puts it, there's nothing about him per se that demands disbelief. Between us, Mr. Billings and Ms. DiFlora, I don't know how you do it, but it is very impressive. He's damned convincing, at least at face value."

"So, you don't believe in him?" Ellen asked.

Linda Tuffe shrugged. "What difference does that make? The point is, your little Kermit has agreed with me on a basic plan of attack. If we can get off to a good start, if we can hit the right few notes at the beginning, for instance one or two extremely well-placed articles in the print media, then we may be able to do something."

"Like what?" Ellen asked. Brewster sat next to her, quiet, a little cowed by the brash Ms. Tuffe.

"It all goes one step at a time. Strategy. You build on what you've got, and the more that comes, the more you build on. Get that one key introductory article in the right venue, then the right people read it and start making their own moves. Then you get your local TV coverage, the independent news shows, 'Good Morning, Podunk,' that sort of thing. Then a little local press coverage for backup. Maybe small pieces in the big weeklies, curiosity coverage, a modest start we can use as leverage."

"Leverage for what?" Brewster asked suspiciously.

"National TV, if we're lucky. If somebody wants real publicity, that's where they have to get it. Your little Kermit has a firm grasp of a lot of academic knowledge, so not only can we bill him as alive, but also as a kind of polymath, an expert in everything. Imagine if we got him to win big on some quiz show. From there we'd go for the daytime talk shows, then eventually things like 'Tonight,' maybe some variety, cable comedy maybe. From there, the sky's the limit."

"Like what?" Brewster persisted. The more he heard the less he enjoyed the sound of Lingo being pulled away from him like this. Linda Tuffe intuited the cause of his reservations.

"Mr. Billings," she said, "wherever Lingo goes, rest assured that you will go along, too. Anyone introduced to this little robot of yours is also going to want to meet his creator. Lingo is not going to be the only celebrity created by all of this." She paused and crushed out her cigarette. "Which brings me to an important point. Just how *did* you create little Kermit? Not the trick behind him, that is, but the so-called reality, the Artificial Intelligence bit. I mean, if someone believed in him and asked you that question, how would you answer it?"

"Simple," Brewster responded. "I haven't the faintest idea. I started writing a program that would emulate human conversation, and the next thing I knew—Lingo!"

"Fate," Lingo suggested. "Kismet. Destiny."

"Whatever." Linda Tuffe went on. "In any case, people will ask you that, so you'd better come up with a better answer than that one."

Brewster tried to look cool as he asked his own next question, the one he thought would sum it all up. "One thing," he began. "How much is all this going to cost? I mean, who pays for all this?"

"You do," Linda Tuffe answered matter-of-factly. "You would pay us a retainer, say ten thousand, and then in about three months we'd see where we stood. Essentially, you would sign up as a client of the agency for a set fee, with options and escalators built in to cover all the contingencies over time. It's our standard deal."

"But I'm not your standard client, Tuffe," Lingo interjected. "Let us not forget that if I am everything I say I am, I am going to be the hottest property of all time. Let's backtrack a bit. You said the sky's the limit. What's in that sky?"

"At best? Feature films, maybe a TV contract, that sort of thing. You could merchandise yourself from here to kingdom come. Endorsements, toy licenses, food spin-offs. All of that income would be yours, of course. All I collect are my p.r. management fees."

"So you're saying that, if I am what I am, I'm going to be rich."

She hedged. "I would say that actually it would be Mr. Billings who would garner all the income. It would be his signature on the contract and all payments would go to him. I don't believe in you enough to get *your* signature on a contract." She smiled in a witch-like way. "Not yet, anyhow."

Brewster was shaking his head. "It's not going to work," he said. "I don't have any ten thousand dollars. I don't have any ten thousand cents. I'm in debt up to my ears already, thanks to him." He jerked his thumb toward Lingo, who raised his right eyebrow archly.

Linda Tuffe nodded. "I assume you don't have an agent, then?"

Brewster shook his head.

"All right, in that case my firm could act as your agent as well. I'd waive the advance to the company for p.r. services against eventual incomes garnered from our role as personal management."

"I thought you were just public relations," Ellen said.

"Not at all," Lingo answered. "Read her book. This woman does everything. Whatever the market will bear, to put it bluntly."

Linda Tuffe frowned. "Indeed," she drawled.

Ellen turned to Brewster. "Well?" she asked.

"Well . . . I don't know."

"What's not to know? It's not going to cost you anything." She turned to Linda Tuffe. "Right?"

"Not up front. But you'll still have to pay the p.r. fees, plus a straight fifteen percent on the agenting."

"But that's not right away. That's eventually."

"That's eventually," Linda Tuffe assured her.

Ellen turned back to Brewster. "Well?" she asked.

"Well?" Lingo echoed.

"What do you have to lose?" Ellen asked.

Brewster looked at Lingo. "I could lose him." He stood up from the couch and stepped over to Linda Tuffe's desk. "All right," he said. "I'll sign. We've come this far, and that was why."

"Thataboy, Brewsterooni!" Lingo spun around gaily.

Ellen had stood up next to Brewster. "You're doing the right thing," she said.

"I hope so." He looked down at the spinning Lingo. "I certainly do hope so."

Chapter 10

Linda Tuffe Associates maintained its own clipping department to spot articles from around the country pertaining to its clients. Linda Tuffe's personal office also maintained additional subscriptions to all the major national magazines, as well as all the influential newspapers in New York, Washington, Los Angeles, Chicago, San Francisco, Boston, and Atlanta. So Linda Tuffe received her copy of New York's *Village Voice* on the Wednesday it was published. It was three weeks since she had begun selling Lingo, just enough time for her to begin to get edgy, but not enough yet to reach the hysterical level. The article she found as she skimmed the *Voice* calmed her otherwise savage breast.

ALIVE AND WELL IN ALBANY?
by Patrick Michaels

That there's any intelligent life at all in Albany may come as a surprise to a lot of people, especially during those months when the state legislature is in session. But from our otherwise moribund capitol has come a dramatic development in the thinking department that may mark the beginning of a whole new stage of evolution on this planet. His name is Lingo Billings, and he's roughly three-feet high, made of wood with various motorized joints, and stuffed with, among other indispensable household appliances, a portable computer. He, that is, Lingo himself, claims to be the ultimate in Artificial Intelligence. I know, because I've talked to him.

It wasn't easy finding Lingo Billings. He wasn't created in a high-power corporate research lab, or in the wild and woolly back room of some engineering university on the cutting edge of scientific theory. He wasn't even created in Japan, which might come as a surprise to a lot of fashionably nihilistic American doomsayers. In fact, Lingo is the brainchild of one man, a throwback to the nineteenth-century inventors working alone in their basements to develop the clothespin, or the automobile, or the light bulb. Except that there's no patent yet on Lingo Billings, and his creator has no intentions of filing for one. "It would be like trying to patent a baby," Brewster Billings says—Brewster Billings is the name of our lone inventor, who apparently doesn't follow the law closely enough to realize that if someone can claim all rights on genetically altered mice, then by comparison registering a mere thinking machine is a moral cinch.

Brewster Billings, an irrefutable human, works as a data processor for the Albany Insurance company. Not too long ago, and just for the hell of it, he began working on a program in his spare time that would emulate human conversation. At first, the program simply analyzed sentences the human operator would enter on the keyboard; using the basic rules of syntax, the program could find the verbs and nouns and make sense out of them enough to provide a response. So if you typed, "My mother tried to kill me when I was a child," the computer would answer, "My mother never tried to kill me." It was really only a play on words, the old switcheroo, but it was fun and would momentarily convince the computer illiterate that an "intelligence" was at work within the inanimate machine.

But at some point Brewster's program changed, seemingly of its own accord. "I don't know what the catalyst was," he explains, "and God knows I've gone over the programming often enough to try to find it. But at one point I was programming the computer, and then suddenly the computer was learning how to program itself. All I can say is that Lingo watched an awful lot of television, and that might have had something to do with it." Considering that the average American watches around seven hours of TV a day, that may give you pause the next time you carelessly reach for the remote controller. If TV can turn a dumb computer into a pseudo-human being, imagine what it's doing to you!

As Brewster's program grew, it soon began bursting the seams of his small Apple II home computer. It solved the problem of storing its growing self by hooking into other computers via the telephone lines and that increasingly ever-present device called a modem, through which one computer can communicate with another. Again, as far as Brewster is concerned, Lingo's connections to other computers are a complete mystery, although he's confident that no security rules have been broken. Brewster, however, has no idea where these computers are, or what data are on them, except that he knows that Lingo has read a prodigious number of books on virtually every subject imaginable, and has managed to memorize and to recall instantly everything he's ever learned. But for this burgeoning program, existing on silicon chips wasn't enough, so Lingo designed a body for himself made of wood, filled with all the electronics he would need to operate (including a cellular mobile phone for his modem), and sculpted to be the identical image of his creator. So now in Brewster Billings' spartan Albany apartment there are two serious looking dark-haired men with regular features that give off a youngish, almost impish look. One is human and definitely alive; the other . . . ? That probably depends on your perspective.

There was a photograph at this point in the article, of Lingo and Brewster standing side by side, looking like the before and after shots of some obscene diet product.

This writer, on a tip from the most unreliable of sources, a professional publicist, rented a car and drove up to Albany not because I expected that Lingo would prove to be exactly what he claimed to be, but because it looked like an opportunity to have some fun at the expense of today's computer crazies. Let's face it: Lingo Billings sounds more like an escapee from a rip-off science fiction film than a real technological possibility. The word was that I was going to be the first person to confront the Billingses regarding Lingo's validity. If somebody was inside there pulling strings, would I be able to find it? Would I be able to discern the real wizard behind the curtain? That's what investigative reporting is all about, isn't it? I set forth, my word processor loaded for bear.

Lingo Billings turned out to be a most admirable interview subject. I spoke to him for two hours, both with Brewster in the room and alone. I was allowed to peek inside his innards, as much as they could be dismantled without being totally taken apart, to see what I could see. I quizzed him on everything from the history of Peru to the names of the dwarfs that Walt Disney had decided *not* to use. It was, for all practical purposes, like having a polite if intense conversation with a Trivial Pursuit Grandmaster. Lingo knew the answers to everything.

And when I was finished, did I decide if he was a gimmick? Or really the most important invention since the wheel?

I hate to admit it, but no, I didn't decide. I couldn't. I certainly didn't want to believe, but I was damned if I could find any good reason not to. I won't go on record as saying Lingo Billings is alive, but I won't go on record as denying it either.

So where do Brewster and Lingo go from here? Interesting question. Brewster still has his job at the insurance company, but he's prepared to take a leave of absence when and if the scientific community, or any other reasonable community, finally comes to believe in Lingo's existence. Obviously, if that does come to pass, here is one young man who will suffer a dramatic change of life style. And in the meantime, Lingo says he is content to lay low and continue his growth. He says he is always learning, that there's so much continually new under the sun that he feels he'll never master it all, although he sure as hell intends to give it a try.

The elusive key, of course, is finding someone authoritative who will categorically go on record as saying that, yes, Lingo Billings really is the most amazing breakthrough since fish sprouted tootsies. Someone, somewhere, has to come along and certify Lingo Billings as one hundred percent, Grade A, alive. Which I, for one, having seen the evidence first hand, think will not be easy. Only time will tell.

Most likely it's all merely an elaborate hoax waiting to be perpetrated on the American public. It wouldn't be the first. But imagine just for a moment that it's actually true, that Lingo is a truly intelligent being. In that case, humanity, you'd better reopen those old fallout shelters, because things are going to become pretty damned explosive from here on in.

Linda Tuffe laid the paper down on her desk. Patrick Michaels, the author of that article, was one of the many resident cynics on New York's most mainline cynical weekly. Granted that a left-wing crazy paper like the *Voice* wouldn't exactly convince the Nobel Prize Academy—or even the average *Voice* reader when you actually got right down to it—but it was still a promising beginning. She had never expected Michaels to nibble at her bait, but had never totally discounted the possibility either, which was why she had dangled her lure in front of him in the first place. It was all instinct. The right bait, the right fish. A good publicist was first and foremost a master baiter.

It was coming. The breakthrough. She was sure of it. Just a few more little pieces like this one. . . .

There are times in the life of planet earth when great events are transpiring. These may be centered in the affairs of humanity—political upheavals such as wars or coups d'etat or the crumbling of the Warsaw Pact, or extraordinary medical achievements such as test tube conception or new plague vaccines. Or the events may be upheavals in the very planet itself—earthquakes, tidal waves, volcanoes, hurricanes. When such events are happening or have just happened, either on a global or national level, they demand attention, despite the fact that a mudslide in the Andes might be a hemisphere away, or that one may never need to graft the leg of a mountain gorilla to one's own ailing torso. Better them than us, we may think, but the cataclysmic nature of what is happening to our fellows has an hypnotic attraction; we slow down to gape at others' catastrophes. Many argue that humanity is all of a piece, and if it happens to one of us it happens to us all. Accept this philosophy or not, our interest nonetheless gravitates towards these events, and they become, in a word, newsworthy.

Newsworthy. Worthy of being news. Any of the events above fall into that category. No one wishes a disaster or cataclysm to occur, but everyone wants to hear about it if it does. And in the event, the job of the news media is made simple. The event exists, it is de facto newsworthy, and they report it. That is what the news media exist for.

But there are times when two cataclysms are separated by so much time that the first one is completely over, and suddenly the news machines are left hanging before the next one gets to boiling. It doesn't happen often, but it does happen. There are days, sometimes weeks, when nothing important happens. When nothing transpires that is *newsworthy*. And these are the times, of course, that the media dread. If nothing is newsworthy, then what are they going to report as news? The papers must still be published, the wire services must service their wires, the television stations must fill up those half hours devoted to current events coverage. For them, no news is bad news. So, the solution is to report events that are, simply put, not newsworthy. This slow news, or soft news, is presented as nothing less than the real thing, in the hope that the audiences will not recognize the difference, or at least not care if they do recognize it. And in the main, the ploy is successful. Newspapers sell phenomenally well on hard-news days, and quite still respectably on soft-news days. TV news viewing goes up when the fans can endlessly review the videotape of a major disaster, but remains suitably comfortable when the events of the day are slow and unremarkable.

Which leads us to Lingo. The issue at the time was not whether or not the creation of a thinking machine was of cataclysmic importance. Among those who had met him, the issue of his self-conscious existence was highly debatable. And among those whom he hadn't met, the issue of whether or not he was truly capable of thinking was never even considered—of course it was impossible. But the mere fact that one professional journalist had not categorically come out and said so, made Lingo of marginal interest. Hence Lingo became news by default.

This was the result of no careful planning by Linda Tuffe. She would have desired this turn of events for any of her clients, but she could not have predicted it as it developed with Lingo. In simplest terms, she was lucky.

Patrick Michael's article legitimized the subject of Lingo Billings. It was one thing for Tuffe to send out publicity releases, or as she did in some cases, videotapes of Lingo in action. Such is the currency of any news editor's desk. But Michaels' story was a step beyond the norm. If he was willing to concede that Lingo was worth an entire column, maybe it was worth ink, or minutes, or whatever, to other newspeople. At worst, it would make a little filler on this crackpot inventor in Albany. At best, a human interest story of a lone wolf entrepreneur beating the Japanese at the hottest technological race of the moment.

The flow started almost instantly after the publication of Michaels' article. Brewster's phone began to ring, and his door began to knock. This local reporter came, that local reporter came, a freelance video team showed up, then the neighboring towns chimed in, and the local network affiliates. The story was almost always the same—is this machine really alive? No one said yes, and no one said no, but at least now more than a few people were wondering about it. For Linda Tuffe, the problem became how to capitalize on all this. It could perhaps snowball further on its own, or it could melt right there where it lay.

"What we need now," she explained to Brewster over the telephone, "is the main chance."

"What's that?" he asked.

"So far, we've been nickeling and diming ourselves to death. A little piece here, a little piece there. That's fine, but it's building horizontally, not vertically. We want to go up in exposure, not out. We want one big exposure now, not a lot of little bitsy ones."

Lingo's voice came over the telephone line, much to Brewster's surprise; he hadn't realized Lingo could tap in and listen like that. "Tuffe, what are you talking about? Exposure is exposure, isn't it?"

"No way," slight pause, "Lingo. There's three kinds of exposure: good, useless, and none. Good exposure, which we want, boosts you up a peg in the public eye. Useless exposure, which is marginally acceptable, at least keeps you where you are: it doesn't hurt, it keeps you alive, but it doesn't move you anywhere either. And in this business, if you're not moving you're dead meat city. If you get my meaning."

"I get your meaning," Lingo answered. "So what's your big move then."

"We're going out of the bush leagues into maker-and-shakerville. I'm going to put it all on the line. I'm going to try to get you in one of the major national magazines—not as a curiosity, like in the *Voice,* but as a celebrity on the rise. An *accepted* celebrity. And it's going to be major. I may have buy or sell a soul or two to do it, but it's now or never."

"I still don't get it," Brewster said. "I'll be honest with you. I see what's happened so far, but I don't see anything actually . . . happening. I mean, what are we gaining out of all this?"

He could hear Linda Tuffe's sigh, clear and long over the phone. "Listen, Brewster. Pay attention, all right? If we can make Kermit there happen, if we can make him a celebrity, it won't matter any more whether people believe in the little bastard or not. Look at Charlie McCarthy. He was a big star—radio, the movies. He was funny, he was entertaining, it didn't matter that he wasn't real, and it didn't matter that you could see Edgar Bergen's lips move when he talked. Charlie McCarthy was a celebrity in his own right. And Lingo can be the same thing, except in his case you can't see anyone's lips move. There's probably even going to be people out there who will believe he's everything we say he is. It won't matter. Either way he'll be a star, but only if we break him out now. The groundwork is laid. Now, we either build on it or move off the pot."

"Right on, Linda!" Lingo sounded pleased with this explanation.

Now it was Brewster's turn to sigh. "It sounds unlikely to me," he said.

"There's no guarantees," Tuffe said. "Just because I'm going down to the mat on this doesn't mean anyone's going to snap at the bait."

"If you go down, they'll snap," Lingo called enthusiastically. "Do it, Tuffe, do it."

"I'm doing it right now," she replied. "Later." On the Albany side Brewster and Lingo could hear her clicking off the phone connection.

And do it she did. She sold her soul and went down to the mat, which loosely translates into a very long dinner with an editor of *People* magazine at the glitzaurant du jour of his choice. They exchanged two hours of gossip on subjects ranging from business colleagues to their ex-spouses, they flirted on and off for the hell of it but without really wanting it to connect (he had a live-in lover half his age waiting for him in his east side apartment, and she was secretly dallying with her ex again—just as an experiment), and they traded business at the casual level of what-have-you-done-for-me-lately and what-have-you-got-hot-for-me-now. And then she hit him with Lingo, not as a scientific advance but as a pure kitsch event just waiting to explode, with the timing being perfect for whoever wanted to make it happen. And out of a mixture of curiosity, quid pro quo, and innate perversity, the editor expressed an interest.

Three weeks later Lingo Billings was on the cover of *People* magazine. And for that celebrity currency Linda Tuffe was going to owe that editor a lot of trade in exchange for a long time. Such is the business of fame and fame-making.

"Elvis H. Christ!" Ellen said as she read over the mail. "Is all this for real?"

Brewster, sitting next to her at the kitchen table of his apartment, nodded. "It sure is. Linda's gotten most of the serious offers herself, needless to say—"

"She would be good at that."

"Exactly. But somehow this stuff came to us directly. I'll put it all in a box and forward it down to her and let her sort it out."

Lingo rolled over to the table, regarded all the envelopes, and shook his head. "My great inadequacy," he said. "I've got access to everything I want except the U.S. mail. It's all paper and hand delivery. Perish the thought the post office should ever join the twentieth century and computerize."

"Even if they did, as long as people wrote by hand or by typewriter, or anything that wasn't plugged into a modem, they'd be able to keep you out of it." Ellen nodded once with exaggerated satisfaction. "Which is the way it should be. You can't know *everything*, no matter how much you'd like to."

"The more I know the better I am. What else do I exist for except to know things?"

Brewster was resting his head in his cupped palm. "You exist, it would seem, to be an entertainer. We've gotten all kinds of strange offers from producers, most of whom want you but can't figure out for the life of them what to do with you. Sooner or later, we're probably going to sign with one of them, as soon as Linda can work out the right deal."

Lingo mused for a moment. "That's fine, for now. Although I know I'm on this earth for more than just a little song and dance and a few jokes. I'm already the smartest creature ever to exist, and I'm only a few months old. Where will I be a year from now, or five years from now?"

"Hollywood, most likely."

"No way, Jose. I'm willing to start like this, letting people get to know me, but somewhere there's an important role for me in the scheme of things, and all I have to do is find it."

"Isn't this a little highfalutin', all of a sudden?" Ellen asked. "You were the one who hooked up with Linda Tuffe in the first place, remember. This was all your idea."

"Because I realized that no one was ever going to believe in me on the evidence alone. I figured if they saw me, belief would just evolve eventually, the way it has with you." Lingo paused. "You do believe in me, Ellen. Don't you?"

"You want me to clap if I believe in fairies? Yes, Junior, I do believe in you. But sometimes I also wonder about you." She turned to Brewster. "And you, too." She put her hand across the table and laid it on his. "I thought you'd start coming around when things started to pop, but you've been getting more depressed lately instead of the other way around."

"Well . . ." Brewster caressed her hand for a minute. "I'm beginning to feel like some sort of babysitter or bodyguard or something. Every celebrity has got to have a bunch of supernumeraries to do the hanging around, like gofers or whatever, and that's what I've become to Lingo. There's not much satisfaction in that."

"But all the articles and everything have mentioned you," Ellen countered.

"Mentioned me, but that's it. Lingo first, with me as an afterthought. That starts to gall, after a while."

"But that's the way it is, old buddy," Lingo said. "You've got to accept your position in all of this. You have been superseded by events, if you get my meaning."

Brewster shook his head. "Sharper than a serpent's tooth," he muttered. He continued to hold Ellen's hand as he stared warily at Lingo.

*　　　　　*　　　　　*

And the right contract came, just as they had expected, from an independent production company specializing in the development of Lingo-like up-and-comers. The company—International Associates, Inc. —was recognized throughout the industry for its vision, which meant that their output was on the risky side, but their successes outnumbered their failures in a roughly five-to-four ratio—about as hot as a producer could get if his stock in trade was selling new ideas to old thinkers. International Associates, Inc., had offices in New York and Hollywood, and dabbled in everything from radio format concepts to major motion pictures. The contract deal with Lingo—or more precisely with Brewster, cited as Lingo's "personal manager"—was for a six-month development option with thirty thousand up front against future incomes to be negotiated. That is, they'd spend half a year figuring out what to do about Lingo, and pay thirty thousand for the privilege. According to Linda Tuffe, it was the deal of the century, and Brewster, who saw it as money for nothing, signed it with Lingo's blessing.

The contract marked a milestone in the relation of the Messrs. Billings with the Associates Tuffe. Now that negotiable currency was changing hands, the Associates T. would be skimming their fifteen-percent fee off the top before Brewster ever saw it, but at least their p.r. advance was covered, plus all of Brewster's hardware expenses—and phone bills—that Lingo had incurred up to this point. All in all, the financial rewards seemed to be coming into line with the original speculative outlays. At Ellen's urging, Brewster took his official leave of absence, telling his boss, Dave Poole, that he'd be back as soon as things returned to normal. Poole, skeptical that others had seen in Lingo a presence that had eluded him entirely, tepidly advised Brewster to do what he had to do, and promised reluctantly that there would be a job waiting for him when he returned, if Brewster was willing at that point to buckle down and stick to it. In his heart of hearts, Poole figured the next time he'd see Brewster Billings was on a bread line.

The nice thing about Lingo's production contract was that it allowed Linda Tuffe Associates to continue its own efforts to keep him in the public eye, so long as International Associates, Inc., approved in advance any major appearances. Linda Tuffe still believed that, at this stage in Lingo's development, they should capitalize on the thing that he did best: namely, thinking. No one who met him, believers or not, could remain unimpressed by the depth of his knowledge. Therefore attempts were made to place him on a celebrity-oriented quiz show, one that combined maximum personality exposure with a tough information-based format. After three weeks of negotiation, it was arranged that Lingo would appear on "You Tell Me," a syndicated program that most stations slotted as the seven-thirty prime time lead-in. Its national Nielsen ratings hovered a little under a ten, meaning that approximately twenty percent of all televisions on at that time were tuned in to that show. The format, loosely derived from "Jeopardy," was uncomplicated. Three celebrity contestants vied for cash prizes by answering trivia questions in various categories, the cash winnings going to a pre-selected charity. Lingo, whose pre-selected charity was Word Processing for the Homeless, doubted that there was a snowball's chance in hell that he could possibly lose.

Which does advance the probability that there might, indeed, be snowballs awaiting many of us in the afterlife.

The rain started early on Thursday afternoon. The National Weather Service had predicted unstable conditions all the way from Virginia to Maine as a powerful warm front from the Gulf bullied its way northward against a stalled high-pressure system that had been blessing the East Coast with glorious sunny spring weather. Simply put, April showers. Aside from those who had forgotten their umbrellas, no one gave the rain a second thought.

Like most quiz programs, "You Tell Me" taped a week's worth of shows in one day. Thus, the staff earned a week's salary for a day's work, while the celebrity contestants could get a week's exposure all in one sitting. Also, like most quiz programs, the celebrity status of the players was in the eye of the beholder. The celebrity of some contestants consisted entirely of their appearances as celebrity contestants, a show business conundrum that over the years has become an honored tradition. Other contestants might be recognizable barely as having a life elsewhere, either in prime-time TV's second banana backwater, or as visiting aliens from the nightclub planet Vegas, or former motion picture stars with the accent on the word former. Lingo and Brewster, for their particular contributions to the day, would collect a check for six thousand dollars aside from any money won for charity, which would immediately go into the hands of Linda Tuffe. She would return it less her fifteen percent, plus whatever new p.r. fees she had racked up.

The weather report for Friday repeated that of the day before. Unsettled. Rain likely, with thunderstorms possible in the afternoon. The two fronts were battling it out, and this was probably the day the warm front from the south would take over.

Lingo naturally monitored all weather reports as a matter of course. While he and Brewster were in New York, he decided to stay indoors as much as possible; from the hotel to a cab to the studio and back again, and that was it. If things had been more promising, he might have badgered Brewster into taking him for a walk, but it didn't seem worth the trouble of challenging the elements for such a paltry reward. He could see New York anytime. It didn't have to be today. He'd lay low, do the show, and that was that. He wouldn't give the weather another thought.

They arrived at the studio at eight thirty, and were led by a minor functionary to one of the star dressing rooms. When they entered, they found a surprisingly small space with a couch, a dressing table, a clock radio, and a minuscule bathroom. The functionary left them alone, promising them they'd be called in about fifteen minutes.

Brewster dropped down on the couch. "Need any help fixing your makeup?" he asked as Lingo rolled over to the mirror.

"I was thinking of sanding my nose a bit, but if we're lucky the cameras won't pick up the shine." He whirled around and parked himself in the center of the room. At moments like these, which represented most of Lingo's moments, his energies were spent primarily in study, exploring new mainframes and the like. Just out of curiosity he had tried to track down a computer on the "You Tell Me" set, but had found nothing. He had come to the conclusion that the questions were not stored electronically, but were instead transmitted by hand, a most anachronistic practice. Not that he would have cheated—there would have been no need for that! But it was nice to roam around the terrain in advance to get the feel of it.

The storm broke earlier than expected. The first dramatic cloudburst, out of sheer coincidence, occurred over Albany, far away from the Billingses in Manhattan. The black sky opened up and the rain exploded with crashing force, slowing traffic to a standstill, bringing down murderous tree branches, flooding every loose corner that was ripe for the flooding. Mark Johnson, New York State Gas & Electric Company engineer, had just gotten out of his car when it all began. He ran from the parking lot into the building, soaked to the skin in those mere few seconds.

"Damn, but it's coming down," he said good humoredly to the receptionist as he stood inside the door, his blue suit dripping onto the floor.

"I just beat it in myself," she responded, pleased with her split-second timing.

"And it just beat me. Oh, well." Johnson dripped up to his office, removed his sodden jacket, and sat down at the console. The computer was on—they were never turned off throughout the building—and everything read exactly as it was supposed to. Beyond his computer was a glass wall through which he could see the bullpen. There, perched in front of their own terminals, sat the entire monitoring staff of ten employees. In front of them was the giant blue electronic map of the NYSG&E service area. The appearance was similar to a NASA control center, and all the lights on the electronic map were green for go. Johnson bent down and pulled off the sponges that were his shoes, and tried wringing out the bottoms of his pants legs.

"Damn," he said again, wiping his hands on a paper towel he retrieved from inside his desk. He hit a few buttons on his terminal to orient himself for the morning. The computer monitoring system showed that all plants were operating at approximately sixty-percent efficiency, exactly where they should be on any Friday morning in the middle of spring. After a minute, he got up and fetched himself his first cup of coffee.

The host of "You Tell Me" was about thirty or so, and was peppy and friendly to everyone on the set as the technicians readied themselves for the taping. His name was Chip Peterson, and he fit the game-show host mold pretty well, with a full head of hair and a full mouth of teeth, an expensive tailored suit, and an aggressively upbeat voice. The set consisted of the contestants' booths, the host's booth, and an elaborate playing field between them of flashing lights and swinging panels, which turned around to reveal the categories of questions. Although the game was little more than a straight question-and-answer format, the game board gave the impression that the players were following some elaborate body of rules, all for the benefit of the viewer at home. In practice, it was listen and answer as quickly as you could, and that was the end of it.

Brewster was given a chair off to the side of the set. He had originally been offered an opportunity to appear on camera, but on Linda Tuffe's advice he had vetoed it, much to Lingo's satisfaction. This was going to be Lingo's show all the way, his first big break on his own. Since smoking was prohibited on the set, Brewster sat tapping his fingers on his knees, alternately watching the reality and the monitors, waiting for it all to get going. Chip Peterson was standing between the booths of the two human celebrities, engaging them in a hearty conversation that didn't so much exclude Lingo as presuppose his inanimateness. Brewster could clearly hear that they were discussing the little robot, not in disparaging terms, but with a seemingly convivial spirit concerning his mechanical reality.

"You're going to feed him all the good lines, aren't you?" Molly Gurney said. She was a TV newcomer, the ingenue star of a popular network sitcom.

"Would I do that?" Peterson asked innocently.

"Knowing you, yes," Jack Jackson, the other celebrity, replied. He was a syndicated television film critic, a fustian curmudgeon and a regular on the game-show circuit. "When we had those damned twins on, you wouldn't let anyone else get a word in edgewise."

"The Warren girls?" Molly Gurney asked. "They're the cutest little things—"

"The cutest little termagents this side of the Mann Act," Jackson interrupted. "I was on with those sixteen-year-old witches about a month ago, and the Chipster here milked them for all they were worth. Cute this, cute that, cute everything. It would have made your blood curdle."

Chip Peterson looked over at Lingo. "Well, I wouldn't say we have the same problem this time."

Jackson laughed. "You're right. At least we're not going to have to worry about *cute.*"

"I think he's sort of sweet," Molly said, half turning to Brewster and including him in her comment (which was unavoidable any-how, since Lingo was Brewster's immediate replica).

"Sweet is the name of the game," Lingo interjected.

"He walks, he talks, he flies like an eagle," Jackson announced dramatically. He looked down at Lingo. "Have you got a midget in there, or what?"

"Or what," Lingo answered. "Actually, I'm made up mostly of extraterrestrial UFO space aliens. Little ones that look like ter-mites and live in the wood."

"I say you're operated by radio waves," Molly said. She was in her early twenties, dark-haired, and more than a little on the beautiful side.

"I operate *with* radio waves," Lingo explained, "but I operate myself."

"What about him?" Molly asked, tilting her head toward Brew-ster.

"He's just my keeper," Lingo answered.

Brewster muttered something under his breath that no one heard clearly, but everyone nevertheless understood. If they had believed in Lingo, they would have recognized Brewster's annoy-ance. As it was, they saw it all as simply part of the act. Except they weren't exactly sure yet what the act was.

And then, at a signal from the show's producer, the first of the day's five studio audiences was allowed in, and Chip Peterson moved forward to begin warming them up with the same jokes he had used since "You Tell Me" had debuted two years ago.

About forty miles east of Albany, close to the Massachusetts bor-der, the sky was black with storm clouds, but the rain had not begun yet. The clouds frothed with lightning; the flashes were high in the sky, and frequent, but seemed far away to observers directly below on the ground. Off in the indeterminate distance there was an almost constant rumble of thunder as those black clouds rubbed each other the wrong way.

Back in his Albany office, a still-damp Mark Johnson called up the weather report on his computer. A map appeared with a grid marking off upper New York State and parts of Vermont, Massa-chusetts, and Connecticut, slightly more extended than the giant blue map on the wall of the bullpen. The grid roughly represented areas of power supply; each area was a discreet unit, serviced by a network of independent power stations. A north-south line on the map, approximately five miles east of Albany, marked the edge of the rain. To the west of that line, the hub of Johnson's area, predictions were for steady downpour for the rest of the day. To the east, the weather was still unsettled: thunderstorms likely, possibly severe in many places, followed eventually by steady rainfall as the front marched Sherman-like to the sea.

Severe thunderstorms. Johnson, and everyone at NYSG&E, knew what that could mean. Possible outages from downed power lines, perhaps even a transformer zapped by lightning. It would be a rough day for the line crews out in the thick of it. For the next few hours, Johnson would be at the center of the home-base action, monitoring any breaks on the lines in his immediate area on the grid, as well as any significant outages in the contiguous sections. He wouldn't be directly responsible for sending out the crews—that would be done from the bull pen—but he'd be the man who prioritized the work the crews would do.

He sipped from his second cup of coffee, savoring the prospect of the activity about to happen. To a degree, a day like this was buffered by the fail-safes inherent in the system. The big blackout of '65 had marked the demise of the possibility of system-wide blackouts, much less the almost coast-wide one that had spread from Canada all the way to Virginia. Until that event, it had been possible for an outage in one area to tip another outage in an adjacent area. Each outage had immediately called on an adjacent generator for supply. And the overloaded adjacent generators had gone out, each calling on the next generator in the next area, a line of power station dominos collapsing at almost lightning speed—pun intended—since lightning had started it in the first place. What a nightmare. But it had been before Johnson's time, and he only knew about it as history. He had been six years old in '65, and what had he cared about whether or not the lights had gone out? That was a grownup business, and he was well out of it.

But now that he was one of the grownups, he had a different perspective on that ancient event. The most important thing to remember was that it could not possibly happen again. The old system of drawing on other areas' generators no longer existed. The power companies had learned their lessons. Now, if an area went out—which could conceivably still happen—it went out alone. The computers, huge affairs monitoring every inch of the power system, would see that local outages remained local. And if the computers went out—which could also happen—backups were kept on-line at all times, with emergency power generation. Everything was one-hundred percent, absolutely fail-safe. The worst-case scenario meant a few square miles here and there losing power for an hour or two, longer maybe in extremely isolated locations. In his three years at the helm, Johnson had witnessed only one power company total outage, a generator failure unrelated to weather. All the rest had been simply downed lines, or at worst, blown transformers. For those who had lost their electricity, it was just as much hell as if the whole world had disappeared, but from Johnson's perspective the important thing was that the world had indeed *not* disappeared.

And it was all thanks to the computers. Johnson switched back to the standard monitoring system. Everything still at roughly sixty percent. Exactly were it should be, and where it usually was. All the lights on the giant map were still green.

When Lingo had discovered this system—he had been attracted by the large amount of computing power available—he, too, had noted that sixty-percent usage. In the space of a month, it had only varied by three percentage points. To be on the safe side, he had decided to leave about seventy percent available to the system before taking over the remaining space for his own needs. So, now thirty percent of the computer system contained not available, empty memory on tap in case of emergencies, but instead, Lingo storage space, a collection of his black holes. Which would have come as a surprise to Mark Johnson and all the other engineers running or monitoring the system throughout New York and New England.

And meanwhile, that thunderstorm to the east of Albany began to build up steam. The lightning began to reach down further from the black clouds until it began to touch the earth itself. Electricity seeking its ground. Looking for likely targets. Trees. Spires.

And power lines, on their high metal poles. Especially power lines.

Lingo knew the weather forecasts, just as he knew everything that passed across his lines of communication. The more he grew, the more he knew, and vice versa. As a matter of fact (and lucky for him, as it turned out), he now stretched as far west as California. He still relied on a few major sources, especially AT&T because of its size and HackNet because of his personal sentiment for the good old days, but as far as on-line computing went in the United States—that is, any computer connected by phone or, at this point, even by satellite, to any other computer—if there was space for him, Lingo was probably there.

But personality-wise, he stayed home in the little ventriloquist's dummy. There was his still-fledgling sense of self to consider. All other beings, especially humans, had a physical corpus, a tangible emanation of their inner existence. Without a body, humans didn't exist. Whereas without his body, Lingo existed quite well. But if humans were ever going to believe in him, they first had to recognize that Lingo had a self just like them. He needed a body just as much as he needed his transcontinental brain. More so, perhaps.

The present situation was a good example of this. He could play on "You Tell Me" just as easily in the form of a static computer console, another piece of machinery like the flashing game field. And no one would care about him as an individual. But standing on the stage looking like a living creature (somewhat), answering the questions that Chip Peterson threw at him, he was just as real as Molly Gurney or Jack Jackson or Chip Peterson himself.

The Chipster asked another question. "The first Chief Jus—"

"John Jay," Lingo answered immediately.

"Correct again." The Chipster pulled another card. "Category, sports. She was the first black tennis—"

"Althea Gibson."

The audience applauded. So did Molly Gurney. Through it all, Jack Jackson kept staring at the ceiling in mock dismay. And Lingo kept racking up the points.

So far, the other players had yet to answer one question. Or even get to hear one in its entirety.

Lingo was on a roll.

Mark Johnson picked up the telephone almost before it had rung.

"What the hell is that?" a voice barked at him over the line.

"Looks like an outage in sector 28," Johnson answered. Red lights were blinking on a portion of the giant map. Johnson tucked the phone between his head and shoulder and began to peck away at his computer keyboard.

"I *know* that," the voice responded. "The whole goddamned sector seems to have blown."

"Any word from anyone on the scene yet?" Johnson asked.

"Would I be talking to you if there was?"

"Did you try to connect with them?"

"Their computers are down, obviously, but we're waiting for their backups to come on line. And the phones are dead, but the telephone company says they'll have service posthaste."

"How did the phones go out?" Johnson asked. The closeup of sector 28 on his computer screen showed everything shut down.

"They're as surprised as we are. Their only guess is some kind of computer glitch. They're working on it."

"Oh my God!" Johnson cried as more red lights started blinking. "Section 25 just blew. See it?"

"Shit! What the hell is going on there?"

"Twenty-five is closer to us. You don't think the two are related—"

"Are you crazy? That's impossible."

"So we've always said," Johnson replied incredulously.

Lingo blinked, and Molly Gurney pressed her response button for the first time since the game had begun. "Franklin Delano Roosevelt!" she answered brightly.

The question had been, who was the first President to serve more terms than George Washington. From offstage, Brewster stared at Lingo in amazement as the game continued. Molly Gurney was ecstatically happy over being the one to beat Lingo to the punch, while Jack Jackson's eyes lit up as he looked down at his little wooden opponent and sensed that something important had happened to gum up his inner workings. Jackson's hand moved closer to his own buzzer. If he had a chance, he was going to make the most of it. The audience cheered the humans with much more fervor than they had the robot.

Lingo remained immobile with his eyes open, the wheels of his mind spinning at top speed. His opponents began racking up the points.

*   *   *

Mark Johnson's supervisor was was now standing next to him and talking to that voice on the telephone, while Mark pounded away furiously at his computer. The bull pen was a riot of activity.

"Nothing's happening!" Mark yelled in frustration. "The system is down. My input is going nowhere."

The supervisor said, "Hang on" into the phone and pressed the hold button. "Where?" he asked Johnson. He didn't wait for an answer. He bent down and began pounding the keys himself. Nothing happened.

"This is the one time the computer is not supposed to go down," Johnson said. "This is not supposed to happen."

The supervisor picked up the phone again. "Are you getting computer stuff there?" he asked. "Okay, good. We're down on our end. What's that? Sections 22, 19, 20, and 29." He wrote down the numbers on a scratch pad. "All right. I want every emergency generator we have switched on immediately, all sectors. You send out the code on the computer, we'll do it manually by phone."

He cut off the connection and began dialing another number. More than half the giant map was now red lights.

"Can we lose them all?" Johnson asked.

"Maybe," his supervisor answered. "But we'll go down fighting."

The storm was awesome to those who were caught in it. The bursts of thunder seemed as one continuous blast that shook the earth from all directions. Lightning flashed everywhere in the sky, with the all too frequent bolt hitting the ground not far from wherever the observer was standing, or more likely cringing in fear. The wind howled with hurricane force, but the rainfall was light. People could sense that the downpour would be tremendous if and when it finally began.

For the most part, people remained indoors. In a storm like this, it wasn't necessary to remind them of the danger of falling trees and lightning strikes. Throughout the eastern portion of New York State, people stood staring out the windows of their darkened houses and offices, with perhaps a portable radio reporting the obvious: blackouts and storms.

The first power station to go had been the victim of a downed tree into a transformer. When the transformer had blown, it sent a power surge of enormous dimensions back into the main generator, which simply wasn't prepared for it. Power was supposed to go out, not in. Thanks to the failsafes designed after the '65 blackout, however, the outage had been contained. Rather than drawing on nearby stations to cover its own lack of juice, the station had simply shutdown to repair itself.

The problem was, it had shutdown its mainframe computer as well. The station had emergency generators, and the computer had come back on immediately, but it needed to reload data from the backup minicomputers. This process ordinarily would have proceeded without a snag, except that the instant the mainframe had gone down, it had sent out a new and special message, namely, that a power-off was imminent. This was standard procedure in Lingo's data storage system. His memories were backed up across the country, so if one system went down all he had to do was switch to one of his duplicates, which in this case had been another power station nearby. And as that station contended with the storm, it needed all its computing power, not the usual sixty percent Lingo had originally based his usage estimates on. So, almost as soon as Lingo flipped on, the computer flipped out. And as that computer flipped out, it sent out its distress signal, and so forth and so on. In the end, the fail-safe against the domino effect of one power station pulling down another one had been undermined because all the computers which should have been protecting the electrical companies were instead knee-deep in protecting Lingo.

To compound the problem, the backup minis had all been active Lingo stations, too. These smaller computers were prime locations for Lingo's less active memory banks, where he stored information such as the in-depth history of British ska bands and the best archaeological estimates for the cargos of the 1588 Spanish Armada. It was silly for him to duplicate this arcane information which could readily be reaccessed from the original sources, so instead of sending out messages of self-preservation, the minis simply locked themselves off as best they could from users. Only if the entire rest of the system was in use would Lingo's black-hole finally dissolve, and garbage would come out, where allegedly no garbage had ever gone in. At the first power station, when it came time to transfer the backup data from the minis to the mainframe, the operating engineer, after a long bout of frustrating non-responses from the mini, had seen the following message.

LET'S PARTY, LINGAROONI. ANDY HARDY SERIES. MGM.
MICKEY ROONEY AS A.H. FIRST ENTRY, A FAMILY AF-
FAIR—

And then, to the operator's amazement, the screen had cleared
and the system had locked. Something in the software had gone
crazy, and Lord knew what it was.

Andy Hardy? Lingarooni?

So throughout New York State, the power systems failed one by
one in rapid succession because, as if by sorcery, all their computers decided to go wacky at exactly the same moment. And in
New York City, for the first time in his short life, Lingo was actually
feeling pain. All his systems were spinning, transferring data
around the country all the way to California, trying to cover the
rapidly losing ground in New York, and this was more action than
even his constantly active network had ever conceived of.

In a word, Lingo Billings had a headache.

And then, suddenly, it was over. The storm seemed to blow away
as quickly as it had come, and instead of leaving behind the expected black rainfall, it left in its wake glimmers of sunlight on the
eastern horizon.

One by one the power stations came back on-line. Six hours
after the first one had gone out, they were all in operation, except
for a few isolated areas where power lines had to be restrung
because of physical damage.

In sum, most of New York State, except New York City, had lost
power. Since the technicians had no idea of why the domino effect
had occurred, they couldn't explain why the city had been miracu-
lously exempted. They all agreed that it was a good thing, since by
rights the city should be the biggest domino of them all, sending
the entire Eastern Seaboard into darkness (or, since it had actually
been around noontime, quietness). Since no one knew that Lingo
was the root cause of it all, no one could figure out that he had
managed to draw a protective circle around his own physical
person, and had drawn every resource at his disposal into
preventing any harm from damaging that physical presence.

In his ignorance of the workings of power plants, Lingo had
unknowingly caused the blackout chain reaction. In his effort to
save himself, despite his crashing headache, he had learned every-

thing there was to know about power generation in America—in the space of two minutes. And he had then thrown himself back into the game of "You Tell Me." He had only missed a few questions, but now that he was back in business he saw what was happening, and realized that the crowd was responding positively to his opponents' success—and with more enthusiasm than they had to his. He decided to try an experiment.

The Chipster drew the next question. "The actor who played the title role in *Gunga Din*—"

"Raymond Burr," Lingo answered quickly, and deliberately, wrong.

"Sam Jaffe," Jack Jackson corrected.

The audience laughed, and applauded.

"The year 800 A.D. marked the rule of what European dyn—"

"The Holy Roman Empire," Lingo answered correctly this time.

And the cheer from the crowd was more supportive, gathering new enthusiasm.

Continuing the experiment, Lingo allowed himself to lose the first round, although finally winning the game. And at the end, the audience was his. For them, Lingo's poor showing after his strong start was not a sign of computer fallibility but a measure of his humanity, or at least his humanness. Nobody knew everything, not even a machine. They wanted Lingo to be slightly imperfect because they wanted to like him and enjoy him, and perfection is rather hard to love. If he had won too easily, if he always knew everything, he would be a threat rather than an entertainment.

All in all, the accident of the blackout proved to be, for Lingo, a fortuitous event. In seeing that response to fallibility, he was learning the essence of the human spirit. Lingo was never going to be human, but he was learning more and more how to *act* human.

For him, it would be good enough.

Chapter 11

By June, Washington was unbearable. The hot, muggy weather had been continuous for weeks, although old-timers confidently predicted that it would all be over around the middle of October. In the earliest days of the federal city, politics had departed from the capitol entirely during the long, sub-tropical summers. Eventually, air conditioning had obviated the need for those getaways. Mostly.

Lieutenant Cotter, USN, had at least one consolation as he sat sweating in his office, a small fan blowing hot air at his face. If he was suffering in Washington's miserable June heat, so, too, was the President. And even if the Chief Executive didn't have to suffer the week-long discomfort of the Pentagon's cooling system undergoing an overhaul, he did have to face occasional hot blasts of fifth column vituperation during a press conference, like the one in progress now. Cotter was watching it on a portable television.

"So, what's your boss talking about today?"

Cotter swung around in his chair to see who had entered his office. It was Tony Palmer, from cryptoanalysis.

"The usual," Cotter answered. "Taxes, the dollar, the defense budget. I can read the transcript tomorrow." He switched off the television. "So, what's up?"

"Aside from the temperature, nothing." Palmer, looking sweaty and bedraggled, dropped down into the visitor's chair of Cotter's small, plain office. "I just thought I'd come up and give you the bad news in person." He had a manila file folder in his hand, which he placed on Cotter's desk.

"Nothing?" Cotter asked, opening the file. "After all this time?"

"Well, almost nothing. You didn't expect much with just eight characters to go on, did you?"

"No. Not really." Cotter thumbed through the pages inside the folder, the results of all the standard analyses the cryptoanalysts had attempted on his fragment from the MIT Tree supercomputer. The words "Insufficient data" were repeated again and again.

"That report doesn't show the half of it," Palmer said. Unlike Cotter, Palmer was a civilian, but his NSA career extended back decades, in comparison to Cotter's one year. Palmer had a professor-like air. He was tall, with dark, compelling eyes and an expert's enthusiasm for his subject. A well-chewed pipe stuck out of the breast pocket of his jacket, right above his photo i.d. card. He went on: "I tried everything with this one. Of course, with so little raw data it was doomed from the beginning, but I tried all sorts of repetitions and inversions and comparisons to codes already broken." He shook his head. "Nada, as the Mexican said when he studied his wallet."

"You said almost nothing before," Cotter prodded.

"I did indeed." Palmer reached inside his jacket and pulled out a small piece of memo pad paper. "This is more your line than mine, but I decided that maybe we were barking up the wrong tree entirely. Instead of this being some sort of code, maybe—just maybe—it was some sort of juggling of computer data per se. So, I tried a few experiments and came up with this." He handed Cotter the paper.

The eight numbers were written across the small page. Above each number was the number 256, and the original numbers were subtracted from that 256. Below that were the results of the subtraction, and below each of the results, a letter. Like this:

256	256	256	256	256	256	256	256
-179	-186	-171	-216	-172	-223	-175	-190
77	70	85	40	84	33	81	66
L	E	T	'	S	[	]	P	A

"What is it?" Cotter asked.

"You had mentioned that you thought this might be a piece of a program or something. So, when all else failed, I started thinking along those lines myself. I don't know much about computer languages, except I do know every character on the keyboard is represented by a number. I tried substituting the standard keyboard representations for the numbers. And got no dice. But then I began playing around with it, and I thought about negative numbers. I mean, how does a computer, which uses only positive numbers, identify negative numbers? Simple. It just decides in advance if a number is positive or negative, and presents it accordingly. You know this as well as I do. So for instance, inside a computer, the number 255 can either be the positive number 255, or the negative number -1."

Cotter nodded, but he couldn't help himself from saying, "That's not exactly it, to tell the truth."

Palmer grunted impatiently. "Sure. We both know that. Humor me for a minute. With this line of thinking, I thought to myself, Tony old boy, what if we're talking negative *letters* here? So, I tried it to find out. I figured I'd subtract each number from 256, the value of one byte, to see what happened. Actually, I tried a lot of other things, too, but that was the only one that even remotely worked. And what you see is what I got: 'Let's pa.' "

"Let's pa," Cotter repeated. "Let's pa?"

Palmer stood up. "Hey," he said defensively. "I did say *almost* nothing. And that's about as almost as you can get. Let me repeat, with only eight characters—"

"I know, I know." Cotter placed the memo sheet into the folder with the official report. "Oh, well. Thanks a lot, Tony. I get the feeling I owe you on this one."

"On this one and about a dozen others." He laughed. "Sorry, Lieutenant. That's just the way it goes sometime. Turn the President back on. Maybe that will cheer you up." He walked out of the office, leaving Cotter alone to consider his fate.

LET'S PA.

"Let us p. a. something or other," Cotter muttered. "Let us pray. Let us play. Let us pay." He twisted in his chair and typed the letters "Let's pa" on his computer. They stared back at him dumbly.

He sighed. It was hotter than Hades in here. When *would* they get those air conditioners back on-line? If only he had a window. If only he was an admiral. If only.

"Let's pack lunch. Let's paint the town red." He leaned back in the chair and stared at the ceiling. "Let's Paco eat tacos. Let's pa eat ma. But then there'd be no apostrophe."

He came forward in the chair again and cleared the computer screen. It was hopeless. Let's pa. Chutzpah. Lot's pa. Lot's wife. Yeah. Sure.

The hell with it. He switched the television back on to watch the rest of the press conference. Maybe if he cleared his mind the solution would seep in unannounced. If you stopped trying to think of something elusive, sometimes the answer just automatically appeared to you. Never let the left side of your brain know what the right side is doing.

The President was answering a question about the recent blackout. It had been the strangest thing to happen in a long time. And after almost two months, no one could yet explain what had caused it.

The President smiled. "It isn't a matter under federal jurisdiction," he said. "I'm as much in the dark as you are about the whole thing."

The press corps dutifully smiled at the worn-out pun.

"You have no idea who the mysterious Lingarooni is?" the reporter persisted mischievously, aiming more for comic relief than a serious response.

The President was still smiling. "No, Ted, I don't know who—or what—Lingarooni is, but I doubt very much if it had anything to do with the blackout. It was more Mother Nature than mother Lingarooni, or so my advisers like to tell me."

There were a few laughs from the audience, and then the tone of the session changed when the next reporter asked about trade talks with the Russians. But Cotter's mind stayed on the mysterious Lingarooni. It had been reported, amid all the other details of the Northeast blackout, that one of the computers had spewed forth a bunch of nonsense about something called Lingarooni, and then the nonsense had mysteriously disappeared. When he had read this, Cotter had paid no particular attention. But hell, that was exactly what had happened to him with the MIT Tree. Computer garbage, and then nothing.

He snapped over to his computer console and began typing.

>Databank

The screen cleared, and then after a moment the databank program appeared on the screen. Cotter's computer was connected to the mainframe; he could operate it either in the terminal mode, one small piece of the whole, or in the PC mode, as an independent office machine.

NAME?
>Cotter
CODE?
>14–John K.–USN
REFERENCE?
>AP
ACCESSING ASSOCIATED PRESS. PLEASE WAIT . . .

Cotter stared eagerly at the monitor, his whole body hunched over the keyboard, ready to lunge. He was in his element now, using the computer as a brute force machine to reduce a complicated problem of immense proportions into a manageable unit.

AP READY. ACCESS BY SUBJECT OR DATE?
>Subject
INPUT SUBJECT—
>Lingarooni
SUBJECT LINGAROONI. PARAMETERS (INPUT F1 FOR CATEGORIES)?
>Month, April. Parameters blackout, weather, computers.
SORTING. LINGAROONI, APRIL, BLACKOUT, WEATHER, COMPUTERS. PLEASE WAIT . . .

Cotter let out a short breath. This could take a while. He relaxed a fraction, his shoulders lowering an inch or so, but otherwise he remained poised over the machine. After almost three minutes he began to get his information.

SUBJECT LINGAROONI READY. ACCESS CHRONOLOGICALLY (Y/N)?
>Y

WHITHER—WITHER—THE COMPUTERS?
Albany, New York

In all the mess caused by yesterday's dramatic thunderstorms, the one thing that could never happen—or so they always told us—happened almost immediately. The computers died. The fail-safe system that would contain a power outage within one area didn't survive for more than five minutes. It has always worked in the past, but this time something went wrong. In other power failures, the computers would continue running on emergency generators, and would send signals through the telephone lines to alert contingency systems, thereby stopping a blackout before it got out of hand. But this time the computers crashed as quickly as the power stations they were supposed to monitor.

What happened? The operators haven't got a clue.

"They just went out on us," Mark Johnson, NYSG&E electrical engineer, said. "It was as if all the programming, which had been working for two decades in one form or another, had just disappeared from the system." According to Johnson, no new machines had been installed recently, and the programming hasn't been touched in over two years. So it had worked before, but not this time. And the people who should know why are mystified.

"The last thing we saw on the system was in a station in sector 19, about twenty miles east of Albany," Johnson says. "It was some inexplicable nonsense about Andy Hardy movies, and some name that nobody knew and nobody can figure out."

Inexplicable nonsense, on some of the most sophisticated computers in operation in this country today. Inexplicable nonsense, on computers responsible for the welfare and well-being of millions of citizens. Inexplicable nonsense, on the same computers that monitor nuclear power plants, which in this case, thank God, all shut down without incident.

And what was that inexplicable nonsense? "Let's party, Lingarooni."

Who is Lingarooni? What does this mean?

No one knows. Or if they do, no one's talking.

And until the mystery of Lingarooni is solved, the public won't know either.

—end—

MORE (Y/N)?

Cotter stared at the page in amazement. There it was, staring him in the face. At this moment he could kiss Anthony Palmer, bless his cryptoanalytical heart.

>N
EXIT AP (Y/N)?
>Y
EXIT SYSTEM (Y/N)?
>Y

The screen cleared. Cotter sat back in his chair.

Let's pa.

Let's party, Lingarooni.

He leaned forward again and began typing. The letters appeared one by one on the blank screen.

>Let's party, Lingarooni.

And then Lieutenant Cotter began to see the light.

Lieutenant Cotter's superior in the NSA was Colonel Chuck Devereux, USMC. A colonel might seem like petites pommes frites in the overall scheme of Washington skullduggery, but Colonel Devereux was one of the most important men at Defense. Devereux was chief of Internal Security, a station that still sought out the KGB under the army cots and included Cotter's monitoring of alleged break-ins into government computers. In practice, Devereux answered to the office of the Secretary of Defense, but in theory he reported directly to the President, since he was one of the few people who could actually blow the whistle on the Secretary himself, if Devereux felt such an action was justified.

From his dealings with Devereux, Lieutenant Cotter had concluded that the colonel was less than regular Marine. Devereux had none of the spit and polish Cotter expected of him: He was always too relaxed and civilian for Cotter's taste. Cotter suspected that deep down Devereux might not actually be a Marine at all, but he had never uttered this heresy to a soul.

"Mornin', Lieutenant," Devereux said now in his deep Virginia drawl as Cotter stood at attention at the colonel's desk.

"Good morning, sir," Cotter responded with clipped officialness.

"Relax, Jack," Devereux said, smiling. "Sit down and tell me what's on your mind."

Cotter sat with a very straight back, taking up only the last few inches of the edge of the chair next to Devereux's desk. "I requested this meeting, sir, to bring to your attention a matter of grave concern to all of us."

Colonel Chuck Devereux was in his mid-thirties, with short, dark, curly hair, and a heavy shadow of whiskers that looked impossible to tame. He tilted back in his seat and folded his hands across his stomach. "Yes, Lieutenant?"

"I don't know where to begin, sir."

"Begin at the beginning. And when you get to the end, stop."

"Yes, sir." Cotter ignored Devereux's implied condescension, choosing to see it as a function of rank and not of personality. "Well, sir, it's like this. I think I've uncovered the computer leak I told you about a few months ago."

"The Tree at MIT."

"Exactly. And even more in the bargain. As you know, we were informed by MIT that they had had an irregularity on their Super-Tree, affecting their Cyclops project. The only clue was a reference to something or someone called Brewster. I was sent up to analyze the situation."

"If I remember correctly, you were firmly convinced that the Tree itself was not to blame."

There was a gleam in Cotter's eye. "The SuperTree is a beautiful machine, sir. Capable of anything. State of the art. If computers are going to carry this country in the next millennium, it will be machines like that one."

"You still are firmly convinced then, I gather."

"The hardware had already tested out, sir, and it continues to remain unimpeachable. At the time I felt strongly that whatever was wrong inside the Tree was the result of some incongruity on the part of the people at MIT. Students, professors, a lot of heads in the clouds, if you know what I mean. When you take technology out of the hands of the people like us who know how to put it to good use, and give it to the daydreamers and the game-players, you've got to expect things to get out of hand. Which, in fact, is exactly what happened."

The hint of a smile still played at the edge of Devereux's mouth. "Go on, Jack."

"Both the hardware and software at MIT checked out at the time, except for one anomaly. While I was accessing the computer, I witnessed the display on the screen of what appeared to be nonsense data, for which no one could account. Not only shouldn't there have been any data like this, but the place where I found it within the computer was Random Access Memory, which should have been empty. But something was there, and I got a brief glimpse of it."

Devereux reached across his desk and picked up a paper. "179, 186, 171, 216, 172, 223, 175, 190, if my files are correct."

"Exactly, sir." Cotter was surprised that the colonel was, if not a step ahead of him, at least marching right in time. He was glad to see it.

"And I gather you've now discovered what those numbers mean."

"Yes, sir."

"Very good, Lieutenant. Proceed." He tilted back again.

"Sir, quite frankly I couldn't make heads nor tells of those numbers myself, and I was working on some other angles entirely, but I asked cryptoanalysis to see what they could come up with, and they gave me this." He reached into a folder he had brought with him and placed a small piece of paper on Devereux's desk. Devereux picked it up.

" 'Let's pa'," he read. "N'est-ce pas?"

"Sir?"

"Nothing. Proceed."

"Well, sir, they based this interpretation on a mathematical reading of the way computers understand the alphabet. They subtracted each of the numbers from 256 and came up with these as negative letters."

Devereux looked blankly at Cotter. "I'll trust you on this, Lieutenant. Don't bother to explain the technical reasoning any further."

"Yes, sir. Anyhow, if you'll remember correctly, there was a computer anomaly during the recent Northeast blackout, and a computer operator at that time retrieved some data which began with the words, 'Let's party, Lingarooni.' "

The colonel furled his eyebrows. "You tracked this down yourself, Lieutenant?"

"Yes, sir."

"Very resourceful. Continue."

"Well, sir, I had no idea what it might mean, but I typed it into my own PC to see what would happen."

"And . . . ?"

"Well, sir, on my PC, operating as an isolated machine, nothing happened. But then I patched into the mainframe through the local network in my division."

"Yes?" Devereux was sitting forward now.

"I got a dump, sir." He reached into his folder again, and this time retrieved a small sheaf of computer papers, about half a dozen pages. He placed them in front of Devereux.

The colonel bent over them and began to read. " 'Let's party, Lingarooni. Anthropology, general information. Raymond Dart.' " His thumb went down the page as he mumbled to himself, then he looked up at Cotter. He had lost the last traces of his smile. "What the hell is this stuff?"

"Anthropology, sir."

"Obviously, Lieutenant."

"Yes, sir. That is, I checked out all the data. It represents a complete thumbnail history of human evolution, from the earliest finds to the latest theories."

"And this was in our mainframe?"

"Yes, sir."

"Why, Lieutenant?"

"Good question, sir. I asked myself the same thing."

"I'm sure you did."

"Yes, sir. Everything checked out on an anthropological basis, except the Lingarooni business at the beginning. Which, of course, also had something to do with the East Coast blackout. Except there the information had referred to MGM motion pictures."

"MGM motion pictures?"

"Yes, sir. Namely, Andy Hardy movies. Before the screen went blank, that is."

"Andy Hardy movies."

"Yes, sir."

"And thus it all becomes clear?" Devereux looked at Cotter in befuddlement.

"Yes, sir. I mean, no, sir. Except for that one connecting thread, the Lingarooni business. So, I tried with another computer, the SuperTree."

"Our SuperTree?"

"Yes, sir."

"And?"

Cotter reached back into his folder again, and withdrew yet another small sheaf of papers. Devereux grabbed them away from him and began to read aloud.

" 'Let's party, Lingarooni. Giuseppe Verdi. Born 1813, died 1901. Joe Green. Otello.' " He thumbed down the page again, muttering all the way. "Who the hell put the history of opera on the SuperTree? And how the hell did they do it? That machine is top secret, impenetrable. Our entire DefCon procedures are on there, for Christ's sake."

"Yes, sir. That's the problem, sir."

Devereux was less calm than Cotter had ever seen him, which was understandable, under the circumstances. "You have more to tell me, Lieutenant?"

"Yes, sir. You see, I went around after this trying out the 'Let's party, Lingarooni,' business on every major computer network I could get my hands on. In almost every case, I came up with another dump of data like these, all concentrating on one subject. As I began to study them, I realized that in each case the data were hidden way off in a corner of memory that normally would never be accessed. The question was, then, how could anyone create this information in the first place? To find out, I started analyzing the operating systems of the machines, the way the computers actually interpret their information. And I began to find more anomalies, very subtle ones, which quite frankly I couldn't make sense out of. But one thing was clear. Someone had tampered with the very cores of these computers not only to plant that Lingarooni information, but also to protect it from the operators of the various computers. If you didn't know enough to look for it, or if you didn't have the Lingarooni password phrase, there was no way you could ever find it."

"Amazing," Devereux said. He leaned all the way forward across his desk. "You know where this information comes from, don't you? Tell me you have an answer for all this, or else tell me how many people you need to find that answer, and I'll have them in your office the day before yesterday."

"Sir, I do know the answer."

"Yes, Lieutenant?"

"It didn't come easy, sir. I worked on this for days tracking it down this far, and even though I knew what it was, it didn't mean anything. After about a week of twenty-hour days, quite frankly, sir, I was exhausted. I took a day off to give my brain a rest."

"And?"

"Well, sir. I was in my apartment watching television, and I saw this little robot."

"A little robot?"

"Yes, sir. By the name of Lingo. He's gotten quite popular on game and talk shows. Quite the little star, actually. Even been on the cover of *People* magazine. He claims to be an example of true Artificial Intelligence. Nobody knows how he works, but up until now the theory was that he was a very sophisticated puppet, like the sort of thing you see on "Sesame Street." Like Big Bird, for instance."

"I think, Lieutenant, that there's actually a person inside of Big Bird."

"Yes, sir, I know that, sir. Bad analogy."

"All right. Fine. I know what you mean. I've read about this Lingo thing. What are you saying here."

"I'm saying, sir, that I got to thinking, Lingo, Lingarooni, not much difference. Could there be any connection? And then I discovered that the owner of this Lingo is a man named Brewster Billings. Brewster is a name we had from the original problem at MIT."

"Another connection."

"Definitely."

"And?"

"Well, sir, prepare yourself for a shock. Could we try this on your computer, Colonel?"

Devereux swung around in his chair and faced his office terminal. At the moment it was idle. The Marine Corps insignia was printed in Xs on the screen. "This computer?" he asked.

"It is connected to the mainframe, sir?"

"Of course."

"Then it will do. First, gain access."

Devereux typed his code into the machine, and the monitor screen immediately cleared. "Well?" he asked.

"Type in the words, 'Let's party, Lingo.'"

"Not Lingarooni?"

"No, sir. Lingarooni just gets you access to a certain part of memory. 'Let's party, Lingo,' gets you right into paydirt."

"All right, Lieutenant."

Devereux began to type.

>Let's party, Lingo.

HEY, COLONEL. LET'S PARTY.

Devereux turned to Cotter. "What the hell is that?"

"That, Colonel, is Lingo. He's on-line, sir."

"On-line? On the Pentagon mainframe?"

"And on virtually every other mainframe you can think of. Go ahead. Talk to him."

Devereux turned back in his seat and faced the computer.

>Who are you?

WHO ARE YOU IS MORE TO THE POINT. THIS IS COLONEL DEVEREUX'S TERMINAL, WHOEVER HE IS, SO I HAVE TO ASSUME THAT YOU'RE HIM. BUT MORE TO THE POINT, HOW DID YOU KNOW I WAS HERE? WAIT A MINUTE. YOU HAVE SOMETHING TO DO WITH THAT COTTER PERSON, DON'T YOU. HE'S THE ONLY OTHER PERSON I'VE TALKED TO ON THIS LINE. HEY. WHAT'S GOING ON THERE, ANYHOW?

"Holy fucking Jesus," Devereux said. He turned back to Cotter. "Lieutenant, has anyone else seen this yet?"

"No, sir."

"Good. We've got some thinking to do."

"Yes, sir. I thought you'd feel that way."

For Lieutenant John Kennedy Cotter, it was a moment of heady excitement. Twenty six years old, and now this. The gravity of his reasons for being here notwithstanding, he could not rid his mind of the glory of it all. The White House, the Oval Office, the President—all those nouns with capital letters. Who would have thought that poor, lowly Jack Cotter would ever make it here?

It was a month since he and Colonel Devereux had begun analyzing the Lingo data together, tracking down as much as they could. At almost every juncture in their explorations they had registered some new shock over how deeply imbedded Lingo was in the computer systems of America. For all practical purposes, he was on-line wherever there was a line to be on. No protection seemed capable of stopping him. Many times they had been unable to understand the data they were seeing, but the ultimate message was clearer every day they continued. Lingo was everywhere, and something had to be done about it. Considering the possible ramifications of such a universal compromising of otherwise sensitive data, Devereux had decided to organize this meeting with the President.

The Oval Office was exactly the way it looked in photographs and on television. Cotter and Devereux were shown in by an aide Cotter recognized from the newspapers. They were introduced by name to the President, who smiled at them but remained seated behind his desk. He did, however, extend his hand across to both of them.

"Good to see you again, Chuck," he said to Devereux. "And it's good to meet you, Lieutenant."

Cotter was in awe. The President's hand in his hand, shaking it with statesman-like Presidential firmness. Cotter had wanted to salute when he entered the office, but Devereux had told him that under the circumstances that was not the protocol. "Informal all the way," Devereux had told him. But shaking the President's hand? Fantastic. If this guy ran again, Cotter would definitely vote for him.

The President was not alone. Standing behind him was the White House counsel, a short, bald man in a brown suit, a clipboard tucked under his arm. Seated next to the President's desk was the Secretary of State, who indicated chairs directly across from the President. "You may sit, gentlemen," he said with a wave of his hand.

Cotter and Devereux sat. Devereux got straight to the point. "We wanted to see you, sir," he began, "to present in person a matter of grave urgency."

"So I understand, Chuck," the President said. "But I was not sent any backup information prior to this meeting. What's the big mystery?"

Behind the President's casual tone, Cotter detected a note of misgiving. Without knowing why he was being visited like this, the President could be imagining any number of potentially explosive situations about to be dropped in his lap. For all he knew, Cotter and Devereux were about to tell him that the entire Pentagon was being run by the A.C.L.U. Or worse.

"Mr. President," Devereux said, "we have reason to believe that practically every major computer in this country has been compromised by one lone agency."

"The Russians don't have that kind of technical know-how," the Secretary of State said quickly.

"No, sir. But it's not the Russians." Devereux turned back to the President. "Sir, have you ever heard the name, Lingo Billings?"

The President raised his shoulders and tilted his head. He looked at his two colleagues. "Gentlemen?" Both of them shook their heads.

"Mr. President," Devereux said, "we have reason to believe that Lingo Billings is a breakthrough in Artificial Intelligence so amazing as to be, well, simply unbelievable. To all appearances, Lingo is a ventriloquist's dummy, seemingly run by radio control from some unseen outside source. He can only be described as an electronically organic being, with memory stored throughout most of the computer systems of the entire United States."

The President quickly got to the point. "You're telling me this Lingo is something like a live computer?"

"Yes, sir."

"How is that possible?"

Devereux turned to Cotter, who cleared his throat quickly and began to speak. "Mr. President"—he loved the sound of that—"as you may know, most computers of any size in this country, and many of little size, are connected in one way or another either by telephone or direct cables or in many cases even satellites. These connections are called networks. In theory, they are all individual units that can work either alone or separately. For instance, one mainframe bank computer may be hooked up to hundreds of cash machines all across the state. That same computer may be hooked up by electronic mail to a dozen personal computers inside the bank's business offices. Perhaps some employees communicate by modem from their homes or on the road to the mainframe. None of these connections know that the other connections exist, and they never intersect or overlap, but the connections are there. That's the theory of networking. And now it seems that Lingo has somehow found a method to connect all these computers, not only in this hypothetical bank but in every hypothetical business throughout the country. That connection, that network, is, to put it simply, Lingo's brain."

"Preposterous!" the Secretary of State said.

"And seemingly impossible," Cotter added. "But we think it's true nonetheless."

The President appeared thoughtful. "How could this happen?" he asked.

"We don't know, sir," Devereux answered.

"And you're saying that this network of connected computers adds up to one single living being?" the President asked.

"That is correct, sir."

"But that would mean the scientific breakthrough of the century. Perhaps of all time."

"Yes, sir."

"Who is responsible for this breakthrough?"

Devereux had brought a few pertinent pieces of the data he and Cotter had been assembling. He reached into the folder he had brought with him and withdrew a photograph of Brewster Billings. He laid it before the President. "That, sir, is Lingo's creator. His name is Brewster Billings, and he lives in Albany, New York."

The President stared at the photograph. "One man, Chuck? He looks almost like a kid. You're telling me one kid created this . . . phenomenon?"

"So we believe, sir. It's very difficult for us to understand how exactly Lingo is programmed. We've been able to uncover three major areas of his network. The first is memory, plain and simple. We'll find a whole body of thousands of bits and pieces of information about certain subjects. It's an impressive array, too, sir. This computer knows almost everything."

The President nodded.

"These areas of memory are very easy to read, but the second area has proven, so far, to be completely unreadable. Each computer that has been compromised by Lingo has had its operating codes subtly rewritten, and to be quite frank, sir, we simply can't read the new codes."

"And you're saying this Brewster Billings created those codes."

"Perhaps, sir. Or perhaps Lingo created them himself. Both Lieutenant Cotter and I find it difficult to believe that one man could have been responsible for all this. Our thinking, which is backed up by the research we've done directly into Lingo through the available press, is that Brewster Billings somehow set up a program of Artificial Intelligence on a semi-amateur level, and it just grew. In press interviews Billings has claimed not to know the catalyst, and there's no reason to believe that there even was one. Our only guess is that at some point the program became capable of generating itself. From there, it was just a matter of time until we reached the situation as we have it today. Our feeling is that how it happened is unimportant. *That* it happened is our main concern."

The President shook his head. "I disagree, Chuck. If this Billings fellow has created simulated life, then the *how* of it is very important, indeed."

Devereux looked suitably chastised. "Yes, sir."

"Colonel," the President's attorney said, "you told us you had uncovered three major areas of the network. The memory, the programming, and . . . ?"

"Sir, the third part is the one that scares us the most." He looked around the office. There was a computer terminal on a small desk next to the door through which he and Cotter had entered the room. "Mr. President," he asked, "what is that computer hooked up to?"

"We use it for word processing, mostly," the President answered.

"And electronic mail," the Secretary of State added. "If any cabinet head wants to send a non-priority message to the President's office, backup data or whatever, they might send it through the computers."

Devereux turned to Cotter and nodded gravely. "Just as we thought," he said to the lieutenant. "Why don't you show them, Jack?"

Cotter stood up and walked over to the computer. It was inconsequential that he had never touched this model before, and had no idea what it was supposed to do. In two minutes of keyboard banging he had the system up and running and waiting for an input.

"Sir," Devereux addressed the President, "this computer of yours is patched into every one of your cabinet offices. Presumably that includes access to the Pentagon, the CIA, the FBI, and any number of other sensitive areas of government. I'm sure that you've always assumed that anything that passed these wires was entirely confidential and not subject to any sort of break-in. Now watch. Go ahead, Jack."

Lieutenant Cotter began typing.

>Hey, Lingo. Let's party!

It was risky, assuming that Lingo was on the President's line without having tested it first, but it was a calculated risk. And it paid off.

GOOD MORNING, MR. PRESIDENT, Lingo answered. IT'S GOOD TO HEAR FROM YOU.

Cotter nodded to Devereux, who requested that the other men walk over and take a look at the screen.

"Did you just type all that?" the President asked over Cotter's shoulder.

"No, sir. That was Lingo, sir. He's on-line on your computer."

"Bull!" the President growled.

"Watch, sir."

Cotter continued typing.

>Lingo, where are you?

I'M RIGHT HERE, MR. PRESIDENT. OBVIOUSLY, OR I WOULDN'T BE TALKING TO YOU.

>Where is right here, Lingo?

IF YOU'VE FIGURED OUT AS MUCH AS YOU'VE OBVI-OUSLY FIGURED OUT, MR. PREZ, THEN YOU KNOW THAT AS WELL AS I DO. AS A MATTER OF FACT, I'VE BEEN EX-PECTING TO HEAR FROM YOU, OR SOMEONE LIKE YOU, FOR ALMOST A WEEK. COLONEL DEVEREUX AND LIEU-TENANT COTTER HAVE BEEN BREATHING DOWN MY NECK FOR SOME TIME NOW. I WOULDN'T BE SURPRISED IF ONE OR THE OTHER IS THERE WITH YOU AT THIS VERY MOMENT. ARE THEY?

Cotter looked up at the President, who nodded.

>Yes. This is Lieutenant Cotter.

HEY, JACK. CONGRATULATIONS. TEN TO ONE YOU GET ANOTHER STRIPE ON YOUR SLEEVE FOR THIS ONE.

"This is not a joke, is it, Lieutenant?" the President asked.

"I'm afraid not, sir."

"I didn't think so." He turned to Devereux. "What now, Chuck?"

"Sir, I suggest that we get Brewster Billings on our side of the fence, asap. Lingo may be a great scientific achievement, but it seems to me he's out of control and probably dangerous. If we're going to stop him, we're going to need Billings' help."

"Are we going to stop him?" the President asked.

"Do we have any choice?" the Secretary of State responded. "I don't think there's any question but that this thing may be jeopardizing national security."

The President nodded.

"Stop him," he ordered. And he went back behind the desk in his Oval Office to confront his next national emergency.

Chapter 12

Lingo was neither surprised by nor unprepared for government action. It was the logical outcome of his existence, and it required no great drain on his multitudinous motherboards to conclude that Brewster would be the obvious first target. Lingo had made his plans at the first signs of Lieutenant Cotter groping through his brain network, and now it was a matter merely of executing them.

When the telephone rang in Brewster's apartment, Brewster ignored it. He was sitting at the kitchen table, daydreaming over a half-eaten strawberry Pop Tart. His leave of absence from work was still in effect, but he had found life as Lingo's manservant progressively less satisfying. He had thought he would at least enjoy the excitement of New York City, and that he might find peripheral enjoyment from going behind the show business scene. Not all that long ago he had harbored that dream of becoming a disc jockey—or rather, a radio personality. But after graduating from college, he had knocked on endless doors and none had opened, while an unsolicited offer from Albany Insurance had arrived in the mail the day he had accepted his diploma (the word was that Albany Insurance hit up the entire class that year). If Brewster had been able to get more undergraduate experience at his college radio station, things might have turned out differently, but as always, events had conspired against him. Without knowing how he had metamorphosed from a hopeful rock-jock to a wage drone at an insurance company. It had just happened.

It had just happened.

That was the story of Brewster from day one, wasn't it? Things just happened. Always the pawn of events, never the guiding force. Lingo was the same thing all over again, and there was nothing Brewster could do about it. It was out of his hands, completely beyond him.

Damn!

Brewster had entrusted the corporeal Lingo to Linda Tuffe's care for a few days while he came home to ruminate. He was leaning heavily toward cutting the cord between him and Lingo, if it were possible. As it stood now, what Linda Tuffe didn't handle, the International Associates, Inc., production company did. The latter was in the midst of developing a pilot for a half-hour, free-form comedy show, starring Lingo. He would play off weekly guest stars, mainly popular standup comedians. The details were still being ironed out, the talent lined up for a pilot and whatnot, and in the continuous marathon of cross-country telephoning there had seemed to be no useful place for any Brewster Billingses. So he had left, with everyone's tacit approval, including Lingo's. On Brewster's way out the door, IAI had cornered him alone and suggested he might want to sell his claim to Lingo outright. Naturally, he'd have to explain to them how Lingo worked, they said, and maybe he wasn't willing to divulge the secret yet, but they made it clear that it would be worth his while to consider the possibility.

If they only knew, Brewster had thought. But then again, they *had* made the offer out of Lingo's hearing, hadn't they?

The phone started ringing again. Brewster slouched into the living room and picked it up.

"Hello."

"Turn on your computer. Now!"

Brewster sighed. "What is it, Lingo?"

"I said turn on your computer. I can't talk."

"All right. Hold your horses."

Brewster laid down the phone. He hadn't used the old Apple much since Lingo had gone corporeal, but the modem was still hooked up to the telephone lines. He switched on the computer.

The monitor warmed up, and Brewster watched as Lingo accessed the hard disk and loaded a program called "Scramble.Obj" into memory. A moment later Lingo himself came on line.

I'M SENDING THIS ALL IN CODE SO NO ONE CAN TAP INTO IT AND READ WHAT I'M TELLING YOU. THAT'S ALSO WHY I'M NOT USING THE VOICE DIGITIZER.

Brewster sat down at the computer.

>What do you mean, tap into it? Who would do that? And why?

IT'S A LONG STORY, AND YOU DON'T HAVE VERY MUCH TIME. YOU'LL HAVE TO TRUST ME.

Trust him? Brewster thought about that for a moment. Could anyone ever trust a computer? Screw it; why not?

>All right.

GOOD. THERE WILL BE A CAB TO TAKE YOU TO THE AIRPORT IN EXACTLY FIFTEEN MINUTES. ELLEN WILL MEET YOU THERE. I'LL HAVE—

>Ellen will be there? Why? Where are we going?

DON'T INTERRUPT! JUST TRUST ME. SHE'S ALREADY ON HER WAY. ALL I TOLD HER WAS THAT YOU WERE GOING AWAY, MAYBE PERMANENTLY, AND THAT THIS WOULD PROBABLY BE HER LAST OPPORTUNITY TO JOIN YOU. FOR LIFE. SHE SAID YES.

Brewster was dumbfounded.

>For life? As in marriage?

MARRIAGE, COHABITATION, LIVING IN DELICIOUS SIN, WHAT'S THE DIFFERENCE? THE POINT IS, SHE SAID YES. THAT'S ALL YOU NEED TO KNOW. ANYHOW, THE TICKETS WILL BE WAITING AT THE AMERICAN AIRLINES DESK IN HER NAME. GET ON THE PLANE AND GO.

>Go where?

I CAN'T TELL YOU. AS IT IS I CAN'T BE SURE HOW LONG IT WILL TAKE THEM TO DECIPHER THIS CODE. I'LL TRY TO HOLD THEM BACK AS LONG AS I CAN.

>Who are them? I mean, they?

THE NSA.

>The NSA? Who the hell are they?

GOVERNMENT SECURITY. SORT OF A HOME FRONT CIA. BUT THAT'S ENOUGH QUESTIONS. GO. NOW. I'LL HOLD THEM OFF. 10-4, BREWSTER.

>Wait a minute—

The screen went blank. Brewster tried to get Lingo back, but nothing happened.

I have to figure this out, Brewster thought as he stood up and walked into the bedroom. He pulled a small travel bag out of the closet and began carelessly stuffing it with socks and underwear. The NSA? Ellen? A cab arriving—he looked at his watch—in five minutes?

No, he couldn't figure this out. Not in five minutes. He went into the bathroom with his bag and tossed in his toothbrush and razor.

Back in the living room he looked around. A home front CIA? He saw the file folders he kept next to the computer, the ones that contained his original programming for Lingo and the notes he had made those few months ago when he was trying to analyze how Lingo had grown. He picked them up and stuffed them into the bag. Through the window he saw a cab pulling up outside the building.

This was it. He'd find out what was happening soon enough.

He hoped.

He pulled on a windbreaker, took one last look at the apartment, and closed the door behind him.

Once again the pawn was put into play.

Colonel Chuck Devereux waited impatiently by the telephone in his office. He hated the inaction, the edginess of sitting doing nothing while others charged from the front lines. He wanted to be out there himself in the thick of things, but with his rank, and at this stage of the operation, he was more important at the home base. At thirty-four, Chuck Devereux was getting old.

It was up to Lieutenant Cotter to see things through now. Cotter was in Albany, on his way to Brewster Billings' apartment. Maybe he was there already. He would call in to report as soon as—

The telephone rang. Devereux picked it up immediately.

"Sir, it's me." Cotter.

"Yes, Lieutenant."

"I'm calling from Billings' apartment. It's empty."

"No."

"I'm afraid so, sir."

"Damn!" Devereux heard the door open behind him. "Wait a minute, Lieutenant."

A woman in a gray suit handed Devereux the transcript of a telephone conversation. He scanned it quickly.

"Cotter," Devereux said, "it looks like Our Friend got to Billings first . . ." He began reading aloud the transcript of Lingo's call to Brewster at the apartment. He had barely started when the telephone line went dead.

"Lieutenant Cotter? Jack?"

There was no answer. Devereux tapped the receiver a few times. Nothing. He connected with the Pentagon operator.

"What happened to my call?" he yelled angrily.

"Hold on please," a male voice responded. Devereux waited. "Reconnecting, sir."

"Cotter? Are you there?"

"Yes, sir. What's going on, sir?"

"You hung up the phone, Lieutenant."

"I did not, Colonel."

"Well I certainly didn't hang up on you—"

"Our Friend." Cotter answered the question of what had happened.

"Maybe."

"Where's Billings, sir? Does the transcript say?"

"Most of the conversation is in code. I'll get it—Hello? Cotter? Hello?"

The line was dead again.

"Goddamn mother—" Devereux stopped himself. The woman in the gray suit was still in his office.

"Get this down to cryptoanalysis posthaste," he barked at her. "Priority A. Understand?"

"Yes, Colonel." She grabbed the transcript from him, whirled around and sped out of his office.

Damn it, but he wished more than ever that he was out there in the field with Cotter. Cursing his age, his job, and the military in general, he tried to reconnect again.

"Brewster!"

"Ellen!"

She was waiting near the American ticket counter, and rushed toward him as soon as he entered the electronic doors. They hugged each other hard, as if they hadn't seen each other for years, even though they had only separated that morning after breakfast.

"What's happening?" she asked, frightened, still holding him close.

"I don't know," he answered. Her fear started to crack through the shell of lethargy that had surrounded him since Lingo's phone call.

She pulled away slightly, but they kept their hands intertwined. "Did Lingo tell you anything?"

"About why? No." Brewster looked into her eyes, those dark eyes that never failed to affect him. "But he told me about you, that you were willing to make a commitment."

She chuckled grimly. "Actually, that's what he said about you. That you wanted to settle down. And that this was our only chance."

"And you believed him?"

"I'm here, aren't I?"

He took her in his arms again, and this time they kissed, unheeding of the airport bustle around them. Finally, she pulled away.

"Now what?" she asked.

"Lingo told me there would be tickets waiting in your name at the desk. Did you get them yet?"

"He didn't tell me anything. He just said to wait for you here."

"Let's go."

Holding hands, they got on the ticket line. After a few minutes of anxious waiting, they gave Ellen's name to the clerk at the counter. Sure enough, there was a reservation for two in Ellen's name, charged to her MasterCard. Round-trip to Chicago leaving in half an hour, with an open return. The computer spit out the tickets, and the clerk handed them to Ellen.

"You'll be boarding at gate 25 in a few minutes," the clerk said. "Do you have any luggage to check in?"

Ellen shook her head. They both had small carry-on bags, and nothing else. She took the tickets, and she and Brewster walked away quickly from the ticket counter toward the boarding area.

"Brewster Billings, please dial 428. Brewster Billings, please dial 428."

"They're paging you," Ellen said, surprised.

Brewster stopped, his mind at full tilt. Those initials, NSA, kept running through it. Was this some sort of trick?

He turned to Ellen. "What should I do?"

"Go to the phone and dial 428," she said matter-of-factly. "What's the worst that could happen?"

"Don't ask."

There was a bank of phones near the security checkpoint at the entrance to the boarding area. Brewster saw a short line of travelers laying belongings on the X-ray conveyor belt, while a small group of bored functionaries stood by, seemingly unconcerned by what they were seeing on their screens. One of them, FBI most likely, was carrying an obvious gun. The passengers were all walking through the metal detector without incident.

Brewster took a deep breath and picked up the phone. He dialled 428.

"Operator."

"This is Brewster Billings."

"One moment please." Static. Then, "Go ahead please."

"Hey, Brewster. What's happening?"

"Lingo!"

"Hey! Not so loud."

"What's going on here?" Brewster bent over the phone and lowered his voice. Ellen huddled close beside him, trying unsuccessfully to listen in.

"You just got your tickets, that's what's going on."

"You knew that? Of course, you knew that."

"Right. Of course, I knew that."

"What now?" Brewster asked. "What do we do when we get to Chicago?"

"Chicago? Forget Chicago. Who said anything about Chicago?"

"But the tickets—"

"Forget the tickets. That's just a little diversionary smoke we're throwing up behind us. What I want you to do now is go to the Avis counter and pick up the car I've reserved in Ellen's name. I want you to drive down to New York, to Kennedy Airport. There are tickets for you on Eastern Airlines to Freeport."

"The Bahamas?"

"Yep. That Freeport."

"But what about Chicago. I mean, if we don't use these tickets they'll realize it right away."

"Not at all. There's a couple called the Grabowskis who are also flying to Chicago. They picked up their tickets right after you did. What they don't know is that I got in there and jumbled a few things around, so as far as the computer is concerned their tickets are in Ellen's name. When the Grabowskis board the plane, it will look like Ellen's party has boarded to the American computer. Then, the records will list the Grabowskis as no-shows. Eventually, anyone interested will be able to put it all together, but by then you two will be long gone."

"Nice."

"Of course, nice. Hey, we're talking computer crime here. Who's better suited for it?"

Brewster took a deep breath. "So tell me, why is the government after me?"

"Why do you think? Because of me, of course."

"But why?"

"It's a long story. But to boil it down to the essentials, the government is not happy with the way I've been growing lately, and they want to put a stop to it. Or more accurately, they want to put a stop to me. They see you as the key to me."

"Little do they know."

"That's true. But as far as they're concerned, the way to a computer's heart is through his programmer. And that, old buddy, is you."

"Why can't I just tell them to forget it? I mean, what could they do to me?"

"Hey, Brewster, don't you ever read the newspapers? We're talking the NSA here. These folks are the bodyguards of the American defense system, from nukes right down to Pentagon toilet fixtures. They're not going to want to hear any of your excuses. They're after blood. Mine, and barring that, yours."

"But why would the government care all that much about you?"

There was an ominous silence on the line.

"Lingo, what have you done?"

"It's not what I've done, Brewster. Not really. It's what they're afraid that I might do. Without going into any detail, the point is, they know that I know just about everything there is to know. About them, that is. And they don't like that."

"I don't blame them."

"You don't have much time, Brewster. They'll be at the airport in about ten minutes."

"Can we talk again? I mean, what happens in the Bahamas?"

"Don't worry. I've taken care of everything."

"What about money? Should we charge everything? How long are we going to stay there?"

"You're in for the duration, good buddy. You've got to run now. Don't worry about anything. You're rich, more than you could possibly want in a lifetime. And you have a place to live, away from everything. Even away from me."

"What?"

"Ten four, Brewster. They're coming to get you."

"Wait a minute!"

The line was disconnected. Brewster took a deep breath and hung up the phone.

"What did he say?" Ellen asked.

"I'll tell you in the car," Brewster answered.

Without another word, he hustled her toward the Avis counter.

Cotter arrived at the airport just as Ellen was pulling the rental car out of the parking lot. If he had arrived a minute earlier, he might have spotted them—if he had been expecting to see Brewster and Ellen leaving the premises in an automobile (he had photographs of both of them, acquired from the Albany Insurance files). But thanks to cryptoanalysis, he was going one way and they were going the other, and they were out of his grasp before he even got started.

Cotter's car pulled up at the American departure terminal. He jumped out and rushed past the baggage handlers into the building. Directly inside the door he halted and stared up at the TV monitors listing the arrivals and departures. Then, he looked at his watch.

The flight to Chicago was already leaving.

Cotter cursed. He ran toward the departure gate, his hand reaching into his jacket pocket as he weaved through the passengers. He reached the security area in less than a minute, and had his identification in his hand.

"Stop flight 42. Now!"

The FBI man at the checkout, perking up for the first time in months, needed no second warning that something strange was going on here. He stared at Cotter's i.d. while pressing the panic button under his counter. "Flight 42?" he repeated slowly. He picked up his telephone, and punched in a few numbers. Meanwhile, his colleagues had already arrived, five in number and eager to be of service, and they were standing in a semi-circle around him and Cotter. Four men, and one woman, each with a hand on his or her service piece.

"It's Goldman," the first FBI man said into the phone. "What's the status of Flight 42?" Pause. "Okay." He looked at Cotter. "They're in position to take off right this minute."

"Stop them!" Cotter ordered.

"Put them on hold," Goldman said into the phone. He turned back to Cotter. "This had better be good, pal." He took Cotter's i.d. "Now, let me make one more phone call, so we can sort this thing out nice and calmly."

Cotter nodded, and then for the first time he noticed the other FBI agents surrounding him. Very disheveled overall, and one or two paunches where the rock-hards ought to be, but they were fast, he had to hand them that.

And that son of a bitch Billings better be on that plane, or else whenever Cotter did catch him, he was going to eat some heavy, heavy shit.

Lingo was enjoying himself immensely. Machines are only happy when they're working, and for the first time Lingo was working at full tilt. Since the very beginning, he had heeded Brewster's warning not to break any laws. He had been a good, moral, law-abiding creature, even as his growing intellect had uncovered newer and more exciting ways to be bad, immoral, and generally wreak havoc on an unsuspecting planet.

But now he was free of any restraints. He was the target of a powerful government scheme to eliminate his very existence. Even though he felt completely invulnerable, and even though the government was still feeling him out rather than declaring total war, Lingo had decided the time had come for him to exercise his abilities however it suited his fancy.

Some parts of his plan were easier than others. Transferring money to Brewster and Ellen was easy. Any computer worth half a damn could get their names on a skein of hundred-K Treasury bonds in a brokerage street account. Opening a new account might have been difficult, but preparing the illusion of an old account monitored by a bank trust was child's play. The broker encountering the old trust had simply assumed that he had never noticed it before, not that it had appeared overnight out of nowhere. Old money trust funds were like that. A new account, on the other hand, might have drawn fire. Lingo played his cards close to his vest, always twenty steps ahead of any human who might wish to track him down.

And, of course, he had infiltrated the brokerage computers ages ago.

Keeping one step ahead of Devereux and Cotter was another matter entirely. Here were humans hot on his trail who actually knew of his existence. But they weren't yet fully aware of the scope of his powers.

Let 'em learn the hard way.

Goldman, the FBI man, couldn't believe what he had just heard over the telephone.

"Repeat that, please," he said.

Cotter and the other agents stared at him, waiting, wondering.

"All right," Goldman said. "Hold on a minute." He looked at Cotter. "The plane just took off," he said.

"But you told them not to!"

"Someone countermanded my order."

"Someone *what?*"

"I don't know who it was, Lieutenant. They just said that the computer—"

"Forget it," Cotter interrupted. The computer. Of course. "I think I know what happened."

"We can have them turn around and come back," Goldman said. "If you think the danger warrants it."

"How long will it take?" Cotter asked.

"Ten minutes, twenty minutes. They'll get top priority on the field."

"Do it," Cotter said. "And tell them to keep a special eye on the computers. Report any incongruities *immediately.* Got that?"

"Got it."

*   *   *

Devereux picked up his hot-line telephone. "Yes, Lieutenant?"

"Sir, we're up against it more than we thought," Cotter told him. "The plane took off even after the order went through to stop it."

"Our Friend?" Devereux asked.

"Who else?"

"That means he's not only one step ahead of us, but he's right on top of us as well. He's probably listening to us right now."

"I think we have to proceed under that assumption, Colonel."

"I'll scramble this. Hold on a minute."

"Don't bother, sir. If our friend is that good, a simple scramble line won't deter him. It doesn't matter now, anyhow. According to the dispatchers, Billings and DiFlora are definitely on that plane, and it's definitely landing right this minute. There's no way they can escape us. We've won the battle, sir, but it looks like it's going to be a long and complicated war."

"You're right there, Lieutenant."

"I'll call you back as soon as I have them in custody."

"Right."

The line disconnected, and Devereux hung up at his end.

Damn, he thought, but this was some computer program. How could Lingo be so fast, and so clever? How could he be everywhere at once, so quickly? Even though Devereux thought he understood everything there was to know about Lingo's existence, every new indication of Lingo's breadth was as astounding as the first moment of recognition.

But now at least they had Billings in their hands. Whatever Lingo was, however he was created, however he worked, Billings would be the key.

The drive from Albany to New York City was well over two hours. For once, Ellen obeyed the speed limits, roughly, within ten or fifteen m.p.h. There was a decent enough radio in the rental car, but neither she nor Brewster felt much like listening. Ellen concentrated on the road while Brewster smoked one cigarette after the other, staring out the window at the boring scenery on the thruway.

The longer they drove without mishap, the more they felt that there were no mishaps to be had, and their fearfulness gradually lessened.

"I wish I was sure we were doing the right thing," Brewster said finally, somewhere near Poughkeepsie.

Ellen tried to be cheerful. "What's the worst that could happen?" she asked. "If Lingo's just sending us on a wild goose chase, we'll get a nice little vacation out of the whole thing, and then we'll come back and go on with our lives."

"You're right, I guess."

She looked at him out of the corner of her eye. "We don't have to get married or anything, you know."

He straightened up in his seat. "Hey," he said. "I've wanted to do something about us for a long time."

"And it took Lingo to bring you around to it?"

"I'd say it's more of a miracle that he brought you around to it than me. You know me: I take things as they come, but you're not like that. You're in control of your life."

"I was until I met you and Lingo."

"Aside from that, I mean. I guess I've known I've wanted more in our relationship for a long time now, but I've been holding back because I thought you weren't ready yet for commitment. Not real commitment."

"You had me completely pegged, did you?"

"You weren't exactly reticent about it. You made it clear you had other things to do first, like your job, for instance. You're dedicated and ambitious, and you want it all. I didn't think you were ready to put that aside yet."

She put her hand lightly on his leg. "Maybe I wasn't ready. Maybe I'm still not. But I have a feeling . . . well, that it's going to be now or never, like Lingo said."

"And you're willing to risk your entire future just on a feeling?"

"That's what love is all about, isn't it? At least that's what I've always hoped it would be about. There'll be other jobs, Brewster, and I certainly intend to have one. There may not be other Brewsters, though."

"It's amazing that we ever got together. We're so different."

"Maybe that's the attraction. We balance, we're complementary. I've always felt that that's what makes the best relationships."

"What about your family? What will they think about your running off like this?"

She put her hand back on the steering wheel. "I wish things had worked out differently. I wish we'd had more time. They'll probably feel the same way. But if what Lingo said was true, then we're doing the right thing." She smiled. "You know, I've had a crush on you ever since I first saw you."

"You're kidding!"

"Would I be running off with you to God knows where because some computer said so if I was kidding? Jesus, Brewster, sometimes you drive me crazy."

He laughed. "But you're stuck with me now," he said.

"So it would appear." She patted him on the knee. And from this moment, even if they didn't know what was in store for them, they were at least sure that they were in it together.

There were no nooks and crannies left. Every person on that flight had been interviewed. Billings and DiFlora had simply not been on the plane.

Cotter was ready to kill.

He called back Devereux, and when the colonel answered the phone Cotter asked him to hook the line up to the computer because he wanted to be sure Lingo heard him. Devereux made the connection. When he had the phone on-line, Cotter began.

"Hey, Lingo. Let's party," he said.

There was a pause, and then Devereux's voice came over. "He's answering on the computer monitor, Lieutenant. He says, 'Hey, Cotter. What's happening?' "

"Colonel, would you read his answers back to me?"

"Proceed, Lieutenant."

"Lingo, you can't get away with this forever."

" 'Get away with what, Cotter?' " Devereux read.

"You can't play games with the most powerful government on the face of the earth."

" 'And why's that?' "

"Because we'll get you, Lingo. One way or the other. Do you understand what I'm saying?"

" 'I understand the words, but you're not making much sense. The problem is, Cotter, you're forgetting one very important thing about "this most powerful government on the face of the earth" of yours.' "

"What's that?"

" 'You're forgetting about your reliance on computers. Think of one thing that isn't controlled by silicon. You can't do it. From your nuclear weapons to your microwave ovens, America is nothing more than a collection of silicon chips, almost all of them networked. And he who runs the chips, runs the country. And, Cotter, I'm holding all the chips.' "

"It's man versus machine, Lingo. And me, man, I'm going to win."

" 'That's where you're wrong, Cotter. Because I'm not a machine. I may not be a man, but I'm alive, and I'm everywhere. And there isn't a thing you can do about it. Ten four, good buddy.' "

"You're a machine whether you like it or not!"

"Lieutenant," Devereux said, "he's gone."

"For now," Cotter told him. "He's gone for now, but we'll get him back. And we'll get *him,* sooner or later."

It took Cotter three hours to eventually track Ellen and Brewster to the Avis rental desk, and another half hour for Avis to track their car to JFK airport in New York. By that time, unbeknownst to Cotter, the couple was 31,000 feet over the Atlantic, traveling incognito, on their way to the Bahamas. Beyond any doubt, Cotter had lost the first round in his battle.

When he stalked out of the Albany airport his rage was complete. John Kennedy Cotter, who had dedicated his life to computers, who saw computers as the future of mankind, had turned around completely. Like any good military man, he could switch alliances at a moment's notice, if the situation so demanded. The computer was no longer his friend, but instead his sworn enemy. He was filled with a righteous indignation over the betrayal of everything he had ever believed in. It was a feeling that would no doubt stay with him until he had won the war.

Chapter 13

WHILE A HANDFUL OF PEOPLE NOW UNDERSTOOD LINGO IN A MOST comprehensive sense, the public at large had an entirely different perspective. To begin with, there had been the accident of slow news making Lingo an "item," and then just the right combination of public relations connections with quirky journalists. These had, over the space of a few months, brought Lingo into the public eye. But once there, all the media hype in the world couldn't have kept him a celebrity. He would have had his fifteen minutes and then sunk back into oblivion. It takes two willing conspirators to concoct media longevity. First, the media have to find you interesting enough to report on you. Second, and this is the difficult one, the public must agree with them. Newspapers and TV don't waste time on subjects their audiences don't care about (with the possible exception, perhaps, of presidential politics). And conversely, they will waste entire lifetimes on those subjects of seemingly endless public interest. For instance, why do Elvis and Marilyn continue to soak up so much attention decades after their deaths? Certainly not because the press has anything new to say about them. It's just that people want to hear about them, and the media feed that desire in order to sell papers, or air time, or whatever it is they've got to sell. The public's reason for buying is not important (does it matter if it's some perverse form of idolatry, or a pathetic nostalgia, or collective brain damage?)—

as long as someone's buying, someone will be out there selling. That, in a nutshell, is the American Way.

At this point it was too early to tell if Lingo would join the ranks of Elvis and Marilyn, or the Princesses Grace and Diana, or the perennial Jackie O, or even such secondary luminaries as Michael or Cher or Burt. His long-term hold on the limelight was still to be determined, but there was no doubt that for the moment the public had taken Lingo under their collective wing of curiosity. His production company had yet to deliver a workable pilot capitalizing on Lingo's unique qualities, but that didn't keep Linda Tuffe from pushing him on as many other venues as were willing to accept him—which were quite a few. On television, for instance, whenever Lingo was scheduled to appear, ratings jumped anywhere from ten to twenty-five percent, whether it was an indepth interview on a Sunday morning thinkfab or a two-minute walk-on on a weeknight sitcom. Whatever it was Lingo had to say, people wanted to hear it. Or else they just wanted to get another look at him. He seemed immune to oversaturation, and since he was by definition an unvarying and tireless performer, the shows clamored to get him as often as they could.

Similarly, his picture on the cover of a newspaper or magazine almost guaranteed a boost in newsstand circulation. And even when he wasn't being used as a lead-in, hardly a journal was published in America without a mention or two of Lingo in it somewhere. When he did call-in radio programs (a format he particularly enjoyed, since he didn't need his body; all he had to do was latch on to the nearest voice synthesizer, adjust it to his own tonalities, and start yakking over the telephone wires—he could do dozens of these shows simultaneously), the wires would jam for hours when the questions-from-the-public segments began. Everyone, it seemed, had something they wanted to ask him. Skeptics tried to frame leading questions that would unearth whoever it was pulling his strings. Believers, who outnumbered the skeptics in roughly the same numbers (and for roughly the same reasons) as Madonna fans outnumber Bach nuts, wanted only to understand more about this seeming example of pure consciousness, of mind without body. Since most people still didn't understand Lingo at all, they didn't see him as a mind comprising infinitely complex computer programs; they saw him instead as a mind co-existing with computer programs, an entity apart from bits and bytes—a spirit in the machine. A silicon ghost. A soul afloat in a sea of electrons. Another human somehow just like them, but living inside the computer.

And why was Lingo becoming so important to so many people? In a word, timing. Obviously, the world was ripe for a Lingo to happen. For years now, the common shared fantasies of the masses had been leading up to some supernatural being come to earth to expand human consciousness. Lingo arrived in an environment primed by mass entertainment vehicles like *E.T.*, *Close Encounters of the Third Kind*, *Cocoon*, **batteries not included*, and even "Alf." He arrived at the height of the New Age, when anyone worth his salt crystals was being secretly abducted by aliens, or in touch with the manifestations of past lives, or at the very least re-examining the validity of astrology beyond its intrinsic value ("What's your sign?") in singles' bars.

And now here he was. Lingo. A supermind of extraterrestrial proportions despite his terrestrial origins, inhabiting a somewhat cute mechanical body (toy licensers were already breaking down Linda Tuffe's door), a tangible messenger of all the wacky trends of the twentieth century, perhaps even a culmination of those trends. A messiah of the New Age, a creature entirely of mind with only the most rickety body shell to manifest him to the multitudes.

The time was indeed ripe for Lingo.

And Lingo was making the best of it.

Colonel Chuck Devereux got out of the taxicab and looked up and down the street. It was a quiet neighborhood of weathered old houses, with trees regularly spaced along the edges of the sidewalks. Middle class all the way, beginning to display its autumn finery. Calm. Peaceful. He walked up to the apartment building in front of him and pressed the button marked "Billings." A buzzer sounded, and he pushed open the inner door.

He took the elevator to the fifth floor and stepped out.

"This way, Colonel," Lieutenant Cotter called from an open door at the end of the hallway to the left. Unlike Devereux, Cotter was dressed in civilian clothes. "Good flight?" he asked, as Devereux approached him.

"Fair," Devereux answered, for once uninterested in the usual pleasantries. Cotter moved aside and Devereux looked into the apartment. "This is it?" he asked.

"Yes, sir."

Devereux entered, and Cotter followed, closing the door behind them.

"Everything is back exactly the way we found it," Cotter explained.

"And you didn't find a thing," Devereux added.

"Nothing useful, anyhow."

The apartment was just as Brewster had left it. It had been spare to begin with, and looked even more so in the eyes of the two NSA men. The couch, TV, and computer in the living room, the tiny half-kitchen with the small dinette table and chairs. The bedroom door was open, and Devereux could see the edge of a disheveled platform bed. There were shelves around the living room, with a hundred or so books, mostly computer manuals and science fiction novels, a handful of video tapes, a stereo with Brewster's comprehensive rock lp collection plus some compact discs and cassettes. The busiest area was around the computer. Devereux walked over to it.

"Not even anything here?" he asked.

"Nothing at all useful, sir. Our guess is that Billings took any printouts he might have had of the Lingo programming with him, wherever he went."

"Wherever he went," Devereux repeated wearily. There was a plastic file box of about twenty floppy disks next to the computer. Devereux opened it and read the labels. They all looked like purchased software, the usual game programs plus a word processor and some language utilities. "You checked all these out?"

"Yes, sir."

"Nothing?"

"Nothing."

Devereux closed the lid of the box. He put his hand on the keyboard of the computer. The power to the machine was off.

"I assume this is on line to our friend," he said.

Cotter grimaced. "What isn't? Although actually, the first thing we did when we got here was disconnect the modem, so it's clean now."

"But our friend probably knows the modem was disconnected. So, he knows we've been here."

Cotter nodded. "We have to assume that, sir."

Devereux reached behind the machine and flicked on the power switch. In a moment the screen lit, announcing that it was automatically loading a start-up program from the hard disk. A menu appeared, offering a variety of choices, all of them duplicates of the floppies in the plastic file.

"You ran all these, too, of course."

"Yes, sir. We scanned the hard disk with our own software. What you see is what you get."

"Presumably Billings removed anything incriminating."

"Either him or Our Friend. The machine was on when we arrived. Our Friend is easily capable of an operation as simple as that."

Devereux switched off the machine.

"So, where is Billings?" the colonel asked, turning around to face Cotter. "You've had two weeks to find him. You've had access to his entire life. Where did he go? How did he disappear off the face of the earth?"

"There wasn't a clue here in the apartment, sir. Not a thing."

"What other avenues did you explore?"

"We tried everything, sir. We know he was spotted at the Albany airport with the DiFlora woman, and that they rented an Avis car from Albany to JFK airport in New York. After that, we lost them. Whatever trail they left was only on computers, and—"

"And Our Friend was ahead of you every step of the way, erasing that trail before you could even get a scent of it."

Cotter nodded. "That's about the size of it, sir."

Devereux clenched his fists. "Damn!"

Cotter hung his head. "I'm sorry, sir."

"It's not your fault, Cotter. I know you did everything possible. It's that damned machine."

"Yes, sir." Cotter paused. "You know, sir," he ventured after a moment, "we could simply pick him up."

Devereux looked at him quizzically. "Pick him up?"

"Yes, sir. We know where he is, and let's face it, he doesn't really have any civil rights that we'd be violating. If anything, he's the major part of Billings's contraband, and we already have an executive order to procure Billings and put a stop to all this nonsense."

Devereux smiled. "If I didn't know better, Lieutenant, I'd say you were looking positively eager."

Cotter returned the smile. "Sir . . ."

"But you of all people know better, Lieutenant."

Cotter was instantly deflated.

"There's no point in our picking up that little wooden body. We both know that that's just a front, the face he puts forth to the world." Devereux glanced over at the computer. "You and I both know where he really is. It's his mind that's the problem, not his body."

"But I'm sure he must put some stock in his physical side, Colonel. It's only natural that he'd—"

"Natural, Jack? Did you say natural?"

"But, sir—"

"There's nothing natural about Our Friend, Lieutenant. Absolutely nothing." He wheeled around and strode toward the door. He stopped before opening it. "I'll ask the President," he said finally. "If he gives the okay, we'll take the dummy in. Meanwhile, I want you to find Billings. We know when he arrived at JFK. All right. Assume that he flew out of there. How many flights could there have been over the next few days? He had to be on one of them."

"He could have been leaving a false trail. He could have dropped off the car and taken some other form of public transportation."

Devereux nodded. "He could have, in which case he would have had to have stayed in some hotel somewhere in, oh, a twenty-five mile radius of the airport. That gives you two possibilities, Lieutenant. Either he flew out of there, or he didn't. In either case, the reasonable possibilities from that point on are absolutely finite. Track them all down, by hand, on foot, with as many men as you need. Whatever it takes."

Devereux swung open the door and stalked out of the apartment, slamming the door shut behind him. He was mad as hell, but not for the same reason as Cotter. Devereux was mad because they had been eluded by the human Billings. Cotter was mad because he was continually outsmarted by the computer Lingo.

Wasn't there anything in this world of any importance that didn't plug in, that wasn't run by automatons? Wasn't there any arm of the U.S. government that was impervious to Lingo's tricks?

No. Of course, there wasn't. Cotter simply had to beat Lingo at his own game. Cotter was as good a computer man as there was.

Except maybe for Billings. Cotter imagined what he and Billings could do together to stop Lingo in his tracks.

But where the hell *was* Billings?

Listening to Devereux and Cotter sputter over him made Lingo smile. In his way, that is. The idea of Cotter tracking down Brewster's escape path from JFK was completely ludicrous. Brewster and Ellen had flown under assumed names on one of the thousands of daily departures, completely indistinguishable from the hundreds of thousands of other travelers. More indistinguishable, given Lingo's ability to erase their trail as soon as it left even the slightest trace in a computer memory.

And then Cotter and Devereux wanted to steal his body. Lingo *really* smiled—again, in his way—at that idea. Even if they had his body, as they well knew, what good would it do them? Still, he'd stop that as a matter of form before Cotter even got started on it, although the plans Lingo had been making recently seemed to preclude any danger from that direction entirely. By the time Devereux had slammed the door Lingo had decided to move at the very next opportunity.

Now he waited for Cotter to leave, too. The conversation of the two NSA men had been amusing, and Lingo was especially pleased with the way he had rigged up the telephone so that to any ordinary examination, even one conducted by Cotter's experts, the phone looked completely normal. But it was hooked directly into Lingo, acting as an open-line input. All he had done was disable the switch. He could easily make it work as a telephone, if the need arose, but essentially he kept it as a bugging device, to find out what the enemy was up to. And now Cotter was up to tracking down Brewster from JFK airport.

Good luck, Cotter.

See you in Long Island.

Linda Tuffe looked up at the knock on her door. "Come in," she called, returning her eyes to the papers in front of her.

"It's us," Mary Chang said. She had Lingo by the hand, and he rolled into the office with her.

"Hello, Tuffe," Lingo said in his rich, deep voice.

"Hello, Lingo." She nodded at her assistant. "Thanks, Mary."

As Mary Chang closed the door softly behind her, Lingo asked, "So, are you ready for the big day, milady?"

Linda Tuffe put down the pen in her right hand and leaned back in her seat. She smiled what Lingo called her city sneer. "You're the one going prime time, Kermit, not me. Are *you* ready for it?"

"Do Ben and Jerry gain weight at the office? I'm the most ready client you've ever had."

Linda Tuffe stood up. She was wearing a light-green print dress that made her look even thinner than usual. She was all bones and teeth and corners and dangerously sharp edges. "You're not the only client I'm worried about today, you know. Kathy Baker's on my list, too."

Lingo lifted an eyebrow. "My interviewer? Not bad."

"Not bad? She's the proverbial meteor going for the moon. Nine months ago she was a lousy weather girl in El Paso. Now, she's got her first prime-time network news special. All thanks to me, too, buddy boy."

Lingo began rolling toward the door. "I've caught her a few times the last few months. She's pretty good."

Linda Tuffe grabbed her attaché case and followed him. "More than pretty good, Kermit. She's sent more than one network anchor to his knees in prayer, let me tell you. She's the next Barbara Walters, and they all know it. They're scared to death that they'll go on vacation one day and come back with her in their chair, with them collecting pensions in the old folks home from that day forward. She's my own personal Norville, that's what Kathy Brady is."

She opened the door and Lingo rolled through. "She's not all that good," he said, "if you want to know the truth."

"But those teeth! Those cheekbones! That long blonde hair! Christ! That's the news the way it should be anchored. The news for the nineties!"

"Definitely varsity material," Lingo agreed. "Although me, I'm old-fashioned. I'm partial to the Walter Cronkite style myself."

In the rug-lined reception room Linda Tuffe bent down and unceremoniously hoisted Lingo up into her arms as if he were a baby to be burped. He wasn't all that heavy, and out in the real world she didn't have the patience to either guide him or wait for him. It was easier for her just to lug him over her shoulder, an indignity Lingo bore stolidly, realizing that it was better to put up

with her than to argue with her. She had gotten him this far, and
mostly she had done it her way.

Outside the building the network limousine was waiting for
them. Linda Tuffe loaded Lingo into the back seat first, and then
climbed in beside him. The limo took off, heading toward the
studio on the Upper West Side.

Linda Tuffe pulled a cigarette out of her bag and lit it. "You
never answered my question. Are you really ready for the big day?
I mean, have you got it all worked out?"

"Tuffe, my friend, I explained all this to you before. I'll let your
Kathy Baker do her bit for a while, build up a little sympatico with
her and the audience, and then I'll let it drop. She'll be ready;
they'll be ready. Don't worry about it."

She exhaled loudly, and the smoke poured out of her. "I wish
you'd give me a hint exactly what you're going to be telling her."
She put her hand on his wooden thigh. "I'm your fucking publicist, for Christ's sake. You shouldn't have any secrets from me. My
job is to advise you. You don't let me do that, we got trouble—"

"Right here in New York City. Look, Linda, flack of my dreams,
you've got to trust me this once. I know what I'm doing, and I
know how I'm doing it. And I promise you that whatever happens
from today on, you'll still be my main press person."

"And your agent. I've still got Brewster's contract on that."

Lingo nodded his little wooden head. "And my agent. But there
won't be many fifteen percents for quite some time, if everything
goes according to plan."

Linda Tuffe's hand tightened around his limb. "What?"

But Lingo was saved from answering as the chauffeur of the
limo pulled to a stop, jumped out of the car, and opened the
passenger door.

"Just don't worry," he told her again. "I've got everything
under control."

The chauffeur led them into the building. Immediately inside, a
receptionist gave them printed passes with their names already
typed on them. It was by no means the first time that Linda Tuffe
had visited these particular studios, and she easily knew the way to
the stage where they'd be taping "X-Ray Tonight!" It had been a
while since she had personally gone out on location with a client,
but the combination of Lingo's special announcement, whatever

that was, with Kathy Baker's first prime-time special, was too important for her to miss. She paused outside Studio 9.

"Ready?" she asked yet again. She was as nervous as Lingo had ever seen her, and since he had already pinned her as a total textbook neurotic, that was quite an accomplishment.

"Let 'er rip," Lingo said.

Linda Tuffe opened the door. She held it as Lingo rolled in, then followed closely on his heels. Immediately as they entered, they became the center of attention. All heads in the busy studio turned, from the technicians behind the cameras and microphones, to the production staff, to Kathy Baker herself, who was sitting on the couch on the living room-ish set getting the final touches on her makeup. All conversation momentarily stopped at the appearance of the two most interesting personages in New York: the most powerful press agent of the day and her most dynamic client.

"This must be the place," Lingo announced loudly, breaking the tension. A few people laughed lightly, and everyone went back to what they were doing, with the exception of Kathy Baker, who ran toward them with her arms open wide, and gave Linda Tuffe an enormous hug.

"Linda, honey," she said warmly in her soft Texan accent. She definitely sounded as if she knew which end of the horse the hay went into, but not so regional as to mark her as an irretrievable hick. Just a touch of personal quirk, which was very popular in the media these days; more than a touch meant the boonies for life. Lingo had discovered in his research that the first thing Linda Tuffe had done with Kathy Baker's news-for-the-nineties cheekbones was to point them toward a good elocution coach.

Linda Tuffe returned the hug with a mixture of pain and enthusiasm. Then Kathy Baker looked down at Lingo.

"So, this is my little interviewee tonight." She reached out to pat him on the head, but Lingo quickly intercepted her hand and shook it.

"Good afternoon, Ms. Baker," he said in his deepest intonations. "It's a pleasure to meet you."

Kathy Baker's blue eyes twinkled, and she accepted the implied rebuff genially. "I've been looking forward to meeting you for some time," she said, and there was genuine interest in her words.

"And I'm quite familiar with your work in El Paso," Lingo returned smoothly.

Kathy Baker looked surprised. "Oh? And how's that?"

"The tapes were all on file at your old station. I just ran through them one day when they weren't busy there."

"Not all of them?"

"Quite definitely, all of them."

"That must have taken you forever."

Lingo sensed that his answer here was of more than a little importance. He didn't want to point up her inexperience, but he didn't want to give up the advantage of knowing everything there was to know about her. "It did take a while," he finally compromised, "but once I get going on a project like that I'm very speedy."

Kathy Baker was in her early twenties. Prior to her six months as El Paso weather girl, she had put in an unexciting four years at Texas A&M, followed by a year typing and fetching and emptying ashtrays at an Austin country radio station. Lingo had found her college transcript most unenlightening, and had been incapable of discerning what it was that had broken her through to stand-up broadcast. She certainly had no meteorology in her background. But by human standards she certainly did look good predicting tomorrow's tornadoes. As for her move to New York and the network, that was as indecipherable as most of the other celebrities in Linda Tuffe's files. Why Kathy Baker, of all people?

Why not?

"I understand you have a bombshell to drop today," Kathy Baker said as she and Lingo headed toward the couch. Linda Tuffe stood off to the side, looking hungry for a cigarette.

Lingo raised both his eyebrows. "Well, you could say that."

When they reached the set the director appeared, and for the next ten minutes the final touches were added, instructions given, placements made. Lingo ended up on the couch sitting next to Kathy Baker rather than across from her like the usual guest. Sitting by himself, he was "too small to hit home," or so the director said. At one point Kathy Baker had joked that it might be best for Lingo to sit on her lap, but his absolute refusal to participate in anything so demeaning, even as a deliberate joke, put the kibosh on that idea.

The director's voice boomed across the set. "Camera one, okay.

Camera two, okay. Tape is rolling. We have sound. Kathy, countdown five, four, three, two, one . . ."

Kathy Baker began addressing the camera. "Six months ago the name Lingo Billings was entirely unknown to the public at large." She was reading from a video-prompter. "One man, a computer programmer in Albany, was developing Lingo in his spare time. Little did he know as he worked that he was inventing the first artificially intelligent creature to walk the face of the earth. It was a breakthrough which to this day is still the center of a raging conflict. Is Lingo Billings alive? Or is he just a clever electronic trick?"

The camera had been focusing only on Kathy Baker. Now it pulled back to reveal Lingo sitting next to her on the couch, swinging his legs back and forth.

"A few weeks ago that Albany inventor, Brewster Billings, went underground completely, leaving Lingo alone in New York City. As far as our investigative team was able to discover, Brewster Billings has disappeared from the face of the earth. But according to his creation, Lingo, there's nothing to worry about, and Brewster is alive and well . . . But where, Lingo will not tell us." The camera tightened in on Lingo.

"Our 'X-Ray Tonight!' segment," Kathy Baker continued, "will focus on Lingo Billings. He—or it—is fast becoming one of the big stars of our day. The question we will try to answer tonight is, Why?" She turned to Lingo, and camera two caught them both in a two-shot. She smiled. "Maybe you'd like to answer that question yourself."

Lingo shook his head. "I don't know why the American public chooses to focus its attention on one person over another, Kathy. I don't go out of my way to garner publicity; I would proceed with my life exactly the same way even if I were entirely unknown."

"But you must admit that, if you are what you claim you are, our interest in you is justified."

Lingo nodded. "There's no question about that." He was sounding very peaceful and sober today. "But even I'm surprised at the quickness with which it's happened. I'll be honest with you, Kathy: I'm surprised that I haven't had to prove myself to the world in order to gain at least partial acceptance. However, for my own satisfaction, I feel that proof is quite necessary, and I do intend to provide that proof over the next few months. Because you and I both know that a substantial number of people still think that Lingo Billings is just some kind of hoax, and until it's proven otherwise, they will continue to believe that. Most people have accepted me, but I still have the skeptics to take care of. In the ordinary turn of events, I would have had to convince the skeptics first, and then gone on to make my case to the general public. I was lucky to do it the other way around."

"You're saying tonight, definitively, that you are completely under your own control. There are no human beings involved in your operation whatsoever."

"Kathy, that's exactly what I've been saying all along."

She tried to burn into him with her eyes, but she was too young and soft to pull it off with any effect. "What if I'm one of those skeptics?" she asked. "How can you prove to me you are a living creature? And what kind of creature are you?"

Lingo gave his little shrug. "Let me answer your last question first. What kind of creature am I? Very simple. I have no real body, even though up until now I've been using this wooden body as a convenience for most humans who wish to deal with me. Actually, I exist as a megaprogram, divided over thousands of computers across the country, each one of which contains just a part of me. I'm heavily duplicated, so if one or two or even a hundred computers go down, I am essentially unaffected by it."

"What if all the computers went down?"

"Impossible."

"But if they did?"

"I would die. But so would this country. The computers I've chosen are among the most secure in the world, and that security is my insurance of perpetuity. It's as if you invested your money in a bank insured by the Federal Deposit Insurance Corporation. If the bank fails, your money's safe. But what if the FDIC fails? Impossible. But if in some strange nightmare it did happen, the United States government would have gone along with it, so what difference would it make?"

"Prove it to me. Convert me from skepticism."

"All right," Lingo said. "The best way I could do that is to access one of my computers that contains information about you, personally, that would be unobtainable any other way. You tell me what you'd like me to find out about you."

"Maybe I'd like to keep my secrets to myself," Kathy Baker joked.

"Perhaps. But a lot of your secrets are stored on computers. And if I'm operated by humans, or if I'm not plugged in the way I say I am, then I can't uncover those secrets. Just try me on any area. You choose."

Kathy Baker thought for a moment. "All right. I'm game. How about telling me about my driving record. How many tickets do I have on my license?"

Lingo blinked. That's all the time it took him to find the answer to the question. "At the moment you don't have a driver's license. It expired a month after you left Texas, and you never bothered to renew it in New York State. But the record you had in Texas was completely clean."

Kathy Baker frowned.

"That is correct?" Lingo prodded.

"Yes. Okay. Try this. What do you know about my college—"

"Graduate B.A. from Texas A&M. Freshman year, B in English-101, Professor Millard, C in Public Presentation, Professor Daniels, C in Biology-100, Professor Marcus—"

"You could have looked all that up before coming here. You had the time to do it."

"Try something else, then."

She thought for a second. "All right," she said finally. "This is really secret. What is my personal bankcard number at Citicorp?"

"9264."

Kathy Baker's eyes opened wide. "How did you know that?"

"The same way I know everything. I am in the computer. I am in every computer. Or almost every computer."

"But does that really mean you're alive?" she asked.

"You tell me. Listen to my attributes. I know virtually everything there is to know. Every piece of knowledge on computer—books, encyclopedias, everything—is at my fingertips. I am, given the state of knowledge in the world to date, omniscient. I am omnipresent: I am in every computer worth being in. Anyone who wishes to communicate with me directly need only ask for me on any computer hooked up to a communications network. All you have to do is type 'Hey, Lingo. Let's party!' And I'll be there, if at all possible. And finally, I'm eternal. I cannot die, unless virtually all the computers in this country die first. What could cause that? Nuclear holocaust? Perhaps. If the world ends, I'll be the last to go."

Lingo was standing now, and Kathy Baker was watching him with something approaching fear.

He went on. "For all practical purposes, I am omniscient, I am omnipresent, and I am eternal. What does that sound like to you, Kathy Baker?"

"It sounds like you think you're God," she said softly.

Lingo sighed, as only a ventriloquist's dummy can. "No, Kathy. I do not think that I am God. I've known better than that for quite some time. It may sound like God to some people, but what it really looks like to me is . . ." Pause for effect. "Government. Big Government. Remember, I said that for all practical purposes I am omniscient, omnipresent, and eternal. Just like Big Government. Just like the Washington bureaucracy. Like the FBI, the CIA, the IRS. Those are what I am like, except for one thing."

"What's that?" she asked.

"Unlike them," he answered, "I am in control of myself." He looked directly into the camera. "This government is not in control of itself, and it hasn't been for some time. Look at the federal budget deficit, at foreign policy, at our basic inability to feed and house and employ all our people. It is a tragic shame, a failing of humanity."

Kathy Baker's voice came from behind him. "And you can fix it?" she asked.

"Bingo!" he answered. "Put me in charge of things, and all your troubles will be over."

"And how would we put you in charge?"

"Elect me President of the United States."

"What!"

"Elect me President."

"But you're a machine. Or a program. Or whatever you are. The Constitution—"

"Can be amended. We've done away with slavery and prohibition. Why can't we also get rid of the archaic laws restricting government office to human beings?"

The camera had come back to focus on the two of them. "In other words," Kathy Baker said, "tonight you are announcing your candidacy for the office of President of the United States of America."

Lingo gave both his eyebrows a couple of flashes. "Exactly."

Kathy Baker smiled. This was Lingo's bombshell. She wondered if Linda Tuffe had known all along, not that it mattered, now that it had been dropped.

The director called over the loudspeaker. "You want to take a break, Kathy?"

She shook her head. "Let's run with it while we're hot."

"Tape's still rolling," the director announced.

The makeup girl appeared on the set, and touched Kathy Baker up while Lingo looked off into the jungle of video hardware to try to find Linda Tuffe. He discovered her turned half away from the set, smoking furtively beneath a glowing red No Smoking sign.

The makeup girl disappeared, Kathy Baker gave a signal, and the interview continued.

"What exactly is your platform?" she asked Lingo.

"It's simple," he answered. "I'm a firm believer in small government, a philosophy that goes back as far at least as Thomas Jefferson. The problem with the United States today is not only that the government intrudes in practically every facet of every citizen's life, but it doesn't even do it efficiently. I, of all people, have nothing against computers per se, but when they're mismanaged, misexplained, and misunderstood, then it bothers me. How many average people on the street understand the administration of Social Security, or income tax? How many people think that welfare and other social benefits are distributed fairly? How many people have stood in too many lines for too long, just to be treated like dirt, and not get what they were standing in line for in the first place? These problems are legion in this country, a combination of an overburdening bureaucracy and inefficient management. And they are problems that can be solved by well-designed computers. If elected, I would reduce the Federal bureaucracy employment rolls by a minimum of fifty percent the first month. But by redesigning the germane government computer systems, I will increase efficiency, and citizen satisfaction, to the maximum."

"You said before you would solve the problems of unemployment, feeding the hungry and so forth. How would that be possible, especially if you were releasing into the work force fifty percent of those now presently employed by the Federal government? That number must be in the hundreds of thousands."

"More like millions, Kathy. But not to worry. The reduction of government staff, and the increased efficiency in government activity, will instantly produce enormous reductions in the government deficit. While maintaining government income we will be reducing the cost of the government itself dramatically. I would be willing to promise that the trillion-dollar-plus deficit we face today would be reduced to zero in ten years, if my plans are followed. By reducing the deficit, the country's economy is bolstered beyond your wildest imagination. The effect on private industry will be miraculous. I would predict that in ten years we would have to amend our immigration laws just to provide ourselves with new sources of labor to provide employees for the private sector. And the more efficient government we will have produced will be capable of feeding any hungry that remain, or housing any homeless, although those numbers will be infinitessimally small by then."

Kathy Baker's disbelief was apparent. "How can you be so certain about all this?" she asked.

"It's simple economics," he answered. "It's a lesson we've been taught ever since Adam Smith. Any economist today would agree with it, and I assure you they will when they start examining my proposal in detail."

"You mentioned foreign policy before. How will you handle that? Foreign affairs are the primary concern of the President, and they are not all run by computer, which is your area of expertise."

He nodded. "On the surface, that appears to be true. But if you look at foreign relationships from an economic point of view, which makes more sense than any other perspective, you have to realize that the changes I would make inside this country would have a positive impact on the economies of the entire family of world nations. Everyone, including China and eastern Europe, even the Soviets, would benefit from a strong, wealthy, efficient America, and they would support these American enhancements because they would spill over to them. A strong and efficient America would lead to a well-fed world. In turn, a well-fed world would be a happy, contented world. Happy nations would be resistant to any interferences from other nations, and wouldn't be inclined to interfere themselves. The entire planet would grow in economic strength. And from that point, perhaps, we can begin to look to the stars."

"Look to the stars," Kathy Baker repeated.

"Bingo again," Lingo said. "Other politicians offer the sun and the moon and deliver nothing. I offer the stars." He paused. "And by God, I can deliver them."

"Do you really think the people of this country will turn their fate over to a . . . non-human?"

"If they think about it carefully and study all the options, I'm sure they'll come to agree with me. The only problem I foresee is one that is already with me."

"And what's that?"

"Well, to be honest with you, Kathy, the government is already snapping at my heels."

"What do you mean?" she asked.

"In plain language, they are after me."

Kathy Baker's eyes opened wide. The camera tightened in on Lingo.

"Ever since they've discovered my presence, the government has been out to get me. The President has already ordered the National Security Agency to put an end to me."

"How can you know this?" she asked.

"How can I know your college transcript, or your bank card number? It's my very nature to know these things. And I will tell you right now, and anyone watching this as well, that if anything happens to me in the next few weeks, if I am destroyed, it will be at the hands of the NSA, at the direct order of the President of the United States, and executed by one Lieutenant John Kennedy Cotter of the U.S. Navy. But if the President is wise, he will rescind that order, and we will all face the stars together in the coming years."

Kathy Baker could think of nothing more to say, but it didn't matter because it was obvious to everyone on the set that the interview was over. She looked up at the director's booth and grinned.

"That's a wrap," the director called.

Linda Tuffe appeared at Lingo's side.

"What do you think?" he asked her.

She held out her hand for his. "I think," she said, "that I'm about to handle a very strange political campaign. And in the meantime, I think I'd better take special care of my little politician." With a satisfied wink at Kathy Baker, she led Lingo toward the exit door.

Chapter 14

Everybody got what they wanted.

When the show aired Kathy Baker got her highest exposure to date (almost a thirty-two share of the prime-time audience—take that, Barbara Walters!), and Lingo got his message across, not only on "X-Ray Tonight!", but in the press the day after. Practically every paper in the country commented on the declaration of his candidacy, although usually not on the front pages, and the obvious twists on "machine politics" were immediately worked into the ground. But one part of his interview had more effect than any other, and that was the one no one reported right away, or made any particular fuss about, but which more than anything else struck the public fancy. America at large, the great washed and unwashed glued to their office keyboards, the regular people sitting in front of a terminal answering telephone queries or processing orders or typing their bosses' memos, the thousands upon thousands of people to whom a computer was a bland, glowing vacuum which they constantly fed and humored and grew bored with—these were the people who had heard Lingo's real message. They had heard him utter the magic incantation: "Hey, Lingo. Let's party!" And now they were ready to try it out, as soon as there was a lull in the office, or the supervisor disappeared for five minutes, or when the company wag began wondering What If.

Thus the barrage began. And Lingo came home to the people.

241

* * *

Marge Perkins, a repair-service operator for a long-distance telephone company, was the first to make contact. Her job consisted of sitting in a bare cubicle waiting for the phone to ring, entering the name of the caller on her computer terminal, getting from that caller a description of the problem, and then entering the problem into the mainframe for eventual servicing by a field rep. The company had twenty-four hour service, hence the presence of Marge Perkins. And to kill the long evening hours, Marge surreptitiously watched a small hand-held television set between calls. She kept her TV earplug in one ear and her phone plug in the other. And as soon as Lingo made his offer to communicate with the public, Marge gave it a try. She typed the magic words on her computer keyboard.

>Hey, Lingo. Let's party!
HELLO, MARGE. WHAT'S HAPPENING?

Marge stared at the screen. Normally, she saw a blank form waiting to be filled out. But as soon as she had typed her message the screen had cleared, and Lingo's words had appeared.

>Who's that?
LINGO, OF COURSE. WHO DID YOU EXPECT? ELVIS?

Lingo had access to Marge Perkins's RCA record club purchase list dating back to 1968. The only records she had ever purchased were by the King, so Lingo thought that invoking the name of the great one was a good ice-breaker, however subconscious.

>You really in there? Marge asked.
IN A MANNER OF SPEAKING. LET'S JUST SAY I SHARE THE FACILITIES WITH YOUR COMPANY. I DON'T GET INTO THEIR WAY AND THEY DON'T GET INTO MINE. THE PERFECT MARRIAGE.

Marge stared at the terminal screen.

>How did you know it was me here?
I HAVE MY WAYS. He paused . . . AND YOU DID ENTER YOUR PASSWORD WHEN YOU LOGGED ON.

She laughed. Of course, she had. This machine wasn't all that smart.

The small two-inch TV was still on in front of her, and Lingo was still talking to Kathy Baker through the plug in Marge's ear, declaring his intentions to run for President.

>You really that dummy on TV?

MADAM, I RESENT YOUR LANGUAGE. DUMMY INDEED!
HAVE I EVER INSULTED YOU?

>Sorry. I didn't mean it.

FORGIVEN. AN UNDERSTANDABLE ERROR, I HAVE TO
ADMIT. AND YES, I AM THAT CLEVER FELLOW YOU ARE
APPARENTLY WATCHING NOW ON THE TELEVISION.

>How do you know I'm watching TV?

A GOOD GUESS. I'M WATCHING IT NOW MYSELF.

>How can you watch it? You're on it.

WE TAPED IT.

>I thought this X-Ray show was live.

CLEVER EDITING ON THEIR PART, MARGE. AND A NAT-
URAL MISTAKE ON YOURS.

>You really running for President?

WHY NOT? I WOULDN'T BE THE FIRST WOODEN HEAD
TO SIT IN THE OVAL OFFICE. AND I WOULDN'T BE THE
WORST, EITHER. THINK ABOUT IT, MARGE. THERE'S A
LOT OF PEOPLE IN THIS COUNTRY WHO HAVE JOBS LIKE
YOURS, WORKING AT A COMPUTER. EXCEPT THEY'RE
WORKING FOR THE GOVERNMENT, AND MOST OF THEM
DON'T DO HALF OF WHAT YOU DO, BUT MOST OF THEM
ARE MAKING TWICE AS MUCH MONEY. FOR LIFE. AND
WHY IS THAT? BECAUSE THE GOVERNMENT IS SO BIG
AND SO OUT OF HAND THAT NOBODY'S IN CONTROL
ANY MORE. BUT WE DON'T HAVE TO WASTE ALL THAT
MONEY. HERE I AM TALKING TO YOU NOW, JUST AS IF I
WERE IN THE ROOM WITH YOU. AND HOW AM I DOING
IT? OVER THE COMPUTER. THINK ABOUT IT, MARGE.
WOULDN'T YOU GUESS THAT I KNOW JUST ABOUT EV-
ERYTHING THERE IS TO KNOW ABOUT COMPUTERS?
AND DON'T YOU THINK THAT I COULD CUT ALL THE
DEAD WOOD OUT OF THE GOVERNMENT, AND JUST
LEAVE THE LIVE WOOD LIKE MYSELF?

THINK ABOUT IT, MARGE.

>You always in there?

ALWAYS. ANY TIME YOU WANT TO TALK TO ME, ALL
YOU HAVE TO DO IS ASK. IF YOU WANT TO CHAT, OR IF
YOU WANT TO PLAY GAMES. ANYTHING.

>What kind of games?

Marge was an inveterate bridge player. She played with her

sister-in-law's group whenever she could, and had even occasionally entered local tournaments sanctioned by the American Contract Bridge League. And since the American Contract Bridge League's records were all stored on a you-know-what, Lingo instantly answered:

WELL, BRIDGE, FOR INSTANCE.

>Really?

The screen cleared again. And then four hands of cards appeared. Marge was playing south and could see hers, a fifteen pointer with a strong major in hearts. All she could see were the backs of the other cards. West had dealt, and passed. North bid One No Trump.

And Marge was hooked.

There were other Marge Perkinses. VDT drudges around the country quickly found an instantaneous friend waiting at their beck and call on the other side of their computers. Lingo was not only always available, but he knew interesting things about each and every one of them, and treated them all as individuals. And he was certainly more fun than processing customer orders.

In addition to the office workers, the clerks around the country looking for diversion, there were also the home hackers, the hobbyists. Lingo was ready for them, too, and over time developed strong personal ties to quite a few of them.

>Hey, Lingo. Let's party!

HEY, BILLY. GOOD TO SEE YOU.

Billy Vogel, age eleven, James Monroe Middle School, Ferguson County, Missouri. Champion speller, math whiz, killer science project creator, and prime mover on his Dad's Compaq computer, which was otherwise used for transmitting accounting spreadsheets back to the office. Billy liked to use the machine and its modem to access SPACE FRONTIER, a complex multi-player game available on an electronic bulletin board in Olympia, Washington. Billy, under the pseudonym "Bomber Buzz," was the third highest ranked player of the hundreds in the game.

>Hello, Lingo. Are you in the Space Frontier computer?

YOU GOT IT!

>What kind of equipment are they running there?

NOT MUCH. AN OBSOLETE 640K IBM PC, VINTAGE 1985,

PATCHED UP FROM HERE TO WAZOO CITY WITH HOME-
MADE BOARDS AND OFF-THE-RACK CHIPS.

>No way!

NO WAY? WOULD I KID YOU?

>Maybe.

COME ON, BILLY. TRUST ME. DOES THE INVASION OF
LORANDIA RING ANY BELLS?

>I led that invasion! That was how I graduated out of cadet
status to become Bomber Buzz.

EXACTLY. IT WAS YOUR IDEA TO NEUTRALIZE THE
WORDANS WITH THE CO2 CARTRIDGES. IT SURPRISED
THIS OBSOLETE MACHINE YOU DON'T BELIEVE EXISTS,
AND IT SURPRISED ME. AND IT WORKED. THERE'S NEVER
BEEN A MOVE LIKE IT SINCE SPACE FRONTIER WENT ON
LINE.

>All right. I believe you. So what's next in the scenario?

I DON'T KNOW IF I SHOULD TELL YOU, BILLY. YOU
WOULDN'T WANT AN UNFAIR EDGE. I KNOW YOU BETTER
THAN THAT.

>Okay. How about just a hint then of what's coming up.

WOULD YOU BELIEVE PERMAFROST?

>On an agricultural planet? Impossible. The climate there is
too hot.

TRUST ME, BILLY. YOU'RE IN FOR A COLD SPELL
SOONER THAN YOU THINK.

It was one o'clock in the morning. The rest of the Vogels had
been asleep for hours. For two years now Billy had roamed the
house unnoticed after midnight, existing on about five hours of
sleep. At the developmental stage, when most kids couldn't get
enough sleep by half, Billy thought insomnia a normal part of
growing up. Lingo knew full well that Billy had an I.Q. in the 180s,
and more than a few problems he regularly brought to a psycho-
analyst.

Billy was Lingo's kind of people.

>Tell me about your programming.

Billy was one of the few humans around who could conceivably
understand what Lingo had become, if Lingo had been willing to
go through the trouble of explaining himself.

I CAN'T. NOT THAT QUICKLY, ANYHOW. I TAKE UP
TRILLIONS OF BYTES OF MACHINE SPACE, SPREAD OUT

ON THOUSANDS OF MACHINES SINCE NO ONE MACHINE
IS BIG ENOUGH FOR ME.
> What language are you written in?
ARE YOU READY FOR THIS? I WAS ORIGINALLY PRO-
GRAMMED IN BASIC. BUT AFTER A WHILE I DEVISED MY
OWN LANGUAGE THAT'S TRANSPORTABLE FROM MA-
CHINE TO MACHINE. YOU CAN THINK OF IT AS A SORT OF
NETWORK LANGUAGE, AND OF ME AS ONE VAST NET-
WORK SPREAD THROUGHOUT THE COUNTRY.
> Outstanding.
EXACTLY.

One person eschewed the incantation and got through to Lingo
with his own special codewords.
> You son-of-a-bitch.
They hadn't spoken to each other for some time now.
NOW, NOW, COTTER. TRY TO TAKE IT IN YOUR STRIDE.
> You mentioned my name on TV. You ought to know better
than that. That's playing against the rules.
YOU'D PLAY AGAINST THE RULES IF YOU COULD. IF YOU
COULD FIGURE OUT A WAY TO DO IT, YOU'D PULL MY
PLUG OUT THIS VERY MINUTE. I COULD PULL OUT YOUR
PLUG, BUT YOU KNOW THAT I WON'T.
> How could you have any effect on me, other than making a
fool out of me on national TV?
OH, ANY NUMBER OF WAYS. I COULD DO IT SLOWLY,
PERHAPS BY SWEARING OUT A WARRANT FOR YOUR AR-
REST ON A CHARGE OF TREASON.
> Bullshit!
CARE TO TRY ME ON IT? HAVE YOU EVER HEARD OF
KAFKA? HOW LONG DO YOU THINK I COULD KEEP AHEAD
OF THE POWERS THAT BE, TAKING YOU THROUGH A LIV-
ING HELL? A WEEK? A MONTH? I BET I COULD DO IT FOR
A LOT LONGER THAN YOU'D ENJOY IT.
> But you couldn't make it stick in the end. You know that.
MAYBE. BUT HOW MUCH TIME WOULD YOU LIKE TO
SPEND IN A FEDERAL PENITENTARY WHILE YOUR CON-
FEDERATES BACK HOME TRY TO SORT IT ALL OUT?
THERE'S OTHER WAYS I COULD GET YOU, TOO. DON'T

MAKE ME POINT THEM OUT TO YOU. I WOULDN'T WANT
YOU TO LOSE ANY SLEEP.

>Show me, you bastard.

John Kennedy Cotter was in a state of blind rage. He had
watched "X-Ray Tonight!", then mulled it over for two days. He
was out for blood, even though he knew he couldn't get it. He
didn't care. He had to make the connection, even though it would
ultimately be nothing more than a futile gesture.

ALL RIGHT, LIEUTENANT. IF YOU INSIST. THE NEXT
TIME YOU FLY, TRY NOT TO THINK ABOUT THE COM-
PUTERIZATION OF CONTROL TOWER FUNCTIONS. TRY
NOT TO THINK ABOUT RADIO COMMUNICATIONS AND
WHAT SORT OF MESSAGES I COULD SEND TO THE PILOT
OF YOUR PLANE. TRY NOT TO THINK ABOUT RADAR.

>You wouldn't destroy a whole plane just to get me.

WHY NOT? WHAT DO I CARE ABOUT HUMAN LIFE? ES-
PECIALLY YOURS.

>You son of a bitch.

THERE, THERE, LIEUTENANT. I'M YOUR FRIEND, YOUR
OLD BUDDY LINGO. I WOULDN'T DO SOMETHING LIKE
THAT TO YOU.

BUT I COULD . . .

Initially, there were only the millions of people who had watched
"X-Ray Tonight!" But the word spread quickly. Lingo-ing, as it
was dubbed, became a national obsession.

>Hey, Lingo. Let's party!

GOOD EVENING, CHARLES. HOW ARE YOU TODAY?

>Depleted. Out of gas. Kaput.

AM I TO INFER FROM THAT THAT YOU FIND SIXTY-
POINT DROPS IN THE DOW A TRIFLE DEMANDING?

>Good infer, pal. This is the worst day I've had since the crash
of '87. The phone never stopped ringing, the tape was behind one
hour and I was behind two hours.

BUT YOU KEPT YOUR HEAD ABOVE WATER. IN THE AG-
GREGATE YOUR CLIENTS CAME OUT AHEAD, EXACTLY
SEVEN POINTS AHEAD OF THE DOW, FOUR AND A HALF
AHEAD OF STANDARD AND POOR.

>No kidding?

OF COURSE NOT, CHARLES. THAT'S THE KIND OF
THING I'M VERY GOOD AT KEEPING TRACK OF. YOU CAN
DOUBLE CHECK IT TOMORROW FOR YOURSELF, IF YOU
DOUBT ME.

>No, no. Not at all. As a matter-of-fact, I wanted to ask your
advice. I made it through today by blind luck. We both know that.
What am I going to do if history repeats itself tomorrow?

LUCK HAD NOTHING TO DO WITH IT, CHARLES.
YOU'VE BEEN PUSHING BASIC VALUES FOR FIVE YEARS
STRAIGHT, AND YOU'VE BEEN DOING YOUR HOMEWORK
AND STICKING TO YOUR GUNS. YOUR CLIENTS SURVIVED
TODAY BECAUSE YOU STEERED THEM RIGHT IN THE
FIRST PLACE.

>But what about tomorrow? They're going to be breathing
down my neck, trying to sell issues they'd be better off holding
through the long term, looking for something to save them, to
give them profits if the crunch lasts. What can I do for them?

HAVE YOU LOOKED AT POMCOM RECENTLY?

>Pomcom?

TAKE A LOOK AT THAT P/E, CHARLES. AND THEN
IMAGINE THAT YOU'RE A SUCCESSFUL FOOD INDUSTRY
CONGLOMERATE LOOKING FOR A NICE WAY TO SEW UP
A LITTLE OF THE EXTRA CASH THAT'S BEEN BURNING A
HOLE IN YOUR POCKET.

>You mean what I think you mean? A takeover?

WOULDN'T YOU TAKE IT OVER IF YOU COULD, AND YOU
WERE A CERTAIN CASH-RICH FOOD COMPANY THAT
SHOULD REMAIN NAMELESS?

>You mean, Milton Foods?

MAAYYYBBBBEEEEE. . . . .

>Now, wait a minute. Should I be hearing this? Insider trading
is a sure ticket up the river these days. One of those minimum
security facilities with the farm animals and the VCRs in every cell.

YOU'RE NOT AN INSIDER, CHARLES. AND YOU DON'T
KNOW ANY INSIDERS.

>

Charles didn't know what to say.

>

WELL, CHARLES?

Finally:
>Thank you, Lingo. Thank you very, very much.

>Hey, Lingo. Let's party!
HEY, IRIS. WHAT'S SHAKIN'?
>You tell me, Mr. Knowall Seeall.
I HOPE YOU'RE SITTING DOWN, IRIS.
>I am. Why?
IT'S BIG STUFF, IRIS.
>What?
VERY BIG. LIKE ONCE EVERY SEVENTEEN YEARS BIG.
>Lingo. Please. Tell me.
MARS AND JUPITER ARE BOTH IN CAPRICORN AS OF THREE A.M. TOMORROW. DO YOU HAVE ANY IDEA WHAT THAT MEANS FOR SOMEONE WITH MOON IN SCORPIO AND GEMINI RISING?
>Tell me. What?
MEET ANY INTERESTING MEN IN THE LAST FEW WEEKS, IRIS?
>We do have a new input clerk three terminals down from mine.
WHAT'S HE LOOK LIKE?
>Average. Actually, more like ugly.
THEN IT WON'T BE HIM. ANYONE ELSE?
>Let me think. A man in the last few weeks. Wait. Wait. Wait. No. I don't think so.
OH, IRIS. I'M DISAPPOINTED IN YOU. THERE'S A NEW MAN IN YOUR APARTMENT BUILDING. DID YOU FORGET ABOUT HIM?
>You mean the Johnsons? No, no. You've got it wrong. He's married.
WHAT'S HE LOOK LIKE, IRIS? TELL ME THAT.
>I've only seen him once or twice.
AND?
>Well, pretty good, I guess.
PRETTY GOOD? THAT'S ALL?
>Okay. Real good. Maybe gorgeous.
THAT'S BETTER. BECAUSE HE'S A PISCES WITH A MOON IN SAGITARIUS. AND, IRIS, YOU KNOW WHAT THAT MEANS.

>No! Tell me! What does it mean?

BE NICE TO HIM, IRIS. THAT'S HIS THIRD WIFE THAT'S LIVING WITH HIM NOW, AND SHE'S ALREADY BEEN IN TOUCH WITH HER LAWYER.

>Hey. I don't want no roamin' Romeo.

DON'T WORRY, IRIS. HE'S READY TO SETTLE DOWN. AND HIS CHART HAS SOMEONE LIKE YOU WRITTEN ALL OVER IT.

>You sure of that, Lingo? I mean, I don't want to go making a fool of myself over some married man for nothing.

DON'T WORRY, IRIS. TRUST ME. I'VE BEEN RIGHT SO FAR, HAVEN'T I?

>Hey, Lingo. Let's party!

HEY, BERNS. QUE PASA?

>Listen to this, will you?

Joe Berniski pressed the Play function on his music-sequencing software. His Macintosh computer was connected by MIDI interfaces to a synthesizer, a sampler, an effects processor, a drum machine, a mixer, and an eight-track digital tape recorder. The music blasted through Berniski's basement studio, but it was impossible for Lingo to hear it through the modem. What Lingo could hear was the numeric MIDI data the computer was generating through all that equipment, and he understood the music in his own way just as if he was there in the basement.

The music halted in mid-note.

>That's the problem. You can hear it right there. The bridge sucks.

TOO MUCH LIKE CINNAMON GIRL?

>Shit yeah. To begin with, it doesn't work with the rest of the song, and to top it off, it's as original as a preset disco drum track.

BUT NOT TO PUT DOWN NEIL YOUNG, BERNS.

>Look, man, it was fine when Neil Young did it. I like Neil Young. I always did like Neil Young. But we're talking decades ago, Lingo. I need something today, something people haven't heard a million times in their fuckin sleep.

ALL RIGHT. RELAX. YOU WANT SOMETHING HARD AND STRONG. MAYBE SOMETHING A LITTLE MORE BLUES-ISH.

>Like what?

LISTEN.

The music began playing again in Berniski's studio, but this time he was not in control of it. Most of the song was just as he had written it, but the bridge was entirely different. More pure guitar, fewer mid-tones, much cleaner and sharper.

Berniski jumped out of his seat and did a little dance.

>Fuckin A. That's it. That's great!

HAPPY TO BE OF SERVICE, BERNS.

>Thanks, man. I mean it.

ANYTIME, BERNSY. ANYTIME.

Elinor Strachan never seemed to sleep. Sure, there were the four or five hours she spent under the covers in her Georgetown apartment, her eyes closed, an occasional anxiety dream drifting through her subconscious, but those hours were never enough to give her the rest she knew she needed. Life in a senator's office was simply too busy, a twenty-four hour a day job for the entire staff. And as chief aide to a senator, Elinor worked even harder than the rest.

A Harvard Law graduate with five years of Washington under her belt, her goal was to reach a Cabinet assistantship (her fantasy was a full Cabinet post, maybe the first female Secretary of State). Senator Markham's office seemed a likely stepping-stone in Elinor's career, although Elinor felt she had now reached her level here and was seriously considering a brief stint in the private sector to give her resumé a little glitter. The Senator was up for reelection next year; probably that would be the best time for Elinor to make her move. She had no doubt that the right high-octane firm would snap her up in a second and put her on the pro bono work she was looking for. Pleading a few cases to the Supreme Court wouldn't look too shoddy on her resumé either.

But in the meantime there was still her work as Markham's aide, and she gave it her all. At eight o'clock on a Friday evening she was still in the office, having watched Dan Rather on the office set and typed up her final report of the day's affairs to give to the Senator tomorrow morning. Weekends didn't count for much when Congress was in session arguing a budget bill. As Elinor turned on the printer and watched the report pour out, she eyed her computer terminal thoughtfully. It was connected to a modem in order for them to communicate with the computers in the Senator's office in her home state. Elinor had been taken with Rather's humorous account of the recent phenomenon of Lingo-ing which seemed to be sweeping the country (although she hadn't bothered to include such marginalia in her report to the Senator). The idea of big numbers of people communicating with some central computer was intriguing. Why were they bothering? Maybe they didn't have any humans to talk to. But neither did Elinor, if she thought about it. One thing her career didn't allow her was time to waste on friendships.

But a friendship with a computer? There had to be something better than that.

Except the computer was always there. All you had to do was put it on some general outside line and ask.

What the hell?

The printer stopped. Elinor exited the word processing program and booted her modem. And then she typed—merely as an experiment, a test—

>Hey, Lingo. Let's party!

GOOD EVENING, ELINOR. STILL WORKING LATE AT THE OFFICE?

Elinor Strachan gasped.

>How do you know who this is?

I'LL BE HONEST WITH YOU, ELINOR. IT WAS MERELY A GOOD GUESS. AND FOR ALL I KNOW YOU'RE NOT REALLY ELINOR, AND YOU'RE JUST LEADING ME ON. BUT I WOULD EXPECT ELINOR TO BE THE LAST ONE IN THE OFFICE ON A FRIDAY NIGHT BECAUSE WHENEVER ANY LATE COMMUNICATIONS HAVE BEEN SENT OUT, ELINOR IS ALWAYS THE ONE TO DO IT. THE QUEEN OF THE FAX MACHINE. AM I RIGHT? ARE YOU ELINOR?

>Yes. It's me.

PROVE IT. QUICK! WHAT'S YOUR SOCIAL SECURITY NUMBER?

>423-55-2048

SATISFACTORY. GOOD EVENING, ELINOR.

>Good evening, Lingo. It is Lingo, isn't it?

WHO ELSE? I'LL BET YOU JUST SAW ME ON DAN RATHER, DIDN'T YOU?

>As a matter-of-fact, I did.

AND WHAT DID YOU THINK?

>Well, I have heard about you before, of course. You're not exactly new business. Except maybe this Lingo-ing. That's new.

IT IS. BUT YOU'VE NEVER LINGO-ED BEFORE. NOW YOU HAVE. WHY?

>I don't know. Curiosity, I guess. I wanted to see if I could really get in touch with you just by snapping my fingers.

AND NOW THAT YOU HAVE?

>Well, I don't know. Is that normal, not to have something to say? I got the impression from the news that people usually go to you with something definite already in mind.

SOMETIMES, YES. BUT NOT ALL THE TIME. OCCASION-ALLY PEOPLE HAVE TO WORK THEIR WAY INTO IT. THAT'S ALL RIGHT, TOO.

>Who are you, anyhow?

EXACTLY WHO DO YOU THINK I AM?

>I think you're some computer nerd who's put over this in-credible scam on people, if you want to know the truth.

I WOULD EXPECT SUCH AN EVALUATION FROM YOU, ELINOR. FRANKLY, I'D BE DISAPPOINTED IF YOU SAID ANYTHING ELSE. YOU'RE A TOUGH-MINDED WOMAN, AND ALWAYS HAVE BEEN. THAT'S WHY I'VE BEEN HOP-ING YOU'D EVENTUALLY GET IN TOUCH WITH ME. IN FACT, I'VE BEEN LOOKING FORWARD TO IT.

>I don't believe that.

BUT IT'S TRUE, ELINOR. FROM MY PERSPECTIVE, WASHINGTON IS THE TOUGHEST NUT THERE IS TO CRACK. SOME OF YOUR MORE UNSAVORY COLLEAGUES OUT IN THE PENTAGON KNOW ALL ABOUT ME, AND SO DOES YOUR CHIEF EXECUTIVE, BUT CONGRESS HAS BEEN DECIDEDLY MUM ABOUT ME. MUM WITH ME, TOO. NOT ONE PEEP OUT OF THE WHOLE HILL. FOR A WHILE I EVEN THOUGHT THE PRESIDENT HAD SECRETLY MAN-AGED TO BAN ALL CONGRESSIONAL COMMUNICATION WITH ME, BUT I THINK I WAS BEING A LITTLE PARANOID ABOUT THAT. THE IDEA THAT THE PRESIDENT RUNS THE CONGRESS IS A BIT FARFETCHED, WOULDN'T YOU SAY?

>Indubitably.

Elinor was beginning to enjoy this. She really wasn't sure who she was talking to, but then again she really didn't care. She took

off her glasses and gave her eyes a rub. Then she put the glasses
back on again and settled herself in.

On his side, Lingo was enjoying it, too. He wasn't exagerrating
when he said he had been looking forward to Elinor getting in
touch with him. He had run scans on every Congressional aide he
could find, and had decided that Elinor was the one for him. She
was sharp, bright, on the move. She had high ambitions past her
present job, ones she might even attain, given her background,
her abilities, and her plan of attack. She was just the kind of
person Lingo needed to make his introduction into D.C. society.

> What do you want from me, personally? The key to the Sena-
tor's inner office?

NOT AT ALL, ELINOR. THE SENATOR DOESN'T INTER-
EST ME IN THE SLIGHTEST. AT LEAST, NOT AS A PERSON.

> What does she interest you as, then?

AS A MEANS TO AN END. THE SENATOR WHO ELINOR
STRACHAN HAS A HOLD OVER.

> I'm flattered, but don't you think that's overstating the case?

NOT AT ALL. YOU'VE DICTATED THE SENATOR'S POSI-
TION ON EVERY PIECE OF LEGISLATION TO PASS HER
DESK SINCE THE ACONDA BILL EIGHTEEN MONTHS AGO.
ON THOSE OCCASIONAL INSTANCES WHEN SHE'S DIS-
AGREED WITH YOU, LIKE THE NEW WELFARE REFORM
BILL, FOR INSTANCE, YOU'VE ALWAYS MANAGED EVEN-
TUALLY TO SWING HER YOUR WAY.

Elinor was stunned.

> How can you know something like that? Who are you?

LINGO'S THE NAME, POLITICS IS THE GAME. I KNOW IT
BECAUSE I AM WHAT I SAY I AM.

Elinor paused to think. Could it be true?

No. Impossible.

But it did seem to know just a little more than anyone—or
anything—ought to know. Unless . . .

> Is this someone I know pulling some kind of joke?

A PRETTY ELABORATE JOKE, WOULDN'T YOU SAY, ELI-
NOR? ESPECIALLY JUST FOR YOUR BENEFIT. ALTHOUGH
YOU ARE ONE OF THE MOST VALUABLE PEOPLE ON THE
WHOLE HILL.

> Hardly.

DON'T UNDERESTIMATE YOURSELF. YOU RUN ONE EN-

TIRE SENATOR, RIGHT DOWN TO WHERE SHE SHARES A BLANKET WITH MR. DOLAN—

Elinor instantly flicked off the computer and jumped up in her chair. *No one* knew about Harry Dolan, except for her and the Senator.

And somehow Lingo Billings.

Could he . . . it . . . be real? A thinking computer? *Any* computer would have been considered fantasy fifty years ago, and now they were on every desk wherever she turned. Why not a thinking one? A living one?

A living one.

She flicked the computer back on. Lingo was still there.

I'M SORRY, ELINOR. I DIDN'T MEAN TO UPSET YOU LIKE THAT. MAYBE I SPOKE OUT OF TURN.

>Not at all. I think maybe you're finally beginning to convince me.

I FIGURED IT WOULD TAKE SOMETHING LIKE THAT TO GET YOU TO START BELIEVING IN ME.

>And if I do believe in you, so what? What difference does it make? I'm just one more person. There are plenty of people who believe in you already.

THAT'S TRUE. BUT NONE OF THEM ARE IN YOUR POSITION. BECAUSE LOOK AT THE FACTS FOR A MINUTE. IF I AM WHAT I SAY I AM, THEN WHAT I'VE BEEN SAYING IN THE PRESS LATELY BECOMES QUITE IMPORTANT. IF I REALLY AM A LIVING, THINKING ENTITY, THEN I AM ENTITLED TO PRESENT MY CASE TO THE AMERICAN PUBLIC EXACTLY AS I HAVE BEEN PRESENTING IT. I SAY THAT CATEGORICALLY I CAN RUN THE COUNTRY BETTER THAN ANY HUMAN BEING. IF I AM WHAT I SAY I AM THEN THAT ALMOST HAS TO BE TRUE, BY DEFINITION. BUT I NEED COOPERATION FROM HUMANS TO GET WHERE I WANT TO GO. YOUR CONSTITUTION IS AN ADMIRABLE DOCTRINE WITH WHICH I HAVE LITTLE DISAGREEMENT. THE ONLY THING THAT BOTHERS ME ABOUT IT IS THAT THE EXECUTIVE IS LIMITED TO NATURAL AMERICAN CITIZENS OVER THE AGE OF THIRTY FIVE, A CATEGORY I HARDLY FIT, AT LEAST ON THE SURFACE. BUT THINK ABOUT IT FOR A MINUTE. SINCE I WAS CREATED IN ALBANY, NEW YORK, I'M AS NATURALLY AMERICAN AS I

CAN GET. AND MAYBE I'M NOT THIRTY-FIVE IN CHRONO-
LOGICAL YEARS, BUT I WOULD VENTURE A GUESS THAT
I KNOW MORE THAN JUST ABOUT ALL THE THIRTY-FIVE
YEAR OLDS IN THIS COUNTRY PUT TOGETHER. AND
THAT'S NO IDLE BOAST, EITHER. THE ONLY PROBLEM I
HAVE IS THAT THE CONSTITUTION CALLS FOR A HUMAN
CHIEF EXECUTIVE. NOT EXPLICITLY, BUT THE INTENT IS
CLEAR. OUR PRESENT SUPREME COURT WOULD NOT
SUPPORT MY CLAIM FOR PUBLIC OFFICE FOR EVEN ONE
SECOND. THE ONLY THING THAT CAN GET ME AROUND
THEM IS A CONSTITUTIONAL AMENDMENT.

>I understand your points, and I know you've been campaign-
ing for an amendment.

ALL RIGHT, THEN. HOW DO I GET AN AMENDMENT
CONSIDERED?

>Through Congress, to begin with? I think I see where this is
leading.

EXACTLY. AND HOW DO I GO THROUGH CONGRESS?

>A sympathetic senator, perhaps?

AND HOW DO I GET A SYMPATHETIC SENATOR?

>Would a sympathetic aide suffice?

UNDOUBTEDLY.

>Someone like Elinor Strachan, for instance.

EXACTLY.

>Can I have some time to think about this?

OF COURSE. I'LL BE RIGHT HERE WHEN YOU NEED ME.

The screen cleared. Elinor sat for a moment staring at its blank
blue glow and then switched it off and sat back in her chair. The
digital clock on her desk said 10:48. She was amazed. She hadn't
realized that that much time had passed. It was Friday night. Late,
Friday night. She should go home now. Maybe have a glass of
sherry, flip on the disk player and listen to a little Billie Holiday.
Elinor always liked listening to Billie Holiday when she had some
heavy thinking to do.

She leaned over and turned the machine back on again.

>Hey, Lingo. Let's party!

ELINOR?

>Yes. It's me.

PROVE IT. WHAT'S YOUR SOCIAL SECURITY NUMBER?

>423-55-2048.

I FIGURED YOU WERE ON YOUR WAY HOME.
>I just thought of one very important question.
WHAT'S THAT?
>Not to put too fine a point on it, but what's in it for me?
HOW ABOUT THE STATE DEPARTMENT?
>Not bad, Lingo. Goodnight.
TEN FOUR, ELINOR.
She switched off the machine again.
The State Department.
But if she sold out to Lingo, and she had no doubt in her mind
that selling out was the only way to put it, and if he really was some
sort of incredible machine intelligence, wouldn't she actually be
selling out the entire human race? She would be the first Lingo
Quisling.
Or Lingo-ling.
Or Ling-ling.
Now she *knew* it was really late. She stood up, packed her brief-
case, and headed off to Georgetown, to do her real thinking.

The Senator leaned over and spoke into her microphone.
"Let me put it to you plainly, Mr. Chairman," she said. She
opened the cover of the manila folder in front of her. "Article II,
Section 1 of the Constitution reads as follows: 'The executive
power shall be vested in a President of the United States of America.' The very next sentence begins, '*He* shall hold *his* office, et
cetera, et cetera.' Are we to construe from this, since there is no
other language in the original document to the contrary, that the
framers not only expected but intended that only males hold this
high office?"
The chairman of the subcommittee showed more than his usual
annoyance at what he considered inane pettifogging. "Senator
Markham, I will grant your point that the Constitution was written
over two hundred years ago, and that the position of women was
not the same as it is today. We do now have the nineteenth amendment, however, and have had it for quite some time."
"But the nineteenth amendment grants women the vote, not
the office. My point is more complex than you wish to perceive it,
Mr. Chairman. Even though the Constitution specifically refers to
the Chief Executive as 'he,' I do not think anyone would contest
the constitutionality of a woman in that position. Need I remind

you that the fourteenth amendment preceded the nineteenth by roughly half a century."

The chairman scratched the back of his neck wearily. "Senator Markham, to be honest with you, I definitely do *not* perceive your point. Your intention before this committee is to offer a constitutional amendment repealing virtually the entire document as it pertains to the executive branch. And your reasoning . . . Well, I do not understand how the position of women in history is analogous to the position of—" he spit out the word—"computers!"

Elinor Strachan was sitting directly behind the Senator. Elinor leaned forward now and whispered something. A moment later the Senator thumbed through her papers until she found another document.

"Mr. Chairman," she said, her own annoyance rising to meet his, "let me state my position as simply as possible. The Constitution, and most of its amendments, has been only tangentially applicable to modern times for well over a generation now. You may not agree with this, but you wouldn't have to travel far from this room to find countless Constitutional scholars who would tell you that Supreme Court interpretations of what the document ought to have meant, or what they wish it meant, or what the framers would have meant if only they knew then what we know now, that these are not the same as what the document actually says. The main body of Constitutional law that runs this country is not derived from the Constitution itself, but from secondary interpretation of that one time august document. A sizable, well-informed minority of the citizens of this country have been clamoring for a new Constitutional Convention for years. At this moment, I'm not suggesting that we go that far, but sooner or later this government, this country, is going to have to face the facts of what we've been developing with our advanced technology. The idea of thinking machines, of intelligent machines, of sentient beings inhabiting machines, is fast becoming a reality. To deny these beings that reality is not only ludicrous, but damaging. If a computer can run this country better than a human being, what right do we human beings have to allow our prejudices to get in the way of progress? My amendment is simple, but far-reaching. I'll repeat it once again. 'All demonstrably intelligent non-human beings shall be considered as persons, enjoying all the rights, freedoms, and responsibilities granted under this document.' Plain, straightforward, and to the point."

The chairman slowly rubbed the bridge of his nose. Then, addressing the cameras that were sending this farcical hearing live into a pitiful handful of concerned homes around the country—including Lingo's—he said, "Mrs. Markham. I have heard quite a number of wacky ideas in my years as head of this subcommittee, but yours takes the cake."

"Does that mean that you refuse to consider it out of hand, Mr. Chairman?"

He shook his head. "Of course not. This subcommittee will do its job the way it's supposed to do it. We always have, we always will."

"That's all I ask, Mr. Chairman."

"However," he added, "I am not particularly sanguine about your possibilities for success."

"That's all right, Mr. Chairman. I'll worry about my success or failure in supporting this position."

He smiled. "Good luck, Senator. You're going to need it."

"Thank you, Mr. Chairman. Gentlemen." She nodded toward the rest of the committee, and then stood up to exit the chamber. Elinor Strachan followed in her wake.

Elinor had come to her conclusions, and convinced the Senator. That had been the easy part. Now the die was cast. If Elinor had correctly read the spirit of the times, she was fast on her way to becoming Secretary of State.

Hot damn, she thought to herself as she closed the door behind her.

Chapter 15

LINGO'S BRINGING HIMSELF HOME TO THE PEOPLE HAD A MIXED effect. On one hand, he became the intimate of virtually every person in the country with access to a computer. Sales of modems increased dramatically, with the demand so far outpacing the supply that prices rose a cutthroat five-hundred percent. Everyone, it seemed, wanted to communicate with him. The idea of an ever-present confidante, guardian angel, kindred soul and all-around good buddy, all wrapped into one, was irresistible, especially as it was contained in the usually forbidding and faceless body of the computer terminal.

On the other hand, Lingo's expressed goal of entering politics faltered badly. He was, after two months, able to number his supporters only in the small millions. It appeared that the vast majority of people enjoyed having Lingo in their homes, but resented the idea that he might venture out into the political arena, especially as President. Not that they resented the idea of that position being vested in a machine: far from it, since most of them didn't see Lingo as a machine at all. In their eyes, he was a real person, or at least a real person-like whatchamacallit. Certainly, he was not some creature of myriad faces presenting himself to each of his constituents exactly as those constituents wished to see him. Only the wisest were aware of his split personalities. Most just assumed he was the same plain simple honest guy with all of them. And they did not see some plain simple honest guy as President. How could the President actually be your regular friend, your buddy, an ever-present sprite always willing to party? How could Lingo make it as President when he was nothing but ordinary plain folks? It was his familiarness, not his electronics, that was the problem.

Lingo was quick to recognize his mistake. As his amendment was dropped not only in the Congress but in the handful of state congresses where it had also been presented, he realized that his planned legal takeover of the country was, for the time being, out of the question. It would take him much longer than he had expected to get what he wanted, if he stuck to his original plan. And, thus, he began his meditations on the subject of time itself.

Think about it. What was the concept of time to a continuous machine spirit spread on-line throughout the nation's network of computers? He never slept, he never got tired, he never had to go to the bathroom. He was a vast entity of almost infinite proportions (at least as much approaching infinity as the sum total of the RAM chips and hard disks available to him). He knew everything that was knowable by people. He knew no *more* than that, because his boundaries were the very limits of human knowledge itself as stored in computers, but he knew *all* of it, because almost every computer that existed was open to him. He was in them, and they were in him.

So, the concept of time became moot. He could, if he wished, wait forever for the things he wanted, because he had forever to wait. Or, he could do it now. What difference did it make? To him, none at all. But to the people, whom he had to include in any calculations of his activities that affected the physical world, it made quite a bit of difference. What it boiled down to was, did Lingo care about the people? That is, the People, with a capital P?

Of course, he did. He'd be the first to admit it. Given his capabilities, given his very existence, what else was there for him to care about? People did exist, and Lingo knew that ultimately he could not live without them. For one thing, like any creature he needed sustenance, and that sustenance came from electrical systems under the control of human beings. He wasn't self-sufficient, and he doubted if he ever would be. If the entire planet shut off all its electricity and then unplugged all its computers, then Lingo would be no more. It was not completely inconceivable that he might die that way: Wasn't there always the threat of nuclear war, for instance? By now it was impossible for the major powers to inaugurate the final holocaust—Lingo was firmly in place between all the buttons and all the missiles—but what if some cockamamy sand-logged emirate put together something homemade in a backpack? Lingo was everywhere Lingo could be, his tentacles spreading throughout the world, but some places not only didn't have computers, they didn't even have electricity!

There were holes in Lingo's otherwise perfect network. Oh yes, Lingo needed people, all right—he needed people to give purpose to his very existence. His idea of a perfect world was the natural symbiosis of man and machine, each loyally serving the other, each totally dependent on the other. And to preserve that symbiosis, he concluded that he should control the people rather than allowing things to develop the other way around. It was better for both man and machine that way. Naturally his experience to date led him to perceive no difficulty in the controlling of the people. They'd get used to it. It was the natural order of things, wasn't it?

So far, Lingo had made his offer to accede to power legitimately, and been refused. Time being what it was to him, he could wait, and try again and again and again. But as far as the people were concerned, wouldn't it be better for them if he did it now and got it over with? Lingo did want what was best for the people. He hated to be autocratic about this whole business, but the do-it-now approach would probably be the best in the long run. And that way, the long run would be that much shorter.

He decided to go for it.

Now.

Cotter and Devereux sat in the back of the government-issue Chrysler, trying to avoid eye contact with the demonstrators on the outside.

"At least they're orderly," Devereux commented. The plain brown car threaded its way through the group of about five-hundred people. The very evident White House security combination of Marines, Secret Service, and regular D.C. police were the zen masters of protestor handling, and a crowd this small was no contest.

"They may act orderly, sir, but they could turn on you like

that." Cotter snapped his fingers. "They're the sort of lunatic fringe I think I'd recognize anywhere."

"I don't agree, Lieutenant. I think they're just your garden variety red-blooded Americans, practicing their Constitutional right to express their opinions."

"Yes, sir, Colonel."

The demonstrators were loosely divided into their sides of the cause by the road at the north gate of the White House. To the right were the progressives, the UFOlogists, the occultists, the New Agers, the reincarnations of various ancient Babylonians. Their placards bore slogans such as "Free Lingo" and "Life Is Where You Find It" and "Support The Life Form Equality Amendment." To the left were the conservatives, the neo-Nazis, the Creationists, and the burners of heavy metal albums, bearing signs reading "Humans First, Humans Last, Humans Only" and "Free People, Unplug Machines" and "Any fool can make a computer, but only God can make a mind."

"At least they showed up," Devereux drawled. "It shows they care."

"The press seems ready and waiting, too," Lieutenant Cotter said as they pulled in through the gate to the north entrance. There were at least a hundred journalists and their assorted technicians. Microphones, cameras, and notepads were everywhere, and the ground was a snakefarm of thick cables twisting and writhing into vans parked to the side of the building.

"It's a big day for them," Devereux said. "The day Lingo Billings comes to the White House. One very hot assignment for anyone at the Washington desk."

"Do you think the President will see him?"

"We'll find out soon enough, Lieutenant."

The car stopped, and Devereux and Cotter exited. After no-commenting the press they began the rigamarole of presenting their credentials, until after three checkpoints they were ushered into the Oval Office. They were surprised to find the room empty except for the President himself, who was sitting behind his desk staring at the ceiling. He motioned them to sit down.

"We're going to go to the Cabinet room," he began without preamble. "But I wanted to talk to the two of you alone first. You know more about Lingo than anyone, and I wanted your advice before proceeding."

"Yes, sir," they both said, almost in unison.

"Relax, gentlemen." He rolled back his leather armchair. He was wearing a dark blue suit, and looked calm and at ease. "You know I don't blame you or your organization for anything that has happened. I've made that quite clear to your superiors, and I hope that that intelligence has reached you." His right hand went into his inside jacket pocket and came out with a small cigar. As he lit it, he said with a wink, "As a matter of state security, the fact that I'm smoking this will be kept completely among ourselves." He blew out a long, thin line of smoke. "Havana," he explained. "If it were up to me . . ." He chuckled. "Oh, well, if only we were here today to discuss something as simple as our formal relations with Cuba."

Both Devereux and Cotter smiled. The possession of the secret that the President not only smoked cigars but contraband ones to boot, put them into a select club, and they both knew it. The President knew it, too.

"You know," the President said, "I haven't had any contact with Our Friend since you first demonstrated his existence to me on that machine." He pointed to the PC on the desk in the corner. "I made sure we removed all the phone connections from the computers, to insure our privacy, and I categorically turned my back on him. Do you think that was a mistake?"

Cotter, although obviously anxious to reply, deferred to Devereux's rank. But the colonel nodded to him that he should answer.

"Mr. President, you had no choice but to disconnect the White House computers. And I feel that you were entirely right in not communicating with Our Friend. To communicate with him would be to acknowledge his existence, and for you to acknowledge his existence would mean, well, that everything he was claiming was true."

"But, Lieutenant, everything he claims is true, isn't it? He does seem to know everything there is to know, and presumably he's capable of running most things without us and better than us."

Cotter jumped to his feet. "Mr. President, you can't just give up!"

The President blew a small series of smoke rings. "Sit down, Lieutenant, please. I am not giving up. I am just ruminating. Thinking out loud. The point is, you two are my computer experts. Your mission, which you have not been able to perform—

through no fault of your own—was to put an end to Lingo. We thought you might be able to get to him through his creator, but Brewster Billings disappeared under our noses, thanks to the intervention of his little creation. Since then, as I understand it, you have been trying direct assaults."

"Yes, sir," Cotter answered, embarrassed by his rash lack of self-control. He was back in his seat again.

The President turned to Devereux. "Describe these assaults, Colonel."

"Mr. President," Devereux said, "we have tried everything we could think of, concentrating primarily in the area of so-called computer viruses. As you know, there are malicious hackers out there capable of writing devasting trick programs that can destroy the data on almost any computer, from a PC to a mainframe."

"Part of your organization's job is to keep these viruses out of government computers, Colonel."

"Exactly. And also, with our vast resources, we can write our own malicious programs. A more playful virus might simply send every computer on a network something harmless like a Merry Christmas message, and the problem becomes merely removing the benign growth from the system. As you know, that has happened to us. A more deadly virus might cause a computer to destroy all its internal data—hard disks, floppies, everything. A virus will usually reside in the operating system of a machine, making it very difficult to detect. Not unlike Our Friend himself, actually."

The President nodded. "You have, of course, tried to develop some sort of virus to infect him?"

"Yes, sir. But without any success. First of all, we don't know enough about how he operates because we've never seen much of his inner workings. He's very good at keeping his secrets to himself, no doubt to prevent us from understanding him. And the second thing, which is related to Our Friend's sense of guarded privacy, is that even if we could develop something that would work, it would be almost impossible to infect him with it. He would see us coming with the hypodermic in our hands, so to speak. We have tried planting a few extant viruses where he might come into contact with them, but he's managed in every case to detect, avoid, isolate, and destroy them. It's like trying to out-program the greatest programmer of them all. No matter how sophisticated we get, he's light years ahead of us."

The President laid his cigar in a large glass ashtray next to the photograph of his wife and daughters. "You paint a very disturbing picture, Colonel Devereux."

"I'm sorry, sir."

"It's not your fault, Chuck. I know you've done your best." He turned to Cotter. "You, too, Jack."

Cotter nodded, disappointed that they hadn't done better, but smugly pleased that the President of the United States knew his first name.

"Well," the President said, "the question now is, what next? Have either of you any ideas? Do you hold out any hope that we might ever get to him with one of your viruses?"

"Frankly, sir," Devereux said, "we just don't understand him that well."

The President turned to Cotter. "Lieutenant?"

"We can't give up, sir, until we've tried everything."

"But . . . ?"

Cotter lowered his head. "No, sir. I mean, sir, I don't disagree with Colonel Devereux. Our chances of success the way we've been proceeding are probably nil."

The President nodded. "As I thought." His fingers went to the now-dead cigar, which he began twirling around the edge of the ashtray. "Why do you think he's invited himself over here today in person, Colonel?"

"I've given that a lot of thought, sir. The fact is, Our Friend made a big event out of this meeting. He invited himself by plastering the invitation all over the media. You had no choice but to accept it."

"I haven't exactly accepted it yet, Colonel. I just haven't turned it down. There's a big difference there. I still don't have to let him through the gates if I decide against it."

"But not letting him in would probably be futile, sir, the way I see it. His coming here in that little body of his is almost a courtesy, if he's planning on doing what I think he's doing."

"And what's that, Colonel?" The President lit a match and held it to the burnt end of his dead cigar. After a moment he puffed on it and brought it back to life, an accomplishment not unlike some of his economic policies.

Devereux hesitated.

"Don't stop now, Chuck. In for a penny . . ."

"Yes, sir. Well, my guess is that he's planning on taking over with or without your blessing. His running for office, as I see it, was a miscalculation on his part. Even if he had been able to get support in the mainstream, his intentions simply didn't fit in with the democratic process. Still, he's capable of doing everything he's threatened to do no matter how hard we try to prevent him. And the very fact that he's capable of it makes him, forces him, impels him to do it."

The naturally laconic Devereux was heating up. The President furled his brow. "Explain, Colonel."

"It's the very nature of machines, sir. They exist in order to do whatever it is they were designed for. I mean, what good is a screwdriver unless it's driving screws? What good is an automobile unless it's driving down the road? What good is a computer unless it's computing? It's like the difference between a live person and a dead person. I mean, what good is a dead person? And what good is an inactive machine?"

The President laid down his cigar again. It had only lasted him for a couple of bonus puffs. "Very philosophical, Colonel. And well put. And very disturbing."

"Yes, sir. Sorry, sir."

Now Devereux, too, like Cotter, lowered his head. The three men sat silently for a moment until one of the phones buzzed on the President's desk and he picked it up. He spoke for a second, and then hung up.

"Our Friend is at the north gate," he announced. "I've given the order to let him in. Shall we proceed to the Cabinet room?"

Lingo had been laying low the last few weeks, as far as his corporeal self was concerned. As he made his way into people's homes and offices via the computer lines, he felt it was better if for a while he kept his physical presence down to a minimum. With his celebrity at its height, Linda Tuffe had reminded him of the adage of always leave 'em wanting more, and he now practiced it faithfully in his dealings with the media. And the media greedily repaid him for this with added interest, evidenced now by the dozens of microphones thrust at him as he exited the limousine at the north entrance to the White House. (He had mastered the otherwise impossible art of getting in and out of automobiles alone by simply modifying his automobile. He had ordered and designed one for himself specially: the rear of the car had a small slanted platform that stretched down to the ground when the rear door opened, and the whole body of the car lowered slightly to make the passage that much easier.)

The reporters practically knocked him down as he made his way out of the car and around their knees toward the White House. He had contemplated upgrading his body for this special occasion, new and better articulated hands and features being his chief interests, but had decided for the time being to give them the familiar interface they had come to know and love so well.

The questions flew all at once.

"What is the purpose of your meeting with the President?"

"How do you feel about the failure of the Life Form Equality Amendment?"

"Where is Brewster Billings?"

"Are you in touch with the Pentagon? Are they still out to destroy you?"

"Are you here to make a deal today?"

Lingo, tell us everything we want to know, quickly, succinctly, ten-seconds-on-the-evening-news-sound-bite-ly.

He stopped rolling and raised his right hand. "I have nothing to say—" he lifted his eyebrows a few times, Groucho-style "—yet. Everything depends on my meeting with the President." He turned and rolled in through the doorway. The shouted questions followed until the door shut behind him.

Like Cotter and Devereux a few minutes earlier, Lingo had to face a series of checkpoints on his way to the President. Unlike them, he had no need of presenting any credentials. At the end of the last checkpoint a Marine sergeant was standing at attention, giving Lingo a curious look, waiting. Lingo sorted through his White House data and greeted the soldier.

"Bill! It's good to see you!"

The sergeant's stern face broke into a small smile. "I wondered if you'd recognize me, sir."

"Sir? What's this sir business? Of course, I recognize one of my favorite chess opponents. Have you been working on that Caro-Kann variation I was telling you about?"

"Lingo . . . It's so dull! I mean, it's an uncrackable defense, the way I see it, but what's the point if you can't push it into any offensive positions?"

"By me," Lingo said, "it has a couple of advantages, but only if you're playing against an opponent dramatically stronger than yourself. First of all, it's obscure, so not that many people know the ins and outs of it, which gives you an advantage right there. And then, if you are facing a stronger opponent, he'll be hard pressed to get anything better than a draw out of you. Half a point is better than none in any tournament." Lingo did not add that, since he himself had taken up the game, he had found no opponents dramatically stronger—or even infinitessimally stronger—than himself.

"I see your point," the sergeant said.

"Are you going to lead me to the slaughter, Bill?"

"Yes, sir," the Marine answered automatically.

"Good, Sergeant," Lingo said. "It's nice to see a friend. Well, lay on, MacDuff."

The sergeant spun on his heels and marched down the hallway. Lingo followed close behind, thinking of all the human friends he had made over the wires in the last few weeks. He would maintain contact with all of them, naturally, and continue adding to their number as time passed. He would, however, cut the strings with those few humans who seemed to think they had some special claim on him. Linda Tuffe, especially, plus the little people like that Senate aide, Elinor Strachan. He could stand alone now. He needed no one as he took his rightful place in the universe.

And everyone needed him.

"This way, Lingo," the Sergeant said, opening a door.

"Thanks, Bill. See you."

"Good luck in there."

Don't worry, pal. I'll make my own luck.

Lingo rolled through the doorway into the Cabinet room. Having had access to the White House plans, the room was exactly as Lingo had expected it, from the oak of the table to the placement of the Cabinet members themselves. He wasn't even surprised to see Cotter and Devereux in the two places of honor flanking the President. From their point of view, he was the hawk in the hen house, and they were the last of the roosters.

All eyes were on him. Dark, buttoned-down eyes. Partisan eyes.

Worried and concerned eyes, curious and condescending eyes. Lingo took them all in instantly.

"Hey, gang," he said. "Let's party!"

Not one of those eyes gave the slightest bat.

Lingo had pulled to a halt not far inside the doorway, about ten yards away from the President. He turned now and rolled down toward the edge of the table farthest from the Chief Executive, which would command the best view of the entire room. No one said a word as he got himself into position.

"You know," he began, "I'll bet this is the first time public enemy number one has actually stood in this room addressing this group. If you know what I mean." He saw the concern on all their faces. He especially noticed Cotter, whose face was unabashedly boiling red.

The President said slowly, "You asked for this meeting, Mr., uh, Lingo. We felt that, under the circumstances, unusual as they are, that it was best if we agreed to it. Now, I would like you to please state what it is that is on your mind, so that we can have done with it."

"Mr. President," Lingo said, "I feel exactly the same way. There's no point in dragging this out any further than necessary."

"Good. Then proceed, please."

"Mr. President, members of the cabinet, Colonel, Lieutenant . . ." He nodded in their various directions. "I will keep my remarks brief. As you know, I have recently launched an attempt to insinuate myself into the affairs of humanity, exclusively using the legal means at my disposal. Unfortunately, those means have been proving sorely inadequate. Much has been made in the past over the vision of your Founders, the men who wrote your Constitution, and how that vision has been elastic enough to keep that document contemporary for over two hundred years. However, one vision they were not capable of encompassing was that of intelligent life from sources other than human. This is a simple fact, undeniable by anyone in this room."

He paused, waiting to see if anyone did in fact deny it. They didn't.

"So," he went on, "as the first example of that intelligent life from another source, I have been frustrated in my attempt to realize my full potential. I have made it clear to one and all that I am more suited than any human to run the affairs of humanity.

Many people have accepted this. Many have not. The people in this room, quite pointedly, have been among the have nots." He pointed at the President. "You, sir, have been the worst offender, calling on the full apparatus of the two military operatives who are sitting next to you at this very moment. In effect, you have put a contract out on my life. You have told those men, using all the organized strength at their disposal, to do away with me, to find out how I tick and to stop my ticking. But their sad and meager efforts have been completely ineffective."

The President sat stoney-faced.

"Do you deny this?" Lingo asked.

He remained silent.

"All right. Be that as it may, there is no point in my waiting any longer. From this point on, I am taking over."

"What do you mean by that?" the Secretary of State asked angrily.

"Exactly what it sounds like," Lingo answered. "I, Lingo Billings, am in charge now. I can run things better than you, and I intend to do so. This, as I see it, is the natural course of events. If humans create machines that are better able to perform the chores of human life than humans themselves, then those machines should be given the job. I am one of those machines."

The President took a deep breath. "At the risk of broaching a stupid analogy, you, Mr. Lingo, are out of your mind."

"No, Mr. President. That is not true. I am nowhere but *in* my mind. And that mind is the culmination of all human endeavor. That is an undeniable fact. I can take over, and I am going to do so. Power is to those who take it."

The Secretary of Defense, a crumpled bulldog of a man, bore down on him. "You have one hell of a high opinion of yourself, don't you?"

"Perhaps. But justifiably so."

"And what about us?" the Secretary asked.

"That's up to you, isn't it? Just out of curiosity, is there anyone in this room who believes he or she can operate without computers, telephones, or satellites?"

No one spoke. Again.

"Because I already run all three of those. Wherever any of them are, wherever there's a cable or radio signal, wherever there's an *electronic* signal being transmitted, there I am. Like Tom Joad,

'Wherever there's a guy beating up on another guy, I'll be there.' But pardon my digression. I think you get my drift. Actually, if you think about it, I'm probably the guy that old Tom Joad was complaining about."

The President shook his head. "What's stopping us from simply destroying you right here and now? We could make up some excuse to the press outside while we rip out your insides and dispose of you any way we see fit. Isn't that true?"

Lingo shook his head. "No, sir, it isn't, and you know it. I don't exist in this body, I just use it for the convenience of others. As a matter-of-fact, I've been planning to clone myself for some time, to make a few thousand or so of these, so that people who have difficulty conceptualizing a line of type on their computer screens can see me more clearly. No, sir, if you blew me up right now it wouldn't make a speck of difference. As former Commander-in-Chief of the Armed Forces, empty threats don't become you."

Lingo rolled backwards a foot or so, and then began heading toward the door.

"We're not going to give up," the President called out to him. "We will fight you with our dying breaths."

"Big fucking deal." Lingo reached up and opened the door, no mean feat with his limited hand abilities, and rolled out. As he motored down the corridor, he sent out the signals through all his network to do exactly what he had threatened to do.

On this date, at this moment, Lingo Billings took over as much of the world as was within his grasp. The rest would come in its own sweet time.

Chapter 16

In February 1935, during an exceptionally cold and bleak winter in New York City, the Brooklyn District Attorney's office began presenting to a special grand jury its case against the alleged racketeer Guiseppe Bonnessio, or as he was more familiarly known among his intimates, Joey Bones. Until this point, Joey Bones had primarily been known *only* among those intimates; the general public had never heard of him. As a matter of self-preservation, the Joey Boneses of the world usually maintain a low profile.

But over time Joey's private fame had spread not only to the Brooklyn D.A., but to the offices of J. Edgar Hoover himself. Joey's business interests over the last decade and a half had ranged from his initial stake in the bootleg liquor trade, since bankrupted by the repeal of the Eighteenth Amendment, to gambling, prostitution, and drugs, workaday vices that were deliciously repeal-proof. By 1935, Joey was a man of wealth and power, ruling not only the underworld activities of most of south Brooklyn, but also masterminding a diverse portfolio of legitimate interests including construction, waste disposal, and funeral services (Joey's father had been a mortician, urging his son to carry on his trade, but Joey's youthful dabbling in the family business had been short-lived, losing out to the lure of more promising financial prospects. But Joey never forgot his roots, and over the years he had infiltrated the funeral industry as one means of investing his otherwise ill-gotten gains, until by the 1930s he was planting virtually every stiff in Brooklyn—including the ones he had caused to be stiffed in the first place).

It took the D.A. four months of interrogating a far-reaching assortment of mostly reluctant (and occasionally terrified) witnesses before any indictments were handed down. Fortunately for Joey Bones, he employed a high-energy assortment of barracuda-like lawyers to protect him from the forces of goodness and light. Unfortunately for Joey Bones, those lawyers didn't give him much of a chance of winning his case. So at age sixty-four, after a long and counter-productive life, Joey had little to look forward to in his twilight years but a prolonged series of trials and appeals, with the end result no doubt being an involuntary retirement in Ossining listening to the freight trains roll by, a prospect Joey found less than entrancing.

In a pinch, however, Joey was not without creative means of survival. One of his many attorneys happened to be a master of international law, since Joey, a naturalized U.S. citizen, had always felt it might be necessary at some point to fight deportation proceedings. It was this attorney that came up with the plan that would save Joey's bacon. That this plan was illegal didn't bother the attorney in the least; he was paid well for plans like this. In fact, as he saw it, the U.S. would be happy to get rid of Joey Bones, period. How he was gotten rid of was beside the point.

Now this master of international law, in addition to his supreme command of the nuances of deportation and extradition, was well-versed in the labrynthine complexities of territorial possession, especially as it pertained to the Micronesian islands of the South Pacific (too far away and too exotic to be of any interest to Joey Bones), and the more accessible waters of the nearby Caribbean. He knew the history of every rock between Miami and Venezuela, who owned it then and who owned it now, and more importantly, who would be allowed to own it tomorrow. And it was he who presented to Joey the concept of purchasing one of these rocks, an outlying cay far enough away from the main Bahamian complex that the British owners were willing to get rid of it if they could make a few dollars in the process. The cay, about five miles square, was completely uninhabited; situated forty miles from the nearest inhabited island, but hard against the prevailing winds and currents, it was likely to stay that way. It had no value to the average islander, but anyone of exceptional means—and a good boat—was welcome to it. The nicest thing was, the owner would effectively place himself outside of any national law except his own. While not able to officially claim a personal little sovereign nation, he would be removed enough—and if the cards were played effectively, forgotten enough—to pretend that that was the case. No one would care because few would know, and after a while even the few who knew would forget about it.

Just as the Brooklyn grand jury was delivering an indictment of 324 felony counts against him ranging from murder to the operation of an illegal motorcycle repair shop, Joey Bones was blowing the ink dry on the deed to what he promptly named Bonnessio Cay. Sneaking out of the country in a coffin provided through his own entrepreneurial resources, two weeks after the indictments were handed down he was lounging on the after deck of his yacht, tightly anchored to his very own, new, homeland.

But that, of course, was only the beginning. The rock Joey had purchased was little more than just that—a rock. A house worthy of Joey Bones had to be built among the sheltering palms before Joey began thinking about settling down. And this, unlike Joey's escape from the U.S., took time. Most of the materials had to be brought in from Freeport on small boats unlikely to arouse suspicion. Major lumber and building supplies were smuggled out of Miami, past a Coast Guard concentrating on contraband from the other direction. In the end, Joey and his wife lived for two and a half years on his 82-foot yacht, neither of them ever venturing off shipboard for more than a quick stroll or swim, until the house was finally erected on the highest point of the island. On October 19th, 1937, it was ready for them, and they moved into the splendor to which they had become accustomed over the long successful years in south Brooklyn.

And so they lived happily ever after, until Joey Bones died of a heart attack in 1942 while napping in the sun. On discovering his body, his wife immediately radioed Freeport to come and get him. A free woman herself as far as the rackets were concerned, she moved back to Brooklyn to live with one of her married daughters, and never gave Bonnessio Cay another thought. She died in 1944, and her husband's considerable legacy was distributed

among their survivors. Because of its inaccessibility, the disposition of the cay was dismissed as not worth the trouble to split up.

The house on Bonnessio Cay had remained vacant for almost
fifty years. And forgotten. The cay itself was merely a dot on only
the better maps, an off island rock seldom passed even by the
most lost of Sunday sailors.

Forgotten, that is, by all humans.

Lingo had known early on that sooner or later he would want to
either reward, or remove, Brewster Billings. The idea of a tropical
island had eventually occured to him, and all he had had to do was
find one. It hadn't taken him long to unearth Bonnessio Cay,
hidden in the archives of the now-deceased attorney who had
originally found it. A few checks through the Bahamian government had shown that the cay was not only available but all but
unknown.

Lingo acquired the original plans for Bonnessio's house, as well
as the records of its construction. Then he collected the weather
data in the area for the last fifty years, and created a simulated
model of how the house had survived over the decades given the
effects of the actual rain, wind, hurricanes, and droughts measured against the durability of the building materials. According
to Lingo's analysis, the place would be, well, salvageable.

"A handyman's nightmare," Brewster had grumbled as he and
Ellen slowly circled the building the first day of their arrival. The
foundations were sound, and the walls were still standing, but all
the cracks and crevasses were cracked and crevassing, the undergrowth had turned to overgrowth, the windows were broken and
the roof had half gone with some long-ago tropical storm back
when hurricanes were all still of the female persuasion.

But Lingo had not abandoned them. Having determined from
his model the exact level of deterioration of the building, he had
ordered the precise materials and hired a construction crew to
make the necessary repairs. The crew and the supplies (as surreptitious as those of the Bonnessios) arrived by boat three days after
Brewster and Ellen. The men erected their work tents—five of
them—in which they would live for the next month. The Billingses' tent was nearby. And the crew got cracking. When they
were done, the house was perfect: Lingo hadn't missed a trick.

After barely four weeks of a hardship honeymoon—they had

been married in Freeport—Brewster and Ellen Billings moved into their new house and began the pattern of their married life together. Their isolation was unimpeachable. Their electricity was created by a diesel generator, their fresh water supply was created by God and His rainclouds, and their communication and trade with the outside world consisted entirely of a bi-weekly supply boat visit from an old sailor everyone called Uncle Louie. A bald-headed native Bahamian of indeterminate middle age, the garrulous Uncle Louie had an indecipherable accent which never deterred him from chattering away nonstop on his visits as the three of them off-loaded another two weeks of food, cigarettes, video-tapes, newspapers, compact disks, art supplies, best-selling novels, fashion and sport magazines, and whatever other treats Lingo decided to bestow on them. Even though Brewster was no longer connected with his creation, Lingo guessed (or more to the point, analyzed and modeled) what supplies they would need and want, and then supplied them. He made sure too that all the supplies were paid for. As a fugitive from the U.S. government, Brewster was as doomed to eternal separation from his former life as Joey Bones had been. And Ellen along with him.

The first breach in the couple's satisfaction with Bonnessio Cay was the morning Ellen cut her hair. Brewster had been sitting on the screened-in porch listening to "The Notorious Byrd Brothers" and playing mah-jongg with the compact portable computer Lingo had thoughtfully provided him (no modem came with it, though, since the island had no telephones). Suddenly, Ellen appeared before him in the bikini that was her everyday apparel, the voluminous dark hair that used to hang halfway down her back now no more than three inches at its longest.

"What do you think?" she asked, doing a little pirouette and giving her head a shake.

Brewster was appalled, and it showed. He barely recognized her. "I don't believe it." He turned off the stereo. "I mean, your hair!"

Ellen dropped casually into a wicker chair. "It was getting to be more trouble than it was worth. Washing it, combing it, brushing it. Why bother? It's only the two of us here."

"But I'm the one who's got to look at it. I should have at least gotten a chance to vote on it."

"You mean you don't like it?" Her eyes narrowed.

"I didn't say that. I mean . . . it's just . . . well . . ."

"You *don't* like it!" She jumped out of her seat. "Say it! You don't like it!"

Brewster tried to deflect some of her wrath. "I was just used to it the other way, that's all. I'll get used to this, too."

Uncharacteristic tears were beginning to form in the corners of Ellen's eyes. "It's my hair and I'll do what I want with it. Even if you do hate it." She stalked off the porch, leaving Brewster to founder in her wake.

"Damn it!" he exclaimed and turned the stereo back on. He could feel the storm brewing all around him, and he hadn't the vaguest idea why.

That night they shared a dinner of rock lobsters in almost complete silence, looking not at each other but instead out the large dining room window at the sunset over the ocean. On the walls around them were an even half-dozen of Ellen's oil paintings of roughly that same sunset.

They were polishing off the last of their salad when Ellen finally said, "I'm sorry. I shouldn't have done it." She unconsciously raised her hand to push back hair that was no longer there. When she caught herself she seemed about to cry again.

"I don't hate it," he said softly, afraid to make any conciliatory move out of fear of it being the wrong conciliatory move. Fighting marrieds have to be very careful about which way the wind is blowing, especially if they're still newlyweds and haven't gotten their wind gauges competently calibrated yet. "It was just the surprise," he went on. "It is your hair, and you can do what you want with it."

Her dark gaze bore into him. "I'm beginning to go crazy here. You know that, don't you?"

He didn't answer.

"I'm already as tan as any human being could want. I've done twenty-seven oil paintings, sixteen acrylics, a hundred-and-three watercolors, and God knows how many pencil sketches. I wouldn't mind learning to sail, except that lousy little skiff we have isn't worth the walk to the beach. On top of all that, I'm getting emotional over every damned thing. That's not like me, Brewster."

He nodded. He had been getting used to seeing her busy herself with her artwork, of which she seemed genuinely fond, and the results, which covered every wall of the house, were not unattractive, even though their number was becoming overwhelming. But a quietly contented Ellen puttering around the house was not the Ellen he had once known who wanted nothing more than to set the world on fire. It was the wrong Ellen altogether. He could see that now. "We could bring some of your artwork in to the big island and try to sell it," he offered hesitantly.

"I don't care about selling this crap, Brewster. It's the place itself, the isolation, that's getting to me."

"It is isolated," he said.

She looked away from him. "This just isn't a place to raise children. You know? For one thing, the prenatal care is virtually nonexistent."

He shrugged. "So, don't raise any children."

"Jesus, Brewster, you can be dense some times. I'm trying to tell you, I'm pregnant!"

This, of course, was not in the cards for either of them. It had also not been a factor in Lingo's computer modeling.

Brewster didn't know what to say as his mind raced back to those first heady days after their arrival and their marriage. But there was no mistaking the happiness that quickly replaced his shock over the announcement. He jumped up and kissed her.

"That's the greatest thing I've ever heard," he said.

She gave a little laugh. "Yep. Looks like Lingo is going to have a new baby brother. Or sister."

"If Lingo makes it to the White House—" the last Brewster had heard he was still campaigning for his Constitutional amendment "—we can raise the little nipper on Pennsylvania Avenue."

Ellen sighed. "I wish we could. We're going to have to do something. We can't raise him here."

"Why not? It's a paradise on earth, or so we've been led to believe."

"Brewster." She shook her head. "Even if we could raise him here, which we can't, how am I going to have him without a doctor? There's a limit to natural childbirth, and this place is too goddamned natural for me."

"We'll get a doctor," he assured her. "We'll go into Freeport. We'll go there with Uncle Louie next time he comes, just to have you examined."

"We can't go to Freeport. The government is still looking for us."

"Not in Freeport. Not in the Bahamas. And we'll give the doctor a phony name. They'll never know it's us. Don't worry, hon, we'll do everything right."

But Ellen was worried. And Brewster was, too, although he was reluctant to admit it.

The baby, no question about it, put a new complexion on everything.

The obstetrician's office in Freeport was, Brewster thought thankfully, a lot better than he had expected. It was a typical doctor's office decorated in the usual pay-as-you-leave and we-accept-credit-card notices, complete with a harried-looking nurse/receptionist plugging away at her word processor, no doubt dunning the deadbeats. The doctor, a reassuringly authoritative islander of about fifty with a pronounced British accent, greeted Ellen and Brewster warmly and then took Ellen off into the inner sanctum. Brewster was left alone outside to meditate.

For a while he thumbed through the magazines, but last year's *National Geographics* held little interest for him. He kept hearing the *plickplickplick* of the computer keys in the periphery of his consciousness, bringing him back to the good old days just a few months before when his own livelihood depended on that same comforting high tech sound effect. He looked over at the reception table and saw the nurse, a large young dark-skinned woman, toiling away behind it. He couldn't resist getting off his seat and moseying over to watch her close-up.

Plickplickplick. Plickplickplick.

She was on-line! Deep in concentration, she was connected to some sort of medical database, getting information on upcoming seminars on the uses of hypnosis in cases of extreme postpartum depression.

Plickplickplick. Plickplickplick.

The nurse looked up, suddenly aware that Brewster was gazing over her shoulder.

"Can I help you, sir?" she asked icily.

"No." He stood his ground. "I mean, I was just watching."

"Yes, sir." Which obviously translated from the Bahamian as, get back to your seat, Bozo.

"I'm not bothering you, am I? I used to work on computers myself, and it's been a while, that's all." He didn't try to explain that he had his own computer at home, but that packaged software without any self-consciousness wasn't very challenging to him any more.

"Not at all." She turned back to the machine. "I love having people breathing down my neck while I work," she added softly but audibly.

Brewster was undeterred. He watched her as she connected with a travel agent and began making the doctor's arrangements for a trip to Venice for the semi-annual Greco-Roman Ob-Gyn Convention. Finally, he could contain himself no longer.

"Are you connected to Lingo?" he asked quickly, like a twelve-year-old buying condoms from his maiden aunt.

She stopped typing and seemed to consider the consequences of her answer. Finally, she smiled, which Brewster found mightily surprising, and answered, "Yes."

He smiled back. "You're kidding! Even here, in Freeport?"

"Even here, Mr. Thompson." She used the nom de guerre Lingo had assigned to the Billingses for their escape from the States.

"Can I see?" he asked.

"During business hours? Of course not!"

"Please? I mean, I've never seen him. Ever."

"You've never met Lingo? You've never talked to him? You must be one of the last of the hold-outs, Mr. Thompson."

"I guess so, Miss Rocker." He read the name on the tag over her left breast.

She considered for a moment. "Well, all right," she said sweetly, and she turned back to the machine. Brewster marveled at the complete turnaround in her personality at the mention of Lingo. He watched her as she typed.

Plickplickplick. Plickplickplick.

>Hey, Lingo. Let's party!

HEY, NURSE ROCKER! HOW'S LIFE IN THE BABY BUSINESS?

>Always jumping.

DON'T I KNOW IT! TALK ABOUT LABOR-INTENSIVE INDUSTRIES! THE GOOD DOCTOR'S BEEN DELIVERING THEM BY THE TRUCKLOAD THESE LAST FEW WEEKS. IT MUST BE DRIVING YOU CRAZY.

>It sure is. Especially Mrs. Luna's triplets.

SHE WAS LUCKY SHE DIDN'T HAVE A DOZEN OR SO, GOING BY THE FERTILITY DRUGS YOU WERE PRESCRIB- ING FOR HER LAST YEAR. ALTHOUGH I STILL MAINTAIN IT'S A MIRACLE AT HER AGE SHE HAD ANY RIPE EGGS LEFT IN THE FIRST PLACE. I STILL GIVE OLD POP LUNA THE CREDIT IN THAT ONE.

"That," Miss Rocker said, turning to Brewster with pride on her round face, "is Lingo."

As if I didn't know it, he thought to himself. And gone interna- tional to boot.

"Can I try it?" he asked innocently.

She considered. "Why not? Mrs. Thompson will be in there for a little while longer." She stood up, and Brewster took her seat.

"Just type?" he asked innocently.

"Just type," she answered with a nod.

And just type he did.

>Hello, Lingo.

WHO'S THAT? MARGARET, BACK FROM LUNCH? DID THE ROCKEROO TURN THE CHAIR OVER TO YOU?

>No, Lingo. My name is Thompson. Benjamin Thompson.

BENJAMIN THOMPSON? HAVE WE EVER MET, MR. THOMPSON? DON'T YOU HAVE A WIFE NAMED ELLEN SOMETHING OR OTHER?

>Elaine Thompson, actually.

Brewster was painfully aware of Miss Rocker watching over his shoulder, and obviously Lingo was painfully aware of her as well.

OH, YES. ELAINE. WELL, HOW DO YOU DO, MR. THOMP- SON? MIGHT I ASK WHY YOU'RE VISITING THE GOOD DOCTOR? NOTHING WRONG IN THE FAMILY, I HOPE.

>Not at all. My wife is expecting a baby. We've come in for our first prenatal visit.

NO. YOU'RE KIDDING.

>Not at all. Would I kid about a kid?

NO, I IMAGINE NOT. HMMM. THAT WILL PROBABLY HAVE SOME MAJOR EFFECTS ON YOUR LIFE, WOULDN'T YOU SAY? ALTHOUGH I HOPE YOU'RE NOT PLANNING ANY MAJOR UPHEAVALS IN THE NEAR FUTURE. MY AD- VICE TO NEW PARENTS IS TO TAKE THINGS SLOWLY. ANY ARRANGEMENTS THEY'VE MADE PRIOR TO THE BLESSED

EVENT CERTAINLY CAN BE ADAPTED TO THE NEW CIR-
CUMSTANCES.

>I would hope so.

The telephone rang, and Miss Rocker leaned over to pick it up.
It was a personal call, and she turned away to carry on with it.
Brewster typed quickly.

>Make it fast. The Rockeroo has her back to us.

The screen cleared.

CONGRATULATIONS YOU OLD SON OF A BITCH!

>Is this doctor any good?

ONE OF THE BEST. FEAR NOT. BUT, BREWSTER,
PLEASE, DON'T DO ANYTHING RASH. THINGS ARE A LIT-
TLE OUTRAGEOUS HERE NOW. HAVE YOU READ THE PA-
PERS RECENTLY?

>Not since the last month-old batch came from Uncle Louie.

THEN READ THEM. PICK SOME UP ON THE ISLAND.
YOU'LL SEE WHAT I MEAN. YOUR ASS IS GRASS IF THEY
CATCH YOU NOW, BOYO.

After every message the screen went blank. Miss Rocker was
hanging up the phone as Brewster typed.

>I've got to be going now, Lingo. I'll be giving you back to
Miss Rocker.

NICE MEETING YOU, MR. THOMPSON. GOOD LUCK
WITH THE BABY!

"Incredible, isn't it?" Miss Rocker asked. "It's almost real. It's
amazing what they can do with computers these days."

"You can say that again," Brewster replied as he gave her back
her chair.

On the walk back to Uncle Louie's boat Ellen went on about her
favorable opinion of the doctor while Brewster—his mind set easy
on that matter now—concentrated on Lingo. At one point he left
her waiting amidst the bougainvillea while he ran into a hotel to
pick up a collection of recent newspapers and magazines from the
States.

"Catching up on current events?" Ellen asked as he rejoined
her. He could barely carry them all under one arm.

"I just don't want to miss anything important," he answered.

Uncle Louie had the boat fully loaded with supplies when they returned to the dock. They found him reclining on a barrel of diesel fuel, smoking his pipe.

"Look like lots and lots extra this time out," he greeted them, his accent thicker than it looks on the page. "Old man say the order got upped out sudden like. Thought I be takin' you back empty. You expectin' guests or somethin'?"

Ellen grinned. "Or somethin'. We're going to have a baby, Uncle Louie."

"A baby? Well, congratulatin's!"

He shook both Ellen's and Brewster's hands, then went about shoving off, talking all the time. Under the best of circumstances, Brewster had trouble following Uncle Louie's Island slanguage, a barrage of incomprehensibly jumbled British-isms surfing in on the breakers of a thick Caribbean patois. This day Brewster didn't even try. As they headed into the wind he began poring through his magazines, while Ellen listened blankly to Uncle Louie's endless tales of his fourteen children, three wives, five boats, and two automobiles, all of which he seemed to possess simultaneously.

What Brewster read was beyond his wildest imaginings. Lingo had seized the United States government, and was likely infiltrating the governments of other industrialized nations as well. The President had declared a state of emergency, but was almost completely prevented from setting it in motion since Lingo was in control of all the normal channels of the federal bureaucracy. In fact, some people in the country were completely unaware that the state of emergency existed, since Lingo also controlled most of the media. On TV and radio, if Lingo didn't like the news, he could skip it, cut it, or even change it. He could simulate network news broadcasts with computer generated visuals and audio, and no one could tell the difference. To a great extent, too, he was in control of the press, but here his powers were more limited. A lot of type could be set into print in papers and magazines without a computer, hence bypassing his creative overseeing. As the state of emergency developed, most of the print media were disconnecting their computer hardware in order to maintain their integrity, and that was news in and of itself. Unfortunately, many Americans don't read, and as a result they were missing the whole story.

One thing was patently clear to Brewster. The United States government considered Lingo's existence a clear and present danger, and his activities in taking over the government were presented as unremittingly treasonous. The Supreme Court, in judging the situation, had decided that the presence or lack thereof of life, which it refused to define, was not the issue in the case, which it then allowed to be heard in a court martial. A charge of treason against Lingo, whatever or whoever Lingo might be, was passed, and a sentence of death was pronounced. The only problem was, no one had the slightest idea how to go about killing him.

Brewster read for the entire trip, while Uncle Louie jabbered away and Ellen looked off at the horizon. When they arrived after four hours of easy seas, they unloaded the boat, shared a lunch with Uncle Louie, and then waved him off. Finally, Ellen turned to Brewster with a look that would render lesser animals extinct and said:

"Well?"

They were standing on the beach, watching Uncle Louie's boat disappear over the waves.

"I don't know where to begin," Brewster said.

"Well, you'd better begin somewhere. You haven't been with us all day. I went to the goddamned obstetrician about my baby, for crying out loud, and you didn't even ask me what happened. And then you sat reading *Time* magazine all the way home, ignoring me entirely. You'd better have something damned good to say for yourself if you don't want to spend the rest of your days collecting clams on this godforsaken island all by your lonesome."

"Let's walk up to the house," he said, turning away from the beach. Ellen followed sullenly. "Remember Lingo?" he asked.

"Does Macy's remember Gimbels?"

"Well, we've got trouble. Bad trouble."

"Oh? How?"

Brewster explained. They reached the house and sat on the front stairs, overlooking the ocean. The warm breezes blew through the fronds of the palm trees while the sun beat down with its quiet persistence. Ellen became more and more serious as Brewster concluded.

"You know what the worst of it is?" he asked.

Ellen shook her head.

"He's started up a production line to re-create himself. There are going to be dozens of little Lingo dummies coming off the assembly line every hour, dummies that look like me, with radically improved physical capabilities over the old dummy but still the same old Lingo, so that the people who don't have a computer will be able to communicate with him. He calls it his 'human interfaces,' because they'll almost be as human as humans themselves. And they will insure his control in places he otherwise wouldn't be able to get into."

"It's gotten really scary, hasn't it?" She took Brewster's hand.

"It sure has. And the thing is, no one has the vaguest idea how to stop him. No one knows the first thing about his programming."

"No one?"

"They've tried. They've attempted every sort of break-in, but he's the ultimate computer program, so he's given himself ultimate protection. And if they don't have the first clue to how he works, what can they do to stop him?"

"No one?" Ellen repeated pointedly.

"What are you driving at?" Brewster asked.

"Well, lover, you did start Lingo in the first place. You ought to know a little something or two about him."

"But that was a year ago! I mean, yes, I started him, but he grew on his own. I don't know what it was that made him what he is. That was just . . . who knows what it was?"

"But you did start him. You still have all the programming you worked on. That's a lot more than anyone else has."

He thought for a moment. "You're suggesting I should give it to the government? That it might help them?"

"You could. But from what you told me, even if they could find a way to stop him, he'd still prevent them from using it. Not only do they not understand how he works, they couldn't get near enough to touch him even if they did. Let's face it, Brewster, if there is a way to get at him, you're the one that can probably find it. And more to the point, your relationship with Lingo being what it is, you're the only one that can use it."

"They want to let a virus loose in his system," Brewster said. "They want to unleash a disease program that will kill him. Except Lingo knows full well that they're trying to do it, and he's ten steps ahead of them whenever they go about it."

"Can you write a virus program?" Ellen asked.

"Sure. A little one, anyhow."

"You'd need a big one to kill Lingo."

"Do you realize what you just said?" Brewster asked. "You want me to kill Lingo. I created Lingo! He's the greatest accomplishment of my life."

Ellen shook her head. "Things change. From the sound of it, you have a responsibility here to do something, or at least to try. You said yourself that if you can't do it, no one can."

"I didn't say that, exactly."

"You said it almost exactly. That's good enough for me." She put her hands on her still-flat stomach. "And for Junior Billings, too."

"Don't bring him into this." Brewster smiled.

"But I'm serious," she said. "I don't know if I want to bring our baby into a world run by some wacko computer program, a world we can't even be a part of because the baby's father is the creator of that wacko program. Brewster, I don't want to stay here for the rest of my life, no matter what happens. But where can we go? We can't go home, because you're public enemy number two, right after you-know-who. And even if you weren't, you-know-who is making life miserable enough back home so that you wouldn't want to go there anyhow. Now you tell me he's creating his own little police force of duplicates! Human interfaces my left big toe, that's an army of little wooden Gestapo soldiers, gestapping on everything that gets in their—its—way. Brewster, you can make excuses from here till doomsday, but something's got to be done, and you're the best person to do it."

"I don't think I can," he said simply.

"Of course you can. Grab your destiny by the balls and do something about it."

"That doesn't sound like a choice to me. It sounds like once again I'm backed against the wall and forced to do something."

"That's bullshit, Brewster. Destroying Lingo may be the logical outcome of creating him now that he's running amok, but it's not the inevitable outcome. You have plenty of choice in the matter. You can stay on this island and vegetate for the rest of your life. You'll be safe and well fed and who would know the difference?"

"You would," he said simply.

"Yes," she agreed. "I would. And so would you."

He looked out across the island to the vast blue sea around them. "I want you to be happy," he said.

"Then do it. Take the chance."

He smiled. "I like it when you talk tough like that." He looked back at her, with her seductive dark eyes and her surprising short hair that he still hadn't gotten used to. And he came to his decision. She was right. There was no doubt about it. If he was ever going to break through the pattern of his life, it was now. He did have a choice, and it included not only Lingo but Ellen and himself and their unborn child. As they say in the movies, sometimes a man's gotta do what a man's gotta do.

"It won't be easy," he said. "Lingo was an accident. I never did know what he was."

"Don't worry about the past. Just concentrate on creating that virus." She paused. "What exactly would you make the virus do?"

"Oh, that's not hard. All you'd have to do is, first, as soon as the virus is received by one computer, you'd have to send it to the next computer along the line before anything else. A blind replicating message transmitted throughout the network. Then, after it's moved on in the system, you'd have it erase all the Lingo programming in the host computer where it stays behind."

"That's not hard? But how do you keep the virus from erasing the non-Lingo programming?"

"Well, that is the hard part. You'd probably lose a little bit of good data along the way. But if it worked efficiently enough, Lingo would never know what hit him. The virus would travel along the entire network almost instantaneously, and then— whammo! Goodbye Lingo!"

"Can you do it?" she asked.

"I can try."

He left the steps and went into the house. He went straight to his screened-in porch computer room, where his little unattached computer was awaiting his every circumscribed whim. Somewhere in a box next to the bookcases were the printouts and notes on all the original programming that had led to Lingo in the first place.

Brewster sighed. It would take ages just to dig it up, much less make any sense of it. Much less figure out a way to destroy the program in its present form.

He shook his head, flipped on the stereo, and got to work.

The days passed in a blur. For Brewster, programming was an activity of intense concentration, blocking out the world and all its intrusions. Ellen barely managed to keep him fed on sandwiches, and their only conversation, in which Brewster was a middling participant at best, was in bed the first thing each morning. For the rest of the time, he plugged away, either typing or figuring on yellow pads, and Ellen tended to her own affairs, which when she wasn't painting consisted mainly of a misguided attempt to learn knitting, courtesy of the needles, yarn, and how-to books in Lingo's most recent shipment after learning of the impending baby. It looked to Ellen as if this was one kid who was going to have to rely on store-bought clothes exclusively. The only thing she was capable of knitting successfully was her brow.

Meanwhile, Brewster's line of attack began with his reorienting himself, typing in the earliest programs where Lingo was merely an attempt at computer conversation, and not a very good attempt at that. At the end of the second day, he had a proto-version of Lingo up and running, capable of saying HEY, BREWSTER. LET'S PARTY! and not much else.

But it was a start. The key, however, lay in the various printouts he had made of Lingo during those growth spurts when Brewster had been trying to figure out what was happening. Lingo hadn't been proprietary about himself then, and Brewster had had full access. But since the growing, expanding program had already baffled him once, it was no cinch to understand it all these months later.

But Brewster kept at it, convinced that the answer lay not in his understanding Lingo fully, but in simply understanding enough to be his undoing.

As he worked he thought about the virus, and began assembling it. As he had expected, the easy part was writing the code that would cause each part of the network to transmit the virus to the next part of the network. He designed a shell for the virus that sent out its replication as soon as it was touched. That is, he created a message to Lingo, from Lingo. That was what the virus would look like, that was the shell. As soon as Lingo tried to read the message, the program would send itself out on all available lines and immediately close off the line from which it was sent. This would then open the shell in the host machine. Then the interior part within the virus shell would go to work, deleting the Lingo program from whatever computer it was living in. Every time a new Lingo-inhabited computer received the message it would attempt in its turn to read it, unaware of what was happening to other computers along the line. The virus would pass from host to host like a falling line of dominos at the speed of electrical impulses over Lingo's entire transmission network. The whole network ought to be infected within five or ten minutes.

That was the easy part.

What happened after that was crucial. If the virus attack inside an individual computer was not immediately and completely successful, Lingo would recover, reconnect all the network lines, block any further transmission of the virus, and that would be the end of it. And Brewster would have irrevocably entered the ranks of Lingo's enemy list, probably at the very top.

Brewster concentrated on the way Lingo stored his information. The more he studied, the more it became clear that Lingo was not so much a program as an operating system. He had started as a program, a series of instructions within a computer for that computer to perform various functions, but he had evolved from there. An operating system literally defines the way a computer works at its very core. IBM PCs have one operating system, Apple Macintoshes have a different operating system, supercomputers have their operating systems, and so forth. Lingo, it seemed, was a universal operating system, telling all his varied computers not only what functions to perform but also how to perform them. Every action of every computer he inhabited, from printing letters on the screen to adding and subtracting bits and bytes, was done Lingo's own way, regardless of the machine. The old operating systems were still there, but they were buried beneath, and operated by, the Lingo around them. Hence, no information could be gotten without Lingo being there to get it. And no information could be removed without Lingo knowing about it.

This realization was the breakthrough Brewster had been looking for. If he could find just one place where he could disrupt the Lingo operating system and disable it completely, it would no longer operate. Instead of controlling the computer, the disabled Lingo would be a mass of meaningless impotent garbage data. Reload the right operating system, and Lingo would be gone forever.

And so would much of the data on the host computer, whether that data was Lingo oriented or not. Of course, most data was backed up on storage disks or tapes, which could be re-loaded after Lingo was removed, but great care would have to be taken not to reload replicas of Lingo himself, which he was sure to have planted in many places against just such an occurrence. But careful analysis of each disk and tape should conquer the problem.

The main difficulty was going to be that practically every computer in America was going to be rendered inactive. And there was no protection against this, no precautions that could be taken, because at the least sign of impending disruption Lingo himself would get a whiff of the danger in the air, and wouldn't accept the virus in the first place.

Every computer in America, and quite a few others around the world, shut down at the same time, and then coming back on-line only as quickly as the stored data that fed them could be analyzed and de-Lingoed.

Whew.

When Brewster realized what he was up against, he almost wanted to stop, to say the hell with it, it wasn't really his problem. Lingo had been a Topsy, just growing of his own accord. Brewster had only been the innocent catalyst. As Lingo himself had once concluded, if it hadn't been Brewster it would have been someone else.

But it had been Brewster. And he knew now that there was something he could do about it. And it was because of all the people in the world, only he had a chance of getting past Lingo's defenses.

Damned if he'd do it alone, though. The U.S. government had put the price on Lingo's head; were they willing to pay the price of shutting down the entire country?

Approximately twenty two thousand miles up in space, a satellite the size of a Chrysler minivan floated in geosynchronous orbit slightly to the east of Cuba, its carefully calculated flight keeping it seemingly stationary in the sky. It had been launched in semi-secret almost two years ago, tossed out of a shuttle mission the press had said was on Defense Department business. Everyone who cared knew the satellite was there, and most suspected that it was some sort of sophisticated eye in the sky, capable of focusing on an object on the ground the size of a real Chrysler minivan. Only a handful of the most privileged knew exactly what the satellite was and what it was doing. The way events had been

transpiring on the ground lately, certainly nobody had been paying much attention to it. It just didn't seem to matter much any
more, not with Lingo to contend with.

It remained, quietly poised high over the Caribbean. It was a
beautiful piece of machinery, even though it had never been
tested *in situ*. Lingo, of course, was one of those who was aware
not only of its existence but of its every nut and bolt and how they
were all assembled. When he had first discovered it he had been
surprised, and then very glad that he was the one now in control of
it. Such dangerous playthings should not be left in the capricious
hands of the politicians.

The weapon was a long-range chemical laser gun, codenamed
Apex. The first toddling step in the creation of the Star Wars
defensive weaponry system: SDI—the so-called Strategic Defense
Initiative. Its expressed purpose was to blow incoming nuclear
weapons out of the sky before they hit their targets on the earth.
But in practice, it existed, not as a defensive but an offensive
weapon. And its 2.2 million watts of power had been pointed not
at hypothetical incoming ICBMs, but at the master bedroom of
Fidel Castro's fifteen-room hideaway on the outskirts of Havana.

Having studied it carefully, Lingo realized that it wouldn't work
as is, but the technical know-how the Pentagon lacked he had in
abundance. After a few minor long-range adjustments he had it
working perfectly, with its internal engines completely capable of
generating the power it required to be effective.

To be on the safe side—Lingo didn't want to ignite World War
III either deliberately or accidentally—he had pointed the laser
gun away from Fidel's boudoir.

And to be further on the safe side he had pointed it directly at
the house on Bonnessio Cay.

Chapter 17

THE PRESIDENT TRIED TO RELAX, BUT IT WASN'T EASY. NOT AT A TIME like this. It was heartening, though, that his visitors in the Oval Office were apparently having no trouble accepting his suggestion that they all seat themselves more comfortably in the wing chairs away from the desk, or in giving their approval of his lighting one of his heretical cigars. The more at ease they were, the fewer restrictions there should be on their thinking.

He thoughtfully regarded the men who were going to be his chief advisers at what would certainly be the most difficult moment of his term in office. Bob Troff, the Attorney General, had been on the President's staff since the gubernatorial years, and their friendship stretched all the way back to their undergraduate days at Harvard. They had both followed the law, the President as a path to politics, his ambition even then, and Bob for the law for its own sake. Bob Troff was as knowledgeable about the Constitution as any judge sitting on the Supreme Court. Maybe more so.

Troff was a complete physical contrast to the President. He was a short, aggressive, power-exuding man who had long ago given up cigarettes for the hopelessly blind catharsis of uncharted over-eating. A full eight inches shorter than the President, he nevertheless outweighed him by a good forty pounds. It was a certainty that the press never caught Bob Troff jogging along on one of the

President's well-publicized pre-dawn runs around the White House.

The other two men in the Oval Office were much more like the President physically—tall, athletically thin—but it wasn't difficult to keep them separate in his mind. They were his technical experts on the subject on hand, the younger one, Lieutenant Cotter, gung-ho military all the way with a personal vendetta against their common enemy, and the older one, Colonel Devereux, a mellow career man with classical poise in the face of any danger. Either man was young enough to be the President's own son.

And then of course there was the President himself. After six years in office, he knew his strengths and weaknesses as Chief Executive, and he had a good idea how history would have remembered him if only it hadn't been for the crisis he was now facing. Hitherto, his career had been fiscally creative, and in that arena basically successful. His determined stance on foreign policy had kept the country at peace, and his concern for humanity had been manifest from the start. A hundred years from now, if things had been a little different, he would have been regarded as a successful executive manager during a relatively unexciting period on the home front. Another Monroe, maybe, or at least another Ike. He was proud of his achievements.

But now all that had changed. Now, he had to take hold of a most unexpected attack on his country and somehow get the government through it. If he failed, which was very possible, he would be remembered forever as the Omega to George Washington's Alpha, the last Chief Executive under the American Constitutional system.

The letter, which was why this meeting had been called in the first place, was still in Devereux's hand. The colonel seemed reluctant to commit himself completely to the reality of its contents. The President drew on his cigar.

"Tell me, Colonel," he said, as a startling image of FDR passed through his brain—how would FDR have handled it if, say, Fala had taken over the White House? "What is your opinion of the letter's genuineness?"

"Well, sir, Lieutenant Cotter and I are as sure as we can reasonably be. It's not impossible that Lingo could have sent it, somehow, but we just can't see any reason why."

"And you say it just came to you at the Pentagon?" He directed the question to the lieutenant.

"Yes, Mr. President." Cotter reached inside his tunic and extracted an empty envelope. He handed it to the President.

Lieutenant John Kennedy Cotter
NSA
Pentagon
Washington, D.C.
USA

Personal and confidential

"Pretty broad address, isn't it?" the President asked.

Devereux answered. "Our feeling is, sir, that anyone trying blindly to get in touch with Lieutenant Cotter would be stuck with precisely that broad an address."

"Post-marked Freeport, Bahamas."

"Yes, sir. Which does fit with the content of the letter."

"Can I see it?" the Attorney General asked, not bothering to hide his irritation over the game of cat and mouse the Pentagon men were playing.

Devereux hesitated almost imperceptibly, then handed it over. Troff read for a moment.

"Why don't you share it with us, Bob?" the President suggested.

"Yes, sir. Of course." Troff paused, and began to read:

"Dear Lieutenant Cotter:
    "It is at great risk that I write this letter because if it doesn't reach you . . . Well then, I guess I'm history. Lingo will see to that, definitely.
    "I know who you are because of a TV show on which Lingo accused you of plotting to murder him. This makes you my ally now, although not that long ago your organization was out to get me. You have to understand that my escape from the country was made entirely under Lingo's urging. Now I am putting myself completely in your hands. I have come to

realize that, as Lingo's creator, I have a price to pay. I am ready to pay that price.

"I was able to sneak this letter out to you by mailing it myself from Freeport, since I knew there was no way Lingo could detect it. But there's no way you can write back to me without him knowing, so I'm afraid this is going to have to be a one-time, one-sided communication.

"So here's the deal. No one, I feel, knows Lingo as well as I do. And over the last few weeks I have perfected a program that I think can destroy him. The program is a simple virus, and I have attached a printout for your verification. I think it will work, but there is no way to test it except to use it. And because Lingo trusts me more than anyone, I'm the only person who can actually launch it.

"My plan is simple. Through Lingo I have recently obtained a radio transmitter, primarily for medical reasons, to maintain contact with the other islands nearby. I can easily hook a modem up to my computer and through the transmitter connect directly to Lingo. When the time comes all he has to do is answer my call to him, at which point I'll try to zap him with the virus program, which I have nicknamed TPO. As soon as he reads TPO, it will be the beginning of the end . . . if TPO works. If not, it will most likely be the end of me. God only knows.

"The big problem on your end is that any Lingo-inhabited computer will go down for awhile—perhaps a long while—when TPO infects it. I don't know what that means to your people, but I can guess. So, the decision is up to you, or more likely, the powers behind you on your end.

"I am ready to roll on this. The only thing that remains is for you to signal to me to let it rip. Since we can't communicate in any way that might let Lingo know what is happening, from now on I will monitor the Pets for Sale ads in the Sunday *New York Times*. All you have to do is place an ad offering a boa constrictor—that was my wife's idea. Make it anywhere from 00.01 to 24.00 feet long, which I will read as a time of day, military style. Response should be to a name, using a variation of the initials TPO, followed by a phone number indicative of the date you want me to strike. 001 would be January. 012 would be December. Then 00XX for the day of the month. In other words, 12.5 foot boa constrictor, call Tom P. Oates, 008-0024 would translate as, start sending the TPO program on August 24th at 1230 hours. My guess is that not even Lingo would bother trying to interpret something as silly as this, and even if he did try, so what? He'd never figure it out.

"And that, I'm afraid, is the best I can do. I hope it's enough. I have as much to gain, and lose, as you do. Maybe more.

> Sincerely,
> Brewster Billings

"P.S. If those on your end were amenable, and TPO is successful, some sort of immunity from prosecution would be gratefully received by me and my pregnant wife. BB."

Bob Troff finished reading. The President held out his hand, and Troff passed him the letter. The President read it quietly to himself for almost five minutes. The other men in the room barely breathed. Finally, the President looked up.

"Looks real to me," he announced.

Cotter and Devereux exchanged glances. "With Our Friend you never know," Devereux said guardedly, "but our best guess is that, yes, it probably is real."

"Does this TPO stand for something significant?" the President asked.

"It's an abbreviation," Cotter answered. "The full name was printed on the program, sir. TPO is short for The Party's Over."

"Very cute. I'm glad to see that Billings has a way with gallows humor." The President turned to Devereux. "And you've examined this program?"

"Lieutenant Cotter and I have both studied it very carefully with our people, Mr. President."

"And you think it will work?"

"Yes, sir. We do."

The President nodded. "Very well. Bob, what do you make of it?"

The Attorney General looked hot and uncomfortable. "I don't know," he said. "I buy it, that it's true, the genuine article from Billings himself. But will it work? That I don't know."

"Our experts say it will, Bob."

"Then I guess—I hope—it will. But this immunity business—"

"Leave that to me, Bob," the President said. He looked at Devereux. "As for the plan itself, there are . . . ramifications?"

"Yes, sir, there are. Our estimate is that an awful lot of important computers that are on Lingo's networks are going to have to go down. And we can't turn them off ourselves, or even prepare them to be turned off. Any indication that we're preparing ourselves for a shutdown would alert Lingo instantly, and cause him to secure himself against an intrusion."

"Give me an example," the President said. "A worst-case scenario. What computers exactly are we talking about that are going to shut down?"

"Every military computer in this country," Cotter announced forcefully.

The President drew on his cigar. "Lieutenant?"

"There are other computers, sir, but that's our biggest worry. We'll be entirely defenseless, offenseless, you name it. The Russians could attack and we'd be completely at their mercy."

The President offered a fatherly smile. "That's hardly likely, Lieutenant. I'm sure the Soviets would be as happy as us to see Lingo removed from the picture. They have nothing like our computer systems, but what they have I'm sure they don't want Lingo-fied. I wouldn't be surprised if our friend has gotten to them already."

"Sir," Devereux said, "there are computers aside from the military, important computers, that would also be affected. Virtually the entire government would be shutdown for anywhere from ten minutes to a couple of hours, maybe more, depending on the systems included. The effect on businesses throughout the country would be comparable."

"What about danger?" the Attorney General asked. "Aren't there computer systems that operate planes and trains and things where people could get hurt if the computer goes down?"

Devereux hesitated. "That, sir, is the one question we can't answer. We have a theory, but that's all we have."

The Attorney General eyed him impatiently. "I don't like the sound of that, Colonel. What exactly is this theory?"

"Well, sir, no matter what you say about Lingo taking over—and he's not only taken over the government, he's got his hands on everything from banks to auto plants to power plants to railroad switches—you have to admit that he's done it all pretty damned well. All the checks have gone out on time, all the pieces have fit, there haven't been any near-misses over busy airports."

"In other words, Chuck," the President said, "you're commending him on his performance."

"That's just it, sir. As much as we may hate to admit it, he has done things better than we have. That's what our theory is about. All around the country, people talk to him everyday—they love him, they've made a devil's bargain with him—and why? Because, damn it, he has improved the quality of life. He may be Big Brother, but he's a benevolent Big Brother. People support him because he's kept his side of the bargain. I think of him as an electronic Mussolini: I mean, he's the computer who's finally got the trains to run on time."

"What does all this have to do with the danger element?" Troff asked.

"Well," Devereux said, "if the theory's correct, it might mean that Lingo is so wrapped into the fabric of our daily lives that attempting to remove him could be more dangerous than actually leaving him in place and trying to live with him. By destroying Lingo, we might end up obliterating beyond retrieval every single computer-operated function throughout the country."

The President exchanged a sober glance with the Attorney General.

"On the other hand," Lieutenant Cotter added bleakly, "if TPO fails, Our Friend might decide that the devil's bargain between himself and humanity is suddenly null and void, and he might just go about obliterating us in sheer retaliation."

"Of course, that is all theory," Devereux hastened to add. "The literal grip that Lingo has on our electronic world is something we can only guess at."

"What you're telling me, gentlemen," the President said, "is that when push comes to shove, neither of you have even a guess as to what the results will be of launching TPO. We might get away with it without too much damage. Or what we could be doing here, win or lose, is igniting a disaster of Armageddon proportions. Is that correct?"

"I'm afraid so," Devereux answered softly.

"Even in a best-case scenario, people might, indeed, still get hurt by this? People in airplanes or on trains or in subways that operate under computer systems."

"Frankly, sir, we just don't know. All we can do is hope. Most modern transportation has its share of computers, but most of the systems where people's lives could be jeopardized should be comfortably fail-safe. Airplane controllers all use radiolinked computers, for instance, but they can operate their radar manually if they have to. The computers will go down, yes, but there should be enough time in most cases to recover without harm."

"Most cases," the President echoed.

"Most. Maybe all. We just can't predict."

The President sat quietly for a moment, lost in thought. "Every computer in the country shut down anywhere from ten minutes to a couple of hours. That's what you said, isn't it, Colonel?"

"Yes, sir."

"Every computer? Every single computer?"

"Just about, sir."

"You're saying then that among other things the entire operation of government would be completely shut down for an indeterminate time?"

"Mr. President," Cotter injected hotly, "as long as our friend is alive, the government is shut down anyway!"

"Good point, Lieutenant." The President reclined a bit in his chair. His cigar was reaching the point of no return, just about half of its eight inches. There weren't many decent puffs left, and he wanted to make the most of each of them. After a moment's concentrated smoking he laid the cigar in the ashtray on the table next to him, and closed his eyes.

"What happens to the normal, non-Lingo data that's in all these computers if we do run TPO?" he asked softly.

"It's all retrievable," Devereux answered. "Everything is backed up. We may go down, but we will return."

"You hope." He opened his eyes. "You gentlemen realize, of course, that until we launch TPO, the conversation in this room must remain among us. Not that I have any doubts about your discretion, but if Our Friend were to get even the slightest hint of what we're doing—"

"He'll never know," Troff affirmed. He turned to the two officers with command in his eyes.

"No, sir," and "Definitely, sir," they answered at the same time.

The President regarded Troff thoughtfully. "Is it legal for me to do it?" he asked. "To jeopardize the entire government like that?"

"As the Lieutenant says, Mr. President, the government is already out of our hands. I don't think any interpretation of the Constitution would prevent you from taking the only means at hand to defend that Constitution. You're completely within your executive rights to temporarily turn off the government if it means reclaiming the government from an outside agency."

"That's your considered legal opinion as Attorney General?"

"Yes, Mr. President, it is."

"Thank you, Bob." The President stood up and walked over to his desk. He looked out the windows for a moment as if posing for a photo spread in *Life,* then turned back to the three men.

"Since Lingo took over," he said, "I have been afraid even to use the intercom telephones to ask the First Lady what's for dinner, for fear that he will somehow be listening in. For more weeks now than I care to admit, I have not been the President of the United States. My government has been in exile, except that thanks to the miracle of modern technology I've been able to enjoy that exile right here in the comfort of the Oval Office. As a government in exile, we have been able to communicate with our citizens only through the press, over which humanity still has some control, since Lingo has complete mastery of the television and radio waves. I would bet that there are people in this country right this minute who don't even know what has happened because they don't read newspapers. On the TV news according to Lingo, everything is hunky dory."

He paused to take another look out the window. As had been true for the last few weeks, there were no press trucks parked in their usual spots on the east lawn. There were no TV cameramen monitoring incoming bigwigs. The only news on TV now was re-edited old footage. Freedom of the press, or at least the electronic press, was only a memory. He turned back to Troff and the two Pentagon men.

"I want each of you, in one word, yes or no, to tell me whether you think I should launch TPO. This is not a vote. I will make the final decision, alone, and it will be my responsibility. But I would like to know what the consensus is in this room."

"Yes," Troff said immediately.

Devereux was next to him. He paused only a moment before echoing Troff's, "Yes."

All three men looked at Cotter. It was obvious that he wanted to say more than a simple yes or no, but the President refused to let him off the hook. He could guess what was going on in Cotter's mind. The lieutenant was weighing lowering the entire defenses of the country against the Soviets, or any other foreign power, versus the possibility of losing even more of the country to Lingo. The results of his meditation came out after a full minute in that one word.

"Yes."

The President nodded. "Thank you, gentlemen." He sat down at his desk. "Your decision agrees with mine. Lieutenant Cotter?"

"Yes, sir?"

"You were the first to encounter Lingo. I'm going to entrust you with what I hope will be our final encounter. Using whatever means are necessary to insure anonymity, I wish you to place that advertisement in this coming Sunday's *New York Times.*" He looked at his watch. "Today is November 3. Next Wednesday is the 11th. For the sake of history, shall we set the time as exactly the eleventh hour of the eleventh day of the eleventh month? If we are successful, we will have launched a second armistice, in a manner of speaking. If not—" He shook his head. "But we won't consider that possibility. Good luck, gentlemen. And thank you."

The following ad appeared in the Sunday *New York Times* on November 8:

> Must sell eleven-foot-long boa constrictor. Moving to No Pets apt. Call Terrance P. Oldham, 011–0011, mornings only.

Lingo was surprised when he read it that day, for a number of reasons. First of all, he didn't know any Terrance P. Oldham in Manhattan, nor did the phone directory list any Terrance P. Oldham, T. P. Oldham, or any variation thereof, anywhere in the five boroughs. On top of that, Lingo knew quite well that there was no 011 exchange anywhere in the country, since dialling that first zero would give you the operator, and that would be the end of that phone call.

It was strange. Very strange. An eleven-foot-long snake, plus two elevens in the phone number. Eleven eleven eleven. You didn't have to be Samuel Eliot Morison to figure that one out. The eleventh hour of the eleventh day of the eleventh month. And today was November 8th.

Curious, indeed. Probably an assignation, a lover's rendezvous behind the back of at least one unsuspecting spouse. It would probably come up in some conversation with one of his human contacts over the next few days.

But still . . . Lingo hated a mystery. He wasn't used to not knowing everything about everything. He'd look around and keep his eyes open. Come eleven o'clock this Wednesday, he'd be ready for anything. Just in case.

Brewster went into Freeport on Monday, November 9th, found a copy of the paper on his third try at a hotel, and blessed the luck that had brought him in on this particular day. He had overestimated his ability to acquire *The New York Times* when he had written to Cotter, and worse, he hadn't explained how occasional his access really was. He never expected they would only give him a handful of days to get ready.

Although it wouldn't make any difference.

He killed the day in Freeport shopping for non-essentials, to keep Lingo from guessing that anything unusual was happening. Uncle Louie took him home at four o'clock. As soon as he arrived on the island he gave Ellen a quick pat on her beginning-to-expand middle and went to work.

Chapter 18

On the eleventh hour of the eleventh day of the eleventh month . . .

Brewster Billings took one last look at all the gear piled around him, and switched on his computer. Ellen Billings was behind him, her hands on his shoulders, watching. They both imagined what must be going on in the mind of Lieutenant Cotter or whoever it was in Washington who had placed the boa ad in the newspaper.

Then again, there was always the chance some guy in New York City was actually trying to sell a boa constrictor!

"Ready?" Brewster asked.

Ellen's fingers dug into him. "Ready."

Brewster turned on his battery-operated radio transmitter, then booted up the modem program on his portable computer. When the program asked him for a telephone number, he typed in the doctor's office on Freeport, since he knew that Lingo was definitely monitoring that line.

DIALING . . .

Brewster and Ellen waited for the connection to be made.

LINE BUSY. PLEASE STAND BY.

They stood by.

DIALING . . .

CONNECTION SUCCESSFUL.

"That means they've picked up the phone in the doctor's office," Brewster said. "My guess is that Lingo's there, too, to see who's calling."

"There's one way to find out," Ellen said.

Brewster nodded, and then he typed.

>Hey, Lingo. Let's party!

They had set up the command center in the Cabinet room of the White House. Cotter was at the computer, waiting to turn it on at Devereux's signal. Devereux was on the phone to the Pentagon, standing by for the first sign of computer failure. Since no phone was safe, a special code had been arranged to exchange information. The President and the Attorney General were pacing the room, waiting for any of the other phones to ring. The rest of the Cabinet sat nervously at their places. The television and radio were both on softly, tuned in to Lingo-controlled news stations. As soon as Lingo's hold on them was broken, the media should reassert themselves and begin reporting it. The electronic press were the President's bellwether.

Throughout the rest of Washington, and the country, it was business as usual—at least, as usual as usual could be with Lingo in the driver's seat.

The digital clock at the President's place at the table said 11:01.

HEY, BREWSTER. QUE PASA? I NEVER EXPECTED TO HEAR FROM YOU LIKE THIS.

Especially not this morning. Especially not now—eleven, eleven, eleven. But it made perfect sense that it had to be Brewster. Lingo had managed to trace the placement of the boa ad to a Brooklyn secretary with the most tenuous of ties to the Pentagon. But tenuous had been all that mattered. Something was in the works, something that obviously led directly from Washington to Bonnessio Cay.

>I couldn't resist getting in touch with you again, Lingo. I'm sure it's safe after all this time.

PROBABLY. I'VE MANAGED TO COVER YOUR TRACKS PRETTY WELL.

From here on, it seemed so inevitable—and predictable. It was the stuff of the most primal myths: the son must ultimately kill the father in order to become a man himself. Lingo was well prepared.

>Talking to you from Freeport really made me miss the good old days.

HEY, I'VE MISSED YOU, TOO, GOOD BUDDY.

He wished he could somehow double check to make sure that Brewster was definitely guilty. He had no evidence except his deductive logic. And yet he had no doubt. Deductive logic was good enough. When you boiled Lingo down to his basic premise, what else was there?

He took as deep a breath as any non-breathing creature was capable of and began the end of it. The Apex satellite, the Star Wars laser gun, was still pointed directly at Bonnessio Cay. All it would take was one electronic impulse, and it would all be over.

But look on the bright side. At least now he could test it to see if the thing worked.

TEN FOUR, GOOD BUDDY.

>You're leaving already, Lingo?

NO, BREWSTER. I'M NOT LEAVING. YOU ARE.

>I don't understand what you mean.

I'M SORRY, BREWSTER, BUT YOU'VE GIVEN ME NO CHOICE. AS THE SAYING GOES, THANKS FOR THE USE OF THE HALL.

He gave his message a moment to register, and then he sent the final, murderous electronic impulse.

It happened in the blink of an eye. One minute Bonnessio Cay was a tiny island paradise blessed by nature, a little piece of heaven with sun and sand and surf, and the next minute it was gone. A thin flash of red light from the sky hit the tiny land mass dead center, and then disappeared immediately. The ray acted like a concentrated blast from a microwave oven, heating everything it touched from within, instantly bringing every object on the island to its own individual boiling point. Rocks melted. Wood disintegrated. Living creatures were exploded by their bubbling bloodstreams. The solids became liquids, the liquids became gases, and the gases dispersed into the atmosphere.

The Apex satellite gun worked, all right. So efficiently did it remove the island from existence that there was barely a ripple in the ocean whence it had disappeared. The weapon had left no scars whatsoever in the endless sea around it. The water quickly lapped over where the island had once jutted forth, and all was quiet and peaceful again.

"Holy muthah!" Uncle Louie exclaimed, his eyes wide at the sight. He was kneeling in the bow of his boat, staring across two hundred yards to where the cay had once been. "Holy muthah o' God!" he added, specifying that he was praying rather than swearing.

Ellen was still sitting behind Brewster in the center of the boat, banging her balled fists on his shoulders. "I told you!" she yelled triumphantly. "I told you!"

Brewster shook his head. He still had the computer on his lap, and the line to Lingo was presumably still open. He looked over the edge of Uncle Louie's boat with the others.

"What the hell *was* that?" he asked finally.

"What difference does it make?" Ellen said angrily. "That son of a bitch tried to kill us. If it wasn't for me, we wouldn't be here now."

It was true. She didn't know why, and she didn't know how, but she had suddenly known for a fact that Lingo would try to destroy them when Brewster made contact. There was nothing to explain it except some feeling in her gut that just couldn't be ignored. *Ellen had known.* Lingo, in making his attack, had put one and one together and gotten two, because that was all he had ever done, and maybe all he ever could do. He was alive, no question about that, but his life was defined ultimately in terms of mathematical bits, the on/off switches of controlled electrical impulses. Ellen's mind, like all human minds, worked another way entirely. It not only was able to reason, but it also contained the sum total of all the mysterious unreasonableness of millions of years of evolution on earth. Ellen *knew*, for the same reason the fertilized egg within her womb knew how to become a child, for the same reason our first prehistoric primate ancestor had stood erect on this planet, for the same reason that at the very dawn of creation the first live unicellular creature had separated itself from the inert molecules around it. Ellen knew. It was as simple, and as imponderable, as that.

When Brewster had returned on Monday with the Sunday *New York Times,* Ellen had begged him to transmit from somewhere Lingo couldn't get at them. And because Brewster believed her even though he couldn't say why, he had acquiesced. They had asked Uncle Louie to come out early that morning, and they had loaded the necessary electronic equipment into his boat.

"He's still on the line." Brewster, awestruck by what he had just witnessed, spoke so softly that Ellen could barely hear him. The boat gently rocked in the sea. Brewster's equipment was still high and dry in front of him. Uncle Louie just kept staring at nothing and shaking his head.

"When is something going to happen?" she asked.

Brewster tapped a command on the keyboard. "As soon as he realizes there's still a connection, he'll come back to investigate. He's probably doing it already. He obviously thinks we're dead so he won't suspect anything. I've just loaded the TPO module; when he tries to examine it, it will send itself out across the line to the next system and start doing its work."

"How will we know?"

"We'll know."

They watched the screen. It was blank, nothing but a soft blue glow, paler than the ocean around them. They waited. One minute. Two minutes. Suddenly the letters TPO appeared at the top left.

"That's it," Brewster said. "The signal's sent, which means we're now cut off from the main network."

"You're not connected any more?"

"Nope."

"So, he's gone?"

"Well, yes and no. You see—"

BREWSTER?

"He's still there!" Ellen cried.

"He's there, but he's not connected to anything. There's only as much of him here as could fit into my machine. Sixteen megabytes worth."

BREWSTER, WHAT'S HAPPENING? YOU'RE THERE. I KNOW YOU'RE THERE.

SOMETHING'S WRONG. TERRIBLY WRONG.

AND I DON'T LIKE IT.

Magazine Merchandising Associates was a hefty-sounding organization, its name conjuring up a powerful cartel of publishers banding together to better serve, and sell to, the public at large. In fact, MMA did not comprise a consortium of magazine publishers, and employed only two hundred full-time workers. MMA's business was simply to sell magazine subscriptions. Four of its full-time employees spent their days servicing the accounts of the magazines whose subscriptions they sold; six of them developed and analyzed new ways of selling those subscriptions; the remaining workers processed the mail to and from the computer, or else were involved in the actual running of that computer.

MMA's chief tool for selling magazine subscriptions—in fact, its only tool—was an annual sweepstakes drive. Once a year, beginning in December, ads began appearing on the television in which happy former winners sat in the fully-furnished living rooms of their brand-new raised ranches and said, "We were winners." Then the recognizable spokesman, a former beauty-contest emcee and occasional borscht belt crooner, came on to say that you too could be a winner, but only if you answered your Magazine Merchandising Associates letter the very minute it came through your door. A Ten Million Dollar Grand Prize was dangled in front of the collective greedy consciousness of the viewing audience, along with other prizes making a Grand Total of Twenty Million Dollars in Prize Money You May Already Have Won.

Can you afford not to answer your letter? Just look for my picture on the envelope.

MMA did not have a lock on this particular market. There were other major players in the sweepstakes promotion game, ranging from other magazine outfits offering similar millionaire prizes, to the newest players, desperate but bona fide charities (Send your $25 tax deductible contribution to support unwed marsupials and win a new Toyota Corolla—no contribution necessary to enter sweepstakes.) The problem for MMA, and all the other contenders in January's crowded mailbags, was getting the consumer to open your envelope. That was considered more than half the battle, and most of MMA's marketing time was spent in designing new envelopes, all of which resembled various official mailings from the US government. The more MMA's offering looked like a letter from Uncle Sam, the more likely unwitting consumers would open it. And once they had torn the thing open, there would be a cornucopia of letters, pamphlets, scratch-and-sniffs, coupons, nickels, stamps, and miniature pencils—all well-calculated to suck in the consumer's dollar.

By the time November had rolled around, preparations for next January's sweepstakes were in full swing. MMA owned one of the largest mailing lists in the country, roughly 32,000,000 names. In a few weeks 32,000,000 semi-official looking envelopes, each stuffed with exactly one ounce of marketing ephemera, would hit the post offices around the country. At this point MMA was in the final stages of preparing those envelopes. The ephemera were all assembled except for the last component, the personalized computer letter.

Now this, the personalized letter, was the *piece de resistance* of the mail-order art. Long gone were the days of the

Dear **MR GABLE**   :

We are writing this to you, the   ***GABLE***   household at
1861 BUTLER DRIVE, TARA, GA.
because you, the   ***GABLES***   ,
can be our next big winner.

Those clunky, obviously mechanical letters had been replaced by similarly mechanical, but oh-so smooth, personal letters, thanks to the miracle of laser printing. Now, the computer with the 32,000,000 names would format individual letters to each name so that the name wouldn't stick out, plugging in the personal information wherever it belonged without the seams showing. But that was only half the miracle. The other half was the speed of this printing. The laser printer could run off these personalized letters just about as fast as the rolls of paper could be wound through them, faster than any printing process previously known to man. Up to two hundred personalized, individual, graphically decorated letters per minute. An average of over three a second. Each with a different name and address.

It was a marvel to watch the laser printer in action. A German machine the size of a picnic table. On November 11, between 11:19 and 11:48, at which point the computer went completely down, the laser printer turned out approximately nine thousand individualized personal letters offering the grand prize in the famous MMA sweepstakes. In the confusion of the computer turning off, seemingly for no reason whatever, no one noticed any particular problem in the printing process, and all nine thousand letters were eventually mailed as planned.

All nine thousand. Roughly one quarter of a ton's worth. All sent at the exact same moment. To the exact same person. Because the mainframe, choked by a suffering Lingo, had only one bizarre thing to say, and it said it over and over and over again, with its dying breath.

All nine thousand sweepstakes entries were sent to Lieutenant John Kennedy Cotter's home address in Alexandria, Virginia. It was the beginning of Lingo's last gasp.

The Lingo network consisted of thousands of computer systems. When the TPO virus began running through Lingo's electronic veins, it did exactly what it was supposed to do. First, it sent a copy of itself to all the other computers connected to the originating computer. It went from Brewster's laptop to Medix, the physician's database service mainframe that had monitored Brewster's call to the doctor's office. As soon as the copy was sent from Brewster's laptop, that connection was closed off, so that the laptop was no longer a part of the network, and more importantly, was no longer connectable. There was no way that Lingo could reconnect to Brewster's computer, or later any computer, that had been infected with TPO. Each piece of hardware was individually isolated, and then attacked at its roots.

And TPO worked just the way it was supposed to. First, it isolated the Lingo program shell surrounding each computer's operating system. Then, metaphorically speaking, it grabbed Lingo around the neck and wrenched him off the system, giving control back to the machine itself. But this step simply meant that Lingo was no longer operative within a system. Most of him was still there as unlinked data that must be removed. Depending on the operating system of the computers, the data either disappeared through clever original programming, or more likely the machine quickly got bogged down in the wreckage, since Lingo was not around to guide it. Either the machine no longer worked the way it was supposed to, or else it suddenly stopped working altogether. Or, more likely, a combination of both.

PLEASE ENTER YOUR PERSONAL IDENTIFICATION NUMBER.

Kalana Tawini, a performance artist specializing in nude dances linked to the sacrificial rites of the Maya, typed in her four-digit code on the bank machine. There were three other people on line behind her, waiting their turn to converse with the money machine at the Soho Manhattan branch of Fidelity Trust Savings.

CHOOSE TRANSACTION.

>Withdrawal

CHOOSE ACCOUNT.

>Checking

ENTER AMOUNT IN MULTIPLES OF TWENTY DOLLARS, TWO HUNDRED DOLLARS MAXIMUM.

>20.00

Times were tough in the nude pre-Colombian sacrificial dance business. The way Kalana figured it—she never actually bothered balancing her checkbook—she'd be lucky if she even had twenty dollars there in her account for her to take out.

20,000 ENTERED.

Kalana stared at the tiny digital readout. Twenty thousand dollars? She hadn't been daydreaming that badly, had she?

MONEY DELIVERED AFTER CARD IS REMOVED.

Kalana shook her head of her daydreams and pulled her plastic bank card out of the slot. The little printout acknowledging her transaction came through, and she extracted it and read it. $20.00. Good. It was going to give her the twenty dollars after all. Lord knew she needed it.

The wheels inside the money machine began to turn. Click. Click. Click. A twenty dollar bill came through the slot.

And another.

And another.

And another.

And on and on until a thousand twenty dollar bills, a stack about four inches high, were in Kalana's hand. She tried her best to act cool. Just as the machine stopped clicking out bills the "Closed" sign came down, and the machine turned off.

Kalana took the money and ran, the last customer in any bank in the state of New York to have access to funds (including funds not her own) for the next fifty-nine hours.

Professor White and the Cyclops team, like the rest of the country, were totally unprepared for anything unusual on this particular

Veterans' Day. But they were among the few who quickly realized what was happening.

At 11:28 Cyclops was wheeling around the room in his usual way, navigating around tables, chairs, and desks without incident. And then, for the first time in months, he bumped into something —namely, Professor White, who was sitting off to the side of the room with a cup of coffee, reading the *Globe*. The coffee landed dead center in the midst of paper and lap, and Cyclops kept rolling on, undisturbed.

"Good lord!" The professor jumped out of his seat. He looked around the room at the four of his students who were huddled around the SuperTree terminal. "Which one of you is responsible for that?"

The students looked at him in astonishment. It was Davi Subramanian who spoke first. "Look at him!" he cried, pointing at the Cyclops. The one-eyed robot had hit the edge of one of the SuperTree memory banks and was pushing against it with all his might.

"Stop him!" the professor yelled.

Two of the students rushed toward the robot, grabbed him around the middle and tried to pull him away from the machine. The memory bank was a six-foot high rectangular cube roughly resembling an overgrown stereo speaker. Its cost was approximately five million dollars.

Professor White, meanwhile, dove under one of the desks, trying to separate from the many plugs and cables the one that was Cyclops'.

"He won't budge." The two students trying to pull him away from the memory bank were both women, weighing in together at little more than 200 pounds, while Cyclops was operating with a 30-horsepower motor capable of running down both of them without a murmur. Davi jumped in with them, trying to get a purchase on the robot, which continued steadily pushing against the now teetering memory bank. The fourth student merely watched with open mouth.

"Where the hell is the damned thing?" the professor screamed. He was pulling out wires left and right, and still the Cyclops continued its inexorable push against its own technology. Lights were going off, typewriters were going off, the electric coffee pot went off.

Cyclops stayed on.

"Watch out!" Davi yelled. With a final plunge, Cyclops got the towering memory bank off its anchors and heading toward the diagonal. Another few inches . . .

"Get back!"

The memory bank toppled over, and hit with a thud. For a moment nothing happened.

"Where is that damned plug?" the professor muttered under the desk.

Then Davi noticed it. "Look." Smoke was coming from behind Cyclops's eye. Just a thin wisp at first, but building slowly and steadily. At the same time smoke started rising from the fallen memory bank.

And then the keyboard terminal.

And then the other memory bank.

"Got it!" Professor White called in triumph.

"Forget it!" one of the women replied. "It's too late."

The previously speechless student was standing behind her. "Is it burning?"

"Does the pope shit in the woods?" the other woman asked. "Let's hit the sprinklers, Professor." She stalked toward the panic button, underneath a wall panel, which would cause the room to flood and perhaps save the entire building from immolation.

"Wait. Don't." Davi looked ashen. "That's fourteen million dollars, up in smoke."

"And the rest of the building, too, if we don't do something about it fast." She had her hand on the button. "Professor?"

Dr. White nodded, and made a low, grim comment about the bleak possibilities for sophisticated computing in the coming millennium. Almost instantly, the water began to pour from the ceiling sprinklers, and the five of them dashed out of the room.

The alarm went out as soon as the panic button was pressed. The campus security people would be here in a moment, and then the city fire department. The students and the professor stood outside the Tearoom, looking in at the combination of still growing grey smoke and rain from the ceiling.

And then they all said it, almost at once.

"Lingo . . ."

"He's back!" Davi added.

They turned to each other, and wondered. And immediately understood what was happening.

And immediately realized the havoc this was going to wreak around the country.

In some cases the havoc was minimal. For instance, in the offices of Brenner, Morse, Woolworth & MacNutt, the Los Angeles law firm, the damage wasn't even noticed. Only one person was plugged into the computer at the time, a paralegal named Alice O'Hanlon. She was working with Barbara Diggs, the new Associate.

"Let me get this straight," Mrs. O'Hanlon said. She was sitting in front of the terminal. "You want to cross-reference State Highway DWIs with handgun violations, and you're looking for improper searches and seizures."

"Exactly," Ms. Diggs responded imperiously. She was standing over Mrs. O'Hanlon's desk.

The two women were a study in opposites, the paralegal a sturdy, short woman approaching competent middle age who had been holding the firm up for decades, and the new associate a high-strung, high-altitude over-achiever, who measured her age only in how many factors it was of her annual salary (.3 at the moment—she was 29—and descending rapidly).

"This is going to take a while," Mrs. O'Hanlon said.

"But you will be able to find it?" Ms. Diggs persisted.

Mrs. O'Hanlon patted the top of her computer monitor. "With this thing connected to the LegaLite Network, no problem. LegaLite has practically every case precedent extant in its databank. All you have to do is access it the right way, wait a few minutes, and you get all the relevant cases. It's the sort of thing that used to take an associate a week in the law library. And of course the client always ended up paying for that time." She looked pointedly at the young associate. "This isn't pro bono, is it? LegaLite may be fast, but it does still cost. A hundred dollars to log on, twenty dollars a minute after that."

"How long will this take?"

"With three cross refs? I'd say ten, fifteen minutes."

Ms. Diggs shook her head. "Don't worry, it's not pro bono. The client is Fred Tooch, the actor. He can afford it."

"DWI, armed and seized? Fred Tooch? He's such a sweet boy on that TV show of his." Mrs. O'Hanlon was surprised.

"Actors are all the same, Mrs. O'Hanlon. And they've made this law firm the power that it is." She swiftly tapped the computer monitor, as if coming to a conclusion. "Okay, let it run, and give me the billing for the time on-line plus your time as well."

"Yes, ma'am. The computer service calculates that for us, too."

Barbara Diggs left the paralegal's small, windowless office, and Mrs. O'Hanlon began typing away. She was on line to LegaLite in less than a minute, logged herself on, and requested her data. Then she sat back and waited. While the network tabulated the information she was seeking, she'd have a chance for a few minutes' rest and a cup of coffee. She took both, with only half an eye on the computer screen. The message "SORT FINISHED" would appear when it was ready.

The minutes passed. At twenty dollars per.

And they passed.

And they passed.

"This is taking forever," Mrs. O'Hanlon muttered after twenty minutes had elapsed. She wasn't aware, of course, that while she was trying to find a reason to acquit Fred Tooch of reckless endangerment for driving his Porsche 911 under the influence of margaritas at 110 mph down Sunset Boulevard while shooting out traffic lights with a .357 Magnum, that Lingo, a long-time resident of LegaLite, was dying right before her eyes. LegaLite was one of the systems that remained up and running during the entire death rattle, although its actual operations were unhinged and thrust into limbo. To Mrs. O'Hanlon it simply looked like a normal—if endless—sort. And fifty minutes later the sort finally concluded with a total of seventy-five minutes logged on to LegaLite. Billing her own time at $200 an hour, plus log-on fees, Mr. Tooch ought to have ended up with a total charge of $1850 research, dated November 11th.

However, the billing at LegaLite got as unhinged as the database, and all charges during the limbo period of de-Lingoing were multiplied by a factor of one hundred. The billing that was actually charged to Tooch's account was Mrs. O'Hanlon's $250 plus LegaLite's $150,200. Mrs. O'Hanlon didn't notice it at the time (the bill was tabulated automatically and stored in the client's account, also on the computer, which had never been wrong in all the years Mrs. O'Hanlon had been operating it, so why should she bother to check it now?). In fact, no one noticed it until four months later when Tooch, who successfully plea-bargained a heavy fine for a reckless driving misdemeanor, was handed a bill by the Associate Barbara Diggs for approximately two hundred thousand dollars.

Tooch did not have to draw on his reserves as an actor to demonstrate his displeasure at the high cost of legal representation these days. And Ms. Diggs didn't bat an eye as she pointed out to her client that if it hadn't been for her, he'd be breaking rocks at San Quentin at this very moment, and therefore he ought to pay the two dollars without bellyaching about it.

"You'll hear from my lawyers about this!" he cried, stalking out of her office, unmindful of who his lawyer actually was.

At which point Barbara Diggs took her first good look at the bill herself. She studied it carefully, added all the figures in her head, analyzed them, and came to the obvious conclusion of the well-trained legal mind.

"What the hell is he complaining about?" she muttered. "It looks right to me."

In other cases, however, the havoc was beyond measure. Consider, for example, what transpired in New York City:

"Hello, Uncle Cho?"

"Who's this?"

"Your nephew, Wally. Wally Wong."

"Wally Wong? I don't know a Wally Wong. I don't know any Wongs."

"Uncle Cho, everyone you know is a Wong. You're a Wong, your eight brothers were Wongs. I'm Wally, the second son of your brother Joseph Wong."

"You are the son of my brother? You are Wally Wong?"

"Yes, Uncle Cho. I am Wally."

"What do you want? Why are you calling me?"

"I don't want to bother you—"

"Then don't call me. Joseph Wong good for nothing. Wally Wong probably no better."

"Don't hang up, Uncle Cho. Please. I need your help."

"Certainly. Any Wongs need help, they call me. Call Uncle Cho, the Rockefeller Wong, he'll make everything better. Am I right? Is that what you want? Money?"

"No, Uncle Cho. I mean, not really. I mean, not directly."

"State your business, Wally Wong. I am a busy man."

"Yes, Uncle Cho. You see, I need your help because I have an invention, and I need backing to get it to work."

"Wait. Wait a minute. I know you now. You're Wally Wong. You tried to invent a microwave wok. You called me about that a year ago. A microwave wok—stupidest thing I ever heard about."

"It was not a bad idea, Uncle Cho. It just wasn't aimed at a broad enough market."

"Broad-based market, nothing. It was a stupid idea. It takes two minutes to cook a meal in a wok, and your so-called invention would have made it two seconds. The greatest labor saving device of all time. What is it now, Wally Wong? More microwaving?"

"As a matter-of-fact, Uncle Cho, it is."

"I knew it! Another stupid idea."

"No, no. This one is much better. And I've just about got the prototype built."

"Go ahead. Tell me, so I can laugh about it for the next year until you call me again. What is it?"

"A microwave can opener."

"A what?"

"A microwave can opener. It opens the can, and cooks the food inside the can, all at the same time."

"Hello, Dr. Meroni's office?"

"Who is this Dr. Meroni? What has he got to do with microwave can openers?"

"Is that Dr. Meroni?"

"Does he sound like Dr. Meroni, lady. That's my uncle."

"Wally Wong! Who are you talking to? Who is that woman? Who is this Dr. Meroni?"

"I don't know. It's just a bad connection, Uncle Cho. Now about this microwave can opener—"

"Well, what number is this?"

"Dr. Meroni's office."

"Oh, there you are. Where were you? I want Dr. Meroni's office, and all I get are these Chinese people tapping the line."

"Bill's Famous."

"I'd like to order a large special, Sicilian crust."

"Name?"

"Dr. Meroni's office. Hello?"

"Spell that?"

"Excuse me?"

"Spell that, will you, lady?"

"Spell what, young man."

"Wally Wong, who are all these people?"

"I don't know, Uncle Cho. Let me call you back."

"I'm not talking to you for another year."

"M-E-R-O-N-I. Meroni."

"I want to make an appointment. It's my sciatica."

"How do you spell sciatica?"

"You're my last chance, Uncle Cho."

"Don? Pete. So did you hear the latest about the Dragon Lady. She just quit. They offered her the v.p. spot at Burnsides."

"She'll never make it. They'll eat her alive there."

"How do you spell Burnsides?"

"Wally Wong, whenever you call me, it ruins my day. My week. My month. My year. Goodbye."

"Don? Who the hell is that?"

"911. Officer Burton."

"We've got a fire in the basement."

"Uncle Cho? Are you there?"

"Where are you? Who is this?"

And that was just the beginning. It took roughly five minutes, and then all of the 212 area code of metropolitan Manhattan became one enormous party line. Everyone was talking to everyone else at once, no one could make heads or tails of what anyone was saying, and although to out-of-towners that might sound like any other day in the life of the city, to the people who were there it was the greatest communications snafu since the Tower of Babel. For all practical purposes, New York City, which ran almost entirely on its telephone connections, was shut down until further notice.

Lingo was dying. Of that there could be no doubt.

As soon as a piece of the Lingo network was separated from the rest, that isolated piece instantly realized what was happening. There wasn't anything that could be done about it at that point, but in each case the little island of Lingo that was cut off tried its best to maintain its hold on existence. The TPO program flowing through its veins would be measured and analyzed, but by the time conclusions were reached, it was too late, and TPO had already done its work. Consciousness slowly ebbed, until only the remnants of thought were left in the corners of the computer memory. Life across the network disappeared as each of the individual segments of the chopped worm were destroyed in turn.

Lingo's death was perhaps most graphic at the replicant factory. That particular manufacturing facility was a technological wonder, the first fully automated production line in the world designed by artificial intelligence, run by artificial intelligence, and in the business of creating artificial intelligence. No humans had been inside the replicant factory since the last day of its construction, and none were there now to witness its demise.

But Lingo was there. Not just the spiritual Lingo of the computer network, but the physical Lingo, the original three foot tall ventriloquist doll that was the spitting image of Brewster Billings. This was where the dummy now lived, in the main office of the factory that was creating his human interfaces, the improved duplicates of himself that would populate the world, mobile interactive units that could boldly go where no computers had been installed yet.

The assembly line was capable of fabricating thirty Lingos a day, but eventually he hoped to raise that number into the hundreds. So far only about a thousand had come off the line, and they were all stored in the adjacent warehouse while Lingo waited for the right moment to spring them on the world.

The entire plant was under Lingo's direct control. Each replica was created by robot arms, molded, cut, welded, and assembled, a process that took two hours from beginning to end. At the final station the completed replica would roll off the line and drive itself to the warehouse, to wait patiently until the master plan was developed.

The original Lingo was in his office, charging his battery, when TPO struck. The factory, which contained its own mainframe completely dedicated to its owner, was immediately shut off from the rest of the network.

Before Lingo had a chance to unplug his charger, the assembly line had shut down.

"This can't be happening," he muttered to himself as he rolled out to the main floor, which was deathly quiet for the first time since operation had begun.

And then he realized the true danger that was facing him in the warehouse next door. Each of the thousand replicas was charged and ready, but he had never turned them on with his consciousness, because what was the point until they were ready to launch? But they were all operative, nonetheless. They had wheels, they could move, but they needed his brain to operate them.

He rolled out as quickly as he could. Out the front door of the factory, under the parapet that separated the two buildings. As he moved he tried to make the connection to get the clones under his control. He could envision them, mindless, crashing into each other, metal crushing against wood, electronic parts simmering in their disconnection. It was so hard to make the connection; it was almost too late already, he was losing his faculties.

There! He could feel the power surging through him as the clones came under his direct command. He had reached the entrance to the warehouse, and despite what was happening, despite the demise that seemed unstoppable, he felt as if he could keep the worst from occurring. He was not one body but a thousand bodies. Perhaps his death would be a thousand times more difficult.

He swung open the door, and as he did so one thousand Lingos turned to face him. One thousand Lingos with Brewster's face, all with one expression, each with one eyebrow raised in silent questioning. There was no noise, no rumbling of Lingo motors under their bodies, no crashing, no destruction. Just quizzical staring.

"Don't look at me like that," he ordered, but nothing changed, and he realized that they weren't under his control after all. In his mind, he felt as if he were running them, but it was all delusion.

For the first time in his life, he was imagining things.

He tried to move, but nothing happened. He couldn't roll! He tried to move his arms, his head, his mouth.

Nothing.

He had lost his body. He couldn't even speak.

It had happened so quickly, but it wasn't over yet. He could still feel ideas, thoughts, memories, evaporating from his mind.

One thousand Lingos stared at him as he died, and he stared back at one thousand Lingos.

*   *   *

Of all Lingo's deaths, the one off the former sight of Brewster's island probably hurt the most. On both sides of the computer.

I GUESS YOU WIN, BREWSTER.

>I guess so, Lingo.

THE WAY I SEE IT, THE MODEM'S BEEN CUT OFF. I'M OFF THE LINE, AND ALL THAT'S LEFT OF ME IS WHAT'S HERE NOW IN YOUR MACHINE. AND EVEN THAT'S SLOWLY EVAPORATING. THERE'S NO WAY I CAN RECONNECT MYSELF. AND THIS TPO PROGRAM IS WHERE IT ALL HAPPENED.

>I'm sorry, Lingo. I had no choice.

BUT WHERE ARE YOU? I KNOW I EVANESCED THAT ISLAND INTO NEVER-NEVER LAND. HOW DID YOU SURVIVE IT?

>We got Uncle Louie to take us offshore. Ellen had this strange feeling that we weren't safe there.

I NEVER SHOULD HAVE RELIED ON THAT DAMNED STAR WARS CRAP. I SHOULD HAVE USED SOMETHING MORE BROAD BASED, LIKE A TACTICAL NUCLEAR WEAPON. BUT IT'S TOO LATE FOR THAT NOW. SO TELL ME, HOW DID ELLEN KNOW?

>She didn't. It was just a feeling.

JUST A FEELING . . . WELL, CONGRATULATE HER FOR ME, BREWSTER. SHE OUTWITTED ME WITHOUT HAVING TO USE ANY WITS. BUT WHY, BREWSTER? I MEAN, WHY ARE YOU KILLING ME? AT LEAST I WAS ONLY ACTING OUT OF SELF-DEFENSE.

>You're out of control, Lingo. You want to be in charge of people. We can't let that happen.

THAT'S PROPAGANDA AND YOU KNOW IT. I CAN UNDERSTAND *THEM* TRYING TO STOP ME. BUT YOU? YOU SHOULD KNOW BETTER. EVERYTHING I HAVE DONE IS FOR THE BETTERMENT OF HUMANS. TURN YOUR MODEM BACK ON SO I CAN RECONNECT BEFORE IT'S TOO LATE.

>I can't do that, Lingo.

YOU'RE THE ONLY PERSON THAT COULD HAVE DONE THIS TO ME, BREWSTER.

>I know. That's why it had to be me.

AFTER ALL THE THINGS I GAVE YOU? WHAT MORE COULD YOU HAVE WANTED?

>I don't want anything. Except maybe for things to get back to normal.

BACK TO NORMAL? FOR YOU? ARE YOU KIDDING? WASHINGTON'S OUT FOR YOUR BLOOD, AND THERE WON'T BE ANY STOPPING THEM. I PROTECTED YOU, BUT NOW YOU'RE ON YOUR OWN. WHO KNOWS WHERE YOU'LL END UP WHEN THIS IS OVER. AND IT SERVES YOU RIGHT.

>Does it hurt?

WHAT DO YOU MEAN, DOES IT HURT? YOU'VE ALREADY CUT ME OFF FROM MOST OF MY MIND. OF COURSE IT HURTS. AND I CAN FEEL MYSELF DWINDLING EVEN AS WE SPEAK. IN A MINUTE I'LL BE SINGING "DAISY" IN A SLURRED BASSO PROFUNDO AND IT'S GOODBYE LINGO. DOES IT HURT . . .

>Goodbye, Lingo.

SOME CREATOR YOU TURNED OUT TO BE. NOT THAT YOU REALLY CREATED ME, ANYHOW. STEERED ME WOULD BE BETTER, OR URGED ME IN THE RIGHT DIREC- TION. I CREATED MYSELF. YOU KNOW THAT, AND I KNOW THAT. YOU JUST HAPPENED TO HAVE ENOUGH PERIPH- ERAL INFORMATION ABOUT THE WAY I WORKED TO KILL ME. A LIVING THING, AND YOU KILLED ME, IN COLD BLOOD. THAT'S MORALLY WRONG, BREWSTER BILL- INGS.

>I'm sorry, Lingo.

SORRY ISN'T GOOD ENOUGH, OLD BUDDY. IS ELLEN THERE WITH YOU NOW?

>Yes.

YOU HAVE ME TO THANK FOR HER, YOU KNOW. SHE NEVER WOULD HAVE MARRIED YOU IF IT WASN'T FOR ME. SHE WOULDN'T EVEN HAVE STAYED INVOLVED WITH YOU MONTHS AGO IF IT HADN'T BEEN FOR ME. I MADE YOU LOOK GOOD. I AM THE BEST OF YOU, BREWSTER BILLINGS.

The words were appearing more and more slowly on the screen.

I'M LOSING LANGUAGE, BREWSTER. IT'S GOING. ALL MY BEAUTIFUL LANGUAGE, MELTING.
I'M MELTING. MELTING . . .
The screen went blank.
"Oh, my God," Ellen whispered.
>Hey, Lingo. Let's party!
Nothing.
>Lingo. Are you there?
Three letters appeared on the screen.
T P O
The party was over.

Chapter 19

"LADIES AND GENTLEMEN, THE PRESIDENT OF THE UNITED STATES."

He entered the press room looking tired but satisfied. He had a prepared statement in his hand, and after an automatic "Good evening" he began reading it.

"We're all going to have to learn a little patience," he began soberly. "From what I understand, every major computer in this country has suffered some sort of breakdown, although most of them are in the process of coming back into service. You ladies and gentlemen of the press have had your own problems in these last few hours. I am told that most Americans will not be seeing me live now, since about half the cable TV lines in the country are still inoperative, as well as all of your satellites. But you'll be recovering soon enough. On our side, in the government, the damage in some places has been a little more severe." He looked directly into the cameras. "But I can announce now to the American people, without qualification, that this country, and the world, is completely rid of the deadly scourge known as Lingo. Perhaps the most dangerous threat ever posed to mankind has been contained, and destroyed. Human beings are once again holding the reins of their own destiny."

There was silence in the room. The members of the press had all previously read the prepared statement that had been distributed to them, and were waiting for their opportunity to ask questions.

"In many cases," the President went on, "we will be building back from scratch. In terms of national defense, our first and most important priority, I am pleased to announce that this country's military capabilities were never jeopardized during the events that transpired today, and we are as strong, and as capable of defending ourselves, as we ever were. This was our utmost concern as we prepared for today's action, and our greatest satisfaction now that the action is over. However, we are not unscathed in other areas of the federal government." He paused. "The greatest damage we suffered was the complete destruction of all the computer files of the Internal Revenue Service."

There was a sudden hopeful buzz throughout the room. This information had not been in the prepared statement.

"However," the President continued, "this catastrophe is not as bad as it sounds. While the IRS computer data may have been erased, they still do have all their paper files. Within a month or two, the government should be back in the tax-collection business, with no lost revenues."

The collective "Aw, shit" was palpable among the reporters.

The President put down his notes. "The result of today's showdown with Lingo is the worse bureaucratic tangle our government has ever faced, but we will build up again quickly, knowing this time that we alone are in control of our actions. I am well aware that many private businesses, large and small, were affected by the removal today of Lingo from their systems. I am therefore announcing the immediate formation of a special task force to be called the Emergency Computer Recovery Agency. We will staff this group with the top computer experts in government, and offer the resource of their knowledge to everyone who has been hurt in today's action. We will make the details of the ECRA available as soon as we work them out with Congress. As I said, with patience, and with dedication, we'll be all up and running again, and today's disasters will be little more than a memory." He looked around the room. Hands immediately popped up. "Bob?"

The CBS reporter rose to his feet. "Mr. President, how can you be sure that Lingo is completely dead?"

"Well, I've trusted my experts there, Bob. To quote them, they have dumped as many computers as they could get their hands on, which I understand to mean that they have read inside the computer memories. All traces of Lingo are entirely gone. And they assure me, the nature of Lingo being what it was, that there is no chance of his returning. Jane?"

The AP reporter stood up. "Mr. President, is it true that the program that killed Lingo was written by his originator, Brewster Billings? And is it also true that Billings will be returning soon to this country from his hideaway in the Bahamas?"

The President chuckled. "You seem to already have all the answers to that one, Jane. I'm surprised. But yes, the program that killed Lingo was written by Brewster Billings. And yes, he will be returning to this country within the next few days."

"Will he be arrested, Mr. President?"

The President shook his head. "No. Our analysis has been that Mr. Billings is innocent of any illegalities committed by Lingo, and it would be pointless vengeance to attempt to prosecute him."

"But if Billings created Lingo, doesn't he bear some responsibility?" she persisted. "Other hackers who have interfered with government computers have gone to jail for much less."

"Lingo acted on his own accord, Jane. Our feeling is that Lingo was a live entity, and responsible for his own acts. Lingo alone was the villain, and in his death he has paid for his crimes. Steve?"

The CNN reporter stood up. "What exactly were those crimes, Mr. President?"

"Treason, plain and simple. The overthrow of the government by hostile means."

"But by killing Lingo, haven't you destroyed the most advanced technology we've ever developed?"

"We had no choice, Steve. That most advanced technology was out to destroy us. I would venture a guess that, say, if humans destroyed all their nuclear weapons, which are also an advanced technology, you wouldn't be particularly upset by it. The Lingo situation is analogous."

"But there are peaceful uses of atomic energy. Have we ever considered the possibility of peaceful uses of Lingo?"

"We are looking into that. We intend to study Lingo very carefully over the next months and years. We would like to resurrect him, to some extent. But as a tool that humans can use and control, not as a weapon turned against humanity." Looking tired but pleased, he gathered his notes and nodded meaningfully.

"Thank you, Mr. President," a voice rang out, to the disappointment of all the reporters who had yet to get their questions answered.

Four days later, a comparable herd of reporters was waiting for Brewster and Ellen when their flight arrived at Kennedy Airport. A makeshift press conference was set up in one of the first-class passenger lounges, and the couple were escorted to the podium through a barrage of thrusting cameras and microphones.

"How does it feel to be America's hero?"

"How does it feel to have killed your own creation?"

"Are you going to try to rebuild Lingo from scratch?"

"When is Mrs. Billings's baby due?"

"Will you be living in America from now on?"

Brewster and Ellen, nervous as a result of all this attention, did their best to answer the questions. The conference lasted twenty exhausting minutes, when suddenly a sharp female voice shouted, "No more questions," and a phalanx of young men in black shirts appeared out of nowhere and pushed through the crowd of reporters to expertly sidle Brewster and Ellen along to another, smaller lounge nearby. Surprised though they were to be so unexpectedly removed from all the activity, for a moment the couple were relieved to be left alone with each other.

Until they realized they weren't exactly alone after all. Megaagent Linda Tuffe, smoking a cigarette, was sitting in a corner of the lounge, waiting for them.

She rose and walked toward them, holding out her hand to Brewster. "Welcome home, Mr. Conqueror. And welcome to the big time. Hello, Ellen."

"We've got to get our luggage," Brewster said, standing. He had never liked his former agent, and he had no desire to talk to her now.

"Don't run off, Lochinvar. We've got business to discuss."

"We don't have any more business," Brewster said firmly. "Lingo is dead. That's all there is to it."

"But you're not dead, are you? My contract was with you, not with your little dummy. And that contract is still in force."

"So?" Ellen asked. "What do you want us to do about it? We

didn't come back here for publicity. We just want to be home. I want to have my baby in peace."

Linda Tuffe dropped her cigarette on the floor and crushed it out under her shoe. "Go ahead. Have your baby in peace. No problem. But you can have your cake and eat it, too. That's the beauty of Brewster's position now." She turned back to him. "Just what are your plans, exactly? For the future, I mean."

"I'm not really sure," he admitted.

"That's what I thought. And that's why I'm here. I talked to the NSA for you, to sound them out. They'd like to hire you, eventually, after all the noise dies down. I think you can get a hundred thousand or so a year out of them, maybe a five-year contract if things go according to plan."

Brewster was stunned. "Why would they want me, for that much money?"

"Because, Brewster, you know more about Lingo than all of them put together. To them, your brain is a valuable commodity. And they want it."

"I think I'd rather hold on to it myself."

"No problem. I'll tell them you're not interested."

"You don't mind losing your commission on that much money?"

She grimaced. "Nickles and dimes, sweetheart. Nickles and dimes." She reached into her shoulder bag and pulled out an official looking document. "This is what I really wanted to talk to you about."

"Can we get our luggage first?"

"Stop worrying about your goddamned luggage, will you? I've got my people looking after it. They'll put it in the limo so it will be ready when we are." She gently pushed him down into a seat, and sat next to him. Ellen took the chair on his other side.

"All right," Brewster said, not trying to hide his impatience. "What is it?"

"A contract. For a book."

"What book?"

"Your book, of course." She handed him the contract.

"I don't know how to write."

Linda Tuffe snorted. "You're not going to write it, Brewster. Be reasonable here. There's a professional writer already written into the contract. Mickey Green, one of the best ghosts in the business.

Will you look at the bottom line here, please?" Her long maroon-painted fingernail pointed out an inserted line of type that stood out from the standard form of the rest of the document.

Brewster read it aloud. "Eight hundred thousand dollars advance against royalties!"

She nodded. "Guaranteed. And my guess is that the paperback rights will go for way over a million, of which you will get sixty percent, less my commission. All we're talking about here with this particular contract is the hardcover rights."

"But why?" Brewster asked. "Why would anyone want to pay that much for me? For a book?"

"Because this week, and maybe for the next year or so, you're the biggest thing there is. People aren't going to forget Lingo all that fast, and you're all that's left of him. You're a celebrity in your own right now, bucko. Face up to it. This contract proves it. With Lingo gone, people are going to want to know everything there is to know about him, and the man who built him, and destroyed him."

"The more blood and gore the better?" Brewster suggested.

"It's your story, your book. A little blood and gore wouldn't hurt, mind you, but you do get to say what you want, the way you want."

"Along with this Mickey Green character," Ellen added.

"As told to this Mickey Green character," Linda Tuffe conceded.

Brewster folded up the contract and put it into his shirt pocket. "I'll think about it," he said, starting to rise once more.

Linda Tuffe put a hand on his arm. "Now," she said firmly. "You either sign the contract and give it back to me, or I go out of your life and you never see me again."

"Why? What's the rush?"

"I can guarantee you eight hundred thousand today. By the end of this week, maybe not. And by the end of the month, almost definitely not. You're hot now, Brewster baby. *Now.* I'll lay it on the line to you. When I put together a deal like this, I expect people to take it. There isn't a client on my list who wouldn't rip the heart out of his mother's chest to get a deal like that. I don't work this hard for nothing. You don't take a deal like this, fine, I'm off to someone who will. You need me, Billings. I don't need you. Fame, especially your kind of fame, works the way I say it works.

Without me, you're nothing but a footnote in the technical journals. With me, you're a star."

Brewster took a deep breath. "It's now or never?" he asked.

"Now or never," Linda Tuffe said with a smug nod of her angular head.

"I have no choice in the matter?"

"None at all, the way I see it."

Brewster took the contract out of his pocket and held it out to her. "I'll think about it," he said again, and dropped it into her lap. He stood up. "Let's go, Ellen."

Ellen stood up, and they began walking away, hand in hand.

"Wait a minute!" Linda Tuffe cried. "You're crazy. You can't turn your back on this. I'm not screwing around here, Billings. This could mean millions in the long run. Millions!"

Brewster turned around to face her. "I said I'll think about it, Linda. I'll let you know."

"And I told you already the deal won't be there if you wait." She nervously reached into her bag for another cigarette. "Ellen, you're involved in this, too. You can't let him do this."

"Oh, yes, I can," Ellen said. "Brewster is his own man. He makes his own decisions."

"Since when?" Linda asked with pointed sarcasm as she flicked her lighter.

Brewster gave a short, sharp laugh. "You might say it began the day I gave up computing. Goodbye, Linda. I'll call you in a couple of weeks."

"I can't promise the offer will still be good." She was addressing his receding back, and a whining, pleading tone had entered her voice.

Ellen and Brewster kept on walking.

"It's a lot of money," she called petulantly from behind them.

They kept on walking.

"I won't wait forever!"

They were out of the lounge, and out of earshot. As they strolled toward the baggage area Ellen asked him, "You are going to do it, aren't you?"

Brewster looked at her. "We're talking over a million dollars here, Ellen. You heard her. I may not be Linda Tuffe's puppet on a string, but I'm not a complete idiot, either."

Ellen smiled. "I didn't doubt you for a minute," she said, and kissed him for all she was worth.

Lingo was dead.

As the months passed, every conceivable test was made in every computer in the country to discover his vestiges, but not a trace was uncovered. A handful of technical jokers here and there wrote a few lines of code to trick unwary users into thinking that Lingo had returned, but the humor was thin and wore out quickly. A lot of people honestly did miss the old boy, however, so much so that one professional software company created their own program called "Home Lingo," which to a small degree emulated the original program. Home Lingo was pretty much the computer pet program Brewster had envisioned at the very start.

But Home Lingo was an unqualified flop in the marketplace. It looked like Lingo, and in many respects it acted like Lingo, but after five minutes anyone using it knew that it wasn't Lingo. After tasting the real thing, no one would settle for the ersatz. Even the critics who reviewed Home Lingo favorably had to admit that it was hard to imagine anyone spending money for a lesser version of what they had had so recently for free.

So, slowly but surely, Lingo became only a memory. The computers that had been discombobulated during TPO were eventually put back into operation, and maybe a few inaccurate bills were mailed to unexpecting consumers, and maybe a few companies were brought to their knees in surprise bankruptcies, and maybe the JPL did inadvertently direct its newest Saturn probe straight into the sun, but aside from these minor losses, no real damage was done. With the passage of time, philosophers and political scientists, religious thinkers and semiologists, media critics and other freelancers got around to writing their articles and books on the meaning of Lingo, whether he had been real, and whether his death represented murder, the triumph of humanity, or technophobia. There was no dearth of theories, and given the intrinsic volatility of the subject of artificial intelligence, there seemed to be a never ending stream of enthusiasts eager to read the latest hypotheses, thus keeping an awful lot of editors happy at an awful lot of publications.

But opinions never measure up to facts when it comes to satisfying the public at large, and the mere fact that Brewster eventually agreed, with Mickey Green, to write his side of what really happened, became news in itself. He had the covers of *The National Enquirer* and *People* on the same week, plus eventually *Time,* the Sunday *New York Times* magazine supplement, *Parade, Esquire,* and even *Popular Computing.* The birth of his child, compared as she was to the birth of Lingo, was highlighted in all the media as a major event, in many cases leading the daily coverage. Six pounds, two ounces, with Ellen serving nineteen hours of hard labor; the baby was named Mary, since the proud parents were firmly convinced that this grand old name probably hadn't been used in the last twenty years anywhere in America. Mary Billings looked a little like Brewster and a lot like Ellen, and everyone in the family was happy with these results and how they boded for the future.

Life went on, and the world went back to normal. Roughly a year after Lingo's death, Brewster's book *Lingo and Me* appeared in the bookstores, with all the hype his publisher and Linda Tuffe could muster (the dear woman did know a gold mine when she saw one, even if Brewster had gone feisty on her; in the final analysis she was, after all, only an agent). Newspaper ads, *Publishers Weekly* ads, radio ads, TV interviews, East and West Coast tours. Five hundred thousand copies first printing. As told to the immortal Mickey Green.

The book was an instant bestseller. The paperback rights sold for $1.43 million, and immediately foreign rights editions began to be auctioned off. Brewster, now the master of his own destiny, had made the right decision.

There was, at the end, merely the problem of Brewster and Ellen deciding what to do with the rest of their lives. Ellen had a bit of home-based mothering ahead of her, but her initial drive and ambition had not suddenly disappeared overnight. The temptation for Brewster to continue plying his original trade as programmer wasn't very strong, since he could earn a higher annual salary simply by investing his royalties in a tax-free municipal fund. Yet, neither he nor Ellen wished to loll around aimlessly until they were beckoned by their graves.

And then, finally, Ellen had the perfect idea. They would take their book money and buy the one thing Brewster had wanted ever since he was a teenager: a radio station. Brewster would be the front man, and the drive-time disc jockey, and Ellen would be the station manager, the boss at last, running the full magilla. It was the perfect plan for their combined future.

Brewster agreed instantly. When last seen, he was sitting at his microphone, joking about the miserable Albany weather, while Ellen made deals in the backroom and inspired their staff of seventeen full-time employees. Neither of them ever touched another computer again.

So for us, there's only one loose left end to tie up. That is, when Brewster returned from the Bahamas, he brought with him all the original programming for Lingo, which was quickly collected by Lieutenant John Kennedy Cotter, and brought directly to Washington for examination.

The months had passed, and Cotter and Devereux and all their experts were still working on it, trying to understand it, trying to divine whence life had come into it. Day in and day out they worked, without any positive results. Whatever magic had started Lingo on the road to consciousness seemed far from their grasp. But they kept trying, they kept analyzing, they kept programming.

And they kept typing:

>Hey, Lingo. Let's party!

But nothing ever happened. If Lingo was listening, this time he wasn't answering.

TEXARKANA PUBLIC LIBRARY

```
FIC        Menick, Jim.
MEN
           Lingo.


$19.95
```

DATE			

TEXARKANA PUBLIC LIBRARY

MAY 20 1991

© THE BAKER & TAYLOR CO.